PRAISE FOR THE OFF-CAMPUS SERIES

"Elle Kennedy engages your [...] nce! Both deliciously steamy and h [...] s an absolute winner!"

—Katy Evan[...] [...] bestselling author

"More hockey hotness from Elle Kennedy? Yes, please! *The Mistake* is a smart, feel-good, swoon-worthy page-turner that will have fans tossing their hearts onto the rink."

—Sarina Bowen, *USA Today* bestselling author

"Elle Kennedy just never fails to make us smile, laugh, and swoon. *The Score* is just what we needed."

—*Totally Booked Blog*

"Smart, sexy, and utterly addictive, I fell in love with Tucker's strength and patience. But it was his dirty mouth in the bedroom that made me swoon and search for tickets to a hockey game!"

—Vi Keeland, #1 *New York Times* bestselling author

"Just when I thought this series could not get any better, we are given another delectable installment in this witty, sexy, flawlessly written series about opposites attracting."

—*Natasha Is a Book Junkie*

The Legacy

OFF-CAMPUS

ELLE KENNEDY

Bloom books

Sourcebooks and the colophon are registered trademarks of
Sourcebooks. Bloom Books is a trademark of Sourcebooks.

Published by Bloom Books, an imprint of Sourcebooks
P.O. Box 4410, Naperville, Illinois 60567-4410
(630) 961-3900
sourcebooks.com

Originally self-published in 2021 by Elle Kennedy Inc. This is an updated, edited version.

Cataloging-in-Publication Data is on file with the Library of Congress.

Printed and bound in the United States of America.
WOZ 19

PART 1

THE PACT

CHAPTER 1

LOGAN

"She's totally checking me out."

"Suuuuuure, bro."

"She keeps looking over here! She wants me."

"There's no way a hot young thing like her is checking out an old man like you."

"I'm only twenty-eight!"

"Seriously? That's even more ancient than I thought."

I smother a laugh. I've been eavesdropping on this trio of stockbrokers for the past twenty minutes. Well, I don't know if they're actually stockbrokers, but they're wearing tailored suits and drinking expensive liquor in the city's financial district, so chances are they work in finance.

Me, I'm the lumbering jock in ripped jeans and an Under Armour sweater, nursing a bottle of beer at the end of the bar. I was lucky to find an empty seat; the place is packed tonight. With the holiday season in full swing, Boston bars are overflowing with patrons taking time off from work or school.

The three dudes I'm spying on barely glanced my way when I slid onto the neighboring stool, which makes it easier to listen in on their douchey conversation.

"So what's the final score for Baker?" one of the men asks.

He and his blond friend study their dark-haired friend—the ancient one. "Eight percent," the first guy says.

The blond is more generous. "Ten percent."

"Let's split the difference and give him a nine. That's nine-to-one odds."

Although, maybe they're not finance guys. I've been trying to figure out their calculation process, but it seems completely arbitrary and not based in any real mathematics.

"Fuck you both. I've got a way better chance than that," Baker protests. "Have you seen this watch?" He flicks up his left wrist to show off a shiny Rolex.

"Nine to one," the first guy maintains. "Take it or leave it."

Mr. Rolex grumbles in irritation as he slaps some money on the counter. The other two follow suit.

From what I've gleaned, their game goes something like this:

Step 1: One of them picks out a woman in the bar.

Step 2: The other two calculate (I use that word loosely) the odds of the first guy getting her number.

Step 3: They drop oodles of cash on the counter.

Step 4: The guy approaches the girl and inevitably gets rejected. He loses the money he bet, only to get it back in the next round when the next guy also gets rejected.

This entire game is both pointless and stupid.

I sip my beer, watching in amusement as Mr. Rolex saunters over to a stunning woman in a skintight designer dress.

Her nose wrinkles at his approach, which tells me that his buddies are about to win some cash. These guys might be wearing expensive suits, but they're still nowhere close to the same league as the women in this bar. And classy women tend to have no tolerance for immature jackasses, because they know they can do better.

Mr. Rolex's jaw is tight when he returns to the group. Empty-handed. His friends hoot and rake in their winnings.

Just as the blond guy is about to pick a new target, I set my pint glass on the sleek counter and drawl, "Can I play?"

Three heads swivel my way. Mr. Rolex takes in my casual clothes, then smirks. "Yeah, sorry, pal. You can't afford this game."

Rolling my eyes, I slide my wallet out of my pocket and riffle through it—giving them a clear view of all the cash inside. "Try me," I say graciously.

"You've just been sitting there this whole time listening to us?" the blond one demands.

"It's not like you were being quiet about it. And anyway, I like to gamble. Doesn't matter what we're gambling over—I'm there. With that said, what are my chances with…" My gaze conducts a slow sweep of the crowded room. "Her," I finish.

Rather than follow my gaze, three sets of eyes remain glued to me.

They appraise me for several long beats, as if trying to decide if I'm fucking with them. So I hop off the stool and ease closer to the trio. "Look at her. She's fire. Do you think a bum like me could get her number?"

Mr. Rolex is the first to relax his guard. "*Her?*" he says, nodding not so discreetly at the pretty girl who's ordering a drink with the bartender. "You mean Little Miss Innocent?"

He's not wrong. There's definitely an air of innocence to her. A delicate profile reveals a smattering of freckles on her nose, and her light-brown hair is loose around her shoulders rather than up in a complicated style like some of the other chicks in this place. Despite her tight black sweater and short skirt, she's more girl-next-door than sex kitten.

The dark-haired friend snorts. "Yeah, good luck with that."

I flick up my eyebrows. "What, you think I don't have a shot?"

"Dude, look at you. You're, like, a jock, right?"

"Either that or he's on 'roids," the blond guy cracks.

"I'm an athlete," I confirm, but I don't offer more details. Clearly these guys aren't rabid hockey fans, otherwise they'd recognize me as Boston's latest rookie.

Or maybe they wouldn't. It's not like I've been seeing a crazy amount of ice time since I was called up from the farm team to the pros. I'm still trying to prove myself to my coach and teammates. Though I did get an assist last game, which was cool.

But a goal would've been cooler.

"Yeah, a sweet thing like that would be too intimidated," Mr. Rolex informs me. "Odds of you getting her number are…twenty to one."

His buddies agree. "That's a twenty-five percent chance," one says. Because again, their math is nonsensical.

"What if I want more than her number?" I challenge.

The blond snickers. "You want to know your odds of going home with her? A hundred to one."

I gaze at the brunette again. She's wearing black suede ankle boots with chunky heels, one leg crossed over the other as she daintily sips her drink. She's cute as hell.

"Two hundred bucks says I get her to stick her tongue down my throat in less than five minutes," I boast with an arrogant smirk.

My new friends bust out in incredulous laughter.

"Uh, sure, bro." Mr. Rolex chuckles. "In case you haven't noticed, the women in this joint are pure class. Not a single one would hook up with you in public."

I'm already dropping two hundreds on the counter. "Scared of my sexual prowess, huh?" I mock.

"Ha! Fine then. I'll bite," the blond guy says, placing two bills on top of mine. "Go ahead and get your ass rejected, Loverboy."

I pick up my glass and drain the rest of my beer. "Liquid courage," I tell the trio, and Mr. Rolex rolls his eyes. "Now watch and learn."

Winking, I amble off.

Instantly, her attention fixes on me. A hint of a smile, albeit soft with shyness, tugs at her mouth. Fuck, she's got nice lips. Full and pink and glossy.

When our gazes lock, it's as if everyone else in the bar disappears. Her brown eyes are pretty and expressive, and right now they're expressing a sweet hunger that quickens my pulse. I'm trapped in her orbit, my legs speeding up of their own volition.

A second later I'm beside her, greeting her with a rough, "Hey."

"Hi," she replies.

She has to tilt her head to look at me, because she's seated and I'm towering over her. I was always a big guy, but I've bulked up even more since I started playing hockey at a higher level. Skating in the pros is physically demanding.

"Can I buy you a drink?" I offer.

She lifts her full glass. "No, thank you. I've already got one."

"Then I'll buy your next one."

"There won't be a next one. I don't trust myself."

"Why's that?"

"I'm a lightweight. One drink makes me tipsy." Her lips curve slightly. "Two drinks make me do bad things."

Damned if my dick doesn't twitch at that. "How bad?" I drawl.

Although she blushes, she doesn't shy away from the question. "*Very* bad."

I grin at her, then flag the bartender with a fast, exaggerated gesture. "Another drink for the lady," I call.

She laughs, and the melodic sound sends prickles of sensation through me. I'm insanely attracted to her.

Rather than take the empty stool beside her, I remain standing. But I do edge closer, and her knee lightly brushes my hip. I swear I hear her breath hitch at the slight contact.

I glance over and spot my new friends watching us with deep interest. Mr. Rolex taps his watch dramatically as if to remind me the clock is ticking.

"So, listen…" I bring my lips close to her ear so she can hear me.

This time I see her breath hitch. Her perky breasts rise as she sucks in air. "My buddies gave me a twenty-five percent chance of getting your number."

Her eyes dance devilishly. "Wow. They don't have much faith in you, huh? I'm sorry."

"Don't be sorry. I've beaten greater odds than that. But…lemme tell you a secret…" My mouth brushes her earlobe as I whisper, "I don't want your number."

She jolts in surprise, her gaze snapping to mine. "You don't?"

"Nope."

"Then what do you want?" She picks up her drink and takes a hasty sip.

I think it over for a moment. "I want to kiss you."

A startled laugh now. "Uh-huh. You're just saying that because you hope I'll do it, and then you can prove to your friends you're not a loser."

I look over my shoulder again. Mr. Rolex wears a self-satisfied smirk. He taps his watch again. Tick-tock.

My five minutes are almost up. My own watch tells me I've only got two left.

"No," I tell her. "That's not why I want to kiss you."

"Oh really?"

"Really." I lick my bottom lip. "I want to kiss you because you're the hottest woman in this bar." I shrug. "And anyway, it's obvious you want the same thing."

"Says who?" she challenges.

"Says the fact that you haven't stopped staring at my mouth since I walked over here."

She narrows her eyes.

"See, here's the thing." I lightly drag my fingertips along her slender arm. I'm not touching bare skin, yet she visibly shivers. "My buddies think you're Little Miss Innocent. They warned me you'd be intimidated by someone like me. Someone rough and crude. But you know what I think?"

"What?" Her voice is breathy.

"I think you like rough and crude." Once again, I lean in closer. She's wearing a tiny diamond stud, and I can't help but flick the tip of my tongue over the little earring.

There's another sharp intake of breath, and I feel a tug of satisfaction.

"I don't think you're innocent at all," I continue. "I don't think you're a good girl. I think that right now you want nothing more than to shove your tongue in my mouth and rake your nails down my back and let me fuck you right here in front of everyone."

She moans out loud.

The cocky grin is just spreading across my face when she grabs the back of my head and yanks me down for a hard kiss.

"You're right," she murmurs against my lips. "I'm not a good girl at all."

My dick is hard before her tongue even enters my mouth. And when it does, sliding through my parted lips, it's my turn to moan. She tastes like gin and sex, and I kiss her back hungrily, all the while aware of the loud catcalls surrounding us. I'm sure some of those yells are coming from my stockbroker friends, but I'm too busy to bask in their amazement.

As my tongue slicks over hers, I gently nudge one leg between her soft thighs. Letting her feel how hard I am.

"Oh my God," she mumbles. She breaks the kiss, her eyes gleaming with pure lust. "Let's get out of here and finish this somewhere private?"

"No. I want you now." My voice sounds like gravel.

She blinks. "Now?"

"Mm-hmm." I rest one hand on her slim waist, moving my palm in a teasing caress. "I hear the ladies' room has real big, private stalls…"

She presses her own palm to the center of my chest. Not to push me away, though. She teases me too, while her hot gaze roams the length of my body. Then she slants her head and asks, "What would your girlfriend say about that?"

I give her a dirty smile. "She'd say...*hurry, John, I need to come.*"

Grace moans again.

"That's what I thought," I mock, but my girl doesn't look fazed.

Sometimes it's hard to believe she was once that nervous, babbling freshman whose dorm I accidentally wound up in. That the sweet Grace Ivers I fell for is this fearless woman in front of me, the sexy vixen who's about to let me fuck her in the bathroom.

Granted, Grace picked this bar and researched the cleanliness situation of the bathrooms before agreeing to tonight's role-playing exercise. So, yes, she's still that weird girl I met years ago. She just also happens to be my hot, sex-starved girlfriend.

I take her hand and pull her off the stool. I'm still hard as a rock and in need of relief. Judging by her shallow breathing, she's as aroused as I am.

"So what do you say?" I ask, rubbing the inside of her palm with my thumb.

Grace stands on the tips of her high-heeled boots and presses her lips to my ear. "Hurry, John, I need to come."

I swallow a desperate laugh as I follow her toward the rear corridor. Before we pass the doorway, I toss a final glance over my shoulder. The stockbrokers are gaping at me as if I'm an alien from another planet. I gesture to the money on the bar and offer a gracious nod as if to say, *Keep it all.*

I don't need to win some stupid bet. I'm already the luckiest man in the bar.

CHAPTER 2

LOGAN

"You really didn't have to do this," Grace's father insists as I drop the hood of his SUV back in place. "Not that I don't appreciate it, but I feel like a real goofhead for making you do manual labor on Christmas Eve."

Dragging a clean rag over my chin to wipe a streak of motor oil off, I try my hardest not to laugh. I like Tim Ivers a hell of a lot, but there's something very disconcerting about a grown man who uses words like "goofhead."

In the four years I've been dating his daughter, I can count on one hand the times I've heard the man curse, a drastic contrast to my own upbringing. I grew up with an alcoholic father whose every other word was an expletive. My poor mom once had to come in for a meeting with my kindergarten teacher because I'd called another kid a "fucking shit-face." Oh, those were the days... The very bad, unhappy days.

Luckily, everything's changed since then. My dad has been sober for nearly four years, and although we haven't completely mended fences, at least I don't hate him anymore.

If I'm being honest, these days I view Grace's dad as a father figure. He's a decent guy, if you overlook the fact that he prefers football to hockey. But nobody's perfect.

"Tim. My man. I'm not going to let my kinda dad pay money to get an oil change when I can do it for free," I inform him. "I grew up working in our garage. I can change oil with my eyes closed."

"Are you sure?" he pushes, readjusting his wire-rimmed glasses on the bridge of his nose. "You know I would never take advantage, son."

Son. Damn, that does me in every time. There's no good reason Tim should call me that. It's not like Grace and I are married or anything. Back when we first started dating, I thought maybe he was the kind of man who called every younger guy "son." But nope. Just me. And I can't deny I love hearing it.

"I know you wouldn't, which is why I offered," I assure him. "And like I said before, don't you dare go to that money-sucking dealership of yours for repairs ever again. My brother will take care of you. No charge."

"How is your brother these days?" Grace's dad locks his car before heading to the garage door.

I follow him out to the driveway, where the chill in the air instantly cools my face. It still hasn't snowed in Hastings yet this winter, but Grace said the forecast is calling for a huge dump of it tomorrow morning. Perfect. I love a white Christmas.

"Jeff's good," I answer. "He told me to wish you a happy holiday. They're sorry they couldn't be here for dinner tonight."

My brother and his wife, Kylie, are spending the holidays in Mexico this year with Kylie's family. It's her parents' fortieth anniversary, so they decided to do a huge sunny destination celebration. My mom and stepdad, David, are joining us tonight, though, which should be fun. Grace and I always get a kick out of watching her straitlaced molecular biologist father converse with my incredibly bland accountant stepfather. Last year we had a bet to see how many boring subjects they could discuss in one evening. Grace won with a total of twelve. I'd guessed ten, but I underestimated Tim's new fascination with antique milk bottles and David's new ceramic elephant collection.

"Josie's sorry she couldn't make it either," Tim says, referring to Grace's mother, who lives in Paris. Although Tim and Josie divorced years ago, they're still very close.

Unlike my folks, who can't be in the same room together, even with my dad being sober now. Grace and I have had numerous conversations about what'll happen when we get married—*when*, not if, because come on now. We're end game and we both know it. But we've stressed about it, wondering how we'd handle the issue of wedding invites. Eventually, we decided we'd probably elope to avoid all the drama, because there's no way Mom will attend if Dad is there.

Not that I blame my mother. Dad made her life a living hell during their marriage. She was the one who dealt with years of drunken tantrums, blackouts, and rehab stints while trying to raise two sons essentially on her own. I don't think she'll ever come around. It's a miracle Jeff and I managed to find some forgiveness for him.

"Do you know yet if your schedule will allow you to go to Paris with Grace this summer?" he asks as we round the side of the house toward the wraparound porch.

"It all depends if the team makes the playoffs. I mean, on one hand, spending two months in Paris sounds lit. But that would mean us not playing in the post-season, which sucks balls."

Tim chuckles. "See, if you played football, the season would be done in February, and you'd be able to make the trip…"

"One of these days, sir, I'm going to strap you to a chair and force you to watch hockey games on a loop until you have no choice but to love it."

"Still wouldn't work," he says cheerfully.

I grin. "You need to have more faith in my torture abilities."

Just as we reach the porch steps, a big brown van pulls up at the curb in front of the house. For a second I'm confused, thinking it's Mom and David, until I glimpse the UPS logo.

"They're still making deliveries?" Tim marvels. "At six o'clock on Christmas Eve? Poor fellow."

Poor fellow indeed. The delivery man looks frazzled and exhausted as he bounds up the path toward us. He's got a cardboard box in one hand, a bulky phone in the other.

"Hello, folks," he says when he reaches us. "Happy holidays, and sorry to disturb you. You're my last delivery of the day—it's for Grace Ivers?"

"Happy holidays," Tim says. "And that would be my daughter. She's inside, but I can run in and get her if she needs to sign for that?"

"No need. Any signature from the household will do." He hands over the phone and a plastic pen. After Grace's dad scribbles his signature, the delivery man bids us goodbye and hurries back to his truck. No doubt eager to get home and see his family.

"Who's it from?" I ask.

Tim checks the return label. "No name. Just a P.O. Box in Boston."

The package is about two by two feet, and when Tim gives it to me, I notice it doesn't have much heft. I narrow my eyes. "What if it's a bomb?"

"Then it will explode and we'll die, and the atoms of which we are composed will find new uses elsewhere in the universe."

"And Merry Christmas to us all!" I say with exaggerated holiday cheer, before rolling my eyes at him. "You're a real buzzkill, sir, you know that?"

"What's that?" Grace demands when we enter the living room of the big Victorian home.

"Not sure. It just showed up." I hold out the box. "For you."

Grace does that cute lip-biting thing she does when she's thinking. Her gaze travels to the beautifully decorated tree and piles of perfectly wrapped presents beneath it. "I don't think we can put it under there," she finally decides. "My OCD would never allow me to get through tomorrow morning knowing there's one stupid box that doesn't look magical."

I snort. "I can go wrap it if you want."

"There's no wrapping paper left."

"So I'll use newspaper. Or parchment paper."

My girlfriend stares at me. "I'm going to pretend you didn't just say that."

Her father laughs, because he's a traitor.

"Fine, then just open it now," I tell her. "We don't even know who it's from, so technically it might not be an official Christmas present. Fifty percent of me thinks it's a bomb, but don't worry, gorgeous, your father assured me our atoms will be repurposed after we explode."

Grace sighs. "I don't understand you sometimes."

Then she flounces off to the kitchen to look for scissors.

I admire her ass, which looks great in her bright-red leggings. She paired the leggings with a red-and-white striped sweater. Her dad is clad in a similar sweater, but his is green and red and has a badly knitted representation of a reindeer, which I first thought was a cat when he strolled in earlier wearing it. Apparently Grace's mom knit the horrific thing for him when Grace was little. As someone who didn't have many good holidays with my family, I have to admit I'm really into the weird Ivers traditions.

"All right, let's see what we've got here." Grace sounds excited as she slices through the strip of packing tape on the box.

Me, I'm on guard, because I haven't completely ruled out the notion that this could be an assassination attempt.

She opens the cardboard flaps and pulls out a small note card. A frown furrows her brow.

"What does it say?" I demand.

"It says 'I missed you.'"

My guard shoots up ten feet higher. What the fuck? Who the hell is sending my girlfriend gifts with cards that say *I missed you*?

"Maybe it's from your mom?" Tim guesses, looking equally perplexed.

Grace reaches inside and rummages through a sea of packing

paper. The frown deepens when her fingers connect with whatever's inside. A moment later, her hand emerges with its prize. All I glimpse is a flash of white, blue, and black, before Grace shrieks and drops the item as if it burned her palm.

"No!" she growls. "No. No. No. No, no, no, *no*." Her rageful gaze turns to me. She jabs her finger in the air. "Get rid of him, John."

Oh boy. Realization dawns as I approach the box. I have a pretty good sense now of what it contains, and—yep.

It's Alexander.

Grace's father wrinkles his forehead as I lift the porcelain doll from the cardboard. "What is that?" he inquires.

"No," Grace is still saying, pointing at me. "I want him gone. Now."

"What exactly would you like me to do?" I counter. "Throw him in the trash?"

She pales at the suggestion. "You can't do that. What if it makes him angry?"

"Of course it will make him angry. Look at him. He's perpetually angry."

Trying not to shudder, I force myself to look at Alexander's face. I can't believe it's been almost seven blissful months since I've seen it. As far as disturbing antique dolls go, this one tops the list. With a porcelain face so white it looks unnatural, he's got big lifeless blue eyes, weirdly thick black eyebrows, a tiny red mouth, and black hair with an extravagant widow's peak. He's wearing a blue tunic, white neckerchief, black jacket and shorts, and shiny red shoes.

He is the creepiest thing I ever did see.

"That's it," Grace says. "You're not allowed to be friends with Garrett anymore. I'm serious."

"In his defense, Dean started it," I point out.

"You can't be friends with him either. Tucker's okay to keep because I know he hates this as much as I do."

"And you think *I* like it?" I gape at her. "Look at this thing!" I wave Alexander in front of Grace, who ducks and dodges to avoid his flailing stubby arms.

"I don't understand," Tim hedges, reaching for the doll. "This is phenomenal! Look at the craftsmanship." He admires the doll, while his daughter and I stare at him in horror.

"Goddamn it, Dad," Grace sighs. "Now he knows your touch."

"Was this manufactured in Germany?" He continues examining Alexander. "Looks German-made. Nineteenth century?"

"I am very disturbed by your knowledge of antique dolls," I say frankly. "And we're not kidding, sir. Put him down before he imprints on you. It's too late for us—he already knows us. But you still have time to save yourself."

"From what?"

"He's haunted," Grace answers glumly.

I nod. "Sometimes he blinks at you."

Tim runs his fingers over the movable eyelids. "This mechanism is centuries old. If the eyes are opening and closing of their own volition, it's likely due to wear and tear."

"Stop touching him," Grace pleads.

For real. Does he have a death wish or something? I mean, I know *Garrett* does, because clearly he wants me to murder him next time I see him. I love Garrett Graham like a brother. He's my closest friend. He's a teammate. He's fucking awesome. But to do this to us on Christmas?

Granted, I did abuse my spare key privileges a few months ago to sneak Alexander into Garrett and his girlfriend's house for Hannah's birthday. But still.

"Do you mind if I take photos and try to find the value of it?" Tim asks, the geeky academic in him rearing its head.

"Don't bother. He cost four grand," I supply.

His eyebrows shoot up. "Four *thousand* dollars?"

Grace nods in confirmation. "That's another reason we can't throw him out. It feels wrong to throw away that much money."

"Dean bought him a couple years ago at some antique auction," I explain. "The listing said he was haunted, so Dean thought it would be hilarious to get the doll for Tuck's daughter, who was, like, a baby at the time. Sabrina lost her shit, so she waited till Dean and Allie were in town a couple months later and paid off someone at their hotel to leave the doll on Dean's pillow."

Grace giggles. "Allie said he screamed like a little girl when he turned on the light and saw Alexander there."

"And now it's a thing," I finish with a half-grin, half-sigh. "Basically, we all ship Alexander to one another when the other person least expects it."

"What did the seller say about it?" Tim asks curiously. "Does it have a backstory?"

Grace shakes her head. "Dad. Please stop calling him an 'it.' He can hear you."

"He came with some sort of information card," I answer with a shrug. "Can't remember who has it now. But basically, his name is Alexander. He belonged to a little kid named Willie who died on the California Trail back in Gold Rush times. Apparently, the entire family starved to death, except for Willie. Poor kid wandered around for days looking for help and eventually fell down a ravine, broke his leg, and lay there until he died of exposure."

Grace shudders. "They found him clutching Alexander against his chest. The psychotic doll seller said Willie's spirit went into Alexander right before he died."

Tim's eyes widen. "Jeez. That is fucking dark."

My jaw drops. "Sir. Did you just curse?"

"How could I not?" He sets Alexander back in the box and closes the flaps. "Why don't we take him up to the attic? Jean and David will be here any minute. We don't want to expose them to it."

Nodding decisively, Tim Ivers marches off with the box in hand. I honestly don't know if he's serious or just humoring us.

My lips twitch with laughter as I turn to Grace. "There. Alexander's been banished to the attic. Feel better?"

"Is he still in the house?"

"Well, yeah—"

"Then, no. I don't feel better."

Grinning, I grasp her by the waist and pull her toward me. Then I lower my head and brush my lips over hers. "How about now?" I murmur.

"Slightly better," she amends.

When I kiss her again, she melts against me and loops her arms around my neck. Fuck. I miss this so much when I'm on the road. I knew the pro hockey lifestyle would be tough, but I hadn't anticipated how much I'd miss Grace every time I had to leave town.

"I hate that you have to leave again," she says against my lips. Evidently her thoughts are echoing my own.

"Not for a few days," I remind her.

She bites her lip and presses her cheek against my left pec. "Still not enough time," she says, so softly I barely hear her.

I breathe in the sweet scent of her hair and hold her closer. She's right. It's not nearly enough time.

CHAPTER 3

GRACE

A FEW DAYS AFTER CHRISTMAS, LOGAN LEAVES FOR A FIVE-DAY stretch of road games on the West Coast. And of course he does, because conflicting schedules are pretty much a way of life for us now.

School's out for the holidays and I'm home? Logan's gone.

Logan has a couple of nights off and is home? I'm stuck on the Briar University campus in Hastings, a forty-five-minute drive from us.

We chose our cozy brownstone because it's exactly halfway between Hastings and Boston, where Logan's team skates. Winters in New England can be unpredictable, though, so if the weather is shit, our commutes are often double the time, which cuts into the precious time we have together. But until I graduate, this is the compromise we've made.

Luckily, I officially finish school in May, and we're both excited to find a new place in Boston. Although...I don't know what we'll do if I land a job that *isn't* in Boston. We haven't even discussed that possibility. I pray we won't need to.

Although it's winter break, the campus radio and TV station is still open and running as normal, so I drive to work the day after Logan leaves. I'm the station manager this year, which means a lot of responsibility—and a lot of interpersonal bullshit. I'm constantly dealing with an array of egos and the difficult personalities of "the talent," and today is no different. I put out several small fires, including mediating an argument about personal hygiene between Pace and Evelyn, co-hosts of Briar's most popular radio show.

The only bright spot in my hectic morning is brunch with my former roommate Daisy. When it's finally time to meet her, I find myself practically sprinting all the way to the Coffee Hut.

Miraculously, she snagged us a small table in the back. A huge feat, considering the coffeehouse is always jam-packed no matter the day or time.

"Hey!" I say happily as I take off my coat.

Daisy hops up to hug me. She's nice and toasty from being indoors, and I'm an ice statue from my chilly journey across campus.

"Eek! You're freezing! Sit down—I ordered you a latte."

"Thanks," I say gratefully. "I've only got an hour, so let's eat, like, immediately."

"Yes, ma'am."

A moment later we're seated and perusing the menu, which isn't too extensive because the café only serves sandwiches and baked goods. After Daisy goes up to the counter to place our food order, we sip on our respective drinks while we wait.

"You look stressed," she says frankly.

"I am stressed. I just spent the last hour explaining to Pace Dawson why he needs to start wearing deodorant again."

Daisy blanches. "Why did he stop?"

I rub my temples, which are throbbing from all the stupidity I just had to deal with. "To protest the plastic pollution in our oceans."

She snickers. "I don't get it."

"What's not to get?" I say sarcastically. "His deodorant comes in a plastic container. The ocean is full of plastic. Ergo, to protest this travesty, he needs to stink up the studio."

Daisy almost spits out her coffee. "Okay. I know he's obnoxious to work with, but I mean, come on, everything that comes out of that boy's mouth is pure gold."

"Evelyn finally put her foot down and threatened to quit if he didn't start using deodorant again. So I had to sit there and mediate until Pace finally agreed to Evelyn's demand—on the condition that she donates two hundred dollars to an ocean conservation charity."

"I had no idea he cared about the environment that much."

"He doesn't. His new girlfriend watched some documentary about whales last week, and I guess it was life-changing."

Once our food order is ready, we continue catching up as we munch on our sandwiches. We chat about our classes, her new boyfriend, my new position at the station. Eventually the subject of my relationship comes up, but when I say everything's fine, Daisy sees through my crappy poker face.

"What's wrong?" she asks immediately. "Are you and Logan fighting?"

"No," I assure her. "Not at all."

"Then what's going on? Why did you sound so...*blah* when I asked about you guys?"

"Because things are a bit blah," I confess.

"Blah how?"

"We're just both really busy. And he's always traveling. He's been out of town more days this month than he's been home. Christmas was so good, but way too short. He left for road games immediately after the holiday."

Daisy eyes me sympathetically as she takes a bite of her tuna wrap. She chews slowly, swallows, and asks, "How's the sex?"

"Actually, we're good in that department." Very good, in fact. The night we pretended to be strangers at the bar flashes through my mind. The dirty memory triggers a hot shiver.

That was some great sex. Hooking up in public isn't a habit of ours, but when we do it...holy fuck, it's hot as hell. Our sex life has always been amazing. I guess that's what makes this distance between us so terrible. When we're together, everything is as passionate and perfect as it was in the beginning. Our problem is trying to find time to be together. Time is scarce in our world.

I'm not unhappy with Logan. If anything, I want more of him. I miss my boyfriend.

"The time apart is tough," I tell Daisy.

"I can imagine. But what's your solution? It's not like he can quit hockey. And you're not dropping out of college with only five months left in your senior year."

"No," I agree.

"And you don't want to break up."

I'm appalled. "Of course not."

"Maybe you should get married."

That gets a smile out of me. "That's your solution? Get married?"

"I mean, we both know it's going to happen eventually." She shrugs. "Maybe if you guys had a more permanent commitment, it would make this stressful transitory period easier for you. Like, whenever you're feeling the distance, you won't have to stress about drifting too far apart because that extra-solid foundation is there to keep you stable."

"It's not a terrible idea," I admit. "And I do want to marry Logan, absolutely. But our problem is time. Even if we wanted to elope, when would we have the time?" I sigh miserably. "We're always busy and/or in different states."

"So then I guess you have no choice but to suck it up," Daisy says. She's right.

It's difficult, though. I miss him. I don't like coming home from class to an empty apartment. I don't like turning on the TV in order to catch a glimpse of my boyfriend. I don't like cramming for exams and being too tired to go out and see a movie or have dinner with him. I don't like Logan returning home after a particularly tough game and crawling into our bed, bruised and sore and too exhausted to even cuddle.

There simply aren't enough hours in a day, and it's even worse now that I'm running the station. When I started college, I wasn't sure what line of work I wanted to go into after I graduated. Originally, I thought about being a psychologist. But then I got a job sophomore year producing a campus radio show, and it made me realize I'd like to be a television producer. More specifically, I want to produce the news. Now that I've picked a career path, it's harder to blow off class or call in sick to work if Logan suddenly has a free hour or two. We've both got other commitments that are important to us. So, like Daisy said, we just have to suck it up.

"I'm sorry," I say. "I don't mean to be such a bummer. Logan and I are good. It's just hard sometimes—"

My phone beeps with an incoming text. I glance at the screen and smile at Logan's message. He's letting me know the team landed safely in California. He did the same thing yesterday when they got to Nevada. I appreciate that he always checks in like this.

"One sec," I tell my friend as I type out a response. "Just sending a quick text to wish Logan good luck on his game tonight."

He answers instantly.

Logan: Thanks, babe. I really wish you were here.
Me: Me too.
Him: I'll call you after the game?
Me: Depends how late it is here when you call.
Him: Try to stay up? We only talked for like 2 minutes last night :(
Me: I know. I'm sorry. I'll drink a bunch of coffee today so I'm more awake!

But although I keep the first part of that promise—chugging coffee like a fiend—the caffeine only makes me crash harder when I get home from campus that evening. I'm dead on my feet. Barely have enough energy to eat dinner and take a shower.

By the time Logan texts me at midnight to chat, I'm already fast asleep.

CHAPTER 4

LOGAN

Grace: How'd the press conference go?
Me: It went OK. I blew it on a couple questions, spoke too long. G answers everything short and snappy. He's an old pro, tho.
Her: I'm sure you did great <3
Me: Well, Coach didn't pull me aside afterward to fire me, so I assume I passed the media test.
Her: If he fires you, I'll kick his ass.

I SMILE AT THE PHONE. I JUST GOT BACK TO THE HOTEL AFTER tonight's game against San Jose, and I'm still feeling energized. Eventually the exhaustion will crash into me like a tidal wave, but the adrenaline of a game typically takes a while to drain from my system.

Me: Anyway. EAM.
Her: EAM? I'm too tired to try to decode that.
Me: Enough about me. Tell me about your day.
Her: Can we talk about it tomorrow? I'm in bed already. It's 1 a.m. :(

I check my phone display. Dammit. Of course she's in bed. It might only be ten p.m. here, but it's way past her bedtime on the East Coast.

I imagine Grace all snug and warm beneath our flannel bedsheets. It's freezing in New England right now, so she's probably sleeping in her plaid pants and that long-sleeved shirt with the words SQUIRREL POWER! on it. Neither of us knows what it means, because the shirt has a pineapple on it. She won't be wearing any socks, though. She sleeps barefoot no matter the temperature, and her feet are always like little blocks of ice. When we're curled up in bed, she presses them against my calf because she's evil.

I rub my tired eyes. Fuck. I miss her.

I type, I miss you.

She doesn't respond. She must've fallen asleep. I stare at the phone for a while waiting for an answer, but it doesn't come. So I pull up another chat thread and text Garrett.

Me: Quick drink at the bar?
Him: Sure.

We meet downstairs and find a quiet corner in the lobby bar. It's not at all busy, so it doesn't take long for our beers to arrive. We tap our bottles together, and each take a swig, mine longer than his.

Garrett watches me for a second. "What's wrong?"

"Nothing," I lie.

His eyes narrow in suspicion. "Swear to God, if you're about to bitch me out again about Alexander, I refuse to hear it. You broke into our house and planted him there to scare the shit out of Wellsy. If you think I'm gonna apologize for delivering him to you on Christmas, it ain't happening, kiddo."

Trying not to laugh, I cock my head at him. "You done?"

"Yes," he huffs.

"Good. Because I also refuse to apologize. You know why, *kiddo*?

Wait, are we calling each other that now? I don't get it, but okay, sure. Anyway, we've all had to suffer at the creepy porcelain hands of Alexander. Hannah's birthday just happened to be your time of torment."

Garrett's indignation dissolves into a grin. "Who you gonna ship him off to next?"

"I was thinking maybe a wedding gift for Tuck?" Our best friend Tucker is finally marrying his baby mama this spring, after three years of living in unwedded sin, that blasphemous asshole. I'm a bit surprised it took him and Sabrina this long to tie the knot—they've been engaged for-fucking-ever—but I think Sabrina wanted to finish law school first. She graduates from Harvard Law in May.

"Dude. No." I swear Garrett's face turns pale. "You do *not* fuck around with people's weddings."

"But the holidays are fair game?" I counter.

"Chicks are happy and agreeable during birthdays and holidays. Weddings? They turn into lunatics." He shakes his head in warning. "Sabrina will rip your balls off if you do that to her."

He's probably right. "Fine. I'll dump him on Dean. He deserves it more."

"Truth, brother."

A pretty, dark-haired young woman saunters past our table and instantly does a double take when she notices us. I brace myself for the wide eyes and piercing shriek, the plea for an autograph or a selfie with *the* Garrett Graham. But to her credit, she plays it cool.

"Good game tonight," she says tentatively, her awed gaze shifting between me and Garrett.

We both tip up our bottles. "Thanks," Garrett replies with a polite smile.

"You're welcome. Enjoy your night." She waves and keeps walking, her stilettos clacking against the lobby's marble floor. She stops at the front desk to talk to the clerk, all the while continuing to toss quick looks at us over her shoulder.

"Aww, look at that, superstar," I mock. "They don't even ask you for selfies anymore. You're old and washed up."

He rolls his eyes. "Didn't see her asking you for one either, rookie. Now are you gonna tell me why I'm down here drinking with you instead of getting my beauty sleep?"

I swallow another mouthful of beer, then slowly set the bottle down.

"I'm worried Grace is gonna break up with me."

The bleak words hang between us.

Garrett looks shocked. Then, his gray eyes soften with concern. "I didn't realize you two were having problems."

"We're not, really. No fighting or anger or cheating—nothing like that at all. But there's this distance between us," I confess. There aren't many people I feel comfortable turning to for advice, especially about chick problems, but Garrett is a good listener and a damn good friend.

"Distance," he echoes.

"Yeah. Literal and figurative. And it's only gotten worse. It started when I played for Providence, but that schedule is nothing compared to this one." I motion vaguely at our surroundings. I can't even remember the name of this hotel. Hell, some nights I don't remember what city we're in.

The life of a professional hockey player isn't all glitz and glamour. It's a lot of traveling. A lot of time spent on planes. A lot of empty hotel rooms. And, fine, maybe this is sort of like somebody crying about how their diamond shoes are too tight. Boo-fucking-hoo, right? But great money aside, this life *does* take a toll, physically and mentally. And, as it turns out, emotionally.

"Yeah, it's not an easy adjustment," Garrett admits.

"Did you and Wellsy have any problems when you first joined the league?"

"Of course. Being on the road all the time puts a strain on a relationship."

My index finger traces the label of my beer. "How do you *un*strain it?"

He shrugs. "I can't give you an exact answer. My only advice? Spend time together as often as you can. Go on as many adventures as you—"

"Adventures?"

"Yes. I mean, Wellsy and I barely left the house for the first few months. We'd be so tired and just sit around and watch Netflix like a pair of zombies. It wasn't good for us, and I don't think it's good for any relationship, to be honest. We were cooped up at home. She'd be strumming her guitar and I'd be dead on the couch, and yeah, sometimes it's nice just knowing that she's there, sharing the same space as you."

I know exactly what he means. If I'm watching TV and Grace is studying at our dining room table, I often look her way and smile at the little crease of concentration in her forehead. Sometimes I'm tempted to go over there and kiss that tiny groove, smooth it out with my lips. But I leave her to her work, smiling to myself and simply enjoying the fact that she's near me.

"But other times you feel so apart, even though you're together," Garrett continues. He takes another sip of beer. "That's when you need to inject some excitement into the relationship. Go for a walk. Explore a new neighborhood, try a new restaurant. Just keep making memories and sharing experiences. Good or bad, they bring you closer together."

"We do adventurous things," I protest.

"Like what?"

I wink. "Role-playing, for one."

"Nice. But I'm not talking about sex. Sex doesn't hurt, obviously, but…it's a matter of making her a priority. Showing her that hockey isn't your entire world, even when it feels like it is. And if all else fails, a week in the Caribbean does wonders."

"Dude, when do we have time for that? We barely have a night or two off, let alone a week."

"You can make do. We've got two nights off next week for New Year's Eve," he reminds me. "There're lots of places to go close to home."

"Really. In New England. In the winter."

"*Dude,*" he mimics. "Open up Airbnb. You'll find tons of little ski lodges and hotels, all within a few hours' drive."

"True." And Grace does like to ski…

I think it over. We have that break coming up, followed by another long stretch of away games. I definitely want—no, need to spend some quality time with my girl before the next road trip. I'm afraid if I don't, the distance between us will only continue to grow. Until eventually it'll be too far to bridge.

I'm still stressing about it when we part ways upstairs a half hour later. Luckily, I've crashed from the high of the game and now I'm exhausted, so I know I'll pass out the second my head touches the pillow. We have an early flight to Phoenix tomorrow.

"See you tomorrow," Garrett says before disappearing around the corner. The entire team has rooms on the same floor, but G's is on the other side of the elevator bank from mine.

"Later, bro."

I slide my key card out of my back pocket and pass it over the door handle, which releases with a click. My first sense that something's wrong? Walking into darkness. I clearly remember leaving the lights on when I went to meet Garrett. Now, shadows engulf me, raising the little hairs at the back of my neck.

The next warning bell is the soft rustling sound on the bed.

Wait. Am I in the wrong room? But no, that's impossible. I used my own key card to get in—

"C'mon, superstar. Don't keep me waiting all night," coos a throaty female voice.

I almost jump out of my skin. What in the actual *fuck*?

A hit of adrenaline surges in my veins as I slap the wall to flick the switch. A burst of light fills the room, clearly illuminating the naked woman sprawled on my king-sized bed like she's posing for a pinup calendar. She's got one arm crooked behind her head, dark hair cascading over her shoulder and fanned across my pillow. Tits and legs and the curve of an ass assault my vision before I force my gaze to her face. I recognize it instantly.

It's the chick from the lobby.

"What the hell!" I growl. "How did you get in here?"

My midnight intruder is completely unbothered by the anger coloring my tone. "I have my ways," she says coyly.

I can't even believe this shit is happening right now.

I rub my suddenly pounding temples. "Okay. Look. I don't know you, lady. Whatever you thought you were gonna get out of this, it ain't happening. It's time for you to go."

Her lips curl into an exaggerated pout. "You can't be serious," she whines. "I'm your biggest fan. I just want to show you my appreciation."

"I'll pass, thanks." I cross my arms. "You gonna leave on your own or do I need to call security?"

A smug glint flashes in her eyes. "I don't think leaving your bed is an option, honey."

To my sheer disbelief, she lifts her head slightly to show me the arm she'd been leaning against. Or rather, the wrist that's handcuffed to the bedpost.

You've *got* to be kidding me.

Mustering up my last ounce of patience, I ask, "Where's the key?"

Her eyes flick down her body, and the dirty smile she gives me tells me everything I need to know.

No. Nope. Not dealing with this tonight.

Without a word, I stride across the room to the chaise where I left my coat, then grab my duffel from the floor.

"Where are you going?" the shocked puck bunny screeches.

"Away," I answer tersely. I march toward the door, adding over my shoulder, "Don't worry, I'll let the front desk know you're here."

The last thing I hear before the door swings shut behind me is, *"You come back here, John Logan!"*

Un-fucking-real.

Out in the corridor, I release a string of expletives under my breath, then, bypassing the elevators, stomp toward Garrett's room. I'm way too tired for this crap. The thought of going back downstairs and having to explain the situation to the front desk, then ask to see the manager, arrange for a new room, risk them calling Coach or someone at the franchise for a signature or some shit. Forget it. Too much effort, and it'll cost me a solid hour of sleep.

"Are you stalking me?" Garrett grumbles as he opens the door to find me there. He's shirtless, barefoot, and wearing a pair of plaid pants.

"I'm bunking with you tonight," I mutter in lieu of explanation, then muscle my way into his room. I drop my stuff on a chair. "Let me just use the phone first."

"Are you serious right now?"

I ignore his exclamation and reach for the phone, punching in the button for the front desk.

An overeager male voice slides into my ear. "What can we do for you, Mr. Graham?"

"Hi, this is actually John Logan, Garrett's teammate. I'm supposed to be in room fifty-two-twelve, but there's currently a naked woman handcuffed to my bed—"

Garrett barks in surprise, then releases a howl of laughter that he muffles with his forearm.

"Since the sole key card is in my pocket," I continue in a tight voice, "the only assumption I can make is that an employee gave her access to my room. Or she stole one, somehow. Either way, it doesn't look good for you guys."

On the edge of the bed, Garrett is doubled over in laughter.

"Oh boy," the hotel clerk blurts out. "I am so sorry about this, Mr. Logan. We will send security to your room immediately and get you back in there as soon as—"

"It's fine, I'll be crashing here with Mr. Graham," I cut in. "But yes, please send someone to my room. We have an early flight, so if security needs to talk to me about this, I'll find them before we check out."

I hang up without another word, which I know is rude, but now I'm tired and cranky, and I don't want to talk anymore tonight. With anyone.

"You got an extra blanket in there?" I nod toward the closet as I kick off my shoes.

Garrett gets up to check. A moment later, he tosses me a duvet and a pillow, which I carry to the small couch under the window. My legs will be dangling off the side of that thing, but at this point, I don't care. I just need to sleep.

"Swear to God, the puck bunnies in the pros are next level," I gripe.

"Hey, it's a rite of passage, dude. You're not a pro hockey player until a crazy naked girl breaks into your hotel room." A grinning Garrett watches me arrange my makeshift bed. "Welcome to the league."

CHAPTER 5

GRACE

Does #Wesmie Have Some Competition?

New couple alert?!

OK, let's not get our hopes up, ladies and gents, but could it be?? Do Ryan Wesley and Jamie Canning, Toronto's beloved pair of married hockey hotties, have some competition?? Are Boston's star forward Garrett Graham and breakout star John Logan HOOKING UP???!!

Check out these leaked photos from the San Jose Marriott and tell us what you think... Two friends innocently sharing a hotel room due to a mishap, or two teammates caught in a compromising position after Saturday night's game between San Jose and the visiting Bostoners???

The official story is a crazed fan broke into John Logan's room, but our source at the SJ Marriott hinted this could be a big, fat cover story to disguise the fact that GG and JL are indeed together.

"They were spotted in the elevator looking very cozy," the anonymous source told Hockey Hotties. "Several guests reported seeing them."

And hotel security cameras show the couple (omg!!!!) sharing a romantic drink in the lobby bar late that night.

Oh, and did we mention they were also "roommates" in college?!

All we know is, we are shipping this SO HARD!!! How about you??! Comment below with your thoughts!!!!

I DON'T THINK I'VE EVER ROLLED MY EYES THIS HARD. HockeyHotties.com isn't exactly a paragon of journalistic excellence, but I feel like their content just gets more and more ridiculous. I click on the photos accompanying the article and laugh out loud when I see them.

There's two grainy shots of Logan and Garrett in an elevator, standing about three feet apart. And a few shots of them in a lobby bar—clinking beer bottles in a toast. Sipping their drinks. Brows furrowed as they discuss something. Garrett grinning at whatever Logan just said.

In other words, not at all scandalous.

Meanwhile, on the huge flat screen in our living room, the Boston–New York game is in progress. I glance up from my phone to see my boyfriend skate across the screen. As always, he looks sexy as hell in his uniform.

My phone beeps with another incoming message. Our girls' group chat has been lighting up ever since Hannah texted me a link to that hilarious article.

Allie: Why does this writer use so many question and exclamation marks? It's!! So!? Annoying!!!?? And this is coming from a girl who loves exclamation marks.

I laugh at that. Allie is dating Logan's former teammate Dean, and as a tiny, blond tornado of energy, she does tend to use a lot of exclamation marks in her texts.

Sabrina: I think the more important question is—what are Hannah and Grace gonna do now that we know their boyfriends are secretly banging in elevators?
Hannah: I feel so betrayed.
Me: For real. They've been sleeping together this whole time and haven't even let us watch??!?
Hannah: !!!
Sabrina: !!?!!
Allie: !!!??

My gaze strays back to the TV. It's still so surreal seeing Logan on television. Like, that's the man I love, right there on the big screen for everyone to see. A few more games like tonight, and it'll be Logan's name on the signs all those women are holding up. GARRETT I'M YOURS! is the one currently being showcased by the crowd camera.

Logan scored his third goal of the season during the team's last power play. Now he's once again on the ice, charging the net. My heart jumps to my throat as I watch his stick slap the puck at the net. The goalie makes the save. Ugh. New York then secures the rebound and zips off with it.

Hannah: All seriousness, G told me about the girl who snuck into Logan's room. That shit is the worst. Last time it happened to us, I was actually IN THE ROOM when the hockey stalker snuck in. It was that weekend in NYC—remember, Allie? We went to that restaurant with your dad.
Sabrina: "Last time"? How many times have random crazies broken into Garrett's hotel rooms?
Hannah: We're on #3. Which isn't terrible. Shane Lukov's wife said they're almost at a baker's dozen.
Allie: Holy shit. Bitches be cray.

I have to admit, when Logan called me the morning after the

San Jose game to give me the heads-up about his intruder, I wasn't thrilled to hear it. I'm not typically a jealous person, but the thought of some other woman naked in my boyfriend's bed makes me a bit… homicidal. Hearing from Hannah that it's not an uncommon occurrence does bring some comfort, I suppose.

> Me: I don't know… Can we even be sure there WAS a hotel
> stalker? I mean, according to HockeyHotties.com, it's a cover
> for G&L's sordid affair.
> Hannah: Good point.
> Allie: !!?!!!!

I tap out a quick goodbye to the group chat before tucking my phone away and reaching for my laptop. My psych professor sent us a list of the readings for next semester, so I figured I'd get a head start over the holiday break. It's been getting harder and harder to juggle my course load and work responsibilities this year. I can't wait until graduation.

I glance at the TV to check the score, but the rest of the game isn't very competitive. Boston is kicking ass. Logan takes a scary-looking hit in the third period, but he hops right back up and skates away, which tells me he's all right.

As the post-game interviews waft out of the surround sound, I alternate between staring at my laptop and absently scrolling through my Insta feed to see what my mother is up to. Mom spends her days painting in her studio, traveling when she's not feeling creative, and constantly posting photos of her adventures. I really hoped she'd be able to come home for Christmas, but she had a gallery opening scheduled that week. So now I won't be seeing her until after graduation, when I visit her in Paris for a couple of months.

How sad is it that my life is so hectic I need to learn about my mother's escapades via social media? I make a mental note to give her a call tomorrow. With the time difference, it's too late to call now.

Just after midnight, Logan stumbles through the door. My favorite part about home games is seeing him return at a semi-normal hour.

"Hey, gorgeous," he says when he spots me on the couch. He went out for drinks with some teammates after the game and his hazy expression tells me he's buzzed.

"Hey." I click the remote to shut off the TV, which had been playing *Friends* reruns. "How's your arm? That hit in the third looked painful."

Logan flexes his sculpted forearm, then rotates his wrist. "All good," he assures me. "I'm invincible." He walks over to kiss me. As always, my heart sings the moment our lips touch.

I love this guy so frickin' much. I promised myself I wouldn't be that clingy, whiny girlfriend who bitched and complained about how often her boyfriend travels. And don't get me wrong, I *don't* complain. I understand his schedule is brutal, I really do. But that doesn't mean I don't hate every second we're apart.

"How was your night?" he asks, flopping down beside me.

"Boring. All I did was study." I grin at him. "Although it did pick up after Hannah told me about your forbidden love affair with Garrett."

Logan snorts. "You saw that stupid blog post, eh? Lukov showed it to us in the locker room after the game, and everyone had a great time ragging on us for it. Our D-man Hawkins kept asking when the wedding is. Grygor offered to officiate."

"That was sweet of him."

"Had to break his heart and tell him there won't be a wedding, no matter how good G's BJs are."

"Wow. Garrett takes the time to pleasure you with blowjobs, and you won't even marry the guy? Heartless, Johnny. Heartless."

He falls backward with laughter, leaning on his elbows. "Yeah, sorry. But I'm already planning on marrying someone else."

"Oh really?"

"Really." He smirks. "It's you, by the way."

"Oh really," I say again.

"Really." Those deep blue eyes gleam with intensity. "I told you a long time ago—you're it for me, Gracie Elizabeth. I'm going to marry you one day."

Pleasure heats my cheeks. Logan's not the most romantic man on the planet, but when he does express his feelings, he doesn't do it halfway.

"Who says I want to marry you?" I tip my head in challenge.

"Don't you dare pretend we're not forever."

A smile breaks free. He's right. I'm not that good of an actress. "We're definitely forever," I say firmly. "But don't forget—when we get married, we're eloping."

"Perfect. That way my mom doesn't wind up in jail for murdering my father, and we get to spend all the wedding money on a sick honeymoon."

"For what it's worth, the other day Daisy was also saying we should get married."

"Yeah? And what'd you tell her?"

"That even if we wanted to, it'd be a miracle if we could find the time," I confess, offering a self-deprecating smile.

"Aww. There'll be time. I promise. Now c'mere and tell me how your day was," he says, tugging me toward him.

I rest my head on his broad chest as we lie on the couch and chat about our respective days. His was obviously more exciting than mine, but Logan listens to me describe the news radio show I'm producing as if I'm regaling him with tales of exploration and wonder. He's overcompensating, I know this. And I know he feels like shit about being gone all the time, being too exhausted to pay attention sometimes when I tell him about school or work.

"You're not working tomorrow night, right?" he says, cutting me off midsentence.

"Nope, the station's closed on New Year's Eve. Don't need to go back until Friday."

"Perfect." There's satisfaction in his voice.

I sit up and study his face. "Why are you so interested in my schedule?"

Logan's not great at hiding his emotions. I can tell he's fighting a huge grin.

"What's going on?" I ask suspiciously.

"I think the real question is—who's going where?"

"What does that even mean?" This guy is so exasperating sometimes with his random acronyms and cryptic riddles.

His happy smile breaks free. "It means we're going away tomorrow," he announces, sitting up. "I'm stealing you away for two days."

I stare at him in surprise. "For reals?"

"For fucking reals."

"Where are we going?" I demand.

"That's for me to know and for you to find out." Logan pauses. "Well, actually, it's not a secret. We're going skiing in Vermont."

I can't help but laugh. "Oh, are we?"

His smile falters. "Trust me, I'd much rather whisk you away to an island where you could wear a string bikini and I could eye-fuck you all day long, but the team's flying out to Houston on Friday. So two days in Vermont is all I can—"

"Two days in Vermont is *perfect!*" I interrupt, throwing my arms around him.

He nuzzles my neck, placing a soft kiss there. "I found us a bed-and-breakfast near Killington. It's super isolated and rustic, but it looks cozy. Oh, and there's a private ski hill we can use at a nearby resort."

"Sounds awesome." When my hand moves to his face, Logan presses his cheek to my palm and rubs against it like a happy cat.

My fingertips travel to his lips, and he gives them a teasing nip. "It's not fancy," he admits. "I couldn't find anything better on such short notice, but it's got a bed and a fireplace, which is all we really need, right?"

"Bed and fireplace—the staples of life," I agree solemnly. Then I beam at him. "This is such a terrific surprise."

"You sure?" He anxiously searches my expression as if evaluating my honesty.

"I'm positive." I run my fingers through his close-cropped hair and gaze at him reassuringly. "I can't wait."

CHAPTER 6

LOGAN

I'M EXCITED FOR THIS TRIP. SURE, IT'S NOT A TROPICAL BEACH, but the change of scenery will do us good, and I'm looking forward to escaping my obligations for two whole days. No morning skates, no backbreaking games and sore ribs. Just me and Grace for forty-eight stress-free hours, without anyone or anything getting in the way.

When I was in college, I drove a beat-up truck that I fixed up myself. Hell, I rebuilt the entire engine on that old thing—twice. Nowadays I'm driving a brand-new Mercedes. My rookie salary isn't even that much compared to what other players are raking in, and yet it's still more money than most people make in a decade.

But this new vehicle lacks the charm of my old one. The engine barely makes a sound, and when we're off the highway and driving on an uneven, unpaved road, the suspension proves just as efficient. The SUV barely moves as it coasts over various potholes.

Despite the peak performance of my new ride, I let out a wistful sigh. "I miss my pickup."

Grace looks over. "Aww, really?"

"I really do." I couldn't even bear to sell it, so it's currently sitting in my older brother's garage. We both know I'll have to get rid of it eventually because it's just taking up space, but I'm not ready to say goodbye yet.

"Your truck didn't have butt warmers," Grace points out. "Butt warmers are the best."

"They are the best," I agree.

A notification appears on the screen at my dashboard. Since my phone's hooked up to the car, my text messages are synced to it. "Text from Dean," Grace tells me.

"Ignore it." I make a grumbling noise. "He and Tuck are terrorizing me and G in the group chat about the blog post."

"And you expect me to ignore that?" Her eager hand snaps forward. After she taps a button on the screen, Siri begins reciting Dean's words.

"*I just don't get it. We were all roommates in college. I never even suspected you two were boning!*"

Grace chortles happily. "It's even better hearing it from Siri. Ooh. There's one from Tucker." She taps "next message."

"*I always had a feeling. They kept trying so hard to act like they were platonic.*"

"Because we were platonic!" I growl.

"Were?" my girlfriend says sweetly.

"Are," I correct. "We were and are platonic."

Another message from Dean comes in.

"*Sneaky bastards.*"

I hit a button on the screen. "Siri, send text to Best Buds Forever chat."

"Best Buds Forever?" Grace howls. "That's the name of your group chat?"

"Yeah, got a problem with that?" To Siri, I dictate, "Hey dipshit, at least I wasn't sneaking around taking baths with pink dildos." With a smug nod, I press Send. "There. That'll shut him up for a while."

Up ahead, the road gets narrower and windier, summoning a worried frown from Grace. "Where is this place?"

"I told you, it's rustic."

"Rustic."

"Oh, come on, don't give me that look. It's not like we're gonna be sleeping outside in a tent. I told you, we'll have a huge bed, a roaring fireplace..." I waggle my eyebrows enticingly.

"You're really trying to sell me on this fireplace."

"Because it's fucking awesome and I wish we had one in the apartment."

"No, you don't. They're a fire hazard."

"You're a fire hazard." I wink at her. "Because you're so hot."

Grace sighs.

For the next five miles, we chat about nothing in particular, until Grace becomes apprehensive again.

"The snow is picking up," she says.

It is. What started off as light flurries is now falling harder and sticking to the road. The sun has completely set and the sky is pitch-black, the Mercedes' top-of-the-line headlights the only thing illuminating our way. Maybe it's good I don't have my truck anymore—the right headlight was always flickering, and the left one was too pale. We'd be driving blind right now if we were in that pickup. It was a piece of shit, but I loved it.

"Do you think we should turn around?" Grace asks.

I glance at her. "And go where?"

Her teeth worry her bottom lip. "Back to the highway maybe?"

"The highway's an hour away."

"Yeah, but according to the GPS, it's still another hour and a half to the B&B. Technically we're closer to the interstate."

"We can't just bail," I chide. "We're not quitters, babe."

"But it's..." She trails off.

"It's what?"

"It's dark and scary!" she wails. "Look out the window, Logan. I feel like we're in a horror movie."

She's not entirely wrong. Save for the two yellow stripes from the headlights, the road is dark and the snow isn't letting up. If anything, the weather's only getting worse. The wind has picked up, a deafening gust beyond my window. It's troublesome that I can't hear the damn engine and yet I can clearly hear the wind.

"All right, hold on, let's figure this out," I finally say.

I click the emergency blinkers and pull onto the shoulder of the narrow road. Though I probably don't need the emergency lights, considering we haven't seen another car in ages.

I grab my phone from the cup holder. I only have two bars, but it's enough to load the weather app.

"Shit," I say a moment later.

"What is it?" Grace leans toward me to peer at the screen.

"Apparently there's a blizzard tonight. What the hell. It said nothing about a blizzard when I checked the weather earlier."

"Did you..." She stops.

"Did I what?" I demand.

Grace exhales ruefully. "Did you check the weather for Boston or did you check the weather for northern Vermont?"

I pause.

"Boston," I grumble.

"Babe."

"I'm sorry. That was dumb of me." I lick my lips in an overly lewd way. "Want to spank me for being a bad boy?"

A glint of lust lights her eyes. I chuckle softly. We both know she loves how dirty I am. I'm not shy about what I want and what I like, and Grace has gotten pretty good at voicing her desires too. That's why our sex life is so phenomenal.

"Maybe later," she says, her face growing serious. "Let's focus. It looks like this area is expecting more than a foot of snow tonight."

"They always say that, and it's never that much," I argue.

Stricken, she peers out the dark window. "I don't know... It's really piling up out there."

"So what do you want to do? You want to turn around? Because

I think we can beat the snow and get there before the worst of the storm hits."

She chews on her lower lip. It's so goddamn adorable. I'm tempted to lean over and kiss the hell out of her.

"Fine, let's do it," she decides. "Just don't speed, okay? I want to get there alive."

"Deal. I'll spare our lives."

She snickers.

I steer back onto the road, and despite its stupidly expensive winter tires, the SUV actually skids.

Grace yelps. "Logan!"

"Sorry. I'm not speeding, I swear. It's just slippery." I ease up on the gas, proceeding to drive with more caution.

For the next twenty minutes, we don't speak. We're too focused on the drive and the worsening weather. A wall of white has appeared in front of our car. All the snow accumulating on the ground and on the hood of the Mercedes tells me a foot of it isn't a far-fetched estimate. To make matters worse, this area is so isolated, I doubt any snowplows or salt trucks pay it many visits. Eventually the road becomes treacherous, and it isn't long before I'm driving at a crawl.

"John," Grace says in concern.

"I know," I say grimly.

But it's too late to turn back now. The interstate is too far behind us. The GPS says we're about forty minutes from the B&B, but at the pace we're traveling, we won't reach it for several hours.

"Shit," I curse. "Okay. Keep an eye out. Maybe we'll see somewhere we can stop."

"Like where?"

"I don't know. A motel? An inn?"

A note of panic creeps into her voice. "Babe, there's *nothing* here. We're literally in the middle of nowhere—" She jumps when the SUV skids again.

"Sorry." My hands are curled tightly around the steering wheel.

I lean forward and intently stare out the windshield like an elderly lady who forgot her glasses at home.

"Should we pull over and wait it out?" Grace frets.

I think it over. "Probably not a good idea. What if we get snowed in at the side of the road? I say we keep going."

"Sure, let's keep going at this brisk pace of zero miles an hour," she says sarcastically. "We'll get there at dawn."

"It won't take that long—" Something suddenly flies past the windshield.

A gust of blowing snow, I realize half a second later, but it's too late. I'd already instinctively tapped the brakes. Just lightly, yet even that soft touch sends the car into a fishtail.

"*Fuck.*" I attempt to steer out of the skid, but the tires swing sharply, and this time I can't control it. The next thing I know the Mercedes is barreling toward the slope at the shoulder.

"Hang on!" I shout, white-knuckling the wheel as we fly off the road.

CHAPTER 7

GRACE

My pounding heart nearly busts out of my chest horror-movie style as the SUV fishtails dizzyingly out of control. When it finally comes to a stop, my hands are shaking and I'm weak with relief.

I plaster my face to the window. All I see is total darkness, broken only by the thin columns of the headlights. They're pointing at a stretch of white. Nothing but snow fills my line of sight. We're at the bottom of a small slope, but it might as well be a mountain. When I peer up to where I think the road is, it feels impossibly far.

Logan is breathing hard beside me. "Are you okay?"

"I'm fine." We didn't hit anything. We're both in one piece, and so is our vehicle. "We have four-wheel drive, right? Can we make it back up to the road?"

He purses his lips. Assesses the situation. "I mean, we can try. Worst-case scenario, I'll get out and push."

"You're going to *push* an SUV up a snow hill?" I say in dismay. "I mean, I know you're a big sexy beast, but—"

"Thanks, baby." He sputters out a laugh.

"No problem. But I don't think you're strong enough for the job."

"Ye of little faith."

I roll my eyes. "Prove me wrong, then. But let's do it now, because I'd like to try to get out of here before we die."

"We're not going to die." But there's a serious note in his voice.

He moves the gearshift to drive and gently presses the gas pedal. The car eases forward, much to my relief. Good. At least we're not stuck in some inescapable snowdrift.

Logan drives a few feet, then starts to turn toward the slope. It's not at all steep, but the Mercedes ascends only about a foot before it struggles. Logan hits the gas. The car won't budge another inch.

"Shit." He accelerates again.

I feel the tires laboring to try to gain some traction.

But it's not happening.

"Guess I'm pushing," Logan says in resignation. As I look on miserably, he reverses down the slope and puts the car in park. "All right, gorgeous. It's your time to shine."

I laugh weakly.

He zips up his coat and grabs his wool hat from the center console. He shoves it over his head, then takes a pair of gloves out of his pocket.

"Well," he announces with a wry grin, "this is gonna suck."

"I can come and help you push."

"No, I need you to steer and work the pedals."

After he hops out, I climb into the driver's seat and buckle up, then feel a bit stupid for doing so. But better safe than sorry, right? When I open the window so I can hear his instructions, a gust of bitterly cold air slaps me in the face.

"All right," I hear Logan's muffled yell. "On the count of three, hit the gas and I'll give you a little push. Okay?"

"Okay," I call out the window.

He begins to count. "One…two…*three.*"

I slam my boot on the gas. The car shoots forward. A foot, two feet. And then it keeps moving.

"Yes!" I shout. "It's working." We're about halfway up now.

"Keep going!" Logan hollers his encouragement. "We got this, kiddo."

"Did you just call me *kiddo?*"

"Yeah, sorry, G got in my head!"

We're shouting over the wind.

"Oh my God, would it kill you to make any sort of sense ever?"

"Forget it. Just keep your foot on the gas. We got this."

He's right. A few more yards and—

Except we don't got this. I hear a loud curse, and then the car slides backward several feet.

Holy shit, is he still behind me? Alarm tightens my throat. What if I'm running him over?

Before I can blink, the car rolls right back to where we started. Dammit.

Relief pounds into me when Logan's wind-burnt face appears in the driver's side window.

"I slipped," he growls. "Sorry."

"I'm the one who should be sorry," I say, breathing hard. "I wasn't fast enough with the brakes. I could've killed you."

"Let's try again."

"But what if you slip again? I don't want to run you over. I *like* you."

His muscular chest shudders with laughter.

"Besides, I honestly don't think we can do it. Let's just call a tow truck," I advise.

"Fine."

Logan gets back in the car, sliding into the passenger side. He grabs his phone and checks the screen. "Shit, I'm down to one bar. How about you?"

"Zero bars," I answer cheerfully.

"One bar for the win."

Rather than Google the number for a tow truck, he pops open the glove compartment and rummages inside. "I have complimentary road assistance with Mercedes," he says at my questioning look.

"Fancy."

"Number should be in here somewhere."

He finally finds the paperwork. Dials. When someone answers, he provides a policy number and explains the situation. He gives our location, listens for a moment, then rolls his eyes.

"They put me on hold," he tells me.

And while we're on hold, the call drops because of the weak signal, so he's forced to call back and do the whole thing all over again.

"I just called," he grumbles after being asked a bunch of questions. "Someone was checking for me when the call failed and—" He bites out a curse and glares at me. "They put me on hold."

I giggle.

This time he survives the hold, but the response we get is not ideal. "In the morning?" he exclaims. "Seriously?"

"We'll be dead by then," I hiss.

Logan grins at me. "We won't be dead by then—no, no, sorry, I was talking to my girlfriend. But that's way too long. Come on, man. You gotta get someone here sooner. We're stuck at the bottom of a hill in the middle of a blizzard." He pauses. "I understand it's New Year's Eve, but—" He stops for a beat, then snarls like an irate beast. "They put me on fucking hold."

CHAPTER 8

LOGAN

Six hours. The roadside assistance dispatcher managed to reduce our wait time from twelve hours to six. Which is fantastic, except six hours still means we're stuck here until about three a.m.

Looks like we're ringing in the New Year in our car.

We don't have another choice, though. We're stranded, and there's no way we're leaving this vehicle. I've seen movies. Nothing good ever comes from leaving your car in a storm. Outside sucks. Inside the Mercedes is nice and toasty. For now, anyway.

Although we have more than half a tank of gas, I don't want to take any chances, so I turn to Grace and say, "Let's turn it off for now."

"You mean the heat?" She looks horrified. "We'll freeze to death."

"Nah. I'll keep you warm, I promise."

Her eyes twinkle. "Ooooh. How are you gonna do that?"

I gesture to the back seat. "Get back there and make yourself comfy. I've got some goodies in the trunk for us."

As she climbs over the center console, I hop outside and once again endure the frigid night air. Snowflakes dance around my head and stick to my cheeks as I walk into the wind and round the SUV. I've kept an emergency kit in every vehicle I've ever driven, and this one is no different. I grew up in New England—I know the drill. Blanket, candles, water, the usual survival gear. But I also brought some extra treats for our New Year's Eve getaway.

"Incoming," I call, tossing a thick fleece blanket over the partition between the trunk and the back seat.

"Thank you!" she calls back.

I grab the canvas bag and close the trunk, then suffer four more seconds of snow and wind before sliding in next to Grace. "Fuck, it's cold," I gripe.

She's already under the blanket, lifting it so I can join her. I'm too big for the blanket, so my boots stick out the bottom, but I don't care. Cuddling with my girl is all I care about.

"What's in the bag?" she asks curiously.

"First of all—this." I pull out a bottle of cheap champagne. "It's a twist top," I say with a rueful grin. "You know I'd normally spring for the good bubbly, but I didn't want to be blowing corks into the B&B walls."

Grace snickers. "Blowing corks? That sounds so dirty."

"Also, I didn't pack any glasses because I assumed we'd have some in our room. So I guess we're drinking straight out of the bottle."

"Classy!"

"Hey, I'm the son of a mechanic. I grew up with grease and oil on my hands and face and—actually." I shrug. "It was all over me, all the time."

"Hot."

I arch a brow. "Is that so?"

"Are you kidding me? I'd *pay* you to let me rub oil all over you. All those glistening muscles…" She shivers, and I know it's not from the cold.

I make a mental note—Grace wants to see me all oiled up. I bet I could make that happen next time I have a night off. I mean, I'm all about making her feel good. Whatever it takes to get her off, I'm up to the task.

"Should we open this baby now or wait till midnight?"

She mulls it over. "Let's wait. It'll be a little less depressing if we're at least drinking champagne when the clock strikes twelve."

"Whatcha calling depressing? This is romantic." I pull her toward me. "C'mere."

A second later we're snuggled up, my arm wrapped around her shoulders, her cheek pressed against my chest. The car's still warm, and we have our combined body heat, but the warmth only lasts about fifteen minutes. As Grace chats about the news show she's producing for Briar, I notice her breath starting to escape in white puffs.

"One sec," I interrupt, stretching toward the front seat. "Let's turn on the heat for a bit."

We do this for the next hour—let the heat build up, turn it off to conserve it, and then blast hot air again when we start shivering.

"I feel like there's got to be a better way to stay warm," Grace says after I shut the heat for the billionth time.

"Mmm-hmmm?" I give her a wolfish grin.

"That's not what I meant, but…" She grins back. "It's not a bad idea."

"Not a bad idea at all," I agree, and then I thread my fingers through her hair, tilt her head back, and cover her mouth with mine.

I love kissing her. Sometimes when I'm on the team jet trying to sleep or when my mind wanders in the locker room, I think about the first time Grace and I kissed. I'd accidentally shown up at her dorm room thinking it was my buddy's. Instead, I found a freshman watching *Die Hard* movies and eating candy. I joined her, because, why not? She was cute and I was bored. But somehow it went from a movie night to a make-out session. My hand down her pants and her hand down mine.

Man, that was such a good night. When I mistakenly knocked on that door, I never in a million years thought I'd fall in love with the girl behind it. Or that we'd be sharing an apartment, a bed.

Building a life together. And now here we are in the back seat of our roomy Mercedes, and she's falling backward onto her elbows while my body lowers onto hers. Her hands tangle in my hair, eager tongue slipping into my mouth.

"Fuck," I groan against her lips. "You have no idea what you do to me."

She eases our lips apart. "What do I do to you?" she whispers.

"You turn me on something fierce, obviously. But you also…" I trail off. It's so hard to put it into words. "You make me feel…"

I stop, groaning in frustration, because I've never been skilled at expressing myself. Putting emotions to words.

"You make me feel everything," I finally reveal. "You make me smile. You make me hard. You drive me crazy." My voice breaks slightly. "You make me feel safe."

"*I* make you feel safe? You know you're like a thousand times bigger and stronger than me, right?"

"That has nothing to do with anything," I say roughly.

And then I kiss her again.

When I unzip her coat and slide my palms underneath her cable-knit sweater, she shudders hard enough to still my roving hands.

"Too cold?" I ask in concern.

"No, too *good*." She's a tad breathless. "I love it when you touch me."

"Good, because I love touching you."

My palms slide up to cup her breasts, and I toy with her nipples using my thumbs. The puckered buds summon a groan from my throat. I yank her sweater up and hungrily bring one nipple in my mouth. Grace moans when I suckle it. She holds the back of my head, pressing me against her soft flesh. I can't help grinding my aching dick against her belly while I suck on her tit. Meanwhile, my hand travels south toward the waistband of her thick leggings.

I lift my head from her breast and say, "I want to fuck you."

Grace just moans in response.

"Is that a yes?" I ask with a dark chuckle.

"It's always a yes."

I know exactly what she means. I could be in the most foul mood ever, could be having the worst day of my life, and one smile from Grace, one breathy yes, would turn it all around. All she has to say is, "I want your dick," and I'd give it to her.

I slip my hand inside her panties to find her warm and wet and ready for me. She bucks her hips, rocking into me, and the sexy movements get my palm slick.

"Jesus," I choke out. I withdraw my hand and undo my pants, shoving them down to release my dick. It springs up against Grace's hip, and instantly she curls her fingers around the shaft.

"Love this," she breathes, giving me a hard squeeze.

"Fuck yes," I growl back.

Then I grab my cock out of her hand and guide it between her legs. Her pants aren't even off—they're trapped around her knees. But luckily they're stretchy. Mine are just low enough to expose my bare ass.

We both gasp when I plunge inside her. Since we're completely monogamous and she's on the pill, we stopped using condoms a long time ago, and there's no greater feeling than going bare with Grace. Her pussy is tight and welcoming, my favorite place in the whole world.

"You feel good," I groan into her neck.

She tugs my head up by the hair and our mouths crash together again. My tongue's in her mouth as I thrust my hips, plunging into her as deep as I can go. But the awkward position only allows for quick, shallow thrusts.

My cock aches to be deeper, but this still feels incredible. And when Grace starts moaning and restlessly rising up to meet each thrust, I know my shallow strokes are hitting the right spot. The G-spot. Nice. Her orgasms are always more intense when the G-spot's in play. I angle my hips so I can hit that sweet spot even harder, and her eyes roll to the top of her head.

"Oh my God," she pleads. "Keep doing that. Keep doing it."

And I do, hammering into her tight heat as her expression becomes more and more blissed-out. The warmth of her pussy surrounds me. Her mouth is slack, choppy breaths slipping out. Her eyes close briefly, then flutter open and lock with mine. The raw pleasure I see steals my breath.

"That's it," I urge. "Come for me."

I keep fucking her, watching her eyes grow hazier and hazier. When she moans, I swallow the sound with a blistering kiss, feeling her orgasm squeezing and rippling around me. Hot shivers race through my body. Making her feel good is the best feeling in the world. It triggers my own release, and I come with a strangled groan, my balls tingling and chest heaving.

Our recovery time is comically long. We lie there stupidly, still nearly fully dressed, my dick lodged inside her, her arms wrapped around me, as we struggle for breath.

"Okay," Grace says sleepily. "Now we can freeze to death."

CHAPTER 9

GRACE
11:59 P.M.

"One more minute!" Logan exclaims.

I swear, he's one of the few people I know who still gets ridiculously excited about New Year's Eve. Me, I never cared much for the holiday to begin with, and over the years my interest levels have only decreased.

But my boyfriend is grinning happily as he watches the clock on his phone tick down. Thanks to the blizzard raging outside our car, both of our phones lost their signals a long time ago, but at least the battery life is going strong.

The champagne bottle is poised in Logan's hand. Suddenly he looks over, worried. "Who gets the first sip?" he demands. "We don't have glasses!"

"You can have the first sip," I say graciously.

"You sure?"

"I mean, I guess? I really wanted it, but…" In reality I don't give a hoot who gets the first drink of the new year. But if I make him think I'm doing him a huge favor, I could remind him of this moment the next time he vetoes all my movie picks on Netflix. "It's okay. You do it."

He practically beams at me. It takes very little to make this man happy.

"Thirty seconds," he warns. "Sit up, woman."

I swallow a laugh and straighten up. Logan's blue eyes stay glued to his phone. "We're almost at the countdown. I expect some enthusiastic yelling. Ready, babe?"

"Sure. But we don't have to yell—"

"TEN!"

Oh brother.

"NINE!" he shouts, motioning me with his hand to join in.

And because I love this guy with all my heart, I make him happy and scream right along with him. When we finish shouting "ONE!", Logan throws in a "HAPPY NEW YEAR!" and then kisses me deeply.

I return the kiss, pulling back to whisper, "Happy New Year, Johnny."

"Happy New Year, Gracie."

With a little boy smile, he raises the bottle to his lips and takes the first sip of champagne.

2:00 A.M.

The tow truck still hasn't arrived.

It's been hours since the clock struck midnight, and Logan and I have already polished off the entire champagne bottle. Now we're tipsy and warm in the back seat, regaling each other with random childhood tales.

His stories lack the levity that mine possess, which isn't too surprising. Logan's parents are divorced and his father is a recovering alcoholic, so he didn't have the easiest upbringing. But he does have some good memories with his brother. My parents are also divorced, but they remained close friends, so my family stories are much happier.

As we laugh and snuggle and share memories, we're constantly touching each other. He strokes my hair. I play with the stubble rising on his strong jaw. His whiskers scrape my fingertips, but when he ruefully says he needs to shave, I disagree. I think he's sexy and manly, and I can't stop touching him. It's been like that since the moment we met. My college freshman self fell hard for John Logan, and he hasn't left my system since.

Hopefully he never does.

"Do you think they're ever going to show up?" I ask as I press my nose to the cold window. Beyond the pane, the world is an endless swirl of snow.

"They said six hours," he reminds me. "It hasn't been six hours yet."

"It's been five and a half."

"Five and a half isn't six."

"But why aren't they here yet?" I whine.

"Because it hasn't been six hours!"

"Stop saying that!"

Logan bursts out laughing, while I continue to look miserably out the window.

"What if we starve to death?"

"We won't," he assures me.

"What if we die of exposure and—oh my God. I just realized something. What if we're being punished?"

He sighs. "All right. I'll bite. Punished for what and by whom?"

"By Alexander! For hating him. What if he did this?" I gasp suddenly. "Oh my God, Logan, do you think this is how Willie felt when he was lying at the bottom of that ravine with his broken leg? Before his spirit entered Alexander? Do you think he knew he was going to die?"

Logan doesn't speak for a moment. Then he nods. "I've made the decision to ignore you for the next ten minutes, or however long it takes for the terror to leave my body."

2:42 A.M.

I wrest my gaze away from the window and release a long, bleak sigh. "All right. I think it's time."

His brow furrows. "Time for what?"

"To make a pact."

"What pact?"

I pull the blanket tighter around our lower bodies. "We could be stuck here for days. Weeks, even."

"It won't be days or weeks, you crazy woman."

I jut my chin stubbornly. "It *could* be. And if that happens, there's a good chance we'll die from starvation or exposure like Willie did on the California Trail. And unless we decide on a synchronized murder-suicide, obviously one of us will die before the other. So if that happens, we need to make a pact."

"What fucking pact?" he growls.

"If we're dealing with a starvation situation, the person who's still alive has to eat the dead one."

Logan stares at me.

"What?" I say defensively. "It's a matter of survival."

"You want us to eat each other."

"Well, not each other. Only one of us will need to do it. And I just want you to know—if I die first, I give you permission to eat me. Do whatever you need to do to survive. No judgment whatsoever from beyond the grave."

He just stares again.

"So it's a pact? The living one eats the dead one? There's a Swiss Army knife in the emergency kit. Oh, and I think the butt is the best part to cut into. Fleshier."

"No," he says emphatically.

"Yes," I insist. "The butt is the best part—"

"No, as in, I'm not cutting off a piece of your sweet ass and consuming it," he clarifies. "I'd rather we just die in each other's arms, old-people-in-*Titanic* style."

I shake my head in disappointment. "Fine, don't agree to the pact. I'm still doing it."

"A pact requires the agreement of both parties," he argues.

"Not when my *life* is at stake." I stick my tongue out. "Sorry, babe, but I'm eating your ass whether you like it or not."

I don't realize how poorly I worded that until after the words exit my mouth, which earns me howls and howls of laughter from my immature boyfriend.

3:02 A.M.

"Okay, it's obviously been fourteen hours—"

"Six," Logan corrects.

"—and they're still not here." My teeth nearly poke a hole through the inside of my cheek. "I don't think they'll be able to find us."

"They have our exact location."

"Yeah, but the car is covered in snow. They won't see us. And then when the blizzard ends, we'll have to dig our way out." I give him a firm look. "You really need to agree to the pact."

"Never. And we won't have to dig ourselves out. We're fine." But my concerns do spur him into action. He reaches for the door handle and curses when it takes several hard pushes to get it open. "I'll be right back."

"What are you going to do?"

"Scrape the snow off so they can see the car. And I'd better turn on the emergency blinkers now. The cavalry should be here any minute."

I start to push the blanket off. "Let me help."

"No way. It's too cold. Stay here."

He goes outside and starts scraping, until his handsome face eventually appears on the other side of the window. His features are creased with focus, which brings a smile to my lips. No matter what John Logan does, he gives it 110 percent of his concentration.

Fifteen minutes later he's back in the car, shaking snow off himself like a dog shaking off water after a swim. He crawls under the blanket, and I try to warm him up.

"Thanks," he mumbles, his broad frame shivering in my arms.

"Aww, baby." I rub his back in an attempt to infuse him with warmth. It doesn't really work, so I make an executive decision to blast the heat even though I know we're slowly draining our gas tank and battery.

3:46 A.M.

"The tow truck still isn't here. They're almost an hour late and I fear for our lives. Who knows, maybe they'll never show up. We might be trapped here forever. Our bodies will be found years later and—"

"Oh, would you cut it out." Logan grabs the phone from my hand and addresses the camera. "We're not going to die. We are just fine." He pauses for a beat. "But in the event that we do die: Mom, I love you. I want you to know you're the greatest—"

"Hey!" I punch him in the shoulder. "Stop using up my battery for *your* goodbyes. You don't even believe we're going to die." I snatch the phone and talk to it. "He won't even make a pact to eat each other, you guys! What kind of boyfriend is that? I'm offering him sustenance to live and he won't eat me!"

Logan's lips suddenly press against my cheek. "You want me to eat you?" he says silkily. "I'll fucking eat you, baby."

"John," I gasp, aghast. I look at the camera. "Pretend you didn't hear that, Dad!"

Then I stop recording, and Logan and I start making out while the snow continues to fall beyond the car.

4:22 A.M.

"Well, there goes our tank," Logan remarks as the vents release their final burst of hot air. The tow truck still hasn't arrived, and we've officially run out of gas.

"The offer to eat me after I die still stands," I tell him. "That's how much I love you."

He sighs.

4:49 A.M.

I'm curled up in Logan's strong arms, sleepy and contented, as his long fingers play with my hair.

"Missed this," he mumbles.

I twist my head to look at him. "What?"

"Cuddling with you. Being with you."

A lump lodges in my throat. "Me too."

Silence settles between us. The last few years flash through my mind. How we first got together. All the changes in our relationship since Logan graduated from Briar. When he played for Boston's farm team, I thought *that* schedule was hectic. Now he's in the pros, and this schedule is a thousand times more intense.

I reach up to stroke his chiseled jaw. "There's nobody else I'd rather freeze to death with than you."

His chest vibrates from laughter. "Right back atcha, gorgeous."

5:13 A.M.

I'm jolted awake by the sound of honking. Logan nudges me off him and reaches for the door.

"I think they're here," he says.

I fly into a sitting position. "It's about time! They're like eighteen hours late."

"Two," he corrects, grinning at me.

"In blizzard years, that's eighteen."

"Drama queen." He chuckles and hops out of the car before I can take offense.

I zip up my jacket and follow him outside, where my heart immediately does a happy flip. Two beams of light break the pitch-black night. Or morning, rather.

I glimpse a shadowy figure, and then a male voice wafts toward us from the top of the slope.

"You folks called for assistance?"

CHAPTER 10

LOGAN

After a quick stop at a gas station to refuel, and a text to the B&B owners that we're on our way, Grace and I are back on the road. It's completely deserted this morning. I suspect everyone is still in bed after whatever exciting New Year's Eve party and will all wake up nursing unbearable hangovers.

Grace and I aren't hungover, but we look it. Spending the night shivering and crammed in the back seat of a car does that to you. Yet despite my bleary eyes and sore body, it was one of the best nights of my life. Ringing in the New Year with Grace, a bottle of champagne, and a pact to eat each other.

I snicker at the memory.

"What's so funny?" she says from the passenger side.

"Last night." I offer a wry grin. "I was just thinking how much fun it was."

"Fun? We almost died."

"We didn't almost die." I spot a sign for our bed-and-breakfast up ahead and flick the turn signal. "We had an adventure."

The advice Garrett gave me last week was spot-on. Spend as much time together as you can, go on adventures, and make memories. Last night may not have gone as planned, but we still had a blast.

"I have a better pact for us," I announce.

Grace huffs. "Better than cannibalism? Yeah, I doubt it, sweetheart."

A laugh pops out. "Trust me, *sweetheart*, it's way better."

"All right, hit me."

"This is the pact." I gesture between us.

"What do you mean?"

My tone softens. "You and me. The pact is that we spend as much time together as humanly possible. We don't let our busy schedules control our relationship. If there's no time, we make time." I'm startled to hear my voice crack. "Hockey doesn't matter. School, work. None of it matters if you and I are struggling. If we aren't connecting."

I'm equally startled to see tears well up in my girlfriend's eyes.

"Fuck," I mutter. "I didn't mean to make you cry."

"It's okay." She wipes her cheeks. "It's just…you're right. The rest of it doesn't matter. Yes, we have responsibilities to school and work, but we also have a responsibility to ourselves and our happiness. I'm not happy when we're apart."

"Me neither," I say hoarsely. "That's why we need to stick to the pact. You and me matter. I think the moment one of us feels unhappy in the relationship, or if we feel like the distance and time apart is affecting us negatively, then at the first available opportunity, we oughta do something like this."

"Get stuck in a blizzard?" she teases.

"Go on an adventure," I correct. "So what do you say—deal?"

She doesn't hesitate. "Deal."

Snow crunches beneath our tires as I drive down the narrow lane that leads to the B&B. It snowed a ton last night, painting the entire landscape white. It's beautiful. And so is the woman sitting beside me.

"We made it," I say, slowing to a stop in front of the quaint two-story structure. I turn to give Grace a triumphant smile.

The front door of the B&B swings open to reveal a couple

in their late fifties. They're bundled up in parkas and scarves, the woman holding two huge mugs with steam rising from the top.

"John and Grace?" the man calls as we get out of the car.

"That's us," I call back.

"We're so sorry for the early arrival," Grace apologizes.

The woman dismisses that. "Oh, hush, don't be sorry! We're just happy you made it here in one piece. That blizzard last night! Good grief, it was a bad one!" She thrusts out the two mugs. "Some hot tea. I thought you'd need it."

"Thank you." A grateful Grace accepts one of the mugs.

I take the other, welcoming the cloud of steam that warms my face.

"As you've probably figured out, we're your hosts," the woman says. "I'm Amanda, and this is my husband, Pastor Steve."

"We're very pleased to have you," her husband says. "Even if only for a short stay." He offers a sheepish smile in my direction. "I'm a big fan, son."

I won't lie—the praise never gets old. "Thank you, sir. And I—I'm sorry, but your wife's introduction was, um…" Weird, I almost say. "Unclear," I finish. "Should we call you Steve or Pastor?"

"Either works," he says cheerfully.

"You're a pastor?" Grace asks after another eager sip of tea.

"Indeed I am. I lead a small congregation here in our little community."

His wife beams proudly. "He's being modest! He counsels nearly every resident in Bowen County."

I study Pastor Steve's warm brown eyes, then glance over at Grace. Thoughtful. I mean…didn't we literally just have a conversation about taking advantage of every opportunity that comes our way?

"What is it?" It's that same tone she uses when she suspects I'm up to no good.

I flash her a faint smile before turning back to the pastor. "So. Just out of curiosity…" My grin widens. "Do you do weddings?"

PART 2
THE PROPOSAL

CHAPTER 11

DEAN

"Allie, where do I even start? Bottom line: you're incredible. From the day we met, I knew we were meant to be… Okay, well, no, you had a boyfriend when we met and I was a man-whore. But. From the day that we hooked up—shit, no, it was a one-night stand, and you were ashamed and didn't speak to me for days after…"

I take a breath and regroup.

"From the day that you took me back after we broke up because I was an asshole and got high and missed your play."

Nope. Also terrible.

I try again.

"Allie. I don't even know where to start."

"Clearly," comes Garrett's dry voice. "By the way, the answer is no. Go ahead and close that box."

I stare at the open jewelry box in my hand, all plush blue velvet and glittering diamond, trying to tamp down my frustration. I'm still kneeling in front of Garrett, former college roommate and best friend for life, in the living room of his expensive Boston brownstone, while our other best friend watches with amusement from the couch.

"I didn't mind it," Logan says frankly. "It adds sincerity most proposals are lacking."

"It was awful," Garrett corrects. "And I will not be marrying you, Dean Heyward-Di Laurentis. Sorry to break it to you. Now do it again."

"Fine." Normally I wouldn't let G boss me around like this, but I'm a man on an important mission. You can't go into something like this blind.

So, once again, I get in position. One knee. Velvet box in hand. This is my third proposal attempt, because as it turns out, Garrett Graham is goddamn hard to please. I wonder if Hannah has this much trouble satisfying him.

"Allie," I start.

"Look into my eyes," he orders.

I clench my teeth and look into his gray eyes.

"Stop squinting."

I open my eyes wide.

Logan snickers. "Dude, you look like you're possessed. You need to blink."

I blink.

"Allie, you're the greatest thing that's ever happened to me," I begin, keeping my gaze trained on Garrett.

"Ain't that the truth," Logan remarks.

I swivel my head toward him. "No commentary, asshole. You guys are supposed to be offering feedback."

"I am. I'm offering feedback that she's the best thing that's ever happened to your sorry ass. Without that woman, you'd still be screwing your way through life, arguing cases in a courtroom and making an obscene amount of money, driving a Lambo or some other obnoxious sports car and—you know what? That doesn't sound so bad. Maybe you don't need to marry her."

Garrett snorts out a laugh.

I just sigh. These two idiots, along with our friend Tucker, whose wedding I'm in town for, are closer to me than my own brother. Which says a lot, because my brother, Nick, and I are pretty damn close. But they're right. Without Allie, I don't know what my life would look like right now. Before her, I was on track to follow in my parents' footsteps and attend Harvard Law, which I didn't want to do. I also didn't do girlfriends. The one I had in high school tried to kill herself after I broke up with her, and—not gonna lie—that scarred me.

But then a one-night stand changed my entire life. Allie Hayes is it for me. We've been together almost four years now, and there's no doubt in my mind she's the one I'm going to marry, have kids with, grow old with. I was never in a rush to propose before, but lately I've been feeling this urge to start moving things along. To know we're moving forward in our relationship. And, yeah, now that Tucker and Sabrina are finally tying the knot and we're all in Boston to celebrate with them, I guess I have wedding fever. I didn't know that happened to dudes, but there you go. Somehow, I found myself picking out a ring at Tiffany & Co. yesterday morning, and I haven't looked back since.

"Okay. Allie," I try again, looking into the expectant eyes of a grown man. "I love you. I love everything about you. I love your sense of humor. I love how melodramatic you are—"

"Veto," Garrett interrupts. "You can't insult her in the proposal."

"But it's a compliment," I protest. "I love the drama."

"Yeah, but women don't want to hear they're drama."

"He's right," Logan chimes in. "I told Grace she was being dramatic when we got stranded on New Year's and she lost it." He pauses. "Well, technically she lost it because I wouldn't eat her ass."

"I'm sorry—what?" Garrett asks politely.

"Not what it sounds like." He chuckles. "She wanted me to promise that if one of us died in the blizzard, we would eat the other one."

G nods. "Oh. Like that movie."

Logan's face goes blank.

"You know the one. About a football team or something that

crashed in the mountains and cannibalized each other to survive? It's heartwarming."

"Sounds like it," I say dryly.

"Yeah, exactly like that, then," Logan tells G. "But I wouldn't make the promise, and she got pissed. Luckily that didn't stop her from—" He stops abruptly.

"From what?" I prompt.

Logan runs a hand over his buzzed hair. For a second I get the sense he's nervous. Dodging. But then a wolfish grin curves his lips. "From spending all of New Year's Day in bed with me. Anyway. Trust me, girls don't want to be called drama-llama."

I mull over Grace's hypothetical for a second. "Would you eat *me* if I died first?" I ask him.

"Oh, for sure. You too, G."

Garrett sounds intrigued. "You'd eat us for sustenance, but you wouldn't eat your girlfriend?"

"I couldn't. It'd feel completely wrong. The idea of cutting into her perfect flesh…" He shudders. "Nope, can't do it. I'd rather die. Also, if she's dying, I'm dying right along with her. I can't live without her."

"There," Garrett says, jabbing a finger in the air at me. "That's what you say."

"That I won't be able to cut into her perfect flesh and eat it?"

"No, that you can't live without her. Life isn't worth living if she's not with you, blah blah blah."

Finally, some direction. "Got it," I say. "Here. Let me try again."

This time, I lead with the whole can't-live-without-you pitch, while Garrett clasps his hands over his heart, nodding along. Encouraged by his response, I hurry on.

"There's nobody else I want to be with. Nobody else I want to fuck. I love every inch of your body, and I can't wait to spend the rest of our lives seeing you naked—"

"No! You've gone off the rails," Garrett chides. "That's way too sexy. Sexiness plays no role in a proposal."

"I disagree," Logan pipes up. "I say go even sexier."

"Don't listen to him."

"More sexy," Logan argues.

"Less," Garrett shoots back.

My gaze ping-pongs between the two of them, my temples beginning to throb. This is impossible. I don't know how I'm ever going to get through this proposal. I'm not good with romantic words. I'm good with dirty, telling her I want to screw her brains out. I'm good at telling Allie I love her, because I do. I love her with all my heart. Why does a proposal need to involve a whole damn speech?

"You know what, try it on me," Logan suggests. "G is clearly not a good proposal receiver."

"Oh, fuck off, I'm a great proposal receiver. It's just that the proposal sucks. I'm not going to say yes to something that doesn't wow me."

"Go wow yourself," I grumble, flipping up my middle finger.

Garrett beams at me. "I do. Every day when I look in the mirror."

Asshole. He's incorrigible. Although, his massive ego isn't entirely unwarranted. There's a reason he was the big man on campus at Briar for four years. *The* Garrett Graham, constantly swarmed by thirsty girls. Granted, I scored way more often than him, mostly because Garrett was always too busy with hockey and made that clear to any chick who tried getting serious with him. He hooked up, but not nearly as much as me or Logan. But hey, it worked out for him. His dedication to hockey got him signed by the Bruins, and now he's one of the highest paid hockey players in the league and has a girlfriend he adores.

What's wild to me is the fact that G and Logan are teammates again. They played in college together for four years, then went their separate ways for two, only for Logan to wind up playing in Boston—on the same line as Garrett. Talk about serendipity. I think. I always use that word incorrectly.

"As the only one here who's successfully written poetry for a woman, I think I'm best equipped to evaluate a proposal," Logan is saying, jarring me from my thoughts.

Garrett rolls his eyes. "Okay there, Shakespeare."

"He has a point," I tell G.

"See?" Logan crooks a beckoning finger at me. "C'mere, big boy."

I snicker as I lumber over to him. He sits up, long legs dangling over the side of the couch. He's wearing jeans and a long-sleeve black shirt, and when he leans forward, I catch a whiff of him and nod in approval.

"Damn, you smell good, dude. What are you wearing?"

"I ran out of body wash so I'm using Grace's," he answers with a grin. "It's fucking delicious, right?"

"Oh yeah. I can see why Garrett sneaks into your hotel rooms for all those secret man-on-man bone-zone sessions."

"Jealous?" Garrett smirks.

Grinning, I get in position, popping the box open for the millionth time.

The diamond gleams in the light fixture above our heads, causing Logan to gawk at me. "Jesus, that thing is so shiny, it's gonna burn a hole in my retina. It didn't shine this bright when I was across the room."

I nod smugly. "I know how to pick 'em."

"That thing's a monster. You sure Allie's hand is even strong enough to support the weight of it?"

"Trust me, we've talked about engagement rings before. She likes 'em big." I wink. "Big rings too."

Garrett snorts. He wanders over and settles on his leather recliner. "Okay, seriously, dude. You gotta make this one good."

I resist the urge to crack my knuckles the way I used to before a big game. All right. I got this.

"Allie," I say to Logan. "I love you so much. You changed my entire life when you decided to bless me with your love. You make my world better."

"Sexier," Logan murmurs.

"Every time I'm with you, my heart feels like it's going to explode." I pause. "And so does my dick."

From the corner of my eye, I see Garrett shake with laughter.

Logan, however, nods his approval. Our gazes are locked in disturbingly intimate eye contact.

"You're the only one for me, baby."

"More physical contact," he urges.

I don't know if he's messing with me or not. I decide that he is, so I play along.

"You have no idea how stunning you are." I lean forward, still holding the ring box in one hand. I place my other hand flat on his muscular thigh.

Logan narrows his eyes.

You wanted it, I think, battling a grin.

"Every time I look at you, I can't even fathom that you're mine. Your beauty is otherworldly. It makes me want to rip your clothes off. You make me so hard." My hand skims up his chest toward his collarbone. I'm desperately trying not to laugh as I cup his stubble-covered cheek. "Baby. Will you marry me?"

There's a brief silence.

Then Logan's mouth falls open. He turns to Garrett, wide-eyed. Then back at me.

"Chills," he breathes. "Genuine chills, man. Look." He rolls up his shirt sleeve to show me his arm. "That's the one."

"That is not the one!" Garrett growls from the recliner. "Don't you fucking say any of that or you're going to lose the girl."

I hop to my feet, because this entire exercise was completely useless. "I think we're done here," I announce. "You two are truly, and utterly, the worst."

"Or are we the best?" Logan counters.

I roll my eyes. "I'm grabbing a beer, you want one?" I ask them.

When they nod, I pop into Garrett's spacious kitchen and head for the stainless steel refrigerator.

"When are you going to do it?" Logan calls from the other room.

I stick my head in the fridge, searching. I grab three bottles. "I don't know. I'm waiting for the perfect time," I admit as I walk back to the living room. "I was thinking maybe at the wedding?"

Two pairs of eyes stare at me in disbelief.

"The wedding?" Garrett echoes. "Are you nuts? Tucker will rip your balls off."

"You can't ask someone to marry you at somebody else's wedding," Logan balks.

"But isn't it romantic?" I ask blankly. Their response is baffling. "They're swearing their undying love, I'm swearing my undying love. So much undying love in the air. What do you assholes have against undying love?"

"Dude, trust us," Logan says. "You don't want to do this."

I still don't see the big deal.

"All right. Chill. I'll come up with something else."

"You better." Garrett shudders. "That's almost as egregious as Logan wanting to give them Alexander as a wedding gift."

I gape at Logan. "Are you insane? You can't curse their wedding with that demon doll."

"Oh, but you can ruin it by stealing their thunder?" he retorts.

"For fuck's sake, I told you I'm not going to do it," I grumble, sitting on the other end of the sectional.

As I take a long sip of beer, it suddenly occurs to me how monumental this weekend is.

"I can't believe our boy's getting married," I say in amazement.

"I can." Garrett grins. "I mean, he already has a kid."

Good point. And not only does Tucker have a kid, but she's turning three soon. The thought of my little niece Jamie melts my heart. Tuck and I might not be related by blood, but he's family, and I love his daughter to pieces. Hell, these days I even love Sabrina, who I thought was an uptight bitch in college. But we squashed our beef a long time ago, and I can't deny she's been good for Tucker. And a great mom.

"True. But sometimes it feels like we're too young to be doing the whole marriage thing," I answer.

"Says the guy who's about to propose to his girlfriend." Garrett laughs.

"We're twenty-five," Logan objects. "That's not too young, is it? I mean, shit, sometimes I'm so beaten up and bruised after a game, I feel ancient."

I nod solemnly. "You're an old man. Soon you'll have to retire."

"Fuck that, I'm playing well into my thirties."

"Late thirties," Garrett says.

"Forties," Logan says.

I'm about to ask Garrett how long his dad played before he retired but stop myself at the last second. Bringing up Phil Graham is bound to kill the lighthearted mood. The moment Garrett graduated college and was out from under his dad's financial thumb, he basically disowned the man who'd abused him growing up. He doesn't even refer to him as "my father" or "Dad" anymore; the rare times Garrett brings him up, he calls him "Phil."

Unfortunately, G can't be rid of him entirely because Phil Graham is still a legend in the hockey world. But I'm pretty sure Phil played till he was forty-two, which is impressive.

"Oh, thanks for helping with Tuck's surprise, by the way." I rest the beer bottle on my knee. "I can't believe it all worked out."

"Tuck's going to freak," Garrett says.

"Seriously," Logan tells me. "I hate giving your ego any more fuel, but I think this was the best idea you've ever had."

"I know, right? It's a good one."

Ah, I can't wait to see Tucker's face tomorrow night. And I can't wait for Allie to get here already.

Let wedding weekend commence.

CHAPTER 12

ALLIE

"Come play with us."

I glance over at my costar, the eagerness on Trevor's face making me smile. With his thin frame and youthful features, he looks like a teenage boy instead of a twenty-seven-year-old man.

"Malcolm and I are going to that new martini bar on Broadway," he adds. "They've got a VIP lounge, so we won't be hounded by fans." Trevor wiggles his eyebrows enticingly.

I offer a regretful look. "I can't. I'm heading to the airport the moment I change out of this costume."

"Airport?"

"Yeah, remember? I have a wedding this weekend."

We fall into step with each other in the back corridor of the studio I've called home for three years. Trevor is new this season to *The Delaneys*, the cable drama I'd been cast in right out of college. He was cast as my love interest for this final season of the show, and we've grown close these past six months. A part of me wishes the show wasn't ending this year, especially since our ratings are at an all-time high. But our showrunners Brett and Kiersten had always planned for it to be a three-season story arc, and each season has beautifully told the story of this horribly dysfunctional family in which I play the middle daughter.

It's still surreal to think I've been acting on the number one show in the country for the past few years. And it's going to suck so hard to say goodbye, but I'm one of those people who believe in going out with a bang rather than a whimper.

"Ugh. Right," Trevor gripes. "That's this weekend?"

"Yup."

"Who's getting married again?"

"College friends," I answer. "My boyfriend's former teammate."

"Ah, the hockey boyfriend," Trevor teases. "I will never get over the fact that you're with a jock."

"Trust me, I didn't see it coming either." Though is he still considered a jock if he doesn't really play anymore? These days Dean teaches at Parklane Academy, the all-girls private school in Manhattan where he coaches the hockey and volleyball teams.

We reach the corridor that houses the supporting cast's dressing rooms. The bigger stars have trailers on the lot, but we're delegated to these peasant's quarters. I'm joking. The fact that I have my own dressing room, with my name on the door and everything, is the greatest feeling in the whole world. Not a day goes by that I don't wake up overcome with gratitude.

Trevor trails after me into the cozy room I've looked at as a second home for nearly three years. Ugh, I'm dreading the day I have to pack everything up and close the door to this room for the last time. We still have a few more night shoots to do for the finale, but then it'll be a wrap on *The Delaneys*. It's a bittersweet feeling. After playing the same character for so long, I'm going to miss Bianca Delaney. Yet at the same time, I'm ready to tackle something new. Take on a new challenge.

"You bringing the boyfriend to the wrap party next week?" Trevor asks. "Because you know Malcolm's gonna want to get one final look at the golden god."

I snicker. Our costar Malcolm, my on-screen brother, has a huge crush on Dean and scampers after him like a puppy whenever Dean visits set. I don't blame him. Dean Heyward-Di Laurentis is possibly the most attractive man on the face of God's green earth. The first time our director met him, she spent an hour trying to convince Dean to get into acting. She even offered him a role in her next movie. But Dean has no interest being in films.

Unless it's the private kind.

I feel my cheeks heating up at the memory. I swear, our sex life is off-the-charts hot, but I'd expect no less from the man who was once the biggest man-whore at Briar University. As far as sexual partners go, Dean is…spectacular.

More than that, I couldn't ask for a better partner, period. He's attentive, sweet, funny. He even gets along with my dad, which is a huge feat, because Dad is a cranky curmudgeon.

"He'll probably be there, but it depends on his schedule." I shrug. "The hockey team he coaches has a bunch of weekend tournaments once we're back from Boston, but hopefully that doesn't stop him from at least making an appearance."

"Good. And I expect you at the after-after party too," Trevor says firmly, dark eyes twinkling. "Seraphina, Malcolm, and I are going clubbing."

"Ha. I'm not making any promises. Let's see how drunk you maniacs get at the wrap party before I decide if I'm following you down the after-after party rabbit hole."

"No. You have to come. Who knows when we'll get a chance to get our dance on again." He gives an exaggerated pout.

He has a point, though. It's hard to say we'll keep in touch after the show ends. We only met this year, and once we're done filming, he'll go back to LA and I'll stay here in New York. Hollywood friendships tend to be fickle and fleeting.

"I'll think about it," I tell him. "Now shoo. I need to change and scrub off this makeup."

"Have fun this weekend. Love you, babe."

"Love ya."

After he's gone, I quickly change into my street clothes and wipe the makeup from my face. My skin feels raw and looks red and dry when I examine it in the mirror. Frowning, I slather moisturizer all over it. I better not be splotchy for the wedding. That would be unacceptable.

Outside, there's a black town car waiting for me. Everyone involved in the production has access to the studio's car service, but it needs to be booked in advance. When I approach the curb with my rolling suitcase, the driver quickly rounds the vehicle to take my bag.

I greet him with a warm smile. "Hey, Ronald."

"Heya, Allie," he says easily. He's one of our regular drivers, and my favorite one. "The itinerary says you're going to the airport?"

"Yes, please. Teterboro," I say, naming the private airport where billionaires and celebrities slip in and out of the city unnoticed.

"Fancy!" he teases, his eyes twinkling.

I feel myself blushing. Dating Dean comes with perks that go beyond attention and great sex—like the private jet his parents bought a couple of years ago. Yup. The Heyward-Di Laurentis brood owns a jet now. For years they'd been flying back and forth between their Connecticut and Manhattan homes and their place in St. Barth's, so frequently that Dean's dad, Peter, decided it made "fiscal sense" to purchase a jet. I can't even.

Not that I'm complaining. As Dean's girlfriend, I'm wealthy adjacent. Which means I have access to the family jet if it's not in use. So far, I've only flown on it twice, and the one time I tried asking Dean's mom, Lori, how much I owed them for the flights, she laughed at me and told me not to worry about it. I'm terrified of how much it must cost to fuel an entire jet, but Dean assured me that a one-hour flight to Boston wasn't going to break his parents' bank.

Ronald and I chat on the drive, while I simultaneously text with Hannah Wells, my best friend. Since she and her boyfriend live in

Boston already, they didn't have to travel for the wedding. Dean and I are crashing at their place for the weekend, but Dean went a couple of days ahead of me.

> Me: In the car, going to the airport now. I can't wait to see you, Han-Han.
> Her: OMG me too. I miss your dumb face.
> Me: Not as much as I miss YOUR dumb face.

I text Dean next to let him know where I'm at.

> Me: On my way to the airport. See you in a bit.
> Dean: Be safe.
> Dean: Can't wait to fuck you.

I swallow a laugh. I used to be caught off guard by the frank way he talks about sex, but these days I'm used to it.

And if I'm being honest with myself, I sorta kinda love it.

CHAPTER 13

DEAN

ALLIE GETS IN AROUND NINE. EVEN THOUGH SHE ATE DINNER ON the plane, Hannah forces her onto a stool at the breakfast counter while Garrett makes omelets. It feels like old times again. Our college days. I didn't realize until this very moment how much I missed seeing my friends every day.

The last time we all got together was six months ago when Garrett was playing the Islanders. Hannah tagged along, and the four of us had dinner with Allie's dad at a restaurant in Brooklyn. And either I conjured this up in my dirty head, or a naked puck bunny broke into Garrett's hotel room that weekend and accidentally wound up groping a sleeping Hannah instead.

Man, I miss playing hockey. Never knew what to expect.

As we eat, Hannah tells Allie the news she'd already shared with me the other day: she's going to be spending the summer in the studio with an up-and-coming rapper. Along with being a talented songwriter, Hannah's also been working with several music producers, and she'd recently written and co-produced a hit single for singing superstar Delilah Sparks, which opened a ton of doors for her.

Allie grins. "I'm having a hard time picturing you writing hip-hop lyrics."

"God, imagine? But no, just producing some beats and writing some of the choruses. They're bringing in this amazing new singer for one song. I cannot wait to get in the studio with her. She's only fifteen."

We chat for a while longer, but soon my patience wears thin. It's been three days since I've seen my girlfriend, and I'm dying to get her alone. I think I'm still riding a high from the knowledge of that velvet box in my bag upstairs. I was never into all that romance shit, but I swear, picturing that ring on Allie's finger gets me a little hard.

The moment we're alone in the upstairs guest room, my lips are on hers and I'm kissing her like a starved man. Allie kisses me back just as hungrily. When I cup her ass and lift her up, she wraps her legs around me and drags her nails down the front of my shirt. Her hot, eager body is so tempting, I almost fuck her right there against the wall, but she pulls away the moment I reach for the button of her jeans.

"Ugh, I need a shower first," she says breathlessly. "I feel so grimy. I worked all day and then boarded the flight, and now all I can smell is stale airplane coffee."

I bury my nose in her golden hair. I kiss her, breathe her in. Strawberries and roses. The scent was custom made for her by someone her late mom once knew.

"You smell great," I correct. The thing about women is, they hold themselves to a much higher standard than you hold them to.

"Shower," she says firmly.

"Fine. But only if I can join."

Her blue eyes turn smoky. "Deal."

A few minutes later we're naked and wrapped up in each other under the warm spray. I soap her up, playing with her full tits before sliding my hand between her legs and cupping warm, slippery paradise. I bend my head to kiss her, then bring my mouth to her ear so she can hear me over the rush of water.

"I want to fuck you right here. Will you let me?"

"Uh-huh." She makes a noise that's half moan, half whimper. Then she turns around, and the sight of her perky round ass almost makes me come on the spot.

We know from experience that this is the best way we can enjoy sex in the shower. If I'm holding her up, she's too paranoid I'll slip and drop her, and so she never gets into it. In this position, both of us have our feet planted on the ground and we both get what we need.

I grip my aching dick and run it along the crease of her ass. She shivers despite the heat of the shower. I press the palm of my other hand on her tailbone before teasingly skimming it upward along the bumps of her spine.

"I missed you," I say thickly. It's been three torturous days, and I hate being away from her.

"Missed you too," she whispers back.

It's almost pathetic how much I love this girl. How much I crave her. After we hooked up for the first time in college, the craziest thing happened—my dick stopped responding to anyone but Allie. And that's pretty much been the case ever since. I find plenty of other women attractive, but the only woman I want to sleep with is the one who's currently in front of me, jutting her ass out in an unspoken plea to fuck her.

When I enter her, we both moan. I move slowly at first, but there's no chance in hell I'm maintaining that pace. I need her too much, and the sounds she's making are too much of a turn-on. I barely last three slow strokes before my hips move of their own accord and I'm pounding into her with abandon. Breathing hard, I reach one arm around her and cup her breasts, squeeze one, play with the nipple, which contracts and springs against my thumb. I bring my other hand to the juncture of her thighs and rub her clit until her back arches and I know she's close.

"Deeper," she orders in that bossy tone I love to hear from her during sex.

And because I aim to please, I tilt my hips forward and change the angle, giving her the deep strokes she wants. Her breathy noises echo in the stall, mingling with the steam surrounding us. Her gasp of pleasure is all I need. I quickly follow suit, coming inside her. As I recover from the mind-blowing release, I'm too sated to move, so I just stand there, holding her tight to my chest, my face pressed to the back of her neck. Perfection. This girl is perfect.

A bit later, Allie's getting ready for bed while I dress for the big event. "Tucker still has no idea what's going on?" she asks, pulling her hair into a short ponytail.

"No clue," I confirm. "I can't wait to see his face."

"Make sure you film it."

"Obvs." I zip up my jeans, then start buttoning my long-sleeve shirt. "You gonna wait up for me?"

"Depends. When are you gonna be back tonight?"

"Two? Three?"

"Then not a chance. We've got the bachelorette at like, eleven in the morning tomorrow."

"That early?"

"Yeah. We booked the tearoom at the Taj."

"Tea?" This is the first I'm hearing of it. I knew the girls were doing something for Sabrina at a fancy hotel, but I assumed it was a spa thing.

"Yeah, Jamie saw *Alice in Wonderland* for the first time last month," Allie explains. "The cartoon version. So now she's obsessed with tea parties. And since Sabrina said she didn't want to do a late-night thing and look all puffy on her wedding day, we decided to do something low-key and bring the kidlet."

"Jesus. We're talking bachelor and bachelorette parties and nobody is seeing a fucking stripper?" I gripe. "And you're bringing a child? This is a travesty."

"Hey, no one stopped you guys from getting a stripper," she reminds me. "You're the one who decided to make it a sausage party."

"Yeah, and I thought you would compensate for that, not make yours a vagina party!" I give her a magnanimous smile. "It's not too late to change your plans. Go nuts, baby doll. Fondle some packages in sweaty Speedos."

Allie makes a gagging noise. "That is honestly the most unappealing thing I've ever heard. Hard pass."

I snicker. "Fine. Whatever. If a tea party is what Sabrina wants, who are we to deny her that? Jamie will love it, anyway."

"God, that kid is so cute. Sabrina sends daily pics to our girls' group chat and each one is cuter than the last."

"Trust me, I know. Tuck sends at least one a day."

She laughs as she slips into her pajama top. It's one of my old Briar Hockey T-shirts, soft and worn and hanging down to her knees. "He is such a dad."

"For real. You should see *our* group chat. All Tuck does is extol the virtues of dadhood. He thinks all of us should knock up all of you and just pop out kids all over the place."

"Lovely image. How's that going for him? Has he converted anyone yet?"

"Nah. Garrett is all about hockey right now. And I don't know if Logan and Grace even want kids. I guess you and I will have to take up the mantle."

Rolling her eyes, Allie climbs onto the queen-sized guest bed. "Tuck can keep the mantle for now. Kids are the last thing on my mind at the moment."

"Hey, I didn't say it would be soon," I say with a chuckle. "I'm well aware there're a few steps that come before that."

First and foremost, an engagement.

Anticipation bubbles in my gut, and I hope my expression doesn't reveal it. This weekend is about Tucker and Sabrina. But the moment we get back to New York, I'm wasting no time sliding that ring on Allie's finger.

CHAPTER 14

DEAN

It's past midnight and we're in the back of the limo. Just the four of us, because Tucker still believes this is going to be a small affair. For the past ten minutes he's been complaining that we "wasted money" getting a limousine, which he views as an "extravagance" for four people. Eventually Garrett has to shove a glass of champagne in his hand and say, "Oh my God, chill, we didn't even pay for it. I asked the franchise and they arranged it."

Tucker stares at him. "You just asked for a limo and they gave you one?"

Logan snorts. "Do you know who this guy is?" He jerks a thumb at Garrett. "That's Garrett Graham, dude."

I start to laugh.

"Right, I forgot," Tuck says, laughing too. "So, are you finally gonna tell me where we're going or what? I'm assuming some sort of strip club, but…"

"Even better," Garrett promises.

Like the bosses we are, we sip champagne and lounge in the back of the limo while the city whizzes past us. I imagine onlookers seeing us drive by and wondering who's inside. Boston's a hockey town, so girls and guys alike would probably lose their minds if they knew Garrett Graham and John Logan were behind these tinted windows.

"Yo, top me off," I say, holding out my glass.

Logan leans over and pours some more bubbly into it.

"We should be there soon," Garrett tells Tuck. He looks like he's trying not to grin.

I'm also fighting my excitement. This surprise is next-level awesome. It took a lot of coordination and string-pulling, but miraculously we were able to make it happen.

"Oh, okay. Then before we get there," Tuck starts, shifting in his seat so he's facing me, "I need to talk to you about something."

I wrinkle my forehead. "Sure. What's up?"

"G said you were floating the idea of proposing to Allie at the wedding tomorrow."

I instantly shoot Garrett an accusatory glare. "Seriously, dude?"

"Yeah, I'm not apologizing," G says, unfazed. "I had to warn him in case you ignored our advice and went rogue."

"Asshole."

"Hey now," Tuck interjects, his Southern drawl becoming more pronounced. "I'm not pissed. If anything, I think it's a good idea."

Garrett and Logan gawk at him.

I blink in surprise. "Really?"

"Yeah." He brings his glass to his lips, watching me over the rim as he takes a sip. I don't see any bullshit whatsoever in his brown eyes. "It's kinda romantic."

"That's what I said!" I exclaim, feeling vindicated.

He sets his glass in the drink holder beside him, then rests both forearms on his knees and leans forward, his expression serious. "I think you should do it."

"Wait, really?"

"Why not? Sabrina and I would love to share our wedding with you. And it opens so many other doors, y'know? Think about it. All your great achievements, we could share together. Like, when you and Allie get married? We'll be right there with the announcement of our second child. And when you share Allie's pregnancy? We'll be there announcing our new house."

Logan chokes on his champagne mid-sip.

I narrow my eyes. "Point taken."

"No, wait, it gets even better," Tucker says enthusiastically. "When Allie gives birth to your first kid, guess who'll be there! Me again, there to introduce you to our new dog, who I'll name after your baby to honor you. And when your kid grows up, graduates college, gets engaged, and has a wedding of their own, I'll be sitting there in the front row. Faking a heart attack."

Logan shakes his head in utter astonishment. "Holy shit. Tuck is a sociopath. Didn't I always tell you that gingers are crazy?"

Garrett breaks into hysterics.

"All right, I get it," I mutter.

Tucker's smile is downright lethal. "Do you, Di Laurentis? Because if you upset Sabrina tomorrow by asking Allie to marry you, I will be there. I will always be there. At every corner, ruining every important moment of your life until the day you die. And then, when you're on your deathbed, I'll commit suicide right before you go, just to steal your thunder. What do you think, man? How does that future sound?"

Garrett gives me a smug look. "Told you so."

Welp. He was right. And so was Logan, apparently. Like, Tuck is just sitting here now, drinking champagne and smiling at me as if he hadn't just threatened to commit suicide on my deathbed.

Gingers are psychotic.

FIFTEEN MINUTES LATER, THE LIMO SLOWS DOWN AS WE NEAR OUR destination. When Tucker tries to peer out the window, Logan slugs him in the arm and chides, "Not allowed."

"Are we going down a ramp?" Tucker's forehead knits with curiosity.

"Don't you worry about that, little man," Garrett says mysteriously.

"Little man?" He snorts. "I'm as big as all you assholes."

I reach into my shirt pocket for the bandanna I shoved in there earlier. "All right, blindfold on."

His eyebrows shoot up. "No fucking way."

"So distrustful," Logan tsks.

Garrett grins. "We promise this won't end with you being thrown in a pool of Jell-O or anything."

Tucker appraises the group for a moment. He must decide he can trust us, because he nods and dutifully allows me to secure the blindfold. I tie it extra tight as revenge for his psychotic monologue.

After we hop out of the limo, Logan takes Tucker's arm to guide him so he doesn't fall flat on his face. As we walk toward the team entrance of TD Garden, I'm bouncing up and down like a kid on a sugar high. Tonight isn't only for Tuck. It's for all of us.

Voices bounce off the concrete walls as we head down the tunnel toward the locker rooms. We were given access to the visitors' area, which was the best that Garrett could swing, but I'm sure as shit not complaining. The organization went above and beyond to grant Garrett this request. Clearly being the top scorer on the team has its advantages. I wonder what they'd give him if he was the top scorer in the entire league. Maybe the key to the city. But so far, the honor of the league's top scorer this season goes to Jake Connelly over in Edmonton. There's a reason Connelly's nickname is lightning on skates. His rookie season has been explosive.

We reach the locker room door. When Garrett raps his knuckles in an elaborate knock, the voices beyond the door instantly go silent.

A blindfolded Tuck warily moves his head back and forth. "What the heck is going on..."

Chuckling, Garrett opens the door, and Logan and I guide Tuck inside. I almost squeal like a teenage girl at the sea of familiar faces that greet me. It takes all my willpower to stay quiet, and I see my excitement reflected in everyone's eyes. I hold my finger to my lips, indicating to the group to keep their mouths shut.

"You ready?" Garrett asks Tuck.

"Born ready," he drawls.

Someone chuckles.

The moment Tucker pushes the bandanna down, leaving it wrapped around his neck, his breath hitches sharply. Gaping like a koi fish, he stares at the thirty-odd guys filling the locker room. Then he breaks out in the biggest, giddiest smile I've ever seen.

"Are you kidding me!" He slaps his knee and holds his hip like an old lady trying to hold herself upright, happiness rolling off him in waves. "How did you do this?" he demands as his amazed gaze sweeps over our former teammates from Briar.

Considering we played with dozens of guys over the years, it's astounding we managed to get thirty of them to come to Boston. There's Jake Bergeron, a.k.a. Birdie, our team captain before Garrett. Nate Rhodes, team captain after Garrett. Hunter Davenport, the current captain. There's Simms, the goalie who won us three Frozen Four championships. Jesse Wilkes, Kelvin, Brodowski, Pierre. Our other goalie Corsen. Traynor, Niko, Danny. Colin Fitzgerald, who's been dating my sister for the last few years. The list goes on and on.

"I can't believe you're all here." A dazed Tucker begins to greet our old friends, some of whom we haven't seen in years.

Like Mike Hollis, who's back from India where he lived for a year with his wife, Rupi. They moved back to the States recently and live in New Hampshire now, so Boston wasn't a far trek for him.

Tucker hugs every single guy. It's time-consuming and probably unnecessary, but that's just who John Tucker is. He can't simply throw out a "hey" to everybody in a blanket greeting. He needs to personalize each one.

He ends with Fitzy, who helped Tuck renovate his bar here. I know the two of them are pretty close. "So good to see you, man. You don't visit often enough."

"Work's crazy," Fitzy says ruefully. "And Summer monopolizes all my free time."

I glance over with a chuckle. "Hey, I warned you she was high maintenance."

"Worth it," is his easygoing response, which makes me nod in approval. My sister might be a crazy person, but I'd still die to protect her honor and beat up anyone who disparages her, even Fitz.

Beside me, Tucker is now looking around the cavernous room, as finally it dawns on him where we are. "Holy fuck. This is TD Garden."

"Yup." Garrett's answering grin is smug, and not entirely unwarranted. This is an incredible feat.

"Look at the lockers," I urge Tuck.

He follows my gaze, eyes widening when he notices the lockers are filled with equipment. Most guys are sharing a locker, but Tucker has his own, and every single one has a custom jersey hanging inside, with our names on the back. That was Summer's doing. She designed the jerseys and got them done up.

"This is…" I swear his eyes appear a bit watery now. "This is the greatest gift, you guys. I didn't expect to see y'all here and—" He suddenly tenses, guilt crossing his face. "Aw, shit. Are y'all staying for the reception tomorrow? You were all invited, but not everyone RSVP'd. Gonna have to call the caterer, and Sabrina, and…" He trails off, his mind clearly working a million miles a minute to troubleshoot this latest development.

A few guys snicker at his visible anxiety.

"It's all taken care of," I assure him. "We didn't want you to know who was surprising you for the bachelor party, but don't worry, Sabrina has all the RSVPs."

"She knew all about it," Garrett adds, so Tuck knows we didn't just dump thirty extra guests on their wedding.

Relief loosens his broad shoulders.

"And now, no more wedding talk," I say firmly. "Tonight is about the boys hitting the ice again."

"Seriously? We're going to play?" Tucker's entire face lights up. "*Here?*"

I know exactly how he feels. The thought of skating on the same surface where the Bruins play gets my dick semi-hard. This is every hockey fan's wet dream.

"We only have two hours," Garrett tells the group. "So let's gear up already and take advantage of every second before the overnight maintenance crew throws us out."

Without delay, everyone marches to their lockers and clothes start hitting the floor. It's chaotic and awesome, and I'm proud of myself for coming up with such a brilliant idea, which has been months in the planning. Garrett and Logan got us the rink, but I personally flew two-thirds of these guys out to Boston and put them up at a hotel. Not everybody could afford the weekend away, and although some guys protested about letting me pay their way, in the end I convinced them to swallow their pride for Tucker. Definitely doesn't hurt having a trust fund, especially in situations like this.

Now I'm surrounded by old friends, teammates I skated with for four years, and I can't imagine a better night. Forget naked strippers and cringey lap dances where one guy inevitably comes in front of everyone. This is the best bachelor party ever.

CHAPTER 15

ALLIE

Sabrina James, soon to be Sabrina Tucker, is one of those obnoxiously beautiful women who turns every head when she walks into a room. I'm talking glossy dark hair, bottomless brown eyes, and a perfect body that shows zero signs of having ever carried a child. If I didn't know her, I'd probably hate her. Or, at the very least, die of jealousy. And not only is this girl stunning, but she's about to graduate from law school. Ergo, beauty and brains. Some people are just born lucky.

Still, it's very hard to dislike Sabrina once you get to know her. She's a ride-or-die type of friend, loyal to the core, and funnier than her aloof exterior suggests.

When she enters the private tearoom, a brilliant smile lights her face. As if it's an unexpected joy to find all of us here, even though she'd helped plan this.

"I can't believe you're all here." An uncharacteristic note of emotion trembles in her voice. Sabrina is usually cool as a cucumber. Self-assured. She doesn't get emotional. But I'm pretty sure there are tears clinging to her impossibly long lashes as she clutches little Jamie in her arms.

The three-year-old, meanwhile, is clamoring to get down and not get squeezed to death by her mom's anaconda arms.

At Sabrina's request, the guest list was kept small, so our little group barely makes a dent in the large, elegant room. Sabrina's never been a social butterfly, though. She worked her way through college, then had a kid right before starting law school, which doesn't leave much time for socializing. Our group today is comprised of me, Hannah, and Grace; Dean's sister Summer; Hope and Carin, Sabrina's best friends from Briar; and Samantha and Kelsey, two friends from Harvard Law.

But it's Jamie who captures everyone's attention. The toddler has Tucker's dark-red hair and Sabrina's big chocolate-brown eyes. She's the perfect combination of the two of them, and I have no doubt she'll be just as gorgeous. This morning she's wearing a purple dress with a tutu skirt, her hair arranged in two pigtails.

"Auntie Allie!" she shrieks before flinging a pair of chubby arms around my knees.

I bend down so I can hug her proper. "Hey, princess," I say, using Dean's nickname for her. Everyone seems to have their own pet name for Jamie. Garrett calls her gumdrop. Logan calls her squirt. Hope's husband, D'Andre, calls her snickerdoodle, which I think might be my favorite one.

"Oh my goodness, is that a tiara?" I say, admiring the sparkling silver crown atop her auburn head.

"Ya! Daddy got it for me!" Proudly, Jamie shows the tiara off to the entire group, as we all ooh and aah accordingly.

Then we mill around and chat amongst ourselves until an elegantly dressed hotel employee arrives to announce that tea will be served soon.

"Are you excited, little one?" Sabrina asks her daughter. "We're about to have tea. Like Alice."

"Like Alice!" Jamie shouts, because young children don't come with a volume dial. I don't think Jamie Tucker has any concept of the word *loud*.

We all settle around the table at our assigned seats. I'm between Hannah and Summer, with Sabrina and Jamie directly across from us. The moment she settles in her booster seat, Jamie tries to snatch a teacup off the crisp, floral tablecloth on the beautifully set table. Sabrina intervenes like a pro, blocking Jamie's hand as skillfully as a goalie making a clutch save.

"No, this cup is Auntie Hope's," she says, moving the fine china toward the grinning woman with the dark braids. "*This* one is for you."

I hide a smile. Jamie's cup is clearly made of plastic.

"We're going through a butterfingers phase," Sabrina explains, catching my knowing smile. "No china for this one. It'll cost a fortune to replace all the cups she drops."

As a trio of servers appear to pour our tea, I notice Hannah's looking a bit pale. I nudge her gently. "You okay?" I murmur.

"I'm fine. Just a bit queasy," she says. "Not sure wolfing down a fully loaded omelet right before bed last night was a good idea."

"I think they said one of these is a ginger tea? That'll help with the queasiness." I glance at the male server who approaches us. "You said something about ginger? Can we try that one, please?"

"Of course, madam."

Madam. I don't know if that makes me feel fancy or just old.

"Smells good," Hannah says as she brings the teacup to her mouth. She takes a dainty sip. "Perfect. Just what I need."

Across the table, Jamie adorably mimics Hannah. "Mmmmmm!" she announces, slurping her tea. "Perfect!"

Everyone's trying not to laugh.

"She actually likes tea?" Kelsey says from Sabrina's other side, sounding surprised. "It's not too bitter for her?"

"It's G-R-A-P-E J-U-I-C-E," Sabrina spells out, grinning. "There's no way I'm pumping this kid full of caffeine. Are you crazy?"

"There's decaf," Carin points out.

"I'm not taking the chance she accidentally ingests something else. Not after last year's coffee debacle. She was so wired, Tuck almost took her to the ER."

The servers bring out the first round of sandwiches on extravagant three-tiered trays. And for the next hour and a half, the trays keep coming. I feel like I'm acting out a scene from *Downton Abbey* as we munch on tiny cucumber sandwiches and stuffed macaroons. Despite it being Sabrina's day, Jamie is the obvious star of the morning. She's smart as a whip and so damn sweet, reminding me a lot of Tucker. And just when I think she couldn't get any cuter, I discover she has this weird new habit of asking everyone if they're okay, which she proceeds to do while skipping around the table.

"Are you okay, Auntie Samanda?" she asks, pausing next to Samantha's chair.

Sabrina's Harvard friend is clearly fighting a laugh. "I'm wonderful, thank you for asking."

"You're welcome." With a big, beaming smile, Jamie moves to the next seat, which happens to belong to me.

"Are you okay, Auntie Allie?" she inquires.

My lips twitch. "I'm doing great, princess."

She moves over. "Are you okay, Auntie 'Annah?"

Hannah smiles indulgently. "I'm great, gumdrop."

Jamie skips down the line. I gaze at Sabrina and say, "She's a lot calmer than the last time I saw her." It was back in the fall, and Jamie had been a total terror, streaking around the room getting into mischief.

"Trust me, she's still a nightmare," Sabrina answers. "I made sure she got a nap in after breakfast. Tried to wear her out before we got here so she'd be calmer."

Our servers return to top off everyone's teacups, and the conversation shifts from Jamie to tonight's wedding reception. The ceremony itself is taking place about an hour before that, but it's a private event. Just Sabrina and Tucker, and Tucker's mom.

A fact that Carin is pouting over. "I can't believe we won't get to see you recite your vows."

Hope snorts. "I can. No way was this bit—B-I-T-C-H going to pour her heart out in front of two hundred people."

Sabrina grins at that. "You know me well, Hopeless." She shrugs. "It was our compromise. Tuck gets a huge reception, and I get to tell him how much I love him without four hundred pairs of eyes staring at me."

Next to me, Summer is also pouting. "I'm so jealous you're getting married," she tells Sabrina. "Honestly, I cannot believe Fitzy hasn't asked me to marry him yet. The nerve of that man."

I raise an eyebrow. "You're only twenty-two," I remind her.

She tosses her silky golden hair over her shoulder. "So? Twenty-two-year-olds aren't allowed to get married?"

"No, of course they are. It's just… It's young. I'm turning twenty-five soon, and I definitely don't want to get married right now."

Summer waves a flippant hand. "Twenty-five? Oh my God. You're practically an old maid." Her twinkling green eyes tell me she's joking. "I don't know, I just always imagined myself getting married young. And being a young mom," she admits. "I want to have at least four kids."

"Four?" I sputter.

She beams. "Four big strapping boys like their dad."

Sabrina snickers. "Talk to me after the first one. Let's see if you still want the other three."

Summer defends her stance. "I love having two brothers, and Fitz is an only child, so I think he'd enjoy having a big family." She sticks out her bottom lip. "All of that is moot, though, because the jerk is not asking me." She gasps. "Oh my God. What if he doesn't think I'm his forever person?" Before anyone can answer, she releases a rushed breath, then starts to laugh. "Okay, that's just crazy. Of course I'm his forever person. Jeez."

I just nod along. I learned a long time ago that Summer Heyward-Di Laurentis is capable of having entire conversations all by herself.

Suddenly, she turns it on me. "Wait. Are you actually telling me you wouldn't marry Dicky if he asked you right now?" she challenges.

Dean's childhood nickname makes me grin. "Well, he's not asking, so that question is also moot."

"But if he was?" she pushes. "You wouldn't say yes?"

"I…I don't know. Truthfully, I probably wouldn't even let him ask."

"Really?" Hannah looks startled.

I shrug, because I don't know how to put it into words.

It's not that I don't love Dean. Of course I do. And of course I envision us getting married and having a family one day. *One day* being the operative words.

Grace joins the discussion, one eyebrow raised. "Are you saying he might not be your forever person?"

That summons a growl from Summer. "You better not be saying that, because I already have a design in mind for our custom sisters-in-law Christmas onesies."

"I'm not saying that at all," I protest. "Dean is absolutely my forever person. We're end game. But to me, getting engaged isn't just one step. It's, like, three steps all joined together. An engagement should be immediately followed by getting married, which should be closely followed by starting a family, and I'm not ready for any of those steps. Being a mom in the near future sounds terrifying to me." I glance over at Sabrina. "No offense."

"None taken." She offers a dry smile. "It was terrifying to me too. Getting pregnant my senior year of college was definitely not part of the plan. If you're not ready to have a kid, don't let anyone pressure you into it."

"Dean's not pressuring me," I assure her. "But like I said, all those steps are connected for me. I'd rather get married when I know I'm ready for the rest of it. Just do it all at once, know what I mean? I think I'm explaining this badly."

Summer shrugs. "No, that makes sense. See, I don't care if I'm engaged for like five years. I'd just be happy having something sparkly to wear while I wait for the go-ahead to plan the most epic wedding." She holds out her hand, which is already covered in sparkly things. Summer is basically a fashion icon. Expensive clothes and jewelry are her religion.

"You look like you're doing okay for now," I say with a smile.

"That's different. I want one from Fitzy. And I can't wait to design my own wedding gown." She gives Sabrina a stern look. "And you, you'd better be wearing your dress at the reception. I'm dying to see it."

Sabrina flushes slightly. "It's really not anything fancy," she tells Dean's fashionista little sister.

"Doesn't matter. I know you're going to look beautiful in it regardless," Summer proclaims. Her green eyes dance happily. "Oh, I love weddings so much! Are you excited? This is so exciting!"

"SO EXCITING!" Jamie randomly shouts out. Then she peers up at her mom. "What's exciting?"

Sabrina laughs. "Life," she tells her daughter. "And yes, I am excited. Although that's another thing that wasn't part of the plan—getting married. But Tuck and I already have a kid together. And he's the one I want to be with for the rest of my life, so…" She trails off with a shrug.

The answering chorus of awws makes her blush harder.

"Mummy, you're all red." Jamie climbs into her mother's lap and pokes Sabrina's cheek with one sticky finger.

Sabrina narrows her eyes. "And you are covered in chocolate."

I suddenly realize there are chocolate smears all over Jamie's rosebud mouth.

"Where the heck did she get chocolate from?" Sabrina asks.

Everyone looks around the table. Most of the pastries have been devoured, and the ones left are mostly sugar cookies. We'd annihilated anything with chocolate fairly fast.

"Auntie Carin's cookie fell on the floor and I picked it up

and ate it!" Jamie announces proudly, and I almost choke on my laughter.

Sabrina sighs. "All right. Let's get you cleaned up, little one."

She grabs a napkin and wipes Jamie's chocolate-smeared mouth. No sooner does she put the crumpled napkin down than Jamie shoves a cream-filled pastry in her mouth, and now she's got icing sugar all over her face.

Sabrina reaches for another napkin.

Oh man. Kids are exhausting. Witnessing Sabrina's infinite supply of patience is something else. And it just cements my decision to postpone all those pesky steps until later in my life.

Much, much later.

CHAPTER 16

DEAN

At six o'clock, we're all waiting for the newlyweds to enter the ballroom of the boutique hotel where the reception is being held. The private ceremony ended a while ago, but Tucker's mom had popped in afterward with the update that they were taking some pictures up on the hotel roof and would come down shortly

The ballroom currently holds about two hundred guests, many of whom are current or former hockey players all stuffed like sausages in ill-fitted suits. Not me, obviously. I rock a suit like nobody's business. Allie's wearing a sky-blue dress that matches her eyes and silver stilettos that give her some height and make her legs look endless. Her blond hair is pulled back in an elegant twist, revealing the diamond studs in her ears, last year's anniversary gift courtesy of yours truly.

"Is this from the new Tom Ford collection?" my sister asks, running her grubby hands over the front of my very expensive suit jacket. Well, fine, her manicure probably cost more than this suit, but you can't go around pawing at a man's tailored wool, cotton, and silk blend.

"Yes," I answer smugly. "Jealous?"

"Yes, Dicky, I'm so jealous," Summer replies, dramatically rolling her eyes. Then she sighs. "Actually, yeah, I kind of am. You look better than me tonight."

"Thank you for acknowledging that," I say solemnly.

Fitz shakes his head. "You two are insane."

"Ignore him," Summer tells me. "He doesn't understand clothes the way we do."

She's right. Fitz would be happy wearing ripped jeans and old tees for the rest of his life. He has no use for designer clothes. But it's one of the many things Summer and I have in common, along with our lust for life. It'll be nice having her back in New York this summer. After she graduates from Briar next month, she and Fitz are moving to Manhattan.

"I can't wait till we're both in the city together again," Summer says as if reading my mind. "Actually, not just both of us—all of us!" she corrects, her expression shining brighter. "I'm excited to drop by Nicky's office for surprise lunches and shopping trips and watch him make up excuses why he can't go."

Summer gets a kick out of tormenting our workaholic older brother. And tormenting me. And her boyfriend. Basically, she's a holy terror. But we all love her.

A murmur ripples through the crowd.

"They're here," someone says.

All gazes focus on the double doors in the arched doorway. A moment later they fling open, and Jamie Tucker glides into the ballroom looking like an angel princess in a white tulle dress with a full skirt. There's a silver tiara tucked into her auburn hair, and a beaming smile on her cherub face.

Tucker's mother, Gail, scurries after the toddler, chiding, "Jamie! You were supposed to wait for the signal."

Laughter breaks out, which turns into gasps when Sabrina and Tucker appear.

"Oh my God," Allie breathes. "I know she probably hates every-one staring at her, but *look* at her."

She's right. Sabrina is exquisite in a simple white satin gown with a scooped neckline that reveals some pretty delectable cleavage. Her dark hair cascades over one bare shoulder, a section of it clipped to the side with a diamond pin. Even though she's wearing impossibly high heels, Tuck stands at well over six feet and still towers over her. They're holding hands as they enter the ballroom. Sabrina's blushing and Tucker's beaming, and I deeply envy him in that moment.

I squeeze Allie's hand, and when she squeezes back and slants her head toward me with a smile, my heart clenches tight. How did I get this lucky?

"That'll be us someday." I don't want to give away the surprise, but I can't help whispering the teasing words in her ear.

She laughs softly. "One day," she agrees. "Well into the future, though."

I falter for a second. I want to ask her to define "well into the future" but that would tip my hand, so I maintain my light tone. "I don't know… I wouldn't be against seeing you in a wedding dress sooner rather than later. You'd look smoking hot."

"Obviously," she replies, and I grin. Her self-confidence rivals mine. It's one of the reasons I love her.

"Want me to call Vera Wang?" I offer graciously. I'm only half-joking. With my family connections, I could easily get Vera on the line.

Allie's expression grows thoughtful as she studies my face. I don't know what she glimpses there, but whatever it is brings another laugh to her lips. "You might want to hold off on that. I mean, it'll probably take you a while to convince my dad."

Her dad?

She notes my blank look. "Oh, sweetie," she tsks, blue eyes dancing. "You know you'd have to ask for his *blessing*."

My stomach sinks. Oh sweet baby Jesus. I have to ask for his blessing?

Don't get me wrong—Joe Hayes and I have developed a tentative friendship over the years. I mean, he still calls me "pretty boy," but I know he likes me.

Enough to marry his little girl, though? His only child?

Oh, fuck.

Taking pity on me, Allie laces her fingers through mine and tugs me forward. "Come on, let's go congratulate the happy couple."

AND HERE I THOUGHT THAT SKATING IN TD GARDEN WITH MY old team was the greatest night of all time. This wedding reception? Fucking tops that. After a mouth-watering dinner and some of the most hilarious speeches in wedding history, the live band takes the stage and the dance floor comes alive. After a few songs, though, I abandon Allie and she dances with her girlfriends while I try to catch up with as many old friends as I can. Because who knows when or if I'll see them again after tonight.

When college graduation had been looming, I'd worried we'd all drift apart. And some of us have. Birdie and his longtime girlfriend Natalie got married and moved to Oklahoma. Traynor lives in LA and plays for the Kings. Pierre returned to Canada.

Losing touch with college friends is simply one of those depressing inevitabilities of life, but I've also been lucky that many of these guys are still in my life. I see Fitzy frequently because he's dating my sister. Hunter and I still text all the time, so I'm up-to-date on his life. I've met his girlfriend Demi, who couldn't make it tonight, and I know they're moving in together, sharing a house with his teammate Conor and Conor's girlfriend. I talk to Garrett and Logan and Tuck and see them far more often than I thought I would.

There's really only one close friend I can't see, can't speak to, and that's Beau Maxwell, because he's gone. I think Beau would've had fun tonight if he'd been here.

A lump of grief rises in my throat, so I gulp down the rum and Coke I'd been nursing to try to dislodge the heavy emotion.

Luckily, I'm provided a distraction when Coach Jensen interrupts our little hockey reunion by stalking up to the group.

"Hey, Coach," drawls Tucker, beaming at the man who'd challenged and berated us for four years. "I'm glad you could make it. You too, Iris," he adds, smiling at the gorgeous woman at Coach's side.

I can't lie—I was surprised when Coach showed up to the reception with his new girlfriend. It boggles my mind that anyone would choose to date someone as surly and perpetually annoyed as Coach. But Iris March seems cool, and she's definitely a stunner. That part isn't a surprise, though. Chad Jensen's hot for a dude in his forties. Of course he's killing it with the ladies.

"Thanks for having us," Coach says brusquely.

There's a beat of silence.

Then he nods. "All right. Carry on." He rests one big hand on the small of Iris's back, trying to lead her away.

Logan bursts out laughing. "Seriously? You're just gonna walk off without giving a speech? Without congratulating the groom?"

"What kind of sociopath does that?" Nate Rhodes pipes up.

"Despicable," Garrett agrees, nodding gravely.

Coach rubs the bridge of his nose as if warding off a migraine. It's a gesture I've seen thousands of times over the years.

Next to him, Iris laughs softly. "Oh, come on, Chad. Say a few words."

He huffs out a breath. "Fine." But then he doesn't continue.

Still laughing, Iris kicks it off for him. "Let's raise our glasses to Tucker…"

We all raise our glasses or beer bottles.

Finally, Coach Jensen clears his throat. "Well," he says, his shuttered eyes sweeping over the group. "As you know, I don't have any sons. And after coaching all you boys for so many years, I've come to realize I'm glad I don't."

Mike Hollis hoots loudly. I muffle my laughter against my palm.

Coach glares at us.

"With that said," he continues, "out of all the players I've coached, John, you're the one who's given me the least amount of grief. So thanks for that. Congratulations on everything. The lawyer wife. The cute rug rat. I'm proud of you, kid."

Tucker's eyes are a bit shiny. He blinks a couple of times, then says, "Thanks, Coach."

They share a macho side hug. Coach steps back and tugs at his tie in discomfort. "I need another drink," he mutters before taking Iris's arm and making his escape.

We watch him go. "I miss his pep talks," Garrett says glumly.

"They've gotten shorter and drastically less peppy," Hunter tells us.

Logan snickers. "I'm going to grab another drink and find Grace. BRB."

My gaze remains trained on Coach and Iris, who'd just reached the bar. They make a good-looking couple. Coach's muscular body was built for a suit, and Iris's ass looks damn good in her black cocktail dress.

"I can't believe Coach has a girlfriend." Then another thought occurs to me. I go quiet and squint in their direction.

"Are you having a stroke?" Hunter asks politely.

I shake my head. "Nah, I was trying to picture Coach having sex."

Guffaws break out all around me. Hollis, however, is nodding vigorously. "I think about that all the time," he says.

"All the time?" Fitzy echoes.

Hollis ignores his best friend. "Oh yeah. I've spent years trying to solve the mystery."

"Years?" Fitz again.

"What mystery?" Hunter looks amused.

"The mystery of how he fucks," Hollis explains. "Because here's the thing—Coach is like this big burly man's man, you know? So you'd think he'd be a power fucker, right?" Hollis grows more and more animated. "Like, he's going to drill fast and hard."

"I don't like this conversation," Garrett says frankly.

"But maybe that's too obvious," Hollis continues.

"So what are we thinking?" a fascinated Nate asks.

"Submissive," I supply immediately. This might not be appropriate wedding subject matter, but now I'm invested. "I bet he lets her tie him up and have her way with him."

"No way," Hunter argues. "He'd need to be in control."

"Agreed," Hollis says, giving a firm nod. "But here's what I envision: tender."

"Nah," Hunter says.

"Tender," Hollis insists. "He's *all* about the foreplay. He spends hours pleasing his lady. But he's in full control, right? Then, after he's made her come like four times, he slowly enters her—"

"Enters her?" Nate hoots.

Fitz sighs.

"—and they make love," Hollis finishes. "Lovemaking all the way."

I purse my lips. Honestly, I can see it. Coach's exterior is so rough, I bet he throws curveballs in bed.

"Nah," Hunter repeats. "I still vote for power fucker."

"Coach doesn't fuck," Hollis argues. "He makes love."

Someone clears their throat. "Gentlemen."

We jump in surprise when Iris Marsh appears behind us. Biting her lip like she's trying not to bust into laughter, she casually leans past Tucker to grab the silver clutch on the table he's leaning against.

"Left my purse," she says in a light tone.

To Hollis's credit, he's not the least bit abashed. I don't think that dude is capable of feeling shame.

"Uh, enjoying the band?" Garrett asks her, as if we don't all know she'd overheard us dissecting her sex life with Coach.

"They're excellent," she replies. "I loved that Arcade Fire cover."

She tucks the purse under her arm and takes a step back. "Anyway. Sorry to interrupt."

Just before she goes, however, she leans closer to Hollis and murmurs something. So quietly I think I imagined it at first.

"He definitely fucks."

Hollis's jaw drops.

"But you didn't hear that from me," Iris calls over her shoulder, waltzing off in Coach's direction.

"Told you," Hunter says smugly.

CHAPTER 17

ALLIE

"You really do look amazing." I sidle up to the bride, touching her arm.

Sabrina looks over at me, her smile rueful. "Thanks. I feel like everyone is staring at me."

"They are." I grin. "I hate to inform you, but they'd be staring at you even if you weren't wearing that dress. You're hot."

My gaze drifts across the room to where Dean is congregated with a dozen of his former teammates. The comments he'd made earlier about seeing me in a wedding dress are still troubling me. He knows that's not something I want right now. Or at least he *should* know. I made it more than clear that marriage and babies aren't on my agenda when we discussed it last year. But Dean is impulsive. He's the kind of guy who might see Sabrina and Tucker basking in marital bliss and decide to spontaneously propose to me.

"What do you think they're whispering about over there?" I nod toward the group of boys. Their conversation looks intense.

"Hockey, probably." She takes a second to study them, then shakes her head. "No, they're talking about sex."

"Ha! How can you tell?"

"Fitzy's face. He looks like he wants to wither away and die on the spot."

I follow her gaze and laugh again. Yeah, Fitz does tend to get that pained look when he's forced into conversations about topics he'd rather keep private. Usually it's Hollis who drags him in. I shift my gaze. Yup, Mike Hollis seems to be doing the bulk of the talking, which is never good. Honestly, I'm a little disappointed his wife couldn't make it tonight. I would've loved to meet the woman who married Mike Hollis. She either has the patience of a saint, or she's as cuckoo bananas as he is. Summer used to live with her and claims it's the latter.

"Have you seen Hannah?" I ask, searching the crowded ballroom. My best friend has been hard to find tonight. And she hasn't been entirely herself since I arrived in Boston. When I was doing her makeup earlier, she was so distracted that at one point she forgot where we were going tonight.

"I think I saw her heading for the restrooms," Sabrina says.

"Okay. I'm gonna track her down and try to get her onto the dance floor. Be right back." I'm hoping I might be able to get Hannah to sing something too. I'm sure the band would be happy to let her, and I know Tucker would love it.

Outside the ballroom, I welcome the silence. A nice reprieve from the continuous hum of noise and buzz of voices at the reception. As I smooth out the hem of my dress, I catch a glimpse of Logan and Grace standing against a pillar in the wide lobby area. Canoodling, as gossip columnists would say. They haven't spotted me yet, and I'm about to say hello when their voices carry in my direction. What I hear stops me short.

"Should we get outta here soon, Mrs. Logan?"

Um.

What?

"You're never going to get tired of saying that, are you?" Grace is laughing.

"Never." He smacks a kiss on her lips. "Mrs. Logan."

Yup. Didn't imagine it the first time.

I shoot forward like a rocket. "I'm sorry—but…WHAT?" My shocked voice echoes in the cavernous lobby.

They break apart guiltily as I march toward them. I move so fast, I nearly trip on my stilettos. I can't function. Or think straight. My mouth keeps opening and closing as the implications settle.

"Why does he keep calling you that?" I ask Grace. "Oh my God. Did you guys—"

She cuts me off before I can finish. "Come! Let's go powder our noses!" Then she grabs my arm and practically drags me away.

I glance over my shoulder to find Logan grinning sheepishly. He shrugs at me, then winks. That's all I need. Holy shit. Holy *shit*.

"You guys got married?" I exclaim as we burst into the bathroom. Fortunately, it's empty.

"No," Grace says.

I narrow my eyes at her.

"Yes," Grace says.

"Oh my God. How? When?"

Her light-brown eyes focus everywhere else but on me. She pretends to admire the stack of linen towels next to one of the ornate sinks.

"When?" I repeat.

"Over New Year's," she confesses.

"What!" I shriek. "You got married four months ago and didn't tell anyone?" Something terrible then occurs to me. "Wait, does everyone else know and they've just kept it a secret from me and Dean?"

Grace is quick to reassure me. "Nobody knows except us. We didn't want to break it to my dad before graduation. He would freak if he thought I wasn't fully concentrating on school."

Stunned, I sweep my gaze over Grace's girl-next-door features and tentative smile. She's the perfect match for Logan, yes, but she's two years younger than him. And they're married?

"So you two just…eloped?" I'm utterly dumbfounded.

"Sort of? We didn't plan to. It just happened."

"It just happened," I echo. "How does something like that 'just happen'?"

"I mean, we'd discussed marriage before and realized neither of us really wanted a wedding. His parents can't even be in the same room, so Logan didn't want to be in a position where he was forced to choose. And then over the holidays, we wound up at this bed-and-breakfast in Vermont that was owned by a pastor. And not only does he officiate weddings, but he managed to get us a last-minute marriage license because the town clerk is part of his flock, and it was like, serendipity. Is that the word? I hate that word." She's blushing so hard, even the freckles on her nose look redder. "Anyway, I have zero regrets. Neither does he. We're forever."

Emotion clogs my throat and stings my eyes. I've always been a sappy romantic. "That is the most romantic thing I've ever heard," I wail.

"You have to promise not to say anything, Allie. We're not ready to tell anybody, not until after graduation."

"I promise," I say, using the pads of my index fingers to delicately wipe my tears. "It'll stay between us—"

A loud retching noise suddenly echoes in the bathroom.

"—and whoever's throwing up in there," I finish.

Grace pales. She shoots a panicky look at the last stall in the row. I'd been flipping out so hard when she'd dragged me in here, I hadn't even noticed that closed door. I assumed we were alone.

"Everything okay in there?" I call at the stall.

There's a long pause, then, "Yeah, all good. Give me a second."

It's Hannah.

She appears a moment later, still clad in the green sheath dress I'd picked out for her today after Dean informed her if she wore black to a wedding, she was dooming the bride and groom to an eternity of morbid misery. I don't think that's a thing, but it succeeded in convincing Hannah to add some color into her life. The dress is the same shade of green as her eyes, which are currently lined with fatigue as she approaches the wall of sinks and mirrors.

"How much did you hear?" Grace sighs.

Hannah offers a wry smile. "All of it."

She places her cupped hands beneath the automatic faucet and fills them with water. She proceeds to rinse out her mouth before her eyes find ours in the mirror again.

"You okay?" I fret.

She slowly shakes her head. "I'm starting to think no."

A knot forms in my stomach. "What's wrong?"

"I might need a…um…pregnancy test."

Silence crashes over us. It lasts about a second before my loud gasp reverberates in the air.

Grace purses her lips. "I'm pretty sure this was an episode of *Friends*. I've been watching reruns."

My gaze instantly drops to Hannah's stomach even though the rational part of my brain knows that even if she is pregnant, she wouldn't be showing yet.

Hannah catches where my eyes went and fixes me with a stern look. "Don't say anything to Dean." She turns to Grace. "Or Logan. Please. They'll tell Garrett in a heartbeat, and I haven't even taken a test yet. For all I know, it's a false alarm."

"How late are you?" Grace asks.

Hannah bites her lip.

"How late?" I press.

"Three weeks."

I gasp again.

"Seriously, I don't want Garrett knowing anything until I take a test," Hannah says firmly. "Neither of you are allowed to say a word."

"Neither of you are allowed to say a word about my thing either." Grace's expression is equally severe.

"But…" I sputter.

"Not a word until further notice," Hannah orders, while Grace nods in agreement.

I just stand there, gaping at the two of them.

This wedding reception is chock full of HUGE NEWS, and I'm not allowed to tell anyone about it until further notice? Not even Dean?

This is my worst nightmare.

CHAPTER 18

DEAN

"Pretty boy. What are you doing here?"

"I texted you to say I was on my way." Rolling my eyes, I stride through the front door of the Brooklyn brownstone where Allie grew up.

"Yeah, and I asked you why. So. What are you doing here?"

Joe Hayes leans on his cane as he watches me enter. His face displays only mild hostility, which is better than usual. Allie's dad and I didn't hit it off the moment we met, but I like to think that over the years I've grown on him. Although the one time I voiced that thought, Joe had nodded and said, "Like a fungus." He's a real delight.

"Brought you some groceries," I say, kicking off my shoes.

"Why?"

"My God, you're like Tucker's three-year-old. Because I thought you might need food." I turn to him with a mock frown. "Want to know the proper response when someone brings you groceries? *Why, thank you, pretty boy, I appreciate the gesture. How did I get so lucky as to have you in my daughter's life?*"

"Dean. Don't bullshit a bullshitter. You're a nice kid. But you're not a drop-off-groceries-for-no-reason kind of guy. Which means you've got an ulterior motive." He eyes the two paper bags I'm holding. "Any corned beef in there?"

"'Course." I've been here enough times to know what he likes from the deli down the street. "Come on, I'll fix us some sandwiches while I reveal my ulterior motive."

With a chuckle, he hobbles to the kitchen behind me, relying far too heavily on his cane. I almost suggest we go and dust off his wheelchair, but stop myself at the last second because it'll only put him in an even fouler mood. Allie's dad refuses to use that chair. I'm not sure I blame him—it can't feel great going from a fit, physical man to a weakened one with a degenerative disorder. Unfortunately, MS doesn't have a cure, and Joe eventually needs to come to terms with the fact that his condition is only going to get worse. Hell, it already has. His limp is already far more pronounced than when we first met. But he's a proud man. Stubborn like his daughter. I know he's going to hold out on using the wheelchair for as long as humanly possible.

While Joe slowly lowers himself onto a chair, I prepare two sandwiches at the counter, then grab two beers from the fridge.

"It's noon," he points out.

"I need the liquid courage."

Just like that, his expression becomes more pained than usual. "Aw man, no. Is that it? Today's the day?"

I frown. "What day?"

He scrubs one hand over his eyes, the other over his dark beard. "You're gonna ask for my blessing. Aw hell. Just get it over with and ask, then. You really need to drag out the torture and make both of us uncomfortable? I'd rather be waterboarded. Goddamn it. We both know I'm going to say yes, okay? So do it already."

I gape at him for a second. Then a wave of laughter spills out. "With all due respect, sir? You're the fucking worst. I had a whole speech prepared."

But I suppose I'm glad I don't have to recite it. I can't imagine anything more humiliating than pouring your heart out to a man who equates sharing his feelings to literal torture.

I set a plate in front of him before taking a seat across the table. All the wind's out of my sails as I grumble, "So I've got your blessing?"

He takes a bite of his sandwich, chewing slowly. "Got the ring with you?"

"Yup. Want to see it?"

"Bring it out, kid."

I reach into my pocket for the blue velvet box. When I flip it open, his dark eyebrows shoot up like two helium balloons.

"Couldn't find anything bigger?" he asks sarcastically.

"You think she won't like it?" I despair for a moment.

"Oh, she's going to love it. You know AJ. When it comes to jewelry, the bigger and shinier, the better."

"That was my thought process," I say with a grin. I close the ring box and tuck it back in my pocket. "All seriousness—are you truly okay if I ask her to marry me? You weren't exactly my biggest fan when we first met."

"Eh, you're all right." His lips twitch. "You guys are young, though."

"When did you get engaged to Allie's mom?" I ask curiously.

"Twenty-one," he admits. "Married at twenty-two."

I tip my head as if to say, *see?* "That's way younger than us."

"Yeah, but times are different now," he says gruffly. "AJ has a career, goals. And women are having babies later and later these days. There's no rush anymore." Joe shrugs. "But if it's something the two of you want, then I won't stand in your way. AJ loves you. I like you somewhat. Good enough for me."

I smother a burst of laughter. That's about as ringing an endorsement as I'm ever going to get from Joe Hayes.

We clink beer bottles and then talk hockey while we eat our sandwiches.

MY NEXT STOP IS MANHATTAN. ALLIE AND I LIVE ON THE UPPER East Side, but my mother's office is on the west end, which is where the taxi drops me almost an hour later.

Mom smiles happily when the receptionist shows me into her office. "Sweetie! This is a nice surprise!"

She rises from her plush leather chair and rounds the desk to come give me a warm hug. I hug her back and plant a kiss on her cheek. Mom and I are close. Ditto for me and Dad. Truth be told, my parents are awesome. They're both high-profile lawyers, so that means yes, my siblings and I had nannies growing up on account of that. But we also had plenty of family time. Mom and Dad were always there for us when we needed them, and they definitely didn't let us run wild like feral children. Well, maybe Summer, to some extent. That girl's got the folks wrapped around her little finger.

"I have a big favor to ask," I tell my mother as she sits at the corner of her desk. "Can I borrow the penthouse tonight?"

For my entire childhood, we would split our time between our house in Greenwich and our penthouse at the Heyward Plaza Hotel. My mom's side of the family, the Heywards, built a real estate empire that made them billions, and the Heyward Plaza is one of its crown jewels. Although our villa in St. Barth's isn't anything to scoff at either.

"I feel like you're a teenager again," Mom says, narrowing her eyes. They're the same shade of sea green as mine and Summer's. My brother Nick is the only kid who inherited Dad's brown ones. "You're not planning a kegger, are you?"

"Nope. Nothing like that."

"What's the occasion then?"

Unable to contain my grin, I slide my hand in the pocket of my trousers. It emerges with the ring box, which I place on her cherry-stained desk without a single word.

Mom instantly understands. She releases a squeal of joy and suddenly she's hugging me again.

"Oh my God! When are you going to do it? Tonight?" She claps her hands happily. My folks adore Allie, so I'm not surprised by her jubilant response.

"I was hoping. I know it's weird to do it in the middle of the week, but Saturday is Allie's wrap party for the show, and then Sunday my girls have a tournament in Albany, so I'm out of town. I didn't want to wait until Sunday night, so." I shrug. "I figured tonight's the night. I know you're at the penthouse this week, but I was wondering if you could clear out for a few hours while—"

"Say no more. I'll drive back to Greenwich tonight."

"You don't have to leave the city," I protest.

"I was going home on Friday anyway. A few days early won't matter." She claps her hands again. "Oh, your father is going to be so happy!"

"Nope. You're not allowed to tell him until after I do it."

Mom's jaw drops. "You really expect me to keep that kind of secret from him?"

"You have no choice. Dad tells Summer everything, and Summer can't keep her mouth shut to save her life."

After a beat, Mom surrenders. "You're right. Your sister sucks."

I snort out a laugh.

"Fine. I won't tell Dad." She beams at me. "My lips will remain sealed until I receive a call saying my baby boy is engaged."

I sigh. "Mom. You're embarrassing yourself."

That just makes her laugh.

CHAPTER 19

ALLIE

DEAN IS WEARING HIS FAVORITE TOM FORD SUIT AND THAT'S A problem.

Not because he doesn't look good in it. He absolutely does. Dean is the hottest guy in existence, and I'm not saying that as his girlfriend. Like, objectively, I don't think a better-looking man exists. And he looks good in anything. Swim trunks, sweats, khakis—he's a walking catalogue model. But when this man puts on his designer suits, it's dangerous.

As it is, I'm having a tough time controlling my libido at the sight of that wool and silk blend jacket stretching across his broad shoulders. The crisp white shirt, unbuttoned at the top to reveal the strong column of his throat.

But the fact that he's wearing his special occasion suit and had arranged for a romantic dinner at the penthouse tells me I've messed up. Big time.

What occasion am I missing, damn it?

It's not my birthday. I don't think it's our anniversary either, although that date is trickier to pinpoint because we've got a few options. There's the anniversary of when we hooked up for the first time, which I don't count because we were both drunk. Granted, not drunk enough not to know what we were doing, but I can't have alcohol tainting a special day.

Personally, I consider our anniversary to be the first time we had sober sex, which occurred a few weeks after the drunken night. Either way, neither of those dates were in the spring.

Maybe we're celebrating the anniversary of when we got back together after I broke up with Dean that one time? Ugh. But I'm pretty sure that was in April. Today is May 5.

Wait. Cinco de Mayo maybe? Do we celebrate that now?

I feel like the worst girlfriend in the world.

"Are you going to speak?" Dean asks cheerfully.

Which is when I realize it's been nearly four silent minutes of me lost in my thoughts, trying to figure out why we're having dinner. I'm such an asshole.

"Sorry." And then, because I'm always honest with him, I clasp my hands on the tablecloth and say, "I fucked up."

Amusement flickers in his green eyes. "Okay... How so?"

"I don't know why we're here!" I wail.

He chuckles. "Like on Earth? The universe? Is this an existential thing, Allie-Cat?"

"No, I mean here at the penthouse. You called and said to meet you here and told me it's a special occasion and I should dress up. And now I'm wearing this dress, and we're sitting at this table, and I don't know why. Is it for Cinco de Mayo?"

"Cinco de Mayo?" His forehead creases. "I mean, no, but we could start celebrating that if you want."

I huff out a miserable breath. "Did I miss our anniversary?"

"No. That's in October."

"Thank you! So you also count it from the first time we had the real sex?"

"Yeah." He starts to laugh. "The real sex." Then he grins. "Can we just enjoy this dinner, please? It's not an anniversary. Just chillax. Look, I got your favorite bread."

He got my favorite everything. There is an obscene amount of pasta on this table. Grilled zucchini and mushrooms over fettuccini alfredo. Baked ziti in a rose sauce. Penne and spinach-stuffed chicken baked in mozzarella-laden tomato sauce. My mouth waters as I try to decide what I want to try first. Normally I wouldn't allow myself to carb load during filming, but it's our last week on set and I don't need to watch my weight anymore.

I haven't eaten since I got home from the studio hours ago, because Dean said to make sure I have an appetite. So I dig in, piling pasta on my plate. Dean doesn't follow suit. Instead, he watches me eat until I finally shift in discomfort.

"Are you just going to sit there watching me eat? That's weird."

"What's weird about it?"

"It's *weird*! Pick up your fork and eat something."

He obeys, albeit rolling his eyes while doing it. His throat dips as he swallows a piece of bread. It's from our favorite bakery around the corner from our apartment. I think they bake it in a vat of garlic and oil, but I don't care.

"Soooo good," I mumble through a mouthful of bread.

Dean's watching me again, this time with hooded eyes.

"Why are you looking at me like that?" Except I know exactly why. Because my mouth is full, and he's totally picturing me giving him a blowjob.

"I'm picturing you giving me a blowjob," he says.

I almost choke on my pasta from laughter. "God, never change, babe."

"I don't plan on it." He pauses. "Actually, scratch that. Not all changes are bad, right?"

"I guess not." I think he's referring to the fact that *The Delaneys* is ending and I'm going to have to find something new. "You don't have to try to make me feel better about work, though. I already told Ira to send me as many scripts and treatments as he can. I'm sure a meaty new role will come along."

"Oh. Yeah. Of course. But I wasn't just talking about career changes. I meant other changes too."

Where on earth is he going with this?

He takes a small sip of his water, then wipes his mouth with a linen napkin that probably cost more than half the furniture in my dad's house. It always feels so surreal when I come to this multimillion-dollar penthouse. And don't get me started on the Di Laurentis mansion in Greenwich, which has an honest-to-God skating rink on the grounds, and more than one pool.

Wariness crawls up my spine as I study Dean's face. He's acting strange again. One of his big hands moves from the table to rest at the top of his abdomen, as if he's about to slide it down to his pocket and—

Holy shit.

Oh no.

He's not actually going to…

When he reaches into his pocket, I realize, oh yes he is.

Suddenly it all clicks in my brain. Fancy dinner with all my favorite dishes from our favorite spots. Our dressy clothes. This penthouse. I know for a fact Dean's mom is in the city, which means he must've sent her back to Connecticut in order to clear out the place for us.

Dean's hand is about to emerge from his pocket when I stop him with a sharp, "Don't."

He freezes. "What?"

"Is this a proposal?" I demand.

The sheepish gleam in his eyes is all the confirmation I need.

"Dean." It's a warning.

"What?"

"Why are you doing this? And tonight of all nights?"

Confusion clouds his face. "Why? Because it's Cinco de Mayo? Fuck, I didn't realize you cared so much about—"

"I don't care about that! I care that we've had a bunch of

conversations about this subject. We *talked* about it, Dean. We agreed marriage and kids and all that stuff was something we'd discuss in the future."

"It is the future," he points out. "We've been together four years."

Frustration sticks to my throat, making it difficult to speak. Along with it comes a burn of irritation that I know I probably shouldn't feel, but…seriously? Had he not listened to a word I said during all those discussions? I told him I wasn't ready. And I'd reiterated it just before Tucker and Sabrina got married, because I suspected something like this would happen, that the wedding fever would infect all the boys. The four of them are ridiculously close and tend to copy whatever the other does. Like, Garrett gets into a serious relationship in college, and the next thing you know, Logan is professing his love to Grace on the radio and Tucker's knocking up Sabrina. So yeah, I'd made sure to clearly articulate my feelings to Dean.

And it bothers me that either he wasn't listening or decided to completely disregard my wishes.

"You look pissed," he says warily.

"I'm not pissed." I tamp down my annoyance. "I just don't under-stand why you would plan this whole thing when I made it clear I'm not ready to take that step."

"I figured you meant you weren't ready for, like, the babies. The wedding." He rakes a hand through his hair. "I don't see what the big deal about an engagement is."

"Because it's all tied together for me. An engagement is a step toward a marriage, and a marriage is a step toward a baby, and I don't want any of that right now."

"So you're telling me if I pull out this box that's in my pocket and I ask you to marry me, you're going to say no?" His tone is as flat as his expression.

There's a strange clenching in my chest, making my heart contract. I never anticipated having to answer a question like that. I figured when he proposed, it would be because we were both ready. And he would know we were both ready, because I always, always tell him where I'm at emotionally. Apparently he just chose to ignore it.

"I would say...maybe?" I stammer. "I don't know, Dean."

"You would say *maybe*?" His voice is like a knife's edge. Eyes dark and glinting. "I can't believe you just said that."

My jaw hardens. "And I can't believe you didn't listen when I said I wasn't ready to get engaged."

Dean takes a breath. He looks at me for a moment. I glimpse the pain in his eyes, and I know I hurt him. But he masks it quickly, his expression shuttering as he grabs his still-full wineglass and drinks half of it in one gulp.

Still gripping the glass, he meets my gaze again. "Do you love me?"

I stare at him in disbelief. "You know I do."

"Do you see yourself with me in the future?"

"You know I do."

"But you don't want to marry me."

My frustration returns in full force. "You know I want to marry you. Just not right now."

"What difference does it make if it's now or a year from now?" he challenges.

"Do I seriously have to explain it again? I literally just told you how I feel about it. You're just choosing not to listen!" I draw a calming breath. "Every time we talked about it before, you said you were okay with waiting."

"Well, maybe I'm not okay with it. Maybe I want to get married. Soon."

"And it's always about what you want?"

"No, apparently it's always about what you want."

"Oh, bullshit." Now he's just being an ass. "We compromise all the time. Our relationship has always been fifty-fifty, Dean, and you know it."

"What I know is that I wanted to propose to my girlfriend tonight, and she doesn't want to hear it, so...fuck this."

He slams his wineglass down and scrapes back his chair. Doesn't even look my way as he gets up and heads for the doorway.

"Dean!" I yell after him.

But he's already stalking out of the opulent dining room. A moment later, I hear the ding of the elevator that leads to the Heyward Plaza Hotel below us.

I sit there staring at Dean's empty chair and wonder what the hell just happened.

CHAPTER 20

ALLIE

Dean isn't speaking to me. It's been two days since the non-proposal, and he's officially giving me the silent treatment. To make matters worse, we had early morning shoots at work these past couple of days, which meant waking up at four a.m. to make it to the studio for my five o'clock call times. Since Dean doesn't leave for school until eight, he was sound asleep both mornings when I left. And both afternoons when he got home from work, he refused to talk to me.

He's acting like a child. He won't even try to understand my reasoning, or acknowledge that maybe I'm not ready for marriage and engagements and all that grown-up stuff.

So after forty-eight hours of living in a mausoleum, when Trevor texts to invite me to a club that night with some of our costars, I'm grateful for the distraction. I tell him I'm in, and we arrange for his ride share to grab me on the way to the club in Soho.

Of course, the moment Dean finds me in our bedroom slipping into a sparkly dress is the moment he suddenly decides he's speaking to me again.

"Where are you going?" he mutters, leaning in the doorway of our walk-in closet.

"To a club. With Trevor, Seraphina, and Malcolm. And maybe Evie. Do you want to come?"

"No." His stony gaze tracks me as I slide into a pair of silver heels.

"You sure?" I push.

"Yes."

I'm going to rip my hair out if he keeps this up. Gritting my teeth, I try to broach the subject for the fifty billionth time. "Can we please talk about it?"

"Nothing to talk about." Dean shrugs and walks off.

"There's a ton to talk about!" I chase after him as he leaves the bedroom.

He stops, sparing me a cursory glance over his shoulder. "I proposed and you said no," he says flatly.

"No, I didn't even let you propose. I told you not to."

"That's even worse, Allie!" he growls. "Like, I went to your dad and everything! Do you realize what a fucking chump I feel like?" He scrapes both hands through his hair.

My jaw drops. This is the first I'm hearing of it. He hadn't mentioned the "going to my dad" part the night he tried to propose. "You asked my dad for his blessing?"

"Of course! That's how serious I am about this relationship!" He glares at me. "Apparently I'm the only one."

"Oh, that is not fair. You know I'm serious about this relationship. I love you. I'm in it for the long haul. I just don't want to deal with—"

"*Deal with?*"

"That came out wrong." I take a breath. "Look, we just got back from someone else's wedding weekend and that was chaotic and stressful. I don't want that for myself right now. I don't want to plan a wedding or—"

"We don't have to get married right away," he angrily interjects.

"Then what's the point of getting engaged? I don't get why you—" I stop. "You know what, I'm not having this argument again."

"Fine. You don't want to get married. Whatever. Have fun tonight."

With that, he stalks toward the front hall of our apartment, where he grabs a sky-blue windbreaker from the hook on the wall.

"Where are you going?" I call after him.

"Out."

"Oh, that's mature." I clench my fists against my sides. "You're acting like a jerk, you know."

"I don't care."

Then he's out the door.

AT THE CLUB, IN THE VIP LOUNGE AMIDST STROBE LIGHTS AND deafening dance music, I spend more time texting Hannah than I do paying attention to the members of my group. And I can't even claim it's a helpful conversation. None of my chats with Hannah since the wedding have been too productive.

Every time I've asked her if she's taken the test yet, she says no.

Every time I ask if she's told Garrett, she also says no.

Every time she asks if Dean and I have made up, I say no.

It's been an alarming amount of monosyllabic answers to some monumental questions.

Tonight, though, Hannah seems to have plenty to say to me. After telling her about Dean storming out, I'm startled to discover she's not on my side.

Hannah: I mean...can you blame the guy? He planned a whole proposal and you just...you know...

I glower at my phone.

Me: No, I don't know.
Her: You hurt him.
Her: And embarrassed him.

Her: (Don't shoot the messenger.)

Me: He could have spared himself that embarrassment if he'd just listened to me during the DOZENS of talks we had about this very subject. I told him I'm not ready.

Her: Yeah, but it's Dean. You know Dean. Mr. Impulsive. When he's in, he's all in.

She's right. When Dean decided he was into me, he kicked into full pursuit. And after I broke up with him at the end of senior year, he went above and beyond to prove to me he was growing up and changing. He's been an incredible partner ever since. I love him with every fiber of my soul.

So why can't you get engaged to him? a voice pushes.

"Allie! Enough! Am I going to have to throw your phone in this huge bucket of champagne?" Trevor says impatiently.

He's not joking. We have an actual bucket at our booth, filled with four expensive bottles of bubbly. It cost an obscene amount, but Trevor insisted on treating. He likes to spend money.

"Seriously, what's going on with you?" Seraphina's dark eyes sweep over me in concern. She plays my older sister on the show, but despite three seasons of working closely together, we never became close in real life. Sera's very serious, and our senses of humor don't particularly mesh.

With that said, I realize she might be the best person to seek advice from. The thing about Seraphina is, she's been married since she was sixteen years old. Yep. Sixteen. She had to get special permission from her parents to marry her high school boyfriend, but they've been together for fifteen years now.

"I'm in a fight with my boyfriend," I reveal.

"Nooo! The Golden God?" Malcolm gasps. His character on *The Delaneys*, our youngest brother, is dark and edgy. A heroin-addict turned mob enforcer who broods his way through every scene. In real life, Malcolm couldn't be more different.

"What did you do?" he accuses me.

"Why do you assume it's my fault?"

"Because a man like that does not err."

"That's not true," Trevor argues. "What's the thing they always say? To err is human."

"He's not human!" Malcolm retorts, before hopping on the plush semicircle bench of our booth. He proceeds to channel Oprah-era Tom Cruise and jump up and down like a maniac. "He's a beautiful god sent from above to dazzle us mortals with his sheer masculine beauty!"

I mean, I can't argue with that. Dean is quite dazzling.

"What happened?" Seraphina rises from her spot, moving away from Malcolm's bouncing legs to sit beside me.

"He tried to set up a whole romantic proposal, and I wouldn't let him go through with it," I confess.

Then I swallow a groan, because saying it out loud sounds ludicrous.

Their expression confirms my suspicion. I ignore Malcolm's, because he would look just as horrified if I turned down Dean's offer to buy me a Subway sandwich. But Trevor and Seraphina are both eyeing me like I'd gone insane.

"Aren't you madly in love with him?" Trevor asks blankly.

"Yes."

"Then why wouldn't you let him propose?" demands Sera.

After failing to successfully explain it to Dean, I attempt to do a better job at laying out my feelings to my costars. "I've always been a planner," I tell them. "And I'm definitely a relationship girl. But I see relationships as…I don't know, picture a ladder. The relationship is a ladder and the rungs are all the steps." My tone turns a bit grumbly. "First comes love. Then comes engagement. Then comes marriage, and then the stupid baby in the dumb baby carriage."

Trevor bursts out laughing. "Your opinion of children is inspiring."

"Sorry. I'm just cranky because Dean's not speaking to me. But you know what I mean."

Sera's answering smile is kind. "Well, sure. But here's the thing. Yes, those are natural steps in most relationships—"

"Not in mine. I'm polyamorous," Trevor interjects. "Our steps are wild."

She ignores him. "But you get to decide how big the ladder is. How much space there is between the rungs."

"That would be a poorly constructed ladder if the rungs weren't equally spaced," I point out, furrowing my brow. "How would you be able to climb it properly?"

"Oh my God, it's just an analogy," she says, laughing. "All I'm saying is, you don't have to look at it as rung one equals engagement and rung two equals marriage. Maybe the first rung is the engagement, but then you climb for a bit and marriage comes on rung five. It's not set in stone. And just because you had this plan for yourself..." Her gaze softens, while her tone becomes firm but still compassionate. "You're not the only person on the ladder, Allie. Clearly, he doesn't view the rungs the same way you do. You're on the same ladder, climbing to the same place, but Dean's rungs are in different positions and he's on shaky ground. You feel secure on the ladder, but he doesn't. *He* needs you guys to be on the same rung."

Malcolm, who's seated again, stares at her in awe. "Whoa. That is *deep*."

"Like the ocean." Trevor nods.

Oh God, is she right? Is this about more than Dean being his usual impulsive self? I assumed he was proposing because he's spontaneous and was simply jumping on the wedding bandwagon. But what if this is about Dean needing a stronger commitment, needing to know we're moving forward together?

"Gang!"

Jarred from my thoughts, I glance over at Elijah's approach. He's a friend of Malcolm's who tagged along with us tonight and has spent most of the night bragging how his father owns a chain of upscale hotels up and down the Atlantic seaboard. For fifteen full minutes after we'd been introduced, he'd talked my ear off about the Azure Hotel Group until Trevor finally rescued me.

Luckily, Elijah is incapable of sitting still for long. The guy keeps darting off to the bathroom to do lines of cocaine. I'm not just guessing either. Every time he'd left the booth, he winked and said, "Gonna powder my nose. Literally!"

"Why sssso sssserious?" Elijah says in a bad impression of the Joker. "We're at the club!"

Trevor fills him in. "We're giving Allie relationship advice."

Elijah pushes past the guys to plant himself on my other side. When his jean-clad thigh presses against my bare one, I very obviously shift closer to Sera. He's been flirting with me all night and doesn't seem to notice I'm not transmitting a single come-hither vibe.

"Here's my advice: dump the loser and go home with me tonight." He flashes a slimy smile.

"No, but thank you for the offer," I answer politely.

"Aw come on, don't be like that." His hand creeps toward my knee.

Malcolm does me a solid by leaning over and smacking it away. "Elijah," he chastises. "Behave!"

"Do I ever?" he drawls before giving me another lewd smile, this one involving his tongue poking out the side of his mouth.

And that's when I realize something.

What if I was sharing a ladder with this guy?

What if, in some horrible alternate universe, there's an Allie Hayes dating a creepy cokehead who's more likely to sell the ladder for drugs than want to climb it together?

Meanwhile, this Allie Hayes is moping because her boyfriend isn't following the specific steps of her plan?

If a proposal makes Dean feel more secure on our relationship ladder, and if I already know I'm going to marry that man one day, then what the hell is wrong with me?

A lightbulb goes off above my head, flashing the words: I'm such a fucking idiot.

"I need to text Dean." I sigh, reaching for my phone again. This time, none of my friends threaten to drown the phone in the champagne bucket. Sera's faint smile tells me she knows I've seen the error of my ways.

Me: Where are you?

Then, realizing he might ignore the text, I add two words I'm certain he won't ignore.

Me: I'm worried.
Dean: All good here.

I know him well. No matter how pissed he might be at me, Dean would never allow me to worry.

Me: Where's here?
Him: Newark.
Me: ?

There's a short delay, as if he's debating whether I deserve his precious explanation. I'm not annoyed, though. The guilt in my stomach churns harder the more I picture my amazing, sexy Dean alone on his wobbly ladder.

Him: G & Logan played the NJ Devils tonight. We're in Logan's room raiding the minibar now.
Me: Oh nice. What hotel?
Him: Azure Tower near the Prudential Center.

Me: Any idea when you'll be home?

Him: Not late. They have an early flight in the morning.

Him: We done with 20 questions?

Ouch. But I deserve it.

Since I don't want to start any important conversations via text, I guess I have to wait until I see him at home later. He's with his friends, anyway, and—

I gasp.

"Elijah!" I half-shout.

The smarmy, drowning-in-cologne guy beside me looks thrilled to be acknowledged. "What is it, gorgeous?"

"You said your family owns the Azure Group? Does that include Azure Tower in Newark?"

"Damn straight it does."

Oh my God. It's serendipity.

He waggles his eyebrows. "Why? You want a private tour?"

Gag. "No, but…" Excitement tickles my spine. "I need to ask a huge favor."

CHAPTER 21

DEAN

"I don't think he's coming back." Grinning, I nod toward the closed door that leads to the adjoining room. We'd started out an hour ago in Logan's room, but ended up in Garrett's after clearing out the minibar. Or rather, after I cleared out the minibar. Though in my defense, there were only two beers in there and two mini bottles of whiskey. Pathetic. Is that how they're treating professional hockey players at the Azure Tower these days?

Then we realized they'd simply forgotten to replenish Logan's bar, because when we went next door, Garrett's was jam-packed with little bottles of booze. I'm fixing myself a rum and Coke as we wait for Logan. He said he was quickly hopping in the shower before he joined us for a final nightcap, but it's been like twenty minutes.

"I bet he's having phone sex with Grace," Garrett guesses. "Or sending dick pics. You know every time we fly, he sneaks into the jet bathroom and takes pictures of his junk to send her?"

I snort. "Ha, like you don't do the same for Wellsy."

"Well, obviously. I'm not going to deprive my lady of all *this*..." He gestures up and down his body, then strikes a pose in his Bruins T-shirt and plaid pajama pants.

My favorite thing about my social circle? None of us lack confidence.

"Why do you have adjoining rooms anyway?" I glance at Logan's door. "The whole world already knows you guys suck each other's dicks. Just man up and share a room."

"Hilarious."

"Thanks."

"Logan needs my protection," G explains. "He's afraid a puck bunny will sneak into his bed again."

"I'm sorry—what?"

"Happened to him a while back in San Jose." Garrett chuckles. "Grumpy jackass dragged himself all the way down the hall to my room and woke me up. Now he's demanding I'm always next door, so he won't have to go far if he needs to bunk with me."

"Wow. Diva much?"

"Right?"

As I lean against the desk, sipping my drink, Garrett's expression grows serious. "So, what are you going to do? Like, for real. Because you keep dancing around it."

When I got to the hotel, I wasted no time telling my friends what happened with Allie the other night. The whole sordid tale of brutal rejection dished out by the girlfriend who supposedly loves me. But that's about as far as we got.

Garrett swishes the ice cubes in his whiskey glass before bringing it to his lips. "So just to recap, she told you multiple times she wasn't ready for an engagement."

"Yeah," I say warily.

"And you absorbed that information and were like, huh, I guess I should propose, then."

I glower at him. "Oh, fuck off. It wasn't like that."

"I'm trying to understand how it wasn't, because it seems like she told you she wasn't ready, and in response you bought a ring and set up a fancy dinner and ambushed her."

"I can't believe you're Team Allie on this one."

"I'm not. I'm Team Logic. Guess what, dude? We lucked out, man. We could've ended up with chicks who say one thing and mean another. The ones who let out those big sighs and then when you ask what's wrong, they're, like, nottttthing—" He mimics a high-pitched voice. "But we didn't. I've discovered that usually when our girlfriends say something, they're not playing games."

"Right, and Allie has always said she sees us married one day," I mutter.

"Yeah. One day."

"So what does it matter if we're engaged now but get married in ten years?"

"Exactly," he says, head tipped in challenge, "what does it matter? Why do you need that ring on her finger so badly?"

That gives me pause. I suppose he has a point. We don't need to be engaged. We already live together. We know we're in it for the long haul.

It's just a ring, right?

My hand curls tighter around my glass. No, though. It's not.

It's a *symbol*.

A symbol of our commitment. Yes, we live together and are in it for the long haul, and yes, I know engagements get broken all the time, but…Christ, I don't even know anymore. And the irony of this entire situation doesn't escape me. The guy who slept around in college, the self-proclaimed man-whore whose nickname was Dean the Sex Machine, needs a pledge of commitment otherwise his pwecious wittle heart won't feel safe?

"The way I see it, you're at an impasse. You can't force her to get engaged."

"No," I agree.

"Then what are you going to do? Break up with her?"

I glare at him.

"What? It's a valid question."

"I'm not breaking up with her." Frazzled, I gulp down almost half my drink before setting it on the desk. "I guess my only option is to accept she loves me but just isn't ready. And then keep living our lives until that changes."

"Holy shit. That's very mature of you."

I smirk. "I have my moments."

On the nightstand, Garrett's phone buzzes. He leans toward it to check the screen. "That's Wellsy. One sec. Let me just text her back—"

"WHAT THE FUCK!"

We both jump when a male shout echoes beyond Logan's door. It's quickly followed by a female shriek.

A very familiar shriek.

Frowning, I march toward the door and loudly rap my knuckles against it. "Logan, was that my girlfriend?" I demand.

"Dean?" Allie's unmistakable voice.

"Allie-Cat?" I call back. "Is that you in there?"

"Yeah, I'm here with Logan." There's a pause. "And his penis."

Garrett's head pops up from his phone. Sheer delight lights his face. "Oh God. I don't even care that we got our asses handed to us by Jersey. This night officially just became the greatest."

He hops off the bed and races to my side. One of G's favorite pastimes is—to quote the asshole himself—"serving as a bystander to our stupidity."

I knock on the door again. "Unlock this thing."

When I hear a click, I throw the door open and burst into Logan's room, where I find Allie and Logan facing off. My girl stands on one side of the king-sized bed, wearing the sequined dress she'd donned for the club. Only one stiletto, though. I look around, spotting the other heel on the carpet near the far wall by the bathroom.

On the other side of the bed is Logan. He's buck naked.

I lift a brow. "Nice dick," I tell him.

He sighs.

"Any reason why you're showing it to my girlfriend?"

"I didn't show her a damn thing." His bare pecs flex as he lifts both hands to rake through his damp hair. Droplets of water slide down his neck. "I got out of the shower, and she was just right there, sitting on my bed. I thought it was another thirsty bunny."

"So you decided to drop your towel?" Allie challenges.

"I was mid-drop when I walked out of the bathroom. Don't act like I was stripping for you." He scoffs. "You wish."

Garrett snickers. In a helpful gesture, he picks up the towel and tosses it to Logan, who hastily covers up his pretty package.

My attention returns to my girlfriend. "Why are you in Logan's room?"

"Why aren't you in Logan's room?" she shoots back. "Your text said Logan's room!"

"His minibar was empty so we moved over to G's. You didn't think it was weird when you walked in and nobody was there?"

"I saw your jacket on the chair and heard someone in the bathroom. Thought it was you." She crosses her arms defensively. "I certainly didn't expect your friend to walk out with his stupid penis."

"My penis isn't stupid," Logan protests. "How did you even get in here?" His exasperated gaze travels to Garrett. "How do they keep getting in here!"

Garrett shakes with laughter.

"My costar Malcolm brought a friend to the club tonight," Allie tells us. "And turns out the guy's dad owns all the Azure hotels. Don't you dare rat him out, but he asked one of the bellhops to give me a copy of Logan's key card." She smiles broadly. "We met up at the service entrance behind the kitchen, and he handed it over all stealthy-like. It was like a drug deal."

I fight a laugh. Only Allie would enjoy a pseudo drug deal with a total stranger. She probably memorized the entire encounter in case she needs it to prepare for a role one day.

"Awesome," Logan says, his voice dripping with sarcasm.

"Apparently anyone who feels like it can just ask for keys to my room and nobody bats an eye. Who the fuck decided I'm no longer allowed to feel safe in hotels?"

"Oh, boo fucking hoo," Garrett mocks. "It happens to me like every month."

I grin at G. "Brag."

"As fun as this little reunion is," Allie interrupts, her blue eyes focusing on me. "Can we talk? Alone?"

"You guys can use my room," G offers.

I glance over gratefully. "Thanks."

"Wait, let me get my shoe," Allie says, hobbling across the room on one stiletto.

I narrow my eyes. "Why is it all the way over there?"

"Because she threw it at my head," growls Logan.

Garrett hoots. "*Such* a good night," he says happily.

A moment later, Allie has her other shoe, I'm snatching my windbreaker from the chair, and we disappear into the other room. I kick the door closed behind us, then stand in front of her while she timidly sits at the edge of the bed.

After a beat of silence, she says, "I'm sorry."

"You came all the way to Jersey to tell me that?" I ask wryly.

"No, not just that."

"What else?"

"I'm *really* sorry."

I hide a smile. She's so goddamn cute. Her sparkling eyes. Her smoking body in that short dress. She's honestly my favorite person in the whole world.

"There's more," she adds, clasping her dainty hands on her knees. She takes a breath. "I had a forty-minute cab ride to plan out what I was going to say to you, but all my practice speeches sounded so cliché and contrived. I did a couple out loud for my driver, and he told me I was overthinking it."

I wrinkle my forehead. "Overthinking what? Your apology?"

"No." She exhales in a rush. "My proposal."

This time there's absolutely no stopping the smile. It stretches across my face, making my jaw twitch. "Your proposal," I echo.

Allie nods. "I was talking to Seraphina, and she helped me understand something important. My whole life, I've planned for everything. I like doing things in steps. It keeps me focused and, I don't know, I guess it helps me not get overwhelmed each time I'm faced with some major change." She shakes her head, more at herself than me. "But I'm not in this relationship alone. You're here too, and my steps aren't always going to align with your steps. We can't always do everything my way."

I walk over and sink down beside her. "No, I was an ass earlier when I said it was all about you. You were right. It's always been fifty-fifty with us."

"Yeah, but sometimes it shouldn't be. Sometimes one of us needs to give a hundred percent to the other." She reaches for my hand and twines her fingers through mine. "I love you, Dean. I'm one hundred percent yours. And until we have that wedding—which I know Summer and your mom will turn into a gigantic, extravagant production—every time we meet somebody new, I want to introduce you and be able to say, this is the man I'm going to marry."

My heart is beating a little faster now.

"I want to marry you one day. And until that day, I want to be engaged to you." Her throat dips as she gulps nervously. "So. With that said. Will you, Dean Sebastian Kendrick Heyward-Di Laurentis, be my fiancé?"

I have to bite the inside of my cheek to fight the rush of emotion that tightens my throat. I swallow a couple of times, then I bring my free hand to her mouth and rub the pad of my thumb over her bottom lip.

"Of course I will." My voice is so hoarse, I clear my throat before continuing. "If you'll have me."

"Always," Allie says, leaning into my touch. "I'll *always* have you."

Then she throws her arms around my neck, and I bury my face in her hair, breathing in strawberry and roses. When I lift my head, her lips find mine in a kiss that goes from sweet to dirty in two seconds flat. The feel of her tongue slicking over mine sends a jolt of heat to my groin.

Breathless, I pull back and say, "Fuck. I wish I had the ring on me. But it's at home."

Curiosity fills her eyes. "Is it big?" she demands.

"Huge."

"How huge?"

"Massive. Even your dad was impressed."

"You showed your dick to her *father*?"

Allie and I startle when Garrett comes stumbling into the room, a sweatpants-clad Logan flying in after him.

"What the hell?" I snap at them. "You guys were eavesdropping?"

Garrett's defense is, "You're in my room!"

"And I'm just nosy," Logan pipes up. He shoots me a pleased smile. "Good call bringing up the dick at the end. I told you, every proposal needs a dash of sexy."

"We weren't talking about my dick," I growl. "We were talking about the ring!"

"Oh." He blinks. Then glances at Allie. "That thing's ginormous. It'll break your finger."

Allie swivels her gaze back to me, beaming brightly. "You know me too well."

I WAKE UP THE NEXT MORNING WITH ALLIE CURLED UP BESIDE ME in our bed. One slender arm flung over my bare chest, her fingers curled over my hip. When I peer down, I'm nearly blinded by the diamond on her finger. I swear, the second she saw that rock when I pulled it out last night, she got so turned on, she had me naked in a heartbeat, my dick stuffed in her mouth.

Now, I softly skim my fingertips along the curve of her naked back and smile up at the ceiling. We're engaged, baby. Other men might be freaking out a little, but I'm pumped. This blinding ring on Allie's finger is like a billboard announcing to everyone we know and everyone we're gonna know, that this woman is mine. She owns my heart.

The nightstand vibrates. I'm not ready to check my phone yet, because I anticipate a barrage of texts and missed calls. It was too late to make calls when we got home from Jersey last night, but we did text Allie's dad and my entire family to share the news. Then we ignored five FaceTime attempts from my sister and mother, and screwed each other's brains out instead. Right before we fell asleep, we got a text from Joe Hayes. A simple thumbs-up. I love that man.

But as my phone vibrates again, I realize it's not a normal phone call. It's doing that buzzing tone it does when the concierge is calling.

I quickly reach for it. "Hello?" I say drowsily.

"Sorry to disturb you, Mr. Di Laurentis, but there's a courier down here with a delivery for Ms. Hayes. Can I send her up?"

Since our building security is tighter than Fort Knox, I know it's not some bullshit request, so I say, "Yes, no problem. Thank you."

I hang up and attempt to disentangle myself from Allie's possessive grip. She doesn't budge. "Baby doll, you need to move your arm," I tell her, sliding my hand down to lightly pinch her hip.

She murmurs something unintelligible.

"Gotta answer the door. We have a delivery."

Sleepily, Allie rolls over, flashing me her bare ass. Ugh. It takes all my willpower not to rub my suddenly hardening cock over that sweet crease. Stifling a groan, I force myself out of bed and swipe my boxers off the floor. I shove them up my hips then make my way to the front door, scratching my chest and yawning.

"Delivery for Allie Hayes?" a short girl with pink hair and a nose ring says when I open the door.

"That's my fiancée." Yup, never gonna get sick of hearing that. "Does it need a signature?"

"Nope. It's all yours."

The next thing I know, she's shoving a medium-sized box in my hands and heading back to the elevators. I study the label, raising a brow when I discover the sender is Grace Ivers. Clearly Logan wasted no time spilling the big engagement news to his girlfriend.

"Who's it from?" Allie's sitting up when I enter the bedroom, her hair rumpled. She rubs the sleep from her eyes.

"Grace and Logan," I tell her.

"That was fast."

"Right?"

I set the box on the mattress, peel off a corner of packing tape, then rip the entire strip.

"I can't wait to show this off at the wrap party tonight," Allie gushes, admiring her ring as I open the box.

I find a folded piece of paper lying beneath the cardboard flaps. The message inside is short and to the point.

Congratulations on the engagement! The three of us are so happy for you!

"The three of them?" Allie's reading the note over my shoulder, her eager hands now reaching into the box.

A sick feeling creeps up my throat. I have a horrible suspicion I know exactly what—

"No!" she moans when the porcelain doll emerges from the box. "Oh my God, Dean, he's on our bed! We have to burn the sheets now!"

I glower at Alexander's red cheeks and vacant eyes. "Motherfucker," I growl. "You realize Logan would've had to ask Grace to overnight this? This is literal betrayal."

"Next-level betrayal."

We both stare at the doll, neither of us wanting to pick him up and move him. I know I'm the one who opened this grotesque

Pandora's Box when I bought Alexander for Jamie, but how many times do I have to apologize? Why do these sociopaths keep sending him back?

I grit my teeth. "I can't fucking believe Logan would do this to us. And after we complimented his dick?"

My fiancée sighs. "We?"

"Oh, like you weren't impressed too," is my accusatory reply.

"Fine, I was," Allie relents. She offers a shrug. "Mrs. Logan is a lucky woman."

I nod in agreement. "A very lucky—" I stop abruptly. "Wait. What?"

PART 3

THE HONEYMOON

CHAPTER 22

THE DAY BEFORE
TUCKER

NOTHING HUMBLES A MAN LIKE FATHERHOOD. I USED TO WALK the cobblestone paths of Briar University in my hockey jacket while starry-eyed chicks threw themselves at me. Now, I'm walking through our Boston suburb at the beginning of June with a miniature person in pink bedazzled ruffles leading me by the hand. Then again, I could be the dinosaur's dad. All over this indoor playground, the costumed characters that have inhabited our kids like demon possessors fight mythical battles and create complex societies in their secret language that both perplexes and alarms.

The other dads and I are huddled in our corner, watching the children play. Most of the men are in their thirties, which makes me the youngest dad of the bunch. When they found out I had Jamie at twenty-two, half were impressed and the other half asked what I had against condoms. I get it, though. Raising a kid is exhausting.

"Christopher's six weeks into his dinosaur phase," Danny, the dinosaur's father, says when someone finally asks about the stage-worthy outfit. "First he stopped using utensils. Now he eats with his mouth straight off the plate because 'dinosaurs don't use hands.'" He punctuates with air quotes and exasperation. "His mom has all the patience in the world, but I'm gonna draw the line at serving my three-year-old raw meat on the floor."

The rest of us burst out laughing.

Considering the alternative, Jamie's princess phase is light work. Gluing rhinestones back on every night after she's spent all day wreaking havoc in that dress is not the worst daddy detail I could get.

When Jamie saunters over a couple of hours later, eyes heavy and wavy auburn hair falling out of her ponytail, I notice she's short a few accessories.

"What happened to your tiara and jewelry, little darlin'?" I scoop her up because she's liable to fall asleep on her tiny feet. "You lose them in the rope tunnel?"

"I gave them away," she answers, resting her cheek against my shoulder.

"Now why would you do that?"

"Because Lilli and Maria wanted to be princesses too, but they didn't have any princess stuff so I gave them princess stuff."

"Aw man," Danny says to Mark. "How come he gets the sweet princess, and I get the kid who tries to eat the dog?"

"Are you sure you don't mind parting with your things?" I ask Jamie.

"Nope! There should be more princesses." Then she snuggles closer, and I almost melt into a goddamn puddle.

She's such a sweet kid. I hate having to say goodbye to her tomorrow. I'm going to miss the heck out of her, but this honeymoon is long overdue. It's been a month since the wedding. A whole damn month. But now that Sabrina's officially graduated from law school, I can finally pry her away for some adult alone time.

My plan is to spend the next ten days making my wife come six ways to Sunday.

"See you in a couple weeks, fellas," I tell the other dads, before picking up Jamie's pink sequined bag and carting my sleepy daughter out of the building.

When we get home fifteen minutes later, my mom's car is parked in front of the bar. Doesn't matter how many times I see that sign—Tucker's Bar—I still get this surreal feeling washing over me. I opened this place right after Jamie was born, and in nearly three years I'd already turned a profit and opened a second location near Fenway. What I hadn't gotten around to doing yet is moving my little family out of the upstairs apartment. I mean, there isn't anything wrong with living on top of a bar, and sure, our loft space has plenty of room for the three of us. But I want Jamie to have a yard. I want Sabrina to have a proper office. Maybe one for me too.

Now that Sabrina's done with school, it might be time to do some house hunting. I make a mental note of it as I carry Jamie upstairs via the narrow staircase at the side of the brick building. I hear Mom and Sabrina in the kitchen when we step through the front door.

"We're back," I call. I put Jamie down, and she groggily waddles toward the sound of her mother's voice.

"She usually wakes up between seven and eight," Sabrina is telling my mom, standing at the kitchen island. "She'll tell you what she wants for breakfast. She's got cereal and oatmeal in the pantry. Some yogurts in the fridge. I precut fruit for the next couple days, or you can slice some bananas on top. She'll tell you she wants toast or a muffin, which she can have, but she'll only take a couple bites and then demand the yogurt, so you may as well have it ready."

Sabrina hardly notices me. On autopilot, she lifts Jamie in a seat to make her a snack before her afternoon nap.

"We'll get along fine," Mom assures her with only a little annoyance. Sabrina can get kind of high-strung about this stuff.

The closer we've gotten to our trip, the more intense Sabrina has become about planning for Jamie's routine. Our house in plastered with sticky notes reminding Mom where stuff is and when Jamie's bedtime is and whatnot. It's a lot. Thankfully, my mother is taking it in stride.

"This isn't our first rodeo. Right, kiddo?" My mother ruffles Jamie's dark-red hair and gazes down adoringly at her granddaughter. Mom loves this kid as much as we do. Maybe even more. I mean, hell, she relocated from Texas to Boston to be near us, this woman who hates the winter. Like, loathes it.

"Where's all her stuff?" Sabrina asks me after noticing Jamie's accessories are gone.

"She wanted to share with her friends. Mom can take her shopping for more."

Her frown tells me she isn't satisfied with that answer, but the kid's falling asleep in her fruit and veggie plate, so Sabrina picks her up, and I follow them down the hall toward Jamie's room.

"I don't think Gail's heard a word I've said all morning," Sabrina whispers, tucking Jamie into bed.

I fight a smile. "They'll be fine, darlin'. They always have fun together."

"For one night. But ten days is a long time. This was a bad idea." Sabrina bites her lower lip. "I don't know what I was thinking."

I know what I was thinking. I was thinking we've been married for a month, and I haven't been able to properly fuck my wife because little ears hear everything that goes on in this apartment. And Sabrina won't let me lock our bedroom door because she has nightmares about Jamie trying to run in to warn us the house is on fire and not being able to. Like she's a golden retriever. I've been good at not voicing my frustrations, though, because I know how difficult the months leading to graduation have been for Sabrina, especially when she had to juggle law school with motherhood. She works so hard to be superwoman, it feels wrong dumping my shit on her too.

"Come here." Outside Jamie's room, I pull her into my arms and sweep her dark hair away from her face.

I stand there, momentarily mesmerized by her bottomless dark eyes.

"What?" she asks, smiling at me.

I lick my suddenly dry lips. "You're beautiful, you know that? We hardly get five minutes to ourselves these days. I think I keep forgetting how gorgeous you are."

Sabrina rolls her eyes. "Shut up."

"Seriously. Fucking gorgeous. And this isn't a bad idea. You need this trip, darlin'. You've barely had a single day off in years. Same goes for me." I shrug. "We need this."

"Do we?" She's still stressing.

"Absolutely we do. Sun and sand and sleeping in as late as we want," I remind her.

It sounds like heaven saying it out loud. Ten days in St. Barth's at Dean's family vacation home. The plane tickets courtesy of Mom's wedding present. It's going to be the perfect cocktail for rest, relaxation, and generally screwing Sabrina's brains out because having a tiny human running around this place has been a nonstop cockblock. Like, I love the kid, but Mommy and Daddy need to do dirty things to each other.

"Trust me," I assure her. "It'll be magical."

She arches an eyebrow. "I don't know. It's been a while. You might not want to overpromise."

"Ha. If anything, I'm under-promising." I take her around the waist and bend down to kiss her.

Sabrina kisses me back, then pulls away and draws a breath. She closes her eyes. Exhales. "You're right. We deserve a getaway. This'll be good."

It's become a mantra. Convincing herself to take some time away, that her world won't collapse if she does. While planning this trip, she's careened from excitement to dread at least six times a day. If I can get her out the front door, I'll consider it a win.

CHAPTER 23

DAY 1
SABRINA

Tucker started plying me with wine at the airport bar. In the air, he doesn't let a flight attendant walk by without asking for another glass of champagne to shove in my hand. Not that I'm complaining. I admit leaving Jamie was more difficult than I imagined, but he's right: she's in good hands with Gail. And if anything goes wrong, it's a short flight home. We'll survive.

"I saw you staring at her shoes, Harold."

"I swear to God, Marcia, I have never noticed a woman's shoes."

"Don't patronize me. I know what you're into, you pervert."

The middle-aged couple in front of us in first class, however, might not last the flight.

"I'm Team Marcia," Tucker leans in to whisper at my ear. "He's up to some shady foot stuff."

"No way. This is her kink, not his. She likes to start public fights with him to keep the spark alive."

They've been at it since they sat down. Arguing about sugar packets and the in-flight entertainment system. Marcia scolding Harold for asking for a gin and tonic. Harold making loud, animated gagging sounds at her overwhelming perfume that he swears she bought just to aggravate his allergies and kill him.

I'm so glad Tuck and I don't fight like that. Hell, we don't fight at all, although my friends have differing opinions on that. Carin thinks it's a good thing, that it means our relationship is a cut above the rest. Hope, meanwhile, insists it's not normal for couples not to fight. But, really, what can I do about it? Tucker is the most chill man on the planet. I can count on one hand the number of times I've seen him lose his temper.

"A big round booty," Harold says proudly. A flight attendant's head snaps up from making coffee in the galley to stare at him, alarmed. "That's what I like and you know it. If I'm looking at another woman, it's not her shoes, Marcia."

"Are you saying my butt isn't big enough for you? Are you calling me skinny?"

"Would you prefer I called you fat?"

She snarls like a feral cat. "You think I'm fat?"

Tuck leans closer again. "Women, amiright?"

I press my face against his shoulder to smother a laugh. I'm not sure I can survive four more hours of the Harold and Marcia show. Might need some more champagne.

As I glance toward the galley, hoping to catch the attendant's eye, I catch a whiff of smoke. It sneaks up on me in the wake of the man in 3E lumbering down the aisle. I saw him chain-smoking at the curbside check-in when we dropped off our luggage, and either the guy has the runs or he's sucking on a vape every five minutes in the lavatory.

"If we get turned around because of that guy, I'll be pissed," I mutter to Tucker.

"Don't worry, I think the flight crew is on to him." He nods toward the two attendants in the galley doorway, who are whispering to each other while pointedly looking at 3E.

When the male attendant notices us watching, he glides over

and offers that plastic service-industry smile. "More champagne for the newlyweds?"

"Please," I say gratefully.

"Coming right up."

Just as he's moving away, Harold's beefy arm thrusts out to stop him. "Another gin and tonic, please."

"Don't you dare," Marcia warns. "Peter and Trixie-Bell are picking us up when we land in St. Maarten."

"So?"

"So you can't be drunk the first time you meet our son's fiancée!"

"She's a damned stripper, Marcia. Her name is Trixie-Bell! With a hyphen! You think I care about impressing the exotic dancer our stupid idiot boy met two weeks ago at a Caribbean dance club and got it in his fool head to marry?"

It's Tucker's turn to bury his face against my shoulder, trembling with silent laughter. The poor flight attendant stands in the aisle like a deer frozen in a hunter's sights, unsure what to do about the gin and tonic.

"Sir?" he prompts.

"Gin and tonic," Harold says stubbornly.

Except his impassioned speech about their idiot son must've gotten to Marcia, because she raises a hand laden with gold costume jewelry and mutters, "Make that two, please."

Wiping tears of mirth from his eyes, my husband looks over. "Wanna buddy watch a movie?" He gestures to our respective screens, open to the in-flight menu.

"Sure. Give me a sec, though. Just want to log in to the Wi-Fi and see if your mom messaged."

I pull my phone out of the purse at my feet and follow the browser connection instructions. Once the Wi-Fi kicks in, my screen fills up with emails.

"Your inbox is blowing up," Tucker teases.

I scroll through the notifications, but there's nothing from Gail.

"Yeah. HR at Billings, Bower, and Holt keeps sending stuff." I scroll further. "Ugh. Fischer and Associates emailed too."

"When do you have to give them an answer?"

"When we get back."

"Are you leaning more one way or the other?"

"I don't know," I sigh.

"Would you stop fiddling with the screen!" Marcia is chastising her husband again.

"But the movie isn't loading," grumbles Harold. "I want to watch the Avengers, goddammit."

"It won't load if you keep pressing all the buttons!" She huffs. "Look what you've done. Now it's frozen."

"Why don't you mind your damned business and focus on your own screen, woman."

Luckily, our champagne arrives. I take a much-needed sip as I mull over the options for the thousandth time. After graduation, I got a job offer from the number two law firm in Boston. A dream job, as far as a foot in the door goes. It was a no-brainer that I'd take it, until I got a call from a small civil defense firm that now has me considering how my priorities have shifted the last few years.

"What's the difference, practically speaking?" Tucker asks.

"The big firm is right in my wheelhouse. Criminal defense. Major corporate clients. It's where the big money is," I tell him. "The cases I'd be handling would definitely be challenging. Stimulating."

He nods slowly. "Okay. And Fischer?"

"Primarily civil defense. Not sexy stuff, but it's an old legacy firm. They've been in the city for like a hundred years or something. The pay is competitive, which probably means old-money clients."

"Those options don't suck."

"If I take the first one, we're talking eighty hours a week. Minimum. On call day and night. Fighting for a rung on the ladder with a hundred other junior associates."

"Yeah, but you like throwing elbows," Tucker reminds me with a crooked grin.

"If I took the second, I could be home more with you and Jamie."

Throughout law school, I was convinced I wouldn't be fulfilled unless I landed my dream gig. Fighting tough cases tooth and nail, battling in the trenches. Since graduation, though, being home all day with Jamie has changed my attitude. It's got me worrying about the sustainability of balancing work and family long-term.

Tucker, as usual, offers himself up as my rock. My one-man support system. "Don't worry about us," he tells me, his voice roughening. "You've worked your whole life to get to this moment, darlin'. Don't give up on your dream."

I study his expression. "Are you sure you'd be okay if I took the job with more hours? Be honest."

"I'm good no matter what you decide."

I see nothing but sincerity on his face, but one can never truly know with Tucker. He's not great at telling me when something's bothering him, on the rare occasions he gets bothered.

He reaches for my hand, his callused fingertips sweeping over my knuckles. "I can pitch in and do more around the house. Jamie will be fine. Whatever you decide, we'll make it work."

Coming from a broken home in Southie and getting knocked up in college, I could have done a lot worse than to end up with Tucker. At even half capacity, he'd be a great guy, but this big, beautiful man goes and decides to be exceptional anyway.

I can't wait to spend ten days on an island with him all to myself. Sometimes I really miss the early days of our relationship. Before our little monster arrived, and I spent every waking second either in class or bent over a textbook. When we used to have sex in his truck, or when he'd come over after I got off work, push me up against the wall and hike up my skirt. Those moments where nothing else mattered except the overwhelming need to touch each other. It's still there, that need. Other stuff just gets in the way. Part of me isn't sure I even remember how to be spontaneous.

Then Tucker drapes his hand over my knee, dragging his fingers back and forth, and I start eyeing that lighted restroom sign.

I must doze off at some point, because about halfway through the flight I'm jolted awake by some brief turbulence and the raised voices of Marcia and Harold.

"She's knocked up, mark my words."

"Harold! Peter said she wasn't."

"That boy is a pathological liar, Marcia."

"Our son wouldn't lie about this."

"All right then, let's bet on it. If Trixie-Bell doesn't have a bun in the oven, I won't touch a drop of alcohol at this farce of a wedding."

"Ha! As if!"

"But if she is preggo…" He thinks it over. "I get to dump that entire vial of your god-awful perfume in the ocean."

"But it cost three hundred dollars!"

I'm loving this wager. My mind is already trying to figure out how we could learn the outcome. Is there some registry of weddings in St. Maarten? Maybe we can take a private boat over from St. Barth's and crash Peter and Trixie-Bell's ceremony.

I glance over at Tucker to ask if he has any ideas, but he's busy looking around, scanning the aircraft.

"Everything okay?" I ask uneasily.

"You smell that?"

"Oh. Yeah. It's the chain-smoker in 3E."

"I don't think that's cigarette smoke," he says in a hushed voice, peering out the window.

A frown creases his brow. He's sporting that look he used to get after five straight hours of watching aviation disaster documentaries on TV at four in the morning between Jamie's feedings.

The same two flight attendants casually float up and down the aisle with their professional smiles, but now there's a deliberateness to their movements that becomes disconcerting as I watch them. Almost imperceptibly, the plane begins a gradual descent.

"Are we descending?" I hiss at him.

"I think so."

And the odor of smoke is worsening. I swear there's a slight haze to the air, and I'm not the only one to notice. A murmur ripples through the first-class cabin.

"Harold, honey, do you smell that?" I hear a panicky Marcia blurt out.

"Yeah, sweetheart. I do."

Oh no. If the smoke is bad enough to bring terms of endearment out of those two, then things are grim.

My stomach twists as the plane continues to shed its altitude. "Tuck," I fret.

He plasters his face to the window again, then reaches for my hand. "I see runway lights," he says as reassurance that we aren't about to crash in the middle of field or something.

"Folks, this is your captain speaking," a monotone voice says over the intercom. "As I'm sure you've noticed by now, we are indeed descending. Air traffic control has given us clearance to land at Jacksonville International Airport. We've rerouted and will be making an emergency landing shortly due to a mechanical malfunction. Please return to your seats and fasten your seat belts. Flight attendants, please prepare the cabin for landing."

The PA switches off.

I grip Tucker's hand and try to tamp down my rising panic. "This is really happening."

"We're fine. No big deal. Pilots make emergency landings all the time." I'm not sure if Tucker says that for my benefit or his.

The crew carry on about their business with the same artificial smiles, politely gathering up trash and shooing stragglers to put up their tray tables. These sociopaths are determined to keep up the charade even if we splatter into flames and twisted metal.

In front of us, Marcia and Harold embrace each other, their prior ails forgotten as they profess their love.

"I love you, Harold. I'm sorry I called you a pervert."

"Oh, sweetheart, never apologize to me ever again about anything."

"Is it too late to change the beneficiary of our will? What if we wrote something down on this napkin? I don't want that Trixie-Bell inheriting our vacation condo in Galveston!"

I turn to Tuck in horror. "Oh my God. We don't have a will."

Our pilot's voice crackles on the intercom again. "Passengers and crew, please get in brace position."

Tucker puts his hand over mine as we both grip our armrests and brace for impact.

CHAPTER 24

NIGHT 1
TUCKER

WE DON'T DIE.

The airplane touches down safely in Jacksonville to relieved sighs and a few awkward claps and whistles. The crew apologize profusely at the door as we are deplaned and escorted by gate staff to a holding area where we're corralled and bribed with free snacks and coffee. A lady in a blazer doesn't laugh when I ask for a beer instead.

"Who do we want for Jamie?" Sabrina says, after texting my mom to check in. Both Grandma and the kid are fine.

The wife, on the other hand...

"Huh?" I eye her in confusion.

"For our will. We need a custody plan for Jamie." She starts rummaging around in her purse. "I think your mom would be the best guardian, yeah?"

"Here, darlin'. Have some cookies." I grab three bags of mini Oreos from the basket on the chair across from us and toss them in her lap. "You're still feeling the adrenaline. It'll pass."

Sabrina looks up from her bag and fixes me with a death stare. "You're trying to shut me up with cookies? We almost died in a fiery plane crash, and we don't have anything that lays out what happens to our daughter if we both die."

"I assumed she'd become a circus nomad until she finds herself making turquoise jewelry in the desert."

"Gee, John, I'm glad you think this is funny."

Shit. She called me John. Now I know it's serious.

"It's not funny," I assure her. "But this conversation is maybe a little morbid, don't you think?"

"If I can please have everyone's attention." A tall, authoritative-looking representative from the airline in a pantsuit stands in the middle of our holding area. "The maintenance crew has determined there was a minor electrical failure on the aircraft which necessitated the early landing."

"Early." Sabrina scoffs at the euphemism.

"It appears the in-flight entertainment system shorted out."

A loud gasp sounds from the end of our row, courtesy of Marcia. "You did this to us by pressing all those buttons! You froze the screen," she accuses her husband, pointing one red-painted talon at him.

The rotund man glares at her.

"I can assure you," the airline rep says smoothly, "that the failure occurred in the wiring itself and not as a result of any passenger touching the screen."

She then proceeds to tell us our plane is grounded and they're flying in a new one to get us to St. Maarten, where Sabrina and I are hopping a ferry to St. Barth's.

"How long will that take?" someone asks.

The rep is noncommittal about a time frame, which gets groans and arguments from the cranky passengers. Sighing, I start texting to give notice we're not making our scheduled departure. First my mom, then Dean, whose house we're staying at.

"Give me a pen," Sabrina says, nudging me.

"Huh?"

"A pen. I need a pen."

I fish one out of my carry-on, and she snatches it out of my hand. Sabrina, now obsessed with the idea of our untimely deaths, uses the delay to furiously scribble down a will on the back of the flight confirmation we printed off before leaving the house. I'd much rather throw an arm around her, pull her close, and sit there eavesdropping on our fellow passengers, but Sabrina's wholly focused on the task at hand.

"Jamie goes to Mama Tucker?" she prompts. "Garrett and Hannah as backups?"

"I'm good with that."

"All right. That one was easy. What about our finances? You want to leave instructions to sell the bars, or have someone else run them until Jamie comes of age? Fitz maybe? He'd probably like that." She chews on the cap of the pen. "Do you want to leave any monetary gifts to anyone or just give it all to Jamie?"

"I think the most important question is—who do you trust to erase our browser history?"

"What?" Sabrina cocks her head at me, bent over her lap while she writes.

"We can't let my mom do it, and I think Jamie might still be a little young to use the laptops."

Sabrina's nostrils flare. "You're making fun of me."

"Nope," I say innocently. "Just trying to contribute to our death wishes."

She doesn't have to speak to tell me to fuck off. Her brown eyes scream daggers. I hide a grin and open one of the cookie bags.

BY THE TIME WE TOUCH DOWN IN ST. MAARTEN, SABRINA'S PISSED at me because I don't have strong feelings about how I'd like to be buried or who gets my college Xbox game collection. On the private ferry to St. Barth's, she just stares out at the dark water as if she's fantasizing about pushing me overboard. We're both exhausted and sweaty and fully regretting this whole ordeal—until the boat lets us off at our dock and we walk the sandy path up a hill to the house lit in amber against the night sky.

"Are you kidding me?" Coming through the front door, Sabrina drops her bags and does a full spin, staring up at the high ceiling and exposed beams. She takes in the marble floors and enormous breadth of house. "This place is unbelievable."

"Dean's family is hideously rich. You know that."

"I thought I did, but this is *obscene*," she says, skipping ahead of me. "They have a private dock. And a private beach. And—oh my God, there's food!"

I find her in the kitchen, popping open a bottle of Acqua Panna spring water while shoving fruit in her mouth. On the white marble counter, Dean's housekeeping staff had left out a serving tray of cut pineapple, melon, and papaya, along with water and a bottle of Dom Perignon. I'd had my fill of champagne on the plane, so I set the bottle aside. There's also a typed piece of paper lying on top of a thin binder.

As Sabrina bites into a piece of melon, I pick up the sheet and read it aloud. "'Welcome to Villa le Blanc, Sabrina and Tucker! This binder has everything you'll need to know for your stay, and you'll find all necessary keys in the cabinet above the wine fridge. If you have any questions, don't hesitate to ask our housekeeper Isa, or property manager Claudette. Congratulations to the newlyweds! Love, Lori and Peter.'"

Jeez, Dean's parents are super-hosts. The binder is a treasure trove of information. Alarm codes. A map of the sprawling property. Phone numbers for a private chef, local restaurants, tour companies. Contact info for Isa, who apparently brings fresh fruit and newspapers every morning. Instructions on how to have groceries delivered to the villa. How to drive the boat. The ATVs and other beach toys. It's like a mini resort. Goddamn Dean living the life of luxury over here.

We do a quick walk of the first floor, which overlooks the beach out front and is surrounded by palm trees in the back. Sabrina slides open the glass doors to the pool deck to welcome in the cool ocean breeze, white curtains billowing around her.

"You hear that?" she says with a brilliant smile.

I do. I hear the ocean. Waves running up on shore. Distant insects chirping. The soothing near-silence, unbroken by a screaming child or cartoons on TV.

Our earlier trauma dissolves in the night air, all anger and irritability subsiding by the time we shut off the outdoor shower of the master suite and slip naked beneath expensive sheets.

"Do you still regret coming?" I ask, drawing her warm body closer.

She lays her head on my chest, her short fingernails absently stroking the ridges of my abs. "Near-fatal catastrophe aside? No, I'm glad we're here. This place is incredible."

I think the dual showerhead was the tipping point that made the trip worth it for her.

"Thanks for being a good sport," she says by way of an apology.

"No sweat." I know the woman I married. She can be intense, but that's ultimately what I love about her.

"I really am looking forward to spending some quality time together." Sabrina's fingertips skim up my chest toward my face, gently tracing the line of my jaw.

"Just you, me, and this ass." I grab a handful and give it a squeeze, to which she jabs me in the ribs.

"You're such a guy."

"Ha, like you don't want it as bad as I do."

Her quiet laughter tickles my nipple. "True."

And even though we're both exhausted and mentally drained from today's ordeal, that's no excuse for wasting this opportunity. So I tilt her chin up to kiss me, combing my hand through her hair.

It really is the little things I miss about her. The way her hair smells. How soft her skin is at the nape of her neck. I hike her leg up over my hip as I turn on my side. It's almost like I haven't touched her at all in months. The curves of her body so familiar and yet I've missed her. She reaches between us and strokes my erection while I pay special attention to her breasts, sucking on the beaded tips until she's moaning uncontrollably, her fist tight around the aching length of me.

"Get up here and ride my dick," I say hoarsely, pulling her to straddle me.

I grip her hips as she settles on top of me and slowly sinks down. Fuck, I love watching her bounce on my cock. This incredible woman. My wife. I palm her tits as she rocks back and forth, using me to hit the spot that makes her legs shake and her teeth dig into her bottom lip. Her long, dark hair falls around her face while she breathes heavy and determined.

"Get yourself close, baby," I whisper. "Let me see you come."

The dirty request causes her nails to dig into my skin where her palms are planted on my chest. The sting sends a bolt of heat to my balls, which draw up tight to my body. Damn, I'm getting close myself. Too close.

I clench my ass cheeks and bite my lip to ward off the climax. Not yet. Not until Sabrina loses control first.

When her pace slows, I wrap my arm around her waist and flip us over to bury myself deeper inside her. I push her knee up to open her wider as I thrust, leaning in to taste the bead of sweat collecting across her collarbone. Dragging my tongue down her chest to suck on one hard nipple while Sabrina claws at my back.

"Harder," she begs. "Harder."

I lever myself over her body, groaning when I feel her squeezing me and hear her sweet moans of her orgasm. Grasping at fistfuls of the pillow, she writhes beneath me, drawing every ounce of pleasure she can wring out. I rise on my knees, angle her hips up, and watch her pussy slide back and forth on my shaft until my muscles clench and I come inside her, panting.

"You're good to go again, right?" Sabrina teases as I collapse on top of her.

"Darlin', I can do this all night."

"Holding you to that." She pulls me down to kiss me. Pushes my sweaty hair off my forehead. "We might need another shower," she says ruefully.

Yeah, we're both pretty sweaty again. Probably from the humidity rolling in from the open bathroom door that leads to the outside shower. Or maybe it was the hot, primal sex.

"C'mon, let's take another shower under the stars," I say, tugging her out of bed.

Much, much later, when we're back in bed and falling asleep, Sabrina murmurs, "Hell of a honeymoon story to tell, huh?"

"Nah," I answer in a sleepy voice. "I don't think we should tell people about me eating you out in Dean's shower."

She lightly smacks my stomach.

No, I know what she means. "Tomorrow will be better," I promise her. "Couldn't get much worse, right?"

CHAPTER 25

DAY 2
SABRINA

I wake up with every intention to enjoy this honeymoon. While I think mortal terror is a totally reasonable reaction to nearly becoming the lead story on the evening news, part of me feels bad that Tucker put so much effort into planning this trip, only to have it all practically blow up in his face. Now it's time to put our near-death experience out of my mind and take advantage of our time away. The house is gorgeous, the weather is perfect, and we don't have a single responsibility but to get a good tan.

So when Tucker first stirs, stretching through the morning grogginess, I make a peace offering. He moans when I slip my hand under the sheets to cup his balls and stroke his growing erection.

"G'morning, darlin.'"

"Morning," I answer sweetly.

Then I slide down to wrap my lips around the head of his cock, licking the tip.

"Ah, I love your mouth," he says, tangling his fingers in my hair.

I suck him deep, stroking and licking and squeezing until he's thrusting his hips and fisting my hair. It doesn't take long to get him there, and once he recovers, he returns the favor, which leads to skinny-dipping in the suite's private plunge pool, shrouded within the lush vegetation that surrounds the house and affords us complete privacy. There's an actual coconut grove separating us from the nearest neighbors, who are not even close to within earshot of the massive estate.

After toweling off and getting dressed for the day, we amble off to the kitchen to make breakfast. But the second we enter the enormous room, I scream bloody murder.

"What! What is it!" Tucker, whose head was bent over his phone, immediately snaps into fight mode. His long, muscular body gets into a defensive pose as he wildly looks around, ready to protect me from danger.

Without a word, I point to the counter.

His face pales. "No. Unacceptable," he growls.

I feel honest-to-God tears well up in my eyes. "How is he *here*?"

We stand frozen, staring at Alexander, who's propped up against a basket of fresh pineapple. The housekeeper must have brought him, I realize. But why? Why would she do this to us? My distrustful gaze sweeps over the doll's eerie white face and that tiny red mouth, lips pursed in a creepy smirk as if he's harboring a sick secret.

I'm half a second away from channeling my daughter and throwing an epic tantrum when a short woman with dark hair suddenly appears. Wearing a pink pastel tee and white slacks, she comes rushing into the kitchen, her face creased with concern.

"What has happened? Everybody is all right?" Her voice is heavily accented, but I can't place it. Most of the people we'd spoken to on the other island sounded French, but this woman's accent isn't quite that.

"Yes, we're fine," Tucker answers. "Sorry if we scared you. You must be Isa?"

She nods warily.

"I'm Tucker, and this is my wife, Sabrina. Thank you for bringing us pineapple! It looks delicious." His gaze flicks toward the doll. "Um. Any idea how this thing got in here?"

Isa looks confused. "The doll? I bring him. Mister Dean said it was wedding present. He said it is a, what is the word, collector toy? You want me to take away?"

It requires every ounce of willpower not to pick up Alexander and smash his porcelain face against the side of the counter. But poor Isa already looks shaken up, and I don't want her thinking she just brought fresh pineapple for lunatics. It's not her fault. She was unknowingly doing the devil's work, and I can't be angry at her.

Tucker reads my mind. And since it's programmed in his DNA to rescue a lady in distress, he flashes a warm, reassuring smile. "No, no, you can leave him here," he tells Isa. "We were caught off guard, but don't worry, it's fine. Just a little joke between us and Mister Dean."

A joke? Yeah right. There is nothing even remotely comical about the spirit of a dead Gold Rush boy trapped inside a weird doll. I still can't believe Dean actually thought my sweet innocent daughter would like that dreadful thing. She was only eighteen months at the time. Who does that to a baby? Who does that to grown adults?

I take a breath. No. I refuse to let Dean Heyward-Di Laurentis ruin my honeymoon.

I paste on a reassuring smile and direct it at the shaken housekeeper. "Thank you so much for dropping off the fruit and the newspapers. That was very thoughtful."

"I go to boat now."

She still looks unsure, so Tucker once again casts his aw-shucks Texas-boy smile and drawls, "I'll walk you out. By the way, I love your accent. I take it you live on the Dutch side of St. Maarten?"

Dutch. That's it. I forgot our neighboring island has a French side and a Dutch one, each one offering two distinct cultures.

Isa relaxes. "Yes, I do."

"Born and raised? Or did you emigrate from somewhere else?"

He's still chatting with her as they disappear out the front door. Leaving me alone with Alexander.

I try not to shudder. Why is he wearing red shoes? And why are they so shiny? I hate him.

"I hate you," I tell the doll.

His blank eyes burn a hole in the very fabric of my soul. I almost expect them to blink. Logan swears he's seen them move on their own, but the three unfortunate times I've been in possession of Alexander, he hadn't done any brazen haunting.

While I wait for Tucker to return, I move Alexander from the counter—because that's where human beings eat, dammit—to the credenza across the room.

My husband is on the phone when he returns, his features tight with annoyance. "It's one thing to send him out of the blue on a non-occasion," he's saying, "but our honeymoon, dude? Have you no shame?"

"Is that Dean?" I demand. Tuck nods absently. "Put him on speaker. Now!"

Tucker swipes his finger on the screen. "You're on speaker now. Sabrina has something to say."

"Mrs. Tucker!" Dean's asshole voice chirps from the phone. "Happy honeymoon!"

"Don't you dare happy honeymoon us," I snarl.

"Tuck says you don't like mine and Allie's gift. I'm hurt. Almost as hurt as I am about the fact that you didn't give us an engagement gift."

"You haven't even begun to hurt."

"Oh, come on, you two. Let's not be hypocrites now. You've sent him to all of us before."

"We weren't sending *him* to you. We were sending him away from us," Tuck says darkly.

I draw a deep breath. "Dean."

"Yes, Sabrina?" He has the nerve to chuckle.

"This ends today, you hear me? We've all been complicit in this, but no more. I don't care how much he cost. The moment we hang up, I'm taking him outside and throwing him in the ocean."

"You can't pollute the ocean," Dean protests.

"Watch me."

Then I grab the phone and end the call.

Tucker grins at me. "Are we seriously going to give the little dude a burial at sea?"

"You down?"

"Oh yeah."

And that's why, five minutes later, we're carrying Alexander to the beach, only a few steps down the hill from the house. Other than a dark, somewhat-ominous cruise from St. Maarten to the dock last night, I've never really seen the Caribbean Sea up close before. And it's a gazillion times better than the Atlantic. I don't think I've ever seen water this transparent. You can see the bottom, for Pete's sake. I admire the gentle waves rolling ashore and the cloudless blue sky. The sand is crisp white against the turquoise water. Man, Jamie would go completely nuts for the hermit crabs scurrying from one tiny hole to the next.

"Ready?" Tucker says.

"Do it."

Nodding, he winds his arm back and hurls Alexander as far as he possibly can. Then we stand there holding hands, watching the doll bob in the calm waves, slowly carried out to sea.

"Go with God," Tucker says solemnly.

"Babe. He's going to Satan and we both know it."

"Truth, darlin'."

When Alexander is finally out of sight, I don't feel grief. Only relief.

Freedom.

An hour later, we're stuffed from breakfast and lying on a pair of beach chairs. Tuck's on his stomach, dozing. His sculpted back glistens from the sunscreen I rubbed all over it. I'm in a red bikini with a paperback thriller in my lap, but the book starts off too slow and I can't seem to get into it. Eventually I set it on the table between our chairs, pick up my phone instead, and FaceTime home to check in.

"Hello, little one!" I say when Jamie's adorable face fills the screen. "Miss you. Say hi to Daddy."

"Hi, Daddy," she says, waving at the screen.

"Hey, little darlin'," Tuck calls without rolling over. "You being good for Grammy?"

"Yeah."

"You brush your teeth this morning?"

"Yeah."

"Not yet," Tuck's mom says in the background where she's holding the phone up for Jamie, who's already dressed in her bathing suit and a tulle skirt. They were getting ready to go to the neighborhood pool when I called.

"Get upstairs and brush those teeth," Tucker tells her. "Two minutes. And don't use too much toothpaste."

Once Jamie bounds off, Gail assures me the house is still standing and Jamie isn't getting a leg up on her. When she asks how we're doing after the emergency landing, we answer in unison.

"Still shook."

"Already forgotten about it."

"We almost died, Tuck!" I turn to glare at him, but he's still got his face smushed against his forearm. His auburn hair shines in the late morning sun.

"Was it that serious?" Gail sounds concerned. "I thought it was a minor mechanical thing."

"Don't get her started, Mom. It wasn't that bad. Although Sabrina was about to put a handwritten will in a bottle and toss it in the ocean."

"The entertainment system exploded," I inform her.

"It did not." Tucker laughs.

"Grammy! My teeth are clean and they wanna go to the pool!"

Jamie's return signals the end of the conversation. I send a bunch of air kisses into the phone which my daughter pretends to catch and smack onto her rosy cheeks. After we hang up, I settle back on my chair, enjoying the sun beating on my face.

Down the beach a few yards, I notice a guy, maybe early thirties, carry a camera tripod onto the sand. The bizarre sight captures my interest, and I spend the next five minutes blatantly spying on the dude. After attaching an iPhone to the tripod, he proceeds to do a series of push-ups followed by modified burpees, while animatedly narrating for the camera. He's muscular, oiled, and well-tanned. One of those perfect Instagram fitness dudes.

When he catches me staring, I can't even muster up any embarrassment for spying. I wave hello, mesmerized by watching him perform. It's weird, watching from the other side of the screen. Which gets me thinking about an idea for a TikTok that's just the backside of other TikToks. A brilliant idea if I had the time or inclination to pursue such a thing. Oh well.

Beside me, Tucker lets out a groan. "Ah, I'm melting away here, darlin.' Wanna come for a swim?"

"Sure." I'm starting to feel the heat too.

We go down to the water and wade into the surf. The water's warm and crystal clear straight to the sandy bottom, like the kind you only see in cruise commercials. It's incredible.

"Did you see that?" Tucker points over my shoulder as we walk into deeper water.

Dread fills my stomach. "Oh no, is it Alexander?" I search the waves but don't see any nineteenth century porcelain dolls floating by.

"No, something popped out of the water."

"What, a shark?" Oh *hell* no. I frantically back away toward the shore, but Tucker grabs my arm.

"There it was again." When I don't bite, he becomes more emphatic. "Seriously. You didn't hear the splash?"

"I know you're full of shit." I smack water at him.

"Why would I lie?" he insists with those big, innocent eyes. "Look, there." He points again.

I glance over my shoulder, humoring him. The moment I do, something grazes my leg underwater. I cry out louder than my dignity likes, momentarily fearful before rounding on a laughing Tucker.

"You, asshole. I knew you were going to do that."

"But you still fell for it."

I smack another handful of water in his face just as he lets out a pained cry.

"Oh, come on." I roll my eyes at him. "It's just water."

"Fuck. *Fuck.*" Tucker's tone is laced with fake suffering. "Something got me," he grinds out.

"I'm not falling for it twice, babe."

"No. Damn it. Something really fucking got me."

He then darts for shore. I'm not convinced until I see him twisting around to examine the back of his leg. I slosh through the water after him, and when I get closer, I realize there's a big red lash on his flesh, like the mark from a whip.

"I was stung," he growls. "I think I was stung by a jellyfish." Tucker plops down on his ass and lies back on the sand, handsome face contorting in agony. "Fuck, this hurts."

Yeah, he's definitely not lying. The skin is already puckered and swollen, bumps forming around the bright-red marks.

"What do we do?" I blurt out. "Should I pee on it?"

Tucker jumps back into a sitting position. "What? Hell no."

"I think I'm supposed to, aren't I?"

"Babe, I'm not letting you pee on me. That's not even a real thing."

"Pretty sure it is."

He grits his teeth, still staring at the reddish-purple wound. "Man, it hurts."

"Oh my God, do you think this was some sort of cosmic

punishment for drowning Alexander? Did Willie's spirit get its revenge?"

Tucker thinks it over. Then he says, "No." He glares at me. "I think I just got stung by a jellyfish."

"What happens if we don't do something?" I bite my lip in anguish. "I don't think calamine lotion fixes that."

This isn't exactly a little bee sting. What if his whole leg puffs up like that? Do they amputate for jellyfish stings?

"I think urine is the best solution, Tuck." I do an internal body scan and then moan. "You know, I don't think I can," I realize. "I don't have to go—"

I halt when I see the fitness guy approaching us. Oh thank God. I flag him down, waving my arms. His pace quickens as he jogs toward us.

"Sabrina, no," Tucker warns. "Don't you fucking dare."

"Everything okay?" the guy asks when he reaches us. Dark eyes sharply assess Tucker.

"Will you pee on my husband?" I ask the stranger. "He got stung by a jellyfish, but I don't have to go."

"Ignore her. Sabrina, I'm telling you, it's a myth. I'll be fine."

But he looks like he's on the verge of tears and at risk of cracking a tooth with how hard he's biting down, grinding his jaw. His leg looks horrible.

"I don't know if it's a myth," Fitness Guy tells him. "I mean, why would everyone say to do it if it didn't work?"

I implore Tucker with my eyes. "Let him try."

My husband remains stubbornly against the idea. "I'd rather you cut it off with a rusty spoon."

"I'm not bringing you home to Mama Tucker with one leg! Do you remember how long it took her to warm up to me?" I'm practically vibrating from the stress of the situation.

Fitness Guy glances at me. "Take a breath, sweetheart. I can help him out. It's the neighborly thing to do, right?"

Then, to my relief and Tucker's horror, the guy begins to unbutton his cargo shorts—just as another man in a linen shirt and panama hat comes tearing up the sand.

"Bruce, what on Earth are you doing to these people?"

"No, no, it's fine," I assure the newcomer. "I asked him to pee on my husband's leg. He was stung—"

Tucker groans. "I'm still emphatically against this idea, Bruce."

"Better safe than sorry." Bruce shrugs. He's in the process of unzipping now. "Right?"

The new arrival takes off his hat and dabs the sweat from his forehead, biting back a laugh. "That's an old wives' tale. There is absolutely no evidence to suggest urine soothes a jellyfish sting or any other kind. In fact, some studies suggest it would exacerbate the pain and swelling."

At that, Bruce zips up his shorts.

"Really? You're just taking his word for it?" I glower at the man who betrayed me.

"Oh, for sure. Kevin is a walking encyclopedia. He reads scholarly journals for fun."

"See?" Tucker sighs with relief. "For fuck's sake."

"I'm Kevin," the man says, offering his hand to me. He appears to be older than the oiled-up Bruce, maybe in his early forties. "I apologize for him."

"Just trying to help." Bruce gives Tucker an apologetic smile.

"You folks visiting?" Kevin asks.

"We're staying at the Di Laurentis house for a week," I tell them. "Sorry to rope you into all this." I look at Tucker. "I really was just trying to help."

"Let us introduce ourselves properly. We'd love to have you over for dinner tomorrow night," Kevin offers.

I smile. "That'd be great. Thank you."

"Get him sorted out," Kevin says with a sympathetic nod at Tucker. "Run it under a hot shower or soak in a hot tub for about twenty to forty minutes. Take some pain medication. That's about all there is to be done for it. I've been stung twice, so I know the drill."

"We will, thanks."

"That was for the plane, wasn't it?" Tucker accuses as I'm getting him back to the house after we leave Bruce and Kevin.

"I would never."

"You almost let a man pee on me, Sabrina."

"That's how much I love you."

CHAPTER 26

DAY 3
SABRINA

"You don't have to babysit me," Tucker says the next day. He's sprawled on the beach chair next to mine, absently brushing sand off his abdomen. "I'm fine here if you want to go for a swim."

"In that?" I look up from my book to nod at the lovely blue expanse in front of us. All full of terrors untold. "Not a chance."

"So the ocean is the devil now?"

"Yes. Yes it is."

He snorts a laugh at me from behind his dark sunglasses. I choose to ignore that. He thinks it's funny now, but last night he was a crying toddler with his mangled leg. We spent the rest of the day laid up inside, eating and watching movies while I kept working on our will. Not exactly the honeymoon of our dreams.

"The ocean and I have an understanding," I explain. "I stay away from it, and it doesn't try to kill me."

"I've been to the beach a thousand times. First time anything ever got me. You don't have to be scared of it."

"Sounds like something the ocean would say."

I'm flipping to the next page when my phone beeps. The villa Wi-Fi encompasses this section of the beach, so I've been making sure to connect to it every time we're outside just in case there's an emergency back home. I glance at the screen to find a message Grace just sent to our girls' group chat.

> Grace: Wanted to share the news before you saw that stupid Hockey Hotties blog post. And if you've already seen it, then yes, it's true.

What news? And what blog post? Rather than ask for clarification, I click on the automatic link generated by my phone, which takes me to that ridiculous hockey blog run by a group of rabid groupies.

The article in question is at the very top of the page.

Secret Wedding Scandal!!!!!!!

Make sure you're sitting down, ladies and gents!! BECAUSE WE HAVE NEWS!!!

We are sad to inform you that our very own John Logan is off the market!

We'll wait while you go grab the tissues...

Okay, are you back??! Well, it's true, everyone. Our sources have confirmed that JL has indeed married his longtime girlfriend. And not only that, but the sneaky man did it MONTHS AGO!! Like, we're talking wintertime. The nerve of him!!!

Are we happy for that big sexy man?? Well, yeah. Of course!! But we're also CRUSHED!!!!

I stop reading. The excessive punctuation is too much. Besides, I already got the gist of it. If this silly blog is correct, then Grace and Logan got married behind all our backs. This past *winter*.

The nerve of them.

"Tucker!" I growl.

He looks up in alarm. "What is it?"

"Did you know Logan and Grace got married?" I demand.

His jaw drops. "No. Seriously?"

I click back into the group chat and waste no time furiously typing up a storm.

Me: Omg. You made us find out from the internet? What kind of friendship is this??!?

Allie: Seriously!!??

Grace: Oh, shut it, Allie. You knew.

Me: YOU KNEW?

Allie: Hey, in my defense, Hannah knew too.

Me: Yeah, but Hannah's not a gossip. YOU'RE the gossip in the group and that means it was your duty to tell us.

Hannah: Thanks, S.

Allie: Oh come on. How is this on me? They're the ones who got married in secret.

Grace: I'm sorry we didn't say anything earlier. We were waiting to tell my dad until after my graduation. We finally shared the news with him and Mom last night, and both of Logan's parents.

Me: I need details. Now.

Grace: Remember when we went to Vermont for New Year's? It sort of turned into an elopement. Totally unplanned. But zero regrets <3

Beside me, Tucker is trying to peer at my phone. "What's going on?" he pries. "What are they saying?"

"Grace just confirmed it. Apparently she and Logan eloped to Vermont over New Year's."

"New Year's!" he balks. He's already reaching for his phone, no doubt to open his own group chat.

"Yup. They've been keeping it from everyone for months. They only told their parents last night."

We're each typing on our respective phones now.

> Me: Ahh, this is great news! I mean, nefarious tactics aside, I'm so happy for you two <3
> Grace: Thanks! We're pretty happy ourselves.
> Hannah: For what it's worth, Allie and I only stumbled on the news at your wedding, S. They'd already been married for months by then.
> Allie: Yeah, see! I didn't say anything because I didn't want to ruin your big day. You're welcome, bitch.

I send a middle finger emoji, followed by another reprimand.

> Me: Don't use my wedding as an excuse, you traitor. You should have informed everyone the moment you found out. I'm disappointed in you, Allison Jane.
> Allie: Hannah's pregnant.

My shriek nearly sends Tucker flying off his chair. "What?" he says anxiously. "Are you okay?"

I'm about to answer when Hannah's response pops up, causing my jaw to slam closed.

> Hannah: No. No fair. You promised you wouldn't say anything.
> Allie: omg I'm sorry. It just slipped out. My fingers took on a life of their own. Maybe Alexander possessed them.
> Me: Don't you dare try to distract us. Also, Alexander is swimming with the fishes.
> Grace: Wait, what?
> Me: We drowned him.
> Grace: No, the Hannah thing. You're pregnant? I assumed

you took the test after the wedding and it was negative so
that's why you didn't say anything.

Hannah: I'm sorry. I'm not keeping anyone in the dark on
purpose. The test was positive. Allie's the only one who
knows.

Hannah: I haven't even told Garrett yet.

Me: Is this a group chat or a den of secrets and lies?

Hannah: Don't say anything to the guys. Please. Not until I
tell Garrett.

"Sabrina?" Tucker keeps trying to read my screen.

I angle it away. "Sorry. We're all giving Grace grief in the chat for
hiding the marriage from us."

"Yeah, Logan's getting shit from us too." He sends another text.

With Tucker distracted, I return my attention to my own tumul-
tuous chat thread.

Hannah: Please, you guys. Don't say anything. I don't even
know what I'm going to do yet.

The rest of us are quick to reassure her.

Allie: I'm sorry I let it slip here. My lips are officially crazy-
glued shut, babe.

Grace: Mine too.

Me: I won't say a word. Promise.

I bite my lip after sending the response. Normally I don't keep
secrets from Tucker. I trust that man with my life. With our daughter's
life. But I also know what it's like to deal with an unplanned pregnancy.
At least, I get the sense this one is unplanned. And if it is, then Hannah
needs time and space to work through the flood of emotions—and
hormones—she's probably struggling to make sense of right now.

So I banish the news to a little box in my head labeled shut your *damn mouth*. Tuck will understand. He would've hated it with all his heart if he'd learned I was pregnant from anybody but me. Garrett deserves to hear it from his girlfriend, not us.

CHAPTER 27

NIGHT 3
SABRINA

At dinner later with Kevin and Bruce, Tucker still won't let go of the fact that I'm refusing to swim in the ocean for the rest of our honeymoon. Hell, for the rest of our lives.

"I'm the one who got stung, but now she's haunted by the water," he tells them over tuna tartare in their immaculate dining room. The huge open space overlooks the pool deck and the turquois panorama beyond their estate. "I swear, trying to steal my thunder at every turn."

"I want none of your thunder," I say sweetly, smirking at him over the rim of my wineglass. "You go ahead and wear your jellyfish sting as a badge of honor. I'll be over there, safe on land."

Tuck snickers.

I glance at our hosts. "In my defense, I barely escaped a fiery plane crash to get here. My nerves are a little rattled."

"She spent all day writing our will," my husband pipes up. "If I didn't know better, I'd think she was planning to get rid of me."

"You're not serious?" Bruce stares at us in horror then washes it down with a gulp of red wine.

"True story," I say. "There was some kind of electrical fire on the plane, and we had to make an emergency landing."

"Meanwhile, this crazy couple in front of us, who were at each other's throats the entire flight, are suddenly acting like the couple going down on the Titanic. Holding each other and professing their love." Tucker gives a decisive nod. "Fun times."

"See?" Bruce looks plaintively at Kevin, who's laughing at our misfortune. "Nothing exciting ever happens to us."

"I can cut the brake line to one of the cars and not tell you which one," Kevin answers, deadpan.

Tucker barks out a sharp laugh.

"Oh, stop it." Bruce shoves Kevin's arm. "You couldn't live without me." Then to me, "I get it, sweetie. Look how he treats me."

During the main course, Bruce, now a few glasses into what tastes like very expensive wine, starts grilling us. He's clearly the nosier, more outgoing one in the relationship, while Kevin seems to prefer sitting back and letting his partner carry most of the conversation. They make an interesting couple.

"So who did we let into our house?" Bruce asks, swirling his glass while narrowing his eyes at me. "For all we know, we're enjoying a lovely meal with those kids from *Natural Born Killers*."

"Like we've got the Di Laurentises in a pile of corpses in the deep freezer?"

"That was deliciously specific," Bruce says, grinning at me. He's got a dazzling white smile, and he looks much less douchey when he's wearing clothes.

"Ignore him," Kevin says. "He's desperate for someone to want him dead."

"I'm nosy. So shoot me." Bruce glances at Tucker. "So what do you do for a living, Tuck? My guess, judging by that physique? Athlete."

"Nah." Tucker shrugs. "Dean and I played hockey together in college, but now I run a couple bars in Boston."

He proceeds to tell the men about his business. How the first Tucker's Bar that he opened right out of college had become a popular neighborhood hangout that attracted a lot of pro athletes. With its success came the second location, which is doing even better. Bruce looks it up on Instagram, much to the embarrassment of Kevin, who frowns at his partner for pulling out his phone in the middle of dinner.

"Your content and marketing are impressive," Bruce marvels. "You do this all yourself?"

"Somewhat. I hired a couple locals that do video and professional photography for us. In-house staff run our socials. Honestly, a lot of good friends helped us out in the beginning." He shrugs. "A couple of my best friends play for the Bruins, so they talked up the bar, and now we've got some famous clientele popping by."

Bruce looks highly impressed. "You have plans beyond the bars, or is this franchise the baby?"

"He has a ton of ideas," I chime in. "He's nowhere near done yet."

"Definitely thinking of opening more bars in other cities. But…I get bored," Tucker admits.

Frowning, I glance over at him. "You're bored with the bars?" This is the first I'm hearing of it.

"No. I mean, sometimes." He shrugs, reaching for his wine. "It's the double-edged sword of a great staff and an excellent general manager. The bars run without me, and I end up with too much free time on my hands. Gets me antsy."

I gaze down at my plate, hoping it'll shield my expression, whatever it may be. I'm not quite sure how I feel hearing that Tuck's not enjoying his business. I hadn't gotten any sense he felt unfulfilled in his job. Not a single hint of it. I always make a point to ask him about work, and he always just smiles and says it's all good.

"I hear ya," Bruce tells Tuck, nodding. "I'm the same way. Full of ideas. Always on the go."

"Damn man can't sit still," Kevin agrees with a wry smile. "Such is the life of a fitness guru, I suppose."

"Is that what you do?" I ask Bruce, forcing myself to focus on our new friends and not my husband's apparent unhappiness. "I was wondering after seeing you out there with your camera."

As Tuck and I grill him on the ins and outs of being an "influencer," we discover that there's a lot more to the job. Along with having millions of followers across all his social media accounts and making a fortune from sponsored posts, Bruce also works as a personal trainer for an elite clientele.

"He trains two New York Congresswomen and one former president," Kevin boasts, clearly proud of his partner. "Can't say who the prez is, but feel free to guess."

Tucker and I are suitably impressed.

When Bruce turns his cross-examination on me and I mention I just graduated from law school, I discover that Kevin is also a lawyer. Not only that, but a senior partner at a top-three firm in New York.

"We practice criminal law," Kevin tells me. "My section, we exclusively handle wrongful conviction cases. Mostly pro bono work."

I lean forward. "See, that's fascinating. I've known since I started law school I wanted to work in criminal law. Something like that must be incredibly satisfying."

"It's more disappointment than not, if I'm being honest. We have a thorough vetting process, only taking cases we sincerely believe we can prove should be overturned. There's a high bar, however. Courts are often reluctant. Every defeat, though, motivates us to try harder on the next one. Each case is long and arduous, but yes, it's certainly rewarding." He smiles at me. "I imagine a young woman like yourself is quite familiar with hard work. I can't even fathom raising a child while in law school. I barely made it through Harvard myself without having a nervous breakdown, and that was child-free."

"It wasn't easy," I admit. "Tucker was a tremendous support."

"She's being modest," he insists. "Even before we met, she worked two jobs putting herself through college. And then afterward, she was up every morning and night with our daughter, doing feedings and diapers and all that while highlighting textbooks and writing papers. It was exhausting just watching her."

"You're two rather extraordinary young people," Kevin says, as Bruce tops up our glasses. "Not everyone is as motivated or industrious at your age. I certainly wasn't. Took me a few years to find my way."

"I think having our daughter really encouraged both of us to make the best life for her that we can," Tucker answers, clasping my hand under the table. "We want to give her everything. Make sure she's always taken care of."

"Stop," Bruce groans. "You're adorable. I can't stand it."

During dessert, Bruce and Tucker bro out over fitness stuff. Kevin's eyes about roll out of his head when the two men leave the table to start comparing bodyweight resistance techniques. Tucker's in amazing shape, and although he resists the urge to pull his shirt off, Bruce notices and remarks on my husband's incredible abs and biceps. As if anyone could not. I don't take it personally when Bruce blatantly flirts with him while Kevin and I talk law over our mango mousse. For what it's worth, Kevin seems otherwise unfazed by his flirtatious partner. He's a good sport.

"We'll be here for another few days," I let them know as they walk us out after a fantastic meal. "I'm sure we'll run into one another again, but it'd be nice to return the favor. Not sure we can come up with a spread this great, but drinks at our place maybe?"

"Just point me toward the ice bucket," Bruce says, kissing my cheek.

On the walk home under the moonlight, Tucker takes my hand, drawing shapes with his thumb across my knuckles. "You have fun?"

"Definitely." Then I remember something, and my mood dampens slightly. "Why didn't you tell me you were bored with the bars?"

That gets me a shrug. "I'm not bored, exactly. Just restless sometimes."

"Still, you should've said something."

"I didn't say anything because it's really not a big deal. And

I didn't see the point in distracting you during your last year at Harvard."

"You've been feeling this way for a *year*?" I swear, I love this man with all my heart, but would it kill him not to be the strong, supportive type all the time?

Tucker squeezes my hand. "I'm not feeling any sort of way. But see, this is why I didn't bring it up. You would've just tried to fix a minor problem, and we both know your stress levels can't afford to add anything else to your plate. It's already damn full, darlin.'"

My husband being unhappy with his work doesn't sound like a "minor problem." But Tucker doesn't allow me to dwell on it. He stops walking and brings my hand up to his lips, kissing my knuckles.

"Did I mention how hot you look tonight?" he drawls.

"Are you trying to distract me from your work stuff?"

"No, I'm trying to compliment my hot wife."

Sensing he's not going to budge, I decide to let it go. When he's ready to talk about it, he'll talk about it. For now, I'm just going to enjoy this night out with my husband. It's been a long time since we spent an evening with other adults without having to constantly run to check on Jamie. I'd forgotten what it was like to be us as a couple, not just parents.

"Well, it's about time you did." I mock pout. "I went to all the trouble of picking out this dress, and you couldn't be bothered to compliment it?" I have to admit, the long, linen wrap dress I'd chosen does amazing things for my post-pregnancy boobs.

"What a selfish bastard," he agrees, gripping my hips to walk me back until I'm up against a palm tree. "Neglecting to tell you how gorgeous you look."

"Such a bad boy," I whisper.

Tucker kisses me, the flavor of wine still on his tongue. On this sandy path through the wild green shrubs and tall palms between our two houses, a warm breeze creeps over my skin. I hear only the waves nearby and the insect songs. It's secluded, though not exactly private.

"I've wanted to do that all night," he mumbles against my mouth. His hands skim my body to squeeze my ass. "You're beautiful."

I tug on his hand. "We're almost at the house."

"I want to make you come now."

Oh boy. When he talks like that, I can't form coherent thoughts. There are so many facets to John Tucker, and I can honestly say this primal, alpha side of him is one of my favorites. Tucker is so agreeable most of the time, so happy to ignore his own needs and wants in service of mine and Jamie's.

But *this* Tucker knows precisely what he wants and how to get it. The night we met, he seduced me with such effortlessness, I hardly saw it coming. One minute we were flirting at a college sports bar, the next we were naked in his truck while he whispered dirty words to me.

My fingers slide through his hair and grip the back of his neck as I return his kiss, deeper, pulling him closer. He pushes the opening of my dress apart to slip his hand between my legs, dipping his fingers below my skimpy panties. The first brush of his touch against my warm, needy flesh makes me entirely forget about where we are or the rough trunk of the tree at my back. I part my legs farther and encourage him to keep going, rocking against his palm.

"I love you," he whispers, pressing two fingers inside me. "You're so gorgeous."

I don't really hear him. I'm too entranced by what he does to my body. Biting my lip and hanging onto him to stay on my feet. I'm so sensitive that it doesn't take long before my muscles clench and my legs being to shake. I muffle my moans into his shoulder, shuddering through an orgasm that leaves me feeling light-headed.

Eyes shut, I'm still breathing heavy when I hear a *snap* above us.

My eyelids flick open just a heartbeat before something heavy cracks me on the top of the head.

I experience a split second of searing pain before everything goes black.

CHAPTER 28

DAY 4
TUCKER

"Hey. Hey, Sabrina." Cradling her head in my lap, I gently rub her cheek, stroke her forehead.

She's motionless for so long, I consider carrying her back to the house, but I'm afraid to move her.

"Wake up, darlin'. Come on."

Finally, her eyelids flutter. Then her lips part. With a painful groan, she stirs in my lap and peers up at me. It takes a moment for her eyes to focus.

"There you are," I say, letting out a sigh of relief.

"What happened?" She reaches up and feels the top of her head. Instantly flinches, hissing.

"You, uhh…" I clear my throat. Now that I know she hasn't slipped into a coma, I'm having trouble choking back a laugh. "A coconut fell on your head."

There's a beat of silence.

"Seriously?" Moaning, she covers her face with her hands. "For fuck's sake."

"You okay? Fingers and toes?"

She gives them a wiggle, looking down to confirm they're all moving.

"Yep, good."

"Let's try getting you up." I give her my hand and steady her as we stand, but she immediately goes a little sideways.

"Whoa. Yeah, no." Grabbing her head, she leans on me, her legs wobbling. "Everything's spinning."

"I got you."

I scoop her up in my arms and proceed down the dark, sandy path. Back at the house, I carry her upstairs to the master suite, where I help her change out of her dress and put her in bed.

"Let me check the binder for a phone number to a doctor," I say. "We should get you checked out."

"I'm okay," she insists, albeit weakly.

"You could have a concussion."

"I don't think so. And even if I do, they're not going to do anything for it other than monitor me every hour and ask me what day it is. We can do that here."

"Fine. But if I get even the slightest sense you're concussed, we're finding a doctor."

"Fine. Could you grab me some ibuprofen from my bag? I want to get ahead of the migraine that's in store for me."

I duck into the bathroom, returning a moment later with a glass of water and some painkillers for what is going to be a hell of a bump on her head tomorrow.

"Don't laugh at me," Sabrina mumbles afterward, tucked in tight and head elevated on two pillows.

"I would never."

"I know you," she says miserably. "I don't want to hear a sound."

"I swear."

Sabrina drifts off while I'm getting undressed to take a shower. With the bathroom door closed, I cover my mouth and let out a muffled laugh under the sound of the running water. Because that shit was hilarious. Not that my wife got hurt, but come on. A coconut falls on her head and knocks her the fuck out? I release another wave of laughter against my forearm. Jesus. For anyone else, the odds would be astronomical. But for us? Just par for the course on this trip.

THE NEXT MORNING, SABRINA IS AWAKE EARLY. I'M WAITING WITH water and more painkillers when her eyes peel open.

"Close the shades," she grumbles, turning away from the windows. "My head's killing me."

The room darkens as I slide them shut. "What day is it?"

"Wednesday, I think?" She waits for me to confirm or deny.

I just shrug. "Honestly, I don't know myself."

We both grin.

"What's our daughter's name?"

"James. Jamie for short. Your mom's name is Gail. My favorite professor at Harvard was Professor Kingston. My favorite color is green." She sits up and holds out her hand for the pills. "Pretty sure I'm not concussed."

"Can I see your head?" I ask after she swallows the meds.

Without a word, she lets me check her scalp. "What's the prognosis?" she asks with a sigh.

"Yeah, you've got a pretty good bump, but I don't see any open skin. I just want to—" I press down gently around the swollen area.

"Ow! Dick." Sabrina smacks my hand away.

"I don't think you have a fracture."

"Jesus. Warn me next time."

I leave her with the TV remote while I make us some bacon and eggs for breakfast. All the plans we'd made before we got here—snorkeling, off-roading, taking a boat out to explore private coves—have gone to hell since this island is apparently trying to kill us. It's like the moment we left Boston, we've been in a bad *Final Destination* sequel.

"We're terrible at this," she says later as we're finishing breakfast downstairs. Sabrina pops a strawberry into her mouth and chews glumly.

Isa brought us fresh fruit again this morning, along with a basket of freshly baked croissants. I swear our housekeeper has invisibility as a superpower. She glides in and out of this house without making a single sound.

"Terrible at what?" I ask, clearing our plates.

"Vacation. I feel like we've spent most of the trip inside."

"Yeah, because this place is out to get us."

"I'm sorry." Sabrina carries our empty glasses over and sets them next to me at the sink. "I know we were talking about going out on the boat today, but I'm worried my head will be spinning the entire time."

"Hey, no." I grab her around the waist, kiss her forehead. "Take all the time you need. I'm more concerned with you feeling better. I was the one laid up a couple days ago because of my leg." Which, by the way, still looks heinous. But at least the pain's gone away.

While we're cleaning up, voices waft into the kitchen from the back deck. "Anyone home?"

Recognizing Bruce's voice, I call out, "In here."

A moment later, our neighbors stroll in through the open glass doors and cross the dining room toward us. In his polo, khaki shorts, and panama hat, Kevin looks like he's ready for a day of sailing. Bruce, meanwhile, wears a tight tank top that reveals his oiled-up arms and very tight swim trunks.

"We're heading out to do some deep-sea fishing," Bruce says, greeting us with a big smile.

"We've got room for two more," Kevin offers.

I shake my head in regret. "As amazing as that sounds, I think we're staying in today," I tell them. "Sabrina's a little under the weather."

"Oh, no. Really?" Kevin looks concerned. "I've got some echinacea and tea that might help."

"It's not that kind of ailment," I say, while Sabrina glares at me. "We had a little mishap on the way back from your place last night."

"Mishap?" Kevin's shrewd gaze does a sweep of Sabrina.

Mortified, she huffs and looks away.

I fight hard not to laugh. "Coconut fell out of the sky and smacked her right on top of the head. Knocked her out cold for almost a minute."

Bruce gasps. "Oh my God!"

"You're kidding?" Kevin notices Sabrina's murderous expression and chuckles softly. "Not kidding, I see."

"You poor thing," his partner says sympathetically. "You all right?"

"I'm fine," she mutters. "Just a headache."

"It's more common around here than you'd think," Kevin says. "You're lucky it wasn't serious."

He sounds sincere, but I think he says it just to make her feel better.

"Anyway, we're gonna stay in today," I say. "But we appreciate the offer."

Sabrina touches my arm, her features softening. "No, you should go. There's no reason we both have to miss out."

"I don't mind. I'd rather be here if you need anything."

"I'll be fine. I'm just going to hang out by the pool, maybe, and FaceTime Jamie. Probably take a long nap too. If I need anything when you're gone, I can text Isa."

"There," Bruce says, nodding. "It's settled."

"Yes," Kevin tells me. "Come on. It's going to be a beautiful day on the water. And we won't be back too late."

With Sabrina insisting, I eventually capitulate and take them up on it. Getting out on the water sounds great. And truthfully, the thought of watching any more goddamn movies on this beach vacation makes me want to gouge my eyes out.

"Meet you on our dock in five?" Kevin says.

"I'll be right there."

"Keep applying sunscreen," Sabrina reminds me after the men leave. She tails me to our bedroom, watching me get ready. "And try not to get impaled by a marlin or whatever."

"You too. The sunscreen part." I wink at her. "And don't fall asleep under any trees."

OUT ON THE BOAT, THE FISHING IS GREAT. WE MANAGE TO LAND A few grouper and mahi-mahi. A couple of yellowtail snapper. It feels traitorous to even think it, but it's probably the best day I've had since we got here. Spending the afternoon with some beers, feeling the ocean breeze on my face, just shooting the shit. Bruce and Kevin are good guys. And other than a close call when I nearly caught a hook to the face, I manage to return to dry land unscathed.

"Looks like the missus came out to greet you," Bruce jokes as we stride down the long wooden dock toward the shore.

I follow his gaze and spot Sabrina sitting on one of our beach chairs. She's wearing her oversized sunglasses, with her dark hair arranged in a loose side braid and her nose buried in her thriller.

"We're going to grill up that mahi-mahi for dinner," Kevin says, clapping a hand on my shoulder. "You and Sabrina are welcome to join us."

My stomach growls at that. It's only four o'clock, a bit early for dinner, but the lobster salad and breadsticks we had on their boat hadn't filled me up. "Let me go ask the missus."

Sabrina smiles at my approach. "Hey! How was it?"

"Fucking awesome," I admit. "The guys asked if we want to—" I stop in horror. "What the hell happened to you?"

Sabrina, who'd been in the process of twisting around to tuck her book in her beach bag, eyes me in confusion. "What? What do you mean?"

I tug her off the chair and turn her around. The brief glimpse I'd caught of her back hadn't misled me. Now that I have a full, clear view, there's no mistaking the sunburn. Her skin is nearly the same shade of red as her bikini strings.

Sighing, I poke her lightly between the shoulder blades.

"Ow! What was that for?"

"You're sunburnt. It looks bad, darlin'. Didn't you put on sunblock?"

Her nose scrunches, and she looks away while she thinks for a moment. "I fell asleep for a bit after I got off the phone with Jamie. I might have forgotten."

Sighing, I just look at her.

"Don't give me that Dad look," she warns. "Because you're looking a bit red yourself."

"I'm fine."

Eyes narrowed, she lifts the hem of my T-shirt and smacks my stomach.

I flinch. "Fuck, Sabrina. Christ." It feels like she threw scalding water at me.

It's then that I glance down and see the stark white handprint left behind on a very red canvas.

"Well, shit." Guess I forgot too.

Sabrina looks like she doesn't know whether to laugh or cry. She opens her mouth to speak but is interrupted by a commotion from the water's edge. Our attention shifts to Bruce and Kevin, who are examining something on the wet sand.

"Tuck!" Bruce shouts when he catches my gaze. "Sabrina! C'mere! You are not gonna believe this!"

Exchanging a wary look, we walk over to the men to see what all the fuss is about. When we reach them, Bruce is peeling strands of seaweed off some item I can't quite make out.

When he flings the last of the seaweed off, I suck in a breath. Jesus fucking Christ.

"How remarkable is this?" Kevin says, eyes wide. "It just came in with the tide and floated right up to our feet."

A curious Sabrina steps forward before I can stop her. "What is it?"

Then she sees Alexander and starts to cry.

CHAPTER 29

DAY 5
SABRINA

THIS TRIP IS ONE INDIGNITY AFTER ANOTHER. THE DAY AFTER Alexander forces himself back into our lives, Tucker and I both wake up feeling like pieces of fried chicken. We spend the morning slathering aloe on each other while putting towels down so we don't ruin the expensive white couch in the living room. We alternate between that and lying on the cold marble floor.

"Maybe we should just call it," I tell Tucker.

"Call it?"

"Accept defeat and go home."

"You want to leave?" Plastered to the floor, he turns his face to look up at me where I lie facedown on the couch because even the air touching my back feels like a million fire ants feasting on my flesh.

"We're halfway through this trip, and at this rate we'll end up dead before it's over. And I miss Jamie. A few minutes on the phone isn't enough. And who knows what your mom is feeding her."

"I miss her too, but they're fine." He sits up, wincing when the side of his thumb accidentally brushes his sunburnt stomach. "I know there've been a few bumps, but we're not going to get another chance at this for a while once you start your new job."

"Don't remind me."

It's the constant thought that's stalked me every day since graduation. I'm no closer to a decision while the stress of making the wrong choice mounts like my throat is filling with sand. And, frankly, I don't appreciate Tucker piling more guilt on me for our much-delayed honeymoon going to hell.

"What's that look?" he demands, because he can read me like a book.

"Nothing."

"Sabrina."

I sit up too, trying to stop the words biting on my tongue. But they spill out anyway. "I'm sorry my career is ruining everything for you."

"Hey. That's not what I said. But for what it's worth, having to choose between two pretty great opportunities isn't an awful problem to have. At least you're excited about both jobs."

"Unlike you, right? You, who couldn't be bothered to tell me you were unhappy with your job."

He gets to his feet, whiskey-brown eyes narrowing. "What do you want to hear? That I've barely got anything to do at the bars? That they run themselves and I'm bored shitless?" His jaw tightens. "I collect the checks, yeah, but I feel useless."

"And you should've told me all that months ago," I say, my tone a tad sharper than I intend.

"Well, I'm telling you now. I'm dying of boredom, but I don't say anything because I'm trying not to put more pressure on you."

"So now it's my fault you're miserable?"

"Is there a draft in here?" he says with bitter sarcasm. "Where are you hearing this, because those aren't my words."

"Whatever. I guess it's all in my head, right?"

I go upstairs, which effectively tables the discussion. But the can of worms we've opened can't be unopened. We only skirted around the issue, dipped our toes in a pool of resentment I hadn't realized was there.

It's only later, once the sun's gone down, that shit gets real. We decide to take a walk on the beach, because we're both going stir crazy and neither of us want to admit what's been coming since we woke up cranky this morning. The lid rattling on the boiling pot, water threatening to spill over the edge.

"I mean it," I say while staring straight ahead. "Let's just change our tickets and fly home early. If we're just going to sit around the house, we might as well do it at home with our daughter."

The moon is bright and full over our heads. The sun, having just dipped below the horizon, finally giving way to a cool breeze to offer some relief from the thick humidity and our throbbing sunburns.

"Christ, Sabrina, just once can you make us a priority?"

I stop in my tracks, spinning to face him. "Excuse me?"

"You heard me. School, work, Jamie, even a goddamn last will and testament takes precedence over me. Somehow, I always fuckin' end up at the bottom of your priority list. Do you remember why we came here?" Tucker huffs an angry breath. "It was to get some time together. I never see you at home. We can't get five minutes alone. And that's not gonna get any better once you accept that stupid ninety-hour-a-week job."

"Oh, so that's how you really feel, huh? You were the one telling me to take the offer from the bigger firm."

"Because I know it's what you really want," he snaps back, raising his voice.

"So you lied."

"Give me a break, Sabrina." He drags his hands through his hair, yanking. As if I'm not justified in my frustration. "You'd hate practicing civil law. It'd bore you silly."

"What about you?"

"What about me?"

I almost scream. "Oh my God. Stop being Mr. Agreeable and all supportive and, like, *Don't worry, darlin', you do whatever you need to do and I'll be A-okay over here. Just one fucking time, why don't you tell me what you want?"*

Exasperation floods his expression. "I want to have my wife home more than a couple hours a day!"

I rear back, stunned.

Tucker looks equally startled by his uncharacteristic outburst. He draws a breath, his arms dropping to his sides. "But I bite my tongue because I want to support you, no matter what you choose."

"Is this about Tucker's Bar? Do you think me taking this job means you're, what, stuck there?"

"I don't know what I'm going to do about the bar. I care that you're happy."

"How am I supposed to be happy if you're pissed off at me all the time?"

I'm not interested in one of those resentful marriages where we're both suffering in silence, enslaved by our choices until we grow to hate each other. I certainly don't want that for Jamie.

"How am I the bad guy for trying to be supportive?"

"Being passive-aggressive doesn't feel supportive." My frustration reaches sky-high levels. "And what the hell am I supposed to do if you're not being honest with me? You encourage me to prioritize everything but you, and then get mad at me when I take you at your word? How is that fair? I need to be able to trust what you're telling me, damn it."

"Fine." Tucker throws his hands up and turns away. "I give up."

"Where are you going?" Gaping, I watch him stomp in the direction of the house.

"Into town for a drink," he barks over his shoulder. "I'm taking the Jeep."

Of course. This disaster of a honeymoon wouldn't be complete without a fight erupting into a major tantrum. Tucker leaves me there with the waves and moonlight. Sand between my toes. It's at least the prettiest place I've ever been abandoned.

"Lover's quarrel?"

I'm startled when Kevin and Bruce emerge from a nearby cluster of palms, approaching with a flashlight.

I bite my lip. "I think the heat's finally gotten to his head."

"Forgive us," Kevin says. "We happened to overhear you from the terrace and walked down to make sure everything was all right."

Embarrassment warms my cheeks when I realize we're in front of their property. "Sound really carries out here, huh?"

He offers a sympathetic shrug. "It really does."

"Sorry about that," I tell them. A tired sigh slips out. "Turns out we packed all our problems but not enough sunscreen."

Kevin glances over and lightly touches Bruce's massive biceps. "See if you can catch up to him? Make sure he doesn't get into any trouble."

"Would you?" I ask, relieved.

I'm not thrilled about the idea of Tucker running around a strange town alone. Especially if he's drinking. With our luck, he'd end up driving the Jeep off a pier or something. I'd go after him myself, but I get the feeling Bruce will have better luck talking him down from bad decisions. I'd probably accidentally push him to make more.

"No sweat." Bruce gives me a reassuring nod before jogging after Tucker.

KEVIN INVITES ME UP TO THEIR VILLA FOR A GLASS OF WINE TO calm the nerves while we wait for our men to return. Sitting by the pool, I find myself unloading all the pent-up stress of the last several days on this poor, unwitting man.

"It's nothing special, I guess. I'm sure all couples constantly fight about work and time and figuring out the future. And yeah, I know we're pretty fortunate to be in literal paradise complaining about people throwing money at us. I just mean, as a couple, as parents, this stuff matters, right?"

"It does," he says patiently.

"I just wish he would tell me what he was actually feeling instead of pretending like it's all good, all the time."

Kevin chuckles. "In his defense, a lot of men have trouble sharing their emotions. The entire romance self-help industry would crumble if that were not the case. Men are from Mars, remember?"

"I guess. But I didn't realize Tucker was one of them. He's always been so candid with me, or at least I thought he was." I gulp down some more wine. "I'm not a mind reader. If he doesn't feel like he's a priority for me, he needs to tell me. How am I supposed to change my behavior if I don't even realize I'm behaving badly?" A groan slips out. "And now I feel awful. You know what? I should just accept the second job offer. It's less exciting work, but the hours are much better and the money is still good. And then I can be home with Tucker and Jamie more."

Honestly, it's not like Tucker hasn't been accommodating. All through law school and the pregnancy, he never once complained about making dinner or cleaning the apartment. Changing diapers or getting up at four a.m. to rock Jamie back to sleep. Just so I wouldn't have to stop studying. And he did it all with that easy smile of his, taking it in stride.

"He's not so out of line to want me to give a little reciprocation," I admit. "So he has the space to figure out what'll make him happy, find a new business to set up. Whatever it is."

"Sounds like you two care very much about each other's wellbeing," Kevin remarks, smiling. "That's a good place to start."

"It still feels like this trip has been a total bust. At this point we're not even speaking."

"You owe it to yourselves to try salvaging something out of it. I can't deny you've had some bad luck, but it can't last forever. A few good days might be worth the bad, if you give it time." He laughs again. "You want to know what a total bust is? Let me tell you about the first vacation Bruce and I ever took. We were on the Amalfi coast and—"

His phone rings, lighting up. Since it's sitting between us on the pool deck, I clearly see Bruce's photo flashing on the screen.

Kevin wastes no time answering. "Everything—" He barely gets the word out before he's cut off by Bruce on the other end. He listens, then asks, "Where?" His eyes flick to mine.

A knot forms in my gut.

"How much?"

It tightens, stretching against my insides.

"We'll be right there." Kevin ends the call and takes a breath before setting his face in a neutral expression.

"What happened?" My fingernails dig into my palms, bracing.

"Well, here's the thing… Your husband's been arrested."

CHAPTER 30

NIGHT 5
SABRINA

AT THE JAIL IN THE MUNICIPAL COMPLEX, PEOPLE LOITER OUTSIDE on phones while taxis roll through the parking lot, unloading and picking up a steady stream of haggard, stumbling tourists. Kevin and I jump out of his Land Rover and hurry across the cracked, uneven pavement toward the front entrance. It doesn't take long to spot Bruce inside the lobby, looking frantic next to a potted palm and a rotating fan.

"What on earth happened?" Kevin asks his stricken partner.

"I'm not sure I understand." Bruce looks to me, sweat beading on his forehead. "My French sucks."

"You had one job, sweetheart. You two were barely gone an hour," Kevin chides. "How did this happen?"

"We were sitting at the bar. That spot by the marina with karaoke on Thursday nights and the strong mai tais," Bruce rushes to explain. "Short little man comes up and starts shouting at us out of nowhere. No idea who he was or where he came from. Couldn't understand a word he said. He's fuming, pointing his finger at Tucker's chest. I step in and get him to walk away. Then about twenty minutes later, two cops walk in, put Tucker in handcuffs, and walk out. I paid a guy on a scooter thirty bucks to let me hop on and follow them here."

"That's it?" I ask in dismay. "He didn't talk to anyone else? On the street? Sideswipe someone on the road? Tap a bumper?"

"Nope, not a thing. He didn't even get up to use the restroom." Bruce fans a hand over his forehead. Poor guy looks like he ran here from the other side of the island. Face red and shirt damp against his skin. "I'm so sorry, Sabrina. I don't get it."

"We'll get it sorted," Kevin assures me.

With his help translating, we find an officer to escort me back to general holding to see Tucker. He's in a cell with about twenty other men. Mostly young, drunk, and American. Plus the loud Irish guy slurring at the guard, who ignores him while reading a cooking magazine at a small desk against the wall.

When he sees me walk in, Tucker jumps to his feet and hugs the bars. "Sabrina, I swear—"

"Two minutes," the officer barks with a thick accent.

"Don't worry, I know," I tell Tucker. "Bruce filled us in."

He releases a long sigh and slumps against the bars. "Hell of a vacation, huh?" He manages a weak smile. "I'm sorry. I shouldn't have walked away in the middle of the conversation. That wasn't fair."

"It's okay. We both got worked up."

"I don't want to fight anymore." He shakes his head a few times, as if reprimanding himself. "I'm sorry I managed to make this trip worse."

"Time's up," the guard announces from the doorway.

I glance over with narrowed eyes. "That was *not* two minutes."

The uniform-clad man just smirks.

Turning back to Tucker, I give him a reassuring grin. "Baby, I didn't spend three years at Harvard Law to let my husband rot in jail on my honeymoon. Watch your woman work."

With Kevin's assistance again, we get the shift supervisor to come out front to speak with us. Apparently he's the only one around here who's fluent in English.

I'm fired up before the man even says hello, demanding to see the charging documents and whatever evidence they have against Tucker.

In return, he tries blowing us off. "You have to come back tomorrow," he says with a shrug.

"Absolutely not. You're wrongfully holding an American citizen, and I'm not leaving until I know what he's been charged with."

We go around like this a few times until I make myself enough of a pain in the ass that he stomps off to collect the paperwork just to get rid of me. The report ends up being in French, so Kevin translates it for us. Essentially, it says the man who apparently accosted Tucker and Bruce waved down the cops to accuse Tucker of shoplifting from his store and causing some vandalism and destruction of property.

"There's no way," Bruce insists. "I caught Tucker before he left the house, and we drove straight to the bar. We didn't stop anywhere else."

I frown. "And Tuck and I haven't left the house except to go to your place, the beach, or your fishing trip. We've literally been trapped inside since we stepped foot on the island. They've got the wrong guy."

Once more, I tell the officer at the reception desk that I need to speak to the shift supervisor, who is trying to make himself inconspicuous while watching us from the other side of a door behind the desk.

"Listen, you've got my client locked up back there." I narrow my eyes at the desk jockey. "If someone doesn't come talk to me, I'm going to come back here with ten more lawyers and the U.S. Ambassador, and you're going to explain why you've locked up an innocent man without evidence and refused to give him access to his attorney."

The officer reluctantly gets up. An animated conversation takes place behind the door before the shift supervisor again approaches the three of us. And again he tries to shove us off, insisting they have to hold Tucker until his arraignment in the morning.

I cock my head in challenge. "You searched him, right? Were the supposed stolen goods on his person?"

The man's silence is answer enough.

"Did you find them in the Jeep?"

Again, just sullen silence.

"No. Because your plaintiff fingered the wrong man. Now, if you'd like, I can get security camera footage from our house, GPS data from his Jeep and cellphone, plus a dozen witnesses who saw him sitting on a barstool, and then bring a lawsuit against your department for false imprisonment. Or, you can admit your mistake, let him go, and I'll leave you in peace."

After some more back and forth and about forty minutes hanging around the cramped, humid lobby, my husband finally walks out with his personal effects in a plastic bag.

"You're my hero," he says with breathless relief, shoving his wallet and phone back in his pockets before tossing the bag in the trash.

"Marrying a lawyer means never having to spend a night in jail," I tease as he wraps me in his arms.

We step outside, where Kevin and Bruce walk ahead of us toward the parking lot, as if they know we need a minute.

"I'm sorry too, by the way." I stop walking and loop my arms around Tucker's neck. "You're right. I don't want to fight either. I had no idea you felt neglected. I feel so—"

"Hey, let's talk about it at home," he cuts in, then tangles his fingers through my hair. "Right now, I just need *this*."

He brings my chin up to kiss me. His hands, meanwhile, roam to grab my ass like he hasn't seen a woman in months.

I laugh against his hungry lips. "You were only in jail for a few hours."

"I'm a changed man, baby. You don't know the things I've seen."

Then with a smack on my butt, he takes my hand and leads me to Kevin's SUV. After stopping at the marina to pick up our Jeep, we head back to the house.

"I'm sorry I stormed off," he says, watching me drop my purse on the hall table.

"I'm sorry I caused you to storm off."

"You didn't cause it." His lips quirk in a smile. "I was just being an immature ass. To be honest, I'm not even mad about anything."

"That's not true," I chide.

"I'm really not mad," he protests.

"Maybe not mad, but you're definitely frustrated. And not just with your job." I give him a pointed look. "You think I don't make you a priority."

"Sabrina—"

"And there might be some truth to that," I finish, biting my lip. "My life has always been hectic. I can't even remember a time when I wasn't juggling two or three jobs with school and chores and whatever else needed doing. And then we had a kid and"—I groan—"I love her, I really do, but she's a full-time job."

"I get it. Jamie's exhausting."

"And I just assumed that if you were ever unhappy or feeling neglected, you would tell me. I always make a point to ask—"

"I know you do," he interrupts, and it's his turn to groan. "You always ask, and I love you for it. This is on me. I'm the one who always brushes it off because I don't want to stress you out."

"Your happiness shouldn't be brushed off, Tuck."

He shrugs. "Your happiness is more important to me. Can't help it, that's just how I feel. Making you and Jamie happy is what makes me happy."

"Not always." I lift a brow. "You said you want me to make us a priority, remember? Well, that's what I'm going to do from now on. But you need to promise to be more honest about what you need, okay? Because I'm not a mind reader."

"I know." He smiles again, shamefaced. "I'll try to be better at that."

"Good. And I'll try to be better about showing you that you're my number one. Always."

"Good," he mimics.

We stand there for a moment, just grinning at each other. I guess Hope was right—sometimes couples *do* need to fight. Who knows how much deeper the roots of resentment would've dug in if everything hadn't rushed to the surface on this trip.

"So…" He tips his head. "Can we go to bed now?"

"Why are we still even down here?"

In the blink of an eye, he practically chases me up the stairs until he corners me at the foot of the bed and presses his lips to mine. His tongue slides through my parted lips while he roughly peels my clothes off.

"You're incredible," he growls.

"You're just saying that because you almost became someone's prison boyfriend."

"I'm too pretty to be locked up." Tucker kisses his way down my neck, across my shoulder. "Let's not fight anymore. Like, ever." He pauses, meeting my eyes as his hands slide down to my hips. "I hate that we came all this way just to bicker with each other."

"Me too. But we can't just ignore everything. We're going to have to figure out all the job stuff eventually. You know that."

"We will," he assures me. "But it's not something we need to figure out on this trip."

He's right. Our time together needs to be our priority. Half our honeymoon had already fallen victim to disaster. I've got no intention of spoiling the days we have left with heavy life decisions. "Let's save it for home."

He nods. "And just so you know, no matter what, I'm always gonna be there for you. I've got your back."

"I know. And I've got yours. I love you. Always."

Tucker seals his lips over mine. He gently lowers me to the bed while he pulls off his shirt and eases his pants off his hips. Then he drapes his naked body over mine, licking his lips as he props himself up on his forearms. I've never seen a sexier sight.

"You're amazing," I inform him.

A smile curves his mouth. "Don't you forget it, darlin'."

"Never."

CHAPTER 31

DAY 10
TUCKER

I wake up before Sabrina on our last morning, enjoying the weight of her head on my chest and her silky leg draped over mine. I lie there, utterly content, running my fingers through her hair and watching her sleep as the sun slowly fills the room. A while later, she yawns and stretches all the way to her toes. She looks up at me.

"Morning," she murmurs, licking the dryness from the lips.

"Last chance. We could call Dean and tell him we're staying forever."

"Tempting."

Then both our phones start buzzing with the alert that we've got two hours before we need to be at the airport.

"You can have the shower first," I tell Sabrina, kissing her forehead. "I'll make us something to eat. Hopefully Isa dropped off more of those croissants."

"Love you." She slides out of bed naked, letting me watch her saunter off to the bathroom. As long as I live, I'll never tire of that view.

As it turns out, hitting rock bottom on the sticky bench of a Caribbean jail cell was the cure to our honeymoon ails. Since Sabrina sprang me from the joint, there haven't been any stray jellyfish or irate shopkeepers. No coconut assaults or red, splotchy skin. Just clear skies and blue waters and lots of sunscreen. Finally, the vacation we'd been looking for...so of course, it's over too soon and it's time to pack out of here.

As we're getting our bags gathered by the door, our neighbors stop by to say their goodbyes. Kevin and I shake hands, while Bruce and I have a less formal exchange of back slaps and a side hug. I'm going to miss these guys. The four of us became fast friends this week, and yesterday we spent our last afternoon getting drunk and eating fresh oysters on their yacht.

"We wanted to see you off with a little something," Bruce says, handing Sabrina a bottle of the wine she'd loved from dinner that first night. "And, if you have a minute, talk a little business?"

Sabrina and I look at each other, confused.

"I thought about our conversation the other night," Kevin tells Sabrina as we invite them in. "I hope you won't mind, but I did a bit of checking up on you."

"Checking up?"

"Your Harvard transcripts. Spoke with your professors. Who had a lot to say, in fact. A complete background check, of course. We're very thorough."

I'm trying not to laugh. "And that's considered a 'bit' of checking up?"

"I don't understand." Sabrina's voice stiffens. "Who's *we*?"

"I talked it over with the partners at the firm, and we'd like you to come work with us."

Her eyes widen. "I'm sorry—what?"

"We'd like you to come work for Ellison and Kahn, my firm in Manhattan."

"You're offering me a job?" It's rare to catch Sabrina James off guard, but right now she looks like she's struggling to formulate thoughts.

Like me, Kevin is smiling at her shocked expression. "There's a spot available on my team. Representing wrongful convictions. It's challenging work, and not for the faint-hearted. But the hours are manageable, and you'd have some schedule flexibility. If you're up to it."

"I…"

I'm not sure the last time I saw Sabrina speechless.

"That's a generous offer," I speak up while she finds her voice.

"There is, of course, one catch," Kevin adds. "You would have to come to New York."

Now we're both caught off guard. I'd heard the part where he said his firm was in Manhattan, but for some stupid reason I didn't connect those dots.

Sabrina searches me for a response. Leaving Boston was never something we'd even discussed. But I know it had to be in the back of her mind. The best law firms in the world are in New York and LA, and that means there was only so far she could reach, ambition-wise, as long as she stayed in town. This would open a slew of new possibilities.

"Before you answer," Bruce pipes up, "there is one more thing. I'm looking to expand my fitness brand into brick-and-mortar. Give my online regimen a physical presence."

"Gyms?" I guess, all the while wondering how Sabrina and I possibly fit into this.

He nods. "One, to start. Prime real estate in Manhattan. All I need is a partner with a modest investment but who understands how to get a small business off the ground, market it, and make it profitable. Then, hopefully, a nationwide franchise." He grins widely. "From what I've seen, you'd make a hell of a chief operating officer."

"You can't be serious. Just like that?" I can't help but laugh, scratching at the back of my head to make sure I didn't take one of those coconuts and don't remember.

"I'm not much for business," Bruce says, shrugging. "But I know people. I like you, John Tucker. I think the two of us might do good stuff together. If you're up for the challenge."

"Wow. This is a lot to think about," Sabrina tells them, looking as dazed as I feel.

"Sorry to blindside you both, but we couldn't let you leave without catching you," Kevin explains.

"Thank you. Really," I insist. "We can't tell you how much we appreciate this."

"Can we take some time?" Sabrina asks. "We have to consider Jamie. And the bar."

"Of course." Kevin offers his hand. "Talk it over. You have our numbers."

We thank them again, then nearly collapse from the news the moment they're gone.

"Is this seriously happening?" Sabrina stares at me, eyes sparkling. It's maybe the happiest I've seen her since we left Boston.

I start laughing again, marveling at this curveball. Two curve-balls, to be exact. "I guess we were due some good luck on this damn island."

In the taxi on the way to the marina, we attempt to hash out how viable this plan might be.

"My mom would go anywhere to follow her granddaughter," I assure Sabrina when she worries about letting strangers babysit Jamie. Mom moved to Boston from Texas to be closer to us. No reason she wouldn't go to New York.

"And Kevin said the hours were manageable. Flexible." There's an excited chord in Sabrina's voice. "So we might not even need that much babysitting. I'd be able to see you guys a lot more than if I took one of the Boston jobs."

"And I wouldn't have to spend any evenings at the bar. I assume the gig with Bruce would be a daytime one."

"Wait. But Jamie starts preschool in the fall. You think getting her placed in Boston was tough, you have any idea how hard it will be in Manhattan?"

"Dean and Allie are there," I remind her. "I'd bet his family is giving money to someone, some board member, who owes them a favor. If not, we'll make it work. It's a big city."

"And we'd already have friends there," she adds, chewing on her bottom lip. "So it's not like we'd be totally alone."

"It's maybe not a terrible idea."

"Granted, those same friends tried to ruin our honeymoon with Alexander, so really, we should be discussing cutting them out of our lives, not bringing them closer into the fold."

My expression darkens. "I don't like knowing he's in there," I say, nodding toward my carry-on.

"Maybe airport security will think we're smuggling drugs inside his creepy head and confiscate him."

I snicker at her hopeful face. "Babe, if they decide we're drug mules, we'll have bigger problems to deal with than a haunted doll. Don't worry, though. We'll ship him off the moment we get home."

"It better be Dean."

"Nah. They'll expect it." I pause. "Wasn't it Garrett who left him under my pillow when they came over last Thanksgiving?"

Indignation burns in her eyes. "Jamie woke up when she heard me scream, and we couldn't get her back to sleep for hours."

I nod. "G."

She nods back. "I concur. I mean, he and Hannah are over there living their best lives. We can't allow that."

"Someone needs to knock 'em down a peg."

"Exactly."

Grinning, I sling an arm around my partner in crime. "Now, back to the topic at hand. Do we want to move to New York?"

"Ugh. I don't know, Tuck."

We're still talking it out as we board the boat to St. Maarten, until eventually Sabrina holds up a hand and says, "I vote we hold off on a decision until we're back in Boston. Let the idea sit for a while. But…man, it sure is tempting."

"Damn tempting," I agree. "But you're right, let's put a pin in it."

Right now, all I want to do is get home and see our baby girl.

PART 4
THE LEGACY

CHAPTER 32

HANNAH

THERE ARE FEW THINGS LESS DIGNIFIED THAN A LOUD PEE IN A cavernous marble restroom. Somehow, a slinky sequined gown hiked up around my boobs doesn't make this any more glamorous. It was a mad dash from the lobby of the auditorium to this bathroom stall. The entire twenty minutes on the red carpet standing between Garrett and Logan, a smile plastered on my face against shouting reporters and camera flashes, was an agonizing exercise in endurance while every muscle in my body clenched in desperation. I knew that bottle of water in the limo was a bad idea. Lately, I even look at liquid and I've got to pee like a racehorse.

The blogs and articles said this was coming, but I thought, come on, how bad could it be?

The answer: bad.

Awful.

Humiliatingly inconvenient.

Pregnancy blows.

The last place I want to be right now is this exclusive hotel in downtown Boston, but I tell myself to suck it up. Tonight's a big moment for Garrett's career, and I can't let anything dampen the celebration.

Which is just another one of the countless excuses I've been spoon-feeding myself for the last eight weeks.

First, I hadn't wanted to take the test because it was our best friends' wedding weekend. Then I took the test and it was positive, but I certainly couldn't tell Garrett and distract him at such a pivotal moment at the end of the regular season. Couldn't break the news to him while the team was concentrating on the playoffs. Then they busted out in the first round, and Garrett was so crushed, it didn't seem like the right time to announce he better spend the off-season painting a nursery.

I'm going to tell him tonight, though. After we get home, when he's got a few drinks in him and the stars are still shining in his eyes. I'll ease him into it gently.

"Can you believe it's a cash bar?" Two pairs of stiletto heels clack across the shiny floor past my stall and stop at the sinks. "LeBron's wife doesn't put up with this shit."

"LeBron's wife married a basketball player."

"I thought there'd at least be a gift bag."

"Ha! It'd have a can of Molson Ice and a gift certificate to Applebee's."

I swallow a laugh. Women who date or marry into the NHL expecting they'll be rolling around South Beach with Gisele and Victoria Beckham tend to get a rude awakening. The hockey scene is an acquired taste.

Tonight is the NHL Honors, an awards ceremony recognizing achievements in the past season. While it's not exactly the ESPYs, it's a big deal that Garrett is taking home an award for Goal of the Year. This man never stops working to improve his game. Every single day, he puts his body under incredible stress. Pushes himself past the mental barriers that have held him back. The least I can do to watch his dreams come true is suffer one night in a fancy dress and pretend everything's normal. And with Grace in Paris visiting her mom for the summer, I'm pulling double duty as the arm candy.

I just can't eat or drink anything for the rest of the night if I don't want to be running for the toilet every ten minutes.

"Did you see Garrett Graham shaved his beard?" one of the women says while I'm fixing my dress. "He cleans up nice."

He sure does. The team got on some superstition kick about not shaving when they were on a winning streak to clinch the playoffs. Garrett looks hot with some scruff, but this went beyond that. He wouldn't even allow himself to keep the damn thing tidy. It was scraggly and unkempt, and it took all my self-restraint not to mount him in the middle of the night and go at him with a pair of clippers. I love that man, but the beard was nearly the end of us. If I ever see that thing again, I'm lighting it on fire.

"Have you seen his dad? The genes in that family are ridiculous."

"Phil Graham's here?"

"Yeah. Saw him on the red carpet. He's giving out the Lifetime Achievement award."

A dreamy sigh. "I'd go there. Ride the little blue pill jackhammer all the way to Orgasm Town."

"You're demented."

"You know that lucky bitch Garrett showed up with has thought about it. I would."

I bite back a sudden surge of vomit as I exit the stall. I stand beside the two dark-haired women at the sink to wash my hands. I think they're around my age, but one is wearing such heavy makeup, it ages her greatly. The other is a fresh-faced type in a gorgeous red dress.

"Might get a little crowded in that bed," I say lightly. "I saw her show up with the other one too."

"Who?"

"John Logan," I tell them, meeting their gazes in the mirror. "We go way back."

As recognition dawns on their faces, they stare at me with wide headlight eyes.

"Lucky Bitch," I say by way of an introduction. "Nice to meet you."

"Oh my God, this is so embarrassing," one of them blurts out. "Sorry about that."

"I love your dress," the other says meekly, her version of an olive branch.

I shrug. "No worries. You're right, Garrett cleans up nice."

"How long have you been dating?" Red Dress asks.

"Since junior year of college."

Their eyes not-so-discreetly drop to my left hand.

"Not married," I confirm. "Just living together in sin."

Red Dress giggles. "Sinning with Garrett Graham. Not a bad way to live."

Not a bad life, indeed.

When I'm done, I dry my hands and leave the bathroom with a wave. I'm not at all bothered at overhearing them gush over my boyfriend. Truth is, I'm more concerned about the revelation that Garrett's father is in attendance. No one told us he would be. If Garrett runs into Phil unprepared, it'll get ugly.

An usher helps me find my seat where Garrett and Logan are near the end of the row. I squeeze in between the guys, who are discussing Logan's upcoming trip to Paris. He's leaving in a couple of weeks and will be gone for a month. Lucky Grace. I don't know how Logan managed to weasel out of a month's worth of off-season team activities. Garrett hates doing that stuff.

"I can't wait to see the ol' ball and chain," Logan says.

I give him a saccharine smile. "I'm telling Grace you called her that."

He pales. "God, please don't."

Next to me, Garrett is now visibly sulking. "I still can't believe you got married without me," he accuses his best friend.

I fight a laugh. "It's not a team sport, sweetie."

He ignores me. "I was supposed to be your best man." He leans past me to glare at Logan. "You realize this means when Wellsy and I have a wedding, you're not best man number one anymore. I'm giving it to Dean. Dean, Tucker, *then* you."

Logan leans forward too. "No, you're not. It's going to be me first."

Garrett sighs. "It's going to be you first."

"You two want to get a room?" I ask as they practically hang over me, making googly eyes at each other.

"Shhh, Wellsy," Logan chides, as if *I'm* the obnoxious one. "It's starting."

Sure enough, the house lights dim. A moment later, a presentation begins playing on stage, a highlight reel of the last season. I take the opportunity to shift closer to Garrett's broad body, bringing my lips to his ear.

"Did you know your dad was going to be here?" I whisper.

His expression falls flat. The same thin lips and dead eyes I see every time he's forced to play nice with that man at some press function. As much as I hate ruining his good mood, it'll be worse if I don't alert him.

"I had no idea."

"I guess he's presenting an award?"

"Landon should've warned me," he mutters, referring to his agent.

His hand tightens around mine, and I know he's battling all his simmering rage. Nothing flips his switch faster, casts a darkness over him, than having to be around his father.

Sympathy mingles with the lingering nausea in my belly. Tonight was supposed to be another big milestone in Garrett's career, a proud moment for him. Instead, he'll spend it being forced to smile and pose for the cameras with the man who used to beat the hell out of him.

CHAPTER 33

GARRETT

WE CAN'T GET TO THE BAR FAST ENOUGH ONCE THE SHOW ENDS and we're all ushered into a ballroom for the after-party. My girl doesn't usually like me to drink at these things, for fear I'll make an ass of myself to some reporter. Tonight, she takes the award out of my hand and replaces it with a glass of scotch. Maybe she hopes it'll distract me. Or dull my instincts. I doubt it, though. I'm always on high alert when my father is around, wholly aware of his proximity. I spotted him the moment we walked in and have tracked him across the room as he works his way through the pop of camera flashes.

"You don't have to do this," Hannah says, eyeing me cautiously over the rim of her glass of sparkling water. Guess she figures one of us better be sober if I end up in jail tonight. "We can skip this."

"Landon would have a fit if I didn't play ball."

My sports agent would be here pimping me out to the press and working me around the room if he hadn't come down with food poisoning last night. Which I guess is what I pay him for, even if this is the part of the business I would rather live without.

"Is that why he didn't warn you Phil was here?"

I'd wasted no time shooting an angry text to my agent the second the ceremony was over. "He claims he had no idea. Apparently Viktor Ivanov bailed at the last minute, so they swapped in Phil."

My gaze flicks toward him again. He's chatting up the team owner from Dallas, dropping that phony laugh of his.

"We won't stay long," I tell Hannah, rubbing the small of her back with my thumb.

Touching her keeps the more destructive thoughts out of my head. She looks so hot tonight in that long silver dress that clings to all the right places. If I wasn't so tense right now and so hypervigilant of my father's presence, I'd be trying to coax her somewhere private and sliding my hand beneath that slinky fabric. Make her come in a coat closet or go down on her in a supply room somewhere.

"I'll be right here," she promises.

I don't doubt it. Hannah Wells is my rock. I'm not one to brag, but—okay, fine, I'm absolutely one to brag. But I'm pretty sure Wellsy and I have the healthiest relationship of any couple ever. After four years together, it's undeniable: we're simply the best. Our communication skills are top-notch. The sex is fucking unreal. When we first hooked up in college, I never in a million years imagined we'd fall in love, or that we'd eventually move in together, build a life together. Yet here we are.

Don't get me wrong, we're not perfect. We bicker often, but, I mean, that's because she's a stubborn asshole. Though if you ask her, it's because I—supposedly—always need to have the last word. Which is something a stubborn asshole would say.

I stifle a curse when Phil suddenly looks my way and our eyes meet through the crowd.

My fingers tighten over Hannah's, squeezing hard.

"You okay?" she asks.

"Nope," I answer cheerfully.

Getting sucked into Phil's orbit is like being pulled underwater by the vortex of a sinking ship. Or dragged out to sea by a rip current.

Fighting against the inevitable and inescapable force will only lead to exhaustion and kill you faster.

The only way out is through.

"Son," he booms, yanking me into a handshake with a flock of owners and a couple of reporters in tow. He spares a curt nod of greeting for Hannah before turning back to me. Those shark teeth bare in a fake smile. "You remember Don and the boys." The boys, he calls them. A hundred billion net worth. Owners of three of the top five most valuable clubs in the league. "Come get a picture."

"Hell of a season," one of the owners tells me. He's posing for the camera while my dad positions me in the middle of the group and from nowhere shoves my award in my hands while I bite the inside of my cheek.

"Team high record for points and assists in the modern era." The way Phil says it, you'd think he was the one on the ice.

But then, that's always been his problem. The man simply can't let the old days go. Wasn't enough to be beloved in Boston for his time on the ice, he has to live through me too.

Being the son of a legend is a real bitch.

Especially when that legend used to knock you around. When that legend tormented your mother and treated the two of you like trophies he could put on and pull off the shelf whenever he felt like it. If you cracked open the man's chest, you'd find a lump of coal instead of a heart. His soul is black tar.

"Going after your old man's record next year?" another owner asks. He chuckles before tossing back a glass of champagne.

"We'll see," I say, filling my mouth with scotch while keeping one eye on Hannah to avoid looking at Phil.

It's torture. This whole stupid dance. Pretending the old man and I don't despise each other. Letting him play the proud father like I don't still have the scars from his "coaching." Bowing to appearances because no one wants to hear the truth: that Phil Graham was an abusive son of a bitch while the entire sport was throwing flowers at his feet.

Thankfully, my best friend and teammate notices our little group from the bar. Reading the urgency on my face, John Logan makes his way toward us.

"Hey, man," he says with a slightly tipsy grin, swinging a bottle of beer at his side while he inserts himself between us and the camera. "You remember Redhead Fred, right? From the combine. I just ran into him by the crab puffs. Come say hi."

"Right. Fred." I bite back a laugh at how bad he is at subtlety. "Man, I haven't seen him in ages."

I reach for Hannah's hand and slip my way out from between Phil and the owners. Much to his dismay.

"If you'll excuse me," I say politely, and then we get as far away as possible and practically hide behind the decorative potted plants on the other side of the room.

"I'm proud of you," Hannah says, taking the award from my hands and replacing it with a fresh glass of scotch. "Part of me expected you to crack your dad over the head with this thing."

I grin wryly. "Give me a little credit. I'm not a total barbarian."

"Dude, that was awkward," Logan says.

"All good. Thanks for the rescue. You did me a solid."

"Yeah, well, you can make it up to me on the green this weekend. The team doc said I shouldn't carry anything heavy with my back spasms acting up."

I snort. Back spasms, my ass. "I'm not carrying your clubs," I tell him. "That's what rookies are for."

"Please tell me someone is taping this." Hannah laughs, poking me in the ribs. "Last time you tried to golf, we had to pay for that guy's windshield, remember?"

"Not my fault his damned car was in the way of the hole."

Her green eyes fill with exasperation. "His car was where it was supposed to be—in the parking lot. The hole was right in front of your face."

"That's what she said," drawls Logan, wiggling his eyebrows.

"Ew." She smacks his arm.

"Logan hit a tree last time," I tattle to take the heat off myself. "It had a bird's nest in it, and the thing toppled to the grass and all the eggs broke."

He glares at me. "Wow. What part of 'we take this to the grave' do you not understand?"

"You killed a bunch of unborn birds?" Hannah looks horrified.

"Not on purpose," Logan says defensively. To me, he mutters, "Snitches get stitches, G. Don't you forget that."

I roll my eyes. "Whatcha gonna do? Beat me up at the tournament? In front of all the Make-A-Wish kids?"

Although I'm not sure we're playing for Make-A-Wish this time. I think it might be an animal rescue event. Every year, the franchise sets up this charity golf tournament, where big donors pay to play a round of golf with members of the team. Or in the case of some of us, pay to watch us launch balls into trees and parking lots.

"Aw, damn. Who let these dirtbags in here?"

We glance over in time to see Jake Connelly squeeze through the crowd and saunter toward us. He's wearing a navy-blue suit, dark hair slicked away from his clean-shaven face. Like me, he'd ditched the beard after getting knocked out of the playoffs.

Connelly just finished his rookie year with Edmonton, who were three seconds away from making it to the Stanley Cup finals. Literally three seconds. Their series against Ottawa was tied 3-3 and they were up by a goal in Game 7…when in the last three seconds of the game, a Senator scored a fluke goal that every sports network will be replaying for years to come. Damn puck bounced off a guy's ass cheek and sailed past Edmonton's unsuspecting goalie. Ottawa went to win the series in OT, and that's all she wrote.

"Just in time." Logan drains his beer and tries handing the empty to Jake. "Run along and get me a refill, will ya, Rook?"

"Yeah, I would." Connelly holds up his Rookie of the Year award and his own beer bottle. "Hands are kinda full."

"Look at this kid," I say, shaking my head. "Already forgetting where he comes from."

Beside me, Hannah gets those gooey starry eyes she dons every time she's in Connelly's vicinity. And I'm sure that when he walks away, she'll do her usual shtick of poking me in the arm and whispering, "He's so handsome."

I personally don't get it. I mean, he's a good-looking dude, for sure. But has Wellsy seen who she's dating?

"Hey, Jake." Hannah steps forward to give him a hug. "Congratulations. Looks like Edmonton is working out for you."

"Thanks." He shrugs modestly. "Yeah, can't complain."

"Proud of you," I say sincerely. I love seeing fellow players have success entering the league.

"I can't believe you said that to a former Harvard man," Logan tells me, blue eyes gleaming with accusation. He glances back at Jake and arches an eyebrow. "Where's Coach's daughter? She break your heart yet?"

"Oh, shit. That's right." This idiot went and hooked up with Coach Jensen's daughter Brenna like he had a fucking death wish. "You two still together?"

"Yeah, we're good."

I look around. "She here?" I've only met Brenna a couple of times, but she seems cool.

Connelly shakes his head. "She actually flew in from Vienna early this morning just to come to this shindig. She was doing a whole European tour thing with her friend Summer—oh, you know her. Di Laurentis's sister." He shrugs. "Anyway, yeah. She was exhausted, so she went back to the room to get some sleep."

"Let me give you some advice," Hannah says, grinning at him. "When your girlfriend flies in from another continent to see you get an award and says she wants to go to bed early, you go with her."

He looks to me and Logan. We nod solemnly at him. Not going

to find me arguing with Wellsy on this one. I'm still hoping for some congratulations sex when we get home.

"All right then," Jake says, draining his beer and passing it off to Logan. "Guess I'll catch up with you guys later. And congrats," he tells me. He points to my award. "Don't get too comfortable, old man. I'm coming for that thing next year."

"See you on the ice, kiddo."

"He's so handsome," Hannah breathes as he walks away.

"Keep it in your pants," I chide.

No sooner does Connelly leave than Logan taps me on the shoulder to point out the team's GM strutting toward us with Phil. "Got it handled if you want to sneak off," he offers like the ride-or-die he is.

"Call it a night?" I ask my girlfriend.

She gives a firm nod. "Let's get the hell out of here."

Before they can corner us, we slip out the side door and make our escape.

CHAPTER 34

GARRETT

At home later, I still can't release the tension in my shoulders. My chest is tight, like I can't take a deep breath, and there's a kink in my neck I can't shake. I try to forget about Phil as Hannah and I get ready for bed, but there's something else in the room with us that I can't quite discern. Hannah washes her face and brushes her teeth, but it's like she's watching me out of the corner of her eye. Her forehead is creased in that way it gets when she has something on her mind.

"What?" I say, spitting out my mouthwash at the sink.

She eyes my reflection in the mirror. "I didn't say anything."

"I can hear you thinking."

"I'm not."

"You look like you want to tell me something."

"No. I swear."

"Just spit it out."

"I don't know what you're talking about."

For fuck's sake.

"Whatever." If she's going to be difficult, I don't have the energy to fight about it tonight. I wipe my face with a soft towel and then wander into the master bedroom of our brownstone.

I get in bed, staring at the ceiling until Hannah slides in beside me and shuts off the light. She rolls onto her side and places her hand on my bare chest.

"Sorry," she says softly. "I didn't mean to act weird. I was just thinking about you and your dad. I know tonight was difficult for you, but for what it's worth, I thought you handled yourself well."

I pull her toward me, my hand playing with the hem of her thin tank top. "I swear I want to take a swing at him every time he puts his arm around me with that cheesy grin. He's such a hypocrite. And they all love him."

She goes silent for a moment.

"What?" I push.

"I don't know…just thinking. Maybe it's time to have that talk."

"What talk?"

"Tell your father how you feel. That you'd rather he keep his distance."

I can't help but snort out a laugh. "How I feel about anything is irrelevant, as far as he's concerned. It's all about appearances."

"You could try. If you don't put down some boundaries for yourself—"

"Let it go." It comes out more forceful than I intend, and I feel Hannah recoil. I draw her closer, quickly brushing my lips over her soft hair. "I'm sorry. Didn't mean to snap. Trust me when I say if I thought talking to him would help, I would've done it a long time ago."

"No, I get it."

"He doesn't care what I have to say. That's why he traps me like that, corners me at parties with plenty of witnesses. He knows if I snub him, it becomes a story. A story that embarrasses me as much as him when it shows up in the press the next morning."

Hannah grumbles with indignation. "I just hate seeing how much he gets to you. He shouldn't get to have that power."

"I know, babe." I cling to her, because having her warm body curled against mine does a lot to chase the uglier thoughts out of my head. "And I really do appreciate you being there for me tonight. I couldn't have gotten through it without you."

"I've always got your back." She kisses my jaw then settles back into my arms.

Minutes later, an hour, I don't know, I'm still awake. Still staring at the dark ceiling and grinding my teeth as it all plays back in my mind. How smug he is, parading me around for his friends. Not an ounce of shame for what he did to me. To my mom. Not the smallest drop of remorse. What kind of man can be such a shameless bastard?

"Can't sleep?" Hannah whispers. I don't know what wakes her up, or if she ever fell asleep.

"I'm fine," I lie, because there's no sense keeping us both up all night.

She doesn't listen, though. Never does, this stubborn, beautiful woman of mine.

Instead, her fingers trace the lines of my chest and down my abdomen. My muscles clench at the teasing sensation. I grip her tighter around the waist when her hand pushes my plaid pajama pants down to stroke me.

I'm hard the second she touches me.

"You don't have to," I whisper.

"That's cute."

"Not like I'm saying not to." I smirk in the dark. It's like when a friend offers to pick up the tab at dinner. It's polite to refuse the first time.

Hannah pushes the covers back and drags her tongue up my shaft. I grip the sheets, biting my lip at the feel of her mouth on me. No sense arguing with her once she's got her mind made up, after all.

When she reaches the tip, she presses an open-mouthed kiss on it and I nearly explode right then. I breathe in through my nose and silently order my dick to cooperate.

"Go slow," I tell her. "I won't last otherwise."

"Figured." And then her tongue comes out to gently circle the head of my cock. Slow and deliberate. A lazy, torturous exploration. I feel the tension ease from my shoulders. All other thoughts evaporate while I watch the outline of her going down on me.

With her ass in the air beside me, I squeeze a handful, which makes her work me a little quicker. Her delicate fingers glide up my shaft with each upstroke, then her warm, wet mouth slides down hungrily. Oh fuck. She knows I can't last long this way. Hannah's too damn good at this.

"Gonna come," I choke out.

I feel her smiling around my dick, and that's the trigger. I go off like a rocket, groaning from the rush of pleasure. She releases me from her mouth and strokes me through the release, as every muscle contracts and the knot in my gut unravels.

I'm out of breath and wiped out when she cleans me off and comes back to bed.

She cuddles up beside me and presses a kiss to my lips. "Better?"

I'm not sure I manage a response before I fall asleep.

I'VE STILL GOT A HEADACHE FROM LAST NIGHT AND MY PHONE'S blowing up when I throw myself on the couch with a bowl of cereal in the morning. Hannah was gone by the time I woke up. Lately she's been pulling ten- to twelve-hour shifts at the studio producing an album with some new rapper.

> Tucker: Had a virtual watch party for your big night. We drank every time the camera cut to you picking your nose.
> Dean: Those were some tight pants you were sporting last night. Do they come in men's sizes?

I roll my eyes at the messages popping up in the group chat. My friends are dicks. In response, I send them a photo Logan took last night, the one of me flipping him off while holding my award in one hand and a fifth of some expensive bourbon he stole from the bar in the other.

> Dean: Seriously, tho. Congrats.
>
> Tucker: Proud of you.
>
> Me: Thanks, assholes. Really appreciate it.
>
> Logan: How come nobody's congratulating me?
>
> Dean: Did you win an award?
>
> Dean: Yeah, didn't think so.
>
> Tucker: Better luck next year.
>
> Logan: Speaking of my marriage—
>
> Dean: Not a single person was speaking about that!
>
> Tucker: Nobody.
>
> Logan: Don't lie. You were all thinking about it.
>
> Me: We were not.
>
> Tucker: At all.
>
> Logan: We're debating whether this Paris trip is considered a honeymoon. I say yes, because, um, Europe. That's honeymoon central. But Grace says it's not because she was already planning on going to see her mom before we impulsively decided to tie the knot. But it's a honeymoon, right?
>
> Dean: I'll defer to Tuck on this one.
>
> Tucker: Not a honeymoon. Plan something else, you unoriginal bastard.
>
> Logan: Uh-huh because a beach vacay is so original.
>
> Tucker: We almost died in a plane crash and then had a burial at sea for a haunted doll. Try and beat that.
>
> Dean: You asshole. I thought Sabrina was joking. Did you really throw Alexander in the ocean??
>
> Tucker: Sure did.

He punctuates that with a smiley face and the preaching hands emoji.

Wow. I wholly approve of someone finally taking the initiative to do what we've all wanted to do. Just didn't expect it to be Tucker. I thought Logan would snap first. Or maybe Allie. But Tuck for the win.

> Logan: Nice. GRTHR
> Dean: Wtf man. Why you always gotta do that?
> Me: Wait, I think I got this.

I stare at the screen, my brain working to decode Logan's acronym. He and I have a cosmic mental connection. Finally, I hazard a guess.

> Me: Good riddance to horrible rubbish?
> Logan: Close!!! Haunted rubbish.
> Tucker: Gotta go. It's Daddy & Me day at the indoor playground.
> Dean: Lame.

I drop my phone next to my empty cereal bowl and collapse on the couch. With the post-season over, I've got nothing better to do than lie in front of the TV. I'm halfway through the original *Jurassic Park* trilogy when my agent calls.

"Hey, man. What's up?"

"Don't shoot the messenger," Landon starts, his normally brash tone replaced by a timid one.

"What happened?" A dozen scenarios flash through my head. I've been traded. The team is moving. We've been sold. Coach was fired.

"I need you to remember I'm obliged to bring you these offers."

"Just spit it out."

"I got a call from a producer at ESPN for that show *The Legacy*," he says.

"That the one where they're in somebody's living room and the guy's always crying?"

"Uh, yeah. That's the one."

"All right. So they want to have me on? I'm not about to bare my soul in front of a fireplace, but—"

"Here's the thing," Landon cuts me off. Then he doesn't keep going.

I sit up and run a hand through my messy hair. This is the sort of opportunity that could raise the profile of my brand as an athlete, as Landon always put it. It's the kind of thing we hoped would come along after the NHL Honors. Yet something's off.

"Dude, what?" I demand. "You're worrying me."

"They want you and your dad."

"Fuck off." I bark out a humorless laugh.

"Hang on. Hear me out."

Landon starts talking fast, explaining how they want some sort of then-and-now, father-son story comparing our careers. Which even if I didn't hate the man sounds like a stupid idea. It's hard enough growing up in a parent's shadow. Getting compared to them our entire career isn't a trope a son wants to play into.

"The angle they're going for is a 'where you came from and where you're headed' story. Throw some old family photos up there. You as a kid. On the pond where your dad taught you to skate. Then breaking records as a pro. That type of thing. It's a two-hour segment."

"Yeah, hell no."

"Look, I get it," he says with some sympathy. "You know I get it, G."

Landon knows all about my history with Phil Graham, although I didn't disclose it right out of the gate. It got complicated dodging these sorts of requests after I signed my rookie contract, and eventually I had to let him in on the sordid family secrets. Needless to say, the conversation was riddled with awkwardness. It was so damn embarrassing, confessing to my agent that my dad used to beat me. Fucking brutal.

Hannah always says I shouldn't be ashamed of it, that it wasn't my fault, I couldn't have stopped it, blah fucking blah. I love that woman to death, but chicks have a bad habit of turning everything into therapy speak. I know it wasn't my fault, and I know I couldn't have stopped it—at least not until I hit puberty and grew bigger than him. Make no mistake, I stopped the hell out of it after that. But it took years to work through all those feelings of shame, all of which come spiraling to the surface each time I have to tell a new person about my history.

I'm tired of reliving it.

My refusal to do this show shouldn't come as a surprise to Landon, so I wish he'd just take it upon himself to keep this stuff off my plate.

"With that said," he continues, "I do think you need to consider how it's going to look if you say no."

"I don't care how it looks. That's your job." I clench my jaw. "Smiling for a few pictures is one thing. I'll behave myself and play nice. But I'm not getting in front of some reporter and a TV camera and sitting next to that man for hours, pretending he isn't a monster."

"I hear you—"

"Swear to God, Landon. The first time he brings up my mother in the interview, I'd end up slugging him. And then you'd have that to deal with. So why don't you do one of your little risk assessments and decide which fallout will be worse. Saying no, or beating the shit out of him on TV. Take your pick."

"Okay. All right. I'll let them know we have to pass. Tell them you're not doing press right now. I'll think of something."

After I hang up, my temples are throbbing even harder. I reach up to rub them and utter a string of silent expletives. Somehow, I know this is all my dad's doing. I bet he pitched this idea to the network himself. Or if he didn't, then he fucking willed the offer into existence. He does it on purpose. To mess with me. To remind me he's always there, lurking, and always will be.

And it's working.

CHAPTER 35

HANNAH

I'VE GOT ABOUT A DOZEN PEOPLE IN MY CONTROL ROOM BICKERING about lyrics while a six-foot-seven dude named Gumby stands over my shoulder.

"You know what all those buttons do?" he asks, watching me do a rough mix of the verse Yves St. Germain just laid down.

"Nope," I tell him as I punch up the sample track of the violins Nice really liked. "Not a clue."

"Man, stop pestering the lady," Patch tells him. He leans back in the rolling chair beside me, teetering on the edge of falling over. "She don't be trying to tell you how to dress like your mama put your school clothes on layaway in the nineties."

"Yo, for real, though," Gumby says. He reaches for one of the faders, and I smack his hand away from my board. "That's a lot of buttons. How you even learn to do all this?"

Narrowing my eyes, I whisper, "Don't tell anybody, but I don't even work here."

He snorts at me, shaking his head with a smile.

"Y'all get away from her and let the woman do her thing." Nice, as Yves insists I call him, comes back into the control room from a short break. His rapper name is YSG, but his nickname growing up was "Nice." Because he was a nice kid. It's disgustingly wholesome and I love it.

"All good," I say. "Come give this a listen."

We've been at it since about seven this morning. The kid's only nineteen, but he's got a serious work ethic. It's a big part of the reason we get along so well. Both of us would rather be in the studio, tinkering and experimenting, than just about anywhere else.

I play back what we've put down so far on this latest track. His entourage goes silent while they listen, bobbing their heads to the beat. Then those violins come in and Nice whistles, a huge grin spreading across his face.

"Yeah, Hannah. That's sick right there."

"What if you lay down some ad libs under it?" I suggest. "Thicken it up a little."

"I like that. Let's try it." Then he pulls out a box from the pocket of his bright-yellow jacket. "Got you a little something, by the way. For all your hard work."

I can't help but laugh. "I told you to stop giving me gifts!"

This kid gets me "a little something" just about every time I see him. Nice signed a massive recording contract after his single went viral last year. Now he throws money around exactly the way a teenager does when he's got more than he knows what to do with.

"But I gotta let you know I appreciate you." His smile is so earnest, I melt in the face of it.

"Dude, you need to get yourself a financial adviser," I advise. "Put some of that money away for when you're older."

"I keep telling my man to get some of that cryptocurrency," Gumby says.

"Nah, bruh. You know that shit uses as much electricity as it takes to power a whole country for a year?" Nice says gravely. "Screw that."

Inside my box is a beautiful watch. "This is gorgeous," I tell him. "But it's way too expensive. I really shouldn't."

"But you don't want to insult me, so you will," he says, beaming. "It's made from recycled ocean plastic. They only produced twenty of these. Elon Musk has three." Then he pushes up the sleeve of his jacket to show he's wearing four of them. Two on each wrist. Take that, Musk. "They're funding the boat that's pulling the floating garbage island out of the Pacific."

I shake my head in astonishment. "It's amazing. Thank you."

As far as rappers go, Nice is unique. A lot of his lyrics talk about climate change and conservation. Different causes he's passionate about. He's legitimately one of the cleverest teenagers I've ever met, which comes through in his music and the way he puts rhymes together.

"Hey, y'all know Hannah's boyfriend won a hockey award last night?" he says to his friends, who are all crammed on the leather couch with their phones out. The kid travels with an entourage.

"Hockey?" Gumby says, glancing up. "Dump him. I can set ya up with my boy on the Celtics."

"Thank you, but I'm good."

"How'd it go?" Nice asks.

"It was great. I'm pretty proud of him." I grin. "Even if his ego is about to become unbearable."

"You tell him I said congrats. And not to get feeling himself too much."

Which is a trip coming from Nice. Not that he's full of himself, but he's got a lot of diva in him. Some people were just born to be superstars.

We get back to recording, but it isn't long before I'm not feeling quite right. I shift in my chair. It's getting hot in here, and there's a sour taste in my mouth. Oh no. No, no, no. Not here, damn it. But there's no stopping it. In the middle of Nice's chorus, I blurt out, "Gotta pee!" and then dive off my chair. I sprint out of the room, leaving an embarrassing wave of laughter in my wake and Patch remarking, "Lord, these itty-bitty lady bladders, bruh."

Luckily there's a restroom less than five yards away. I stand over the toilet for a few minutes, breathing hard, gulping through the waves of nausea. But nothing comes up. It's been this way for days, and I've had about all the fun I can stand.

After I've washed my hands and dabbed some cold water on my face, I check my phone to see I have a bunch of missed texts.

> **Allie:** Don't leave me hanging. Did you do it??

I sigh. Allie is my best friend and I love her to death, but she's starting to drive me nuts. Ever since I told her I was pregnant, she's been on me to talk to Garrett. Not that it's a ludicrous course of action or anything. I mean, of course I need to tell the father of this baby that he's, well, the father of this baby. But I'm starting to feel the pressure and that just makes me queasier.

> **Me:** No. We ran into his dad at the awards ceremony. Wasn't a good time.

Instead of texting back, she immediately calls me.

I answer with, "Hey. I'm still at the studio so I can't talk for long."

"Oh, don't worry, this won't take long." Her tone becomes part scolding, part pity. "Han-Han. When you start eating pickles and a whole red velvet cake on the couch at two in the morning, he's going to figure it out. You have to tell him."

"Ugh, don't mention food." The thought gets my stomach churning again. "I'm currently in the bathroom trying not to puke."

"Uh-huh. See? Not drinking and going to the bathroom every ten minutes to pee or vomit is something else he's going to notice eventually."

"I know I need to tell him. But it seems like every time I try, there's some reason not to."

"And there always will be if you want there to be."

"Allie."

"I'm just saying. Maybe you need to ask yourself if you're stalling for some reason."

"What do you mean, for 'some' reason? Of course I'm stalling and I know exactly why." Hysterical laughter bubbles in my throat. "I mean, gee, it's not like this is going to completely change our lives forever or anything. Why would that be scary?"

Garrett and I haven't even discussed kids in any serious way. Getting pregnant and springing it on him seems like a hell of a way to broach the subject. How could it not feel like a trap?

"Can I ask?" she says hesitantly. "Do you want to keep it?"

My teeth dig into my bottom lip. That's the thing. The big question. The one that keeps me up at night staring at Garrett while he sleeps and trying to imagine what our life would look like a year from now.

"In a perfect world, at the right time? Sure," I admit, a slight trembling to my voice. "I always thought having a couple of kids would be nice. A boy and a girl." Growing up as an only child, I envied my friends who had siblings. It seemed like so much fun having another kid around.

"But?" Allie prompts when I don't go on.

"But the realities of being a hockey family don't make it easy. He's on the road for months out of the year, which basically means I'd be taking care of a baby by myself. That's not exactly ideal."

Even without a kid, it's a tough lifestyle. Between pre- and post-season, the hockey life is travel, long hours, and exhaustion. By the time Garrett walks through the door, he barely has the energy to put down a meal before he collapses into bed. There's hardly enough time for us, much less a child. A crying newborn on top of that?

Panic starts crawling up my throat. I swallow hard, and my voice shakes when I speak again. "I can't do this by myself, Allie."

"Aw, babe." Her sigh echoes over the line. "It sucks your family doesn't live closer. Give you some help, at least."

"That'd be great, but there's no way."

My parents are stuck in a second mortgage in the crappy small town in Indiana where I grew up. Buried under a mountain of debt that'll probably keep them in that miserable place for the rest of their lives.

"Look. Whatever happens," Allie tells me, "I'm here for you. Anything you need. All you have to do is call, and I'll be on the next flight or train to Boston. I'll hitchhike if I need to."

"I know and I love you for it. Thank you." I blink through my stinging eyes. "I have to go back to work now."

After I end the call, I walk back to the mirror to make sure I don't look like I've been crying. In my reflection I see tired green eyes and pale cheeks and a look of pure terror.

When it comes down to it, I'm scared. Of raising this kid by myself. Of the overwhelming responsibility. Of what Garrett will say when I finally find the right way to tell him. Because I am going to tell him. I just have to find the words.

For the time being, though, there are more pressing issues. Like the exorbitant rate Nice is paying for studio time that is like setting money on fire every minute I'm having an existential meltdown in the bathroom.

We spend the next several hours in the studio banging out a few more songs. When Nice and I get into a rhythm, we work quick. The flow is there, that free creative energy that makes the time pass in a blink. Until suddenly we do blink, and discover that his friends are all passed out on the couch and the night janitor is wandering in to empty the trash cans.

We finally call it quits for the night. I gather up my things and accept Patch's offer to walk me to my car. Can't be too safe these days.

"G'nite, Hannah baby. Lock your door." Patch taps the window frame of my SUV before lumbering back to the building.

I'm just pulling out of the lot when I get a call from my agent. Elise usually calls about this time every evening to check on our progress. She's got the record label calling her every ten minutes wanting to make sure their money isn't being wasted in the studio.

"Are you holding anything hot?" she asks instead of a hello.

"Huh? Like did we write anything good tonight?"

"No, are you literally holding something hot in your hands right now? Coffee? Tea? If so, put it down," she orders.

I experience a jolt of alarm. "I'm driving home. What's wrong?"

"Nothing, if you like money." Elise sounds too pleased with herself, which makes me nervous.

"I like money," I say, albeit warily.

"Good. Because the song you wrote for Delilah took a sledge-hammer to the charts last quarter and I've just sent you an obscene check. You're welcome."

"How obscene is obscene?"

"It's a surprise. Congratulations, Hannah. This is what making it feels like."

I'm hesitant to guess at the number. The pop star I'd written the song for had been all over my social media for months, and I knew the streams and downloads of the single had done well. Which meant the royalty would be pretty nice. But I make it a habit not to pay too much attention to those things. Better to concentrate on the work ahead than obsess about the last gig. The second we get too far up our own asses, the music suffers.

The truth is, this industry is fickle. What's hot today is hot garbage tomorrow. You just have to rack up the credits and enjoy the ride while it lasts.

AT HOME, I CAN'T WAIT TO SHARE THE NEWS WITH GARRETT— and then find a way to slip a baby into the conversation—but when I walk in the door, there are already open beer bottles on the kitchen counter and he's angrily playing video games in the den.

"Fuck," he growls, and throws the controller at the coffee table where it lands with a stinging crack.

"Hey, there." I lean against the doorframe and offer a cautious smile.

Garrett just sighs. He's still in the pajamas he was wearing this morning. Which is never a good sign.

"What's up?" I take a seat on the arm of the sofa to kiss him hello, but our lips barely meet before he's pulling back with an irritated curse.

"He's fucking with me," he spits out.

"Who? That same kid with the lisp? Oh no. He's back?"

For weeks after last Christmas, Garrett had a ten-year-old nemesis taunting him on one of his games. I thought I was going to have to get rid of the console, legitimately worried Garrett would find a way to track the kid down and show up at his house carrying his hockey stick. But then the kid and his lisp just up and disappeared in the spring and I thought the ordeal was over.

"My father," he says darkly. "Nothing satisfies him, so now he's got to rub it in."

My brain is beginning to hurt. "Start from the beginning. What happened?"

"Landon calls me this morning. Says a producer from ESPN wants me to do an episode of *The Legacy*. Only it's not one of their usual career snapshots type of episodes—it's some bullshit father-son feel-good story. So my dad can get on there and talk about raising a prodigy while they throw my baby pictures up behind his head." Garrett's eyes flash a stormy gray. "He's seriously just being sadistic at this point."

"You think Phil set this up?"

"Like it's something novel, going behind my back and trying to interfere in my life?" Garrett tosses over a knowing look. "Doesn't sound familiar?"

He has a point. When we were still in college, Phil Graham all but blackmailed me to break up with Garrett, threatening to cut him off financially if I didn't.

"You're right. It's exactly what he'd do."

"I'm being punished for something. Or maybe he's gone mad with power. Whatever it is, I'm not biting."

"Good," I say, rubbing his shoulders. Nothing takes a toll on Garrett like his dad. "Screw him. Whatever attention he's hoping for, don't give it to him."

But my boyfriend is too agitated to sit still. I trail after his broad, muscular body as he goes to the kitchen to grab the last remaining beer bottle from the fridge. He drinks nearly half of it in one gulp, then rummages around for something to eat.

"It's shit like this that makes me not want to have kids, you know?"

The bitter reflection comes so far out of left field, I'm totally and completely blindsided by it.

It smacks me right in the face, a sharp pang radiating through my chest as I absorb what he just said.

"You're lucky," he says gruffly, turning to face me. He leans against the fridge door. "Your folks are decent people. You've got the good parent genes in your DNA, you know? But what about me? Like, what happens if I turn out just like my dad one day and screw up my kids? Make them grow up to hate me?"

I gulp down the lump of anxiety choking off my airways. "You're not your dad. You're nothing like him."

But Garrett tends to disappear into himself when Phil gets under his skin. He becomes quiet and withdrawn. And I've learned the only cure is time and space. Let him work through the thoughts in his head without pushing him or adding extra pressure.

Which means that once again, we don't quite make it around to the subject of, hey, I've got a kid you most definitely won't screw up brewing in my belly.

CHAPTER 36

GARRETT

Saturday morning, I step off the plane in Palm Springs with the other half dozen of my teammates who got roped into playing this two-day tournament. The charity people set us up at a nice hotel, to which we're ushered by two private cars. Room service brings up some breakfast, while Logan texts me from the room next door to say that Happy Gilmore is on TV, if I want to glean a few pointers before we hit the first tee. I'm about to reply when my agent calls.

"I knew nothing about this," Landon warns before I can say a word.

"What?"

I step onto the balcony where several stories below people are starting to gather for the tournament. The press is setting up. Staff running around, corralling spectators. It's a sunny day. Not too hot and a slight breeze. Good weather for golf. Well, for people who are good at golf.

"When I got to the office, there was a voicemail from that producer," Landon explains.

Christ. These people are incessant.

"The answer's still no."

"Right. I was very clear on that with them." There's a long and disconcerting pause. "Except apparently they're under the impression Phil agreed for both of you."

I damn near chuck my phone off the balcony. I rear back and barely stop myself from releasing, only finding the self-control when I realize there's a good chance it'd knock someone below out cold.

"Fuck no, Landon. You get me?" My grip tightens around the phone, and I feel the plastic case start to crunch. "Tell them to piss off. He doesn't speak for me. Ever."

"Absolutely. I hear you."

"They couldn't get me on that set beside him with a gun to my head."

"I get that, Garrett. I do." Another unnerving pause. "I'll make the call. Whatever you want." He clears his throat. "Here's the thing, though: As far as they understand, you've committed to this. If I go back and tell them you're out, it doesn't look good."

"I don't give a shit."

"No, I know. These are special circumstances. Only, they don't know that. So they might start wondering if there's something more to it."

"Maybe they won't," I mutter through gritted teeth. I'm rubbing my molars down to nubs.

"I promise, it will raise questions. The kind that have a way of snowballing. Are you prepared for what happens when people start wondering if there's bad blood there? Why you'd refuse to do an interview with your father? Because I'll tell you what that looks like. They start calling your teammates and coaches and old college friends and some kid from your third-grade class to ask about your family and relationship with your dad. Can you be sure what they'll say?"

I draw a shallow, ragged breath.

Screw. This.

For the sake of my career, I've been obliged to put on a front for years. There was no getting around it—Phil Graham is one of the biggest names in American hockey. It was either air all our trauma for the world to see or fake the happy family. I'd chosen the latter, because the former is too…Christ, it's too humiliating.

The idea of the entire world viewing me as some sort of victim makes me want to throw up. Hannah has brought it up before, asking if maybe it's time to let my father's actions come to light, to let everyone know what kind of man they've been deifying. But at what cost? Suddenly I go from being "hockey player" to "the hockey player whose daddy used to beat him up." I want to be judged for my skills on the ice, not dissected and pitied. I don't want strangers knowing my business. I feel sick just thinking about it.

These past few years, I'd been fine playing along, putting on that front. Now, for some inexplicable reason, my dad seems intent on making my life especially difficult.

The last thing I want, however, is some nosy sports reporter snooping around in my life. If they track down Coach Jensen at Briar University, I have no doubt my old coach would have my back. Chad Jensen is tight-lipped on a good day. If someone showed up in his arena asking for gossip about a former player, he'd rip them a new one. But I can't say the same for everyone in my life. I played with a lot of guys at Briar who knew I had a violent history with my father.

So despite the acid rising in the back of my throat, I have no choice but to do exactly what that asshole expected when he concocted this farce.

"Fine," I tell Landon. Hating every word as it comes off my tongue. "I'll do it."

After we get off the phone, I pull up my father's name on my contacts list. I can't remember the last time I actually called him. But if he's roping me into this, I'm not going quietly.

"Garrett. Good to hear from you. Ready to hit some balls?" he says, so goddamn unbothered, it spikes my already-heightened anger. He isn't even involved in the tournament, but he makes it his business to always know what I'm up to.

"What the hell are you playing at?" My voice is low. The rage barely restrained.

"I'm sorry?"

He seriously has the nerve to play dumb? "This interview nonsense. Why?"

"They came to me," he replies with feigned innocence. "Didn't see a good reason to say no."

"So you make that decision for me?" My hands are legit shaking. I hate this man so much, it causes a physical disturbance in my body.

"It's the right one. You don't turn down an opportunity like this."

"I decide. Not you. Just because you can't stand not being the center of attention anymore—"

"Garrett." He sighs. So bored with my concerns. "I'd hoped you'd matured over the last year, but I see now I overestimated you."

"Fuck you, old man. I'm not a kid anymore. You can't pull this shit with me."

There was a time the disappointed dad routine worked. Back when I was five years old, six, seven. A little kid desperate to impress his unimpressible father. It drove me into spirals of depression and self-doubt. I would do anything to gain his approval. Until I got older and understood the vicious manipulation at play. On a child. And realized what a bastard he is.

"I won't entertain your tantrums, boy. One day you'll understand everything I've done to give you a career in this sport." Condescension drips from his tone. "Maybe then you'll appreciate how lucky you are to have been born my son."

I'd sooner eat my own foot.

"In any case," he says, with that smug drone that makes my eye twitch. "You will do this interview. You'll sit for the cameras, be charming and personable, and just maybe be smart enough to reach for that next level to become one of the greats. It's what a professional does."

I hang up on him, because if allowed, he'd keep talking to jerk off to the sound of his own voice. Anyway, I've heard this speech before. Be the Michael Jordan of hockey. Fame that transcends the sport.

Which is all well and good, but if Phil Graham is standing beside me when it happens, I can't see myself ever enjoying any of it.

As it is, I can't shake the conversation or the dread of the interview during the tournament and our team finishes the day dead last. I'm double-digits over par and spent most of the afternoon up to my knees in the rough. Logan didn't fare much better, setting up shop in numerous sand traps while the spectators had a good laugh. Which is a bummer for our teammates who paid to play with us, but they were good sports about the whole thing. Keeping them plied with drinks helped, as well as the ribeyes we inhale at a nearby award-winning restaurant after the tournament wraps for the day. The two men are brothers from Texas and own a cattle ranch together, so I trust they know their meat when they tell us this is the best steakhouse in the entire state.

By the time we return to the hotel after dinner, it's quarter past nine and all I want is to shower and get out of these sweaty clothes. I don't bother turning on the light as I stride into my room, tugging my shirt over my head before the door even closes behind me. I'm about half undressed when something suddenly moves in the mirror.

On instinct, I grab a glass water bottle from the desk and spin around, ready to chuck it at whatever is behind me.

"Don't shoot," a female voice drawls in response.

I lower the bottle. Quickly stick an arm out to slap the switch on the wall, flooding the room with light. My heart's pounding and the adrenaline is still pumping hot through my veins, so it takes me a second to comprehend the naked woman lying in my bed, only partially under the covers.

With an unbothered smirk, she raises her hands in surrender. "I'm unarmed."

I draw a calming breath. "Who the hell are you?"

"Your present," she teases before shimmying the rest of the blanket off her to reveal the two red bows stuck to her nipples.

"You're welcome." Then she rolls over and flashes me her bare ass, which has my name written across it in black Sharpie.

Garrett on one cheek, Graham on the other.

I can't.

I just fucking can't.

Without a word, I turn on my heel and stalk out of the room. Pulling my shirt on as I get into the elevator still carrying the bottle of water. Swear to Christ the next person who messes with me is getting clobbered.

Downstairs, my mood gets darker and more turbulent as I get into it with the manager at the front desk, who seems to have mistaken me for someone with patience to spare. Like, dude, we could talk about your woefully inadequate security that let a naked chick in my room with my name on her ass like she's looking to put my skin on a stuffed animal on her bed, or you could just give me a new room so I can go to fucking sleep.

While I'm waiting for them to finally get their act together and move my stuff, I text Logan.

Me: Hockey gods decided to spare you tonight. Just found a groupie in my bed. Bows on her tits and my name in Sharpie on her ass.
Him: Bahahahaha. You go girl.
Him: Permanent marker, eh? Wish my stalkers had that kind of dedication.
Me: Getting a new room now, so don't shout random shit at my door. Won't be there.
Him: Why didn't you just come crash with me?
Me: Cuz I'm a grown man who doesn't need his hand held every time I'm assaulted by a pair of strange tits?
Him: Your loss. We coulda cuddled.

Snorting, I exit the chat thread and find Hannah's name. With all the press crawling around this hotel, I'd expect the rumors to hit the web within the hour.

> Me: Don't look at any of the sports blogs. Maybe stay off social media altogether.
> Her: You shank a ball and kill an endangered egret or something?
> Me: Nah. Found a crazy naked lady in my bed. Hotel is trying to argue that's a feature, not a bug.
> Her: Lmao at least I wasn't in the bed this time.

Guilt settles like a rock in the pit of my stomach.

> Me: I'm sorry. I wish the pro athlete life wasn't so goddamn intrusive. Just didn't want you to get blindsided.
> Her: No worries. I trust you not to cheat on me with some random puck bunny.

Not that I expected anything else, but Hannah being chill about this feels like the one win I've had today. She's the single thing in my life I don't have to stress about. We're just good, always, no matter what. When everything else is out of control, this woman grounds me.

> Me: I mean, if you want to be a little jealous, that's cool too...
> Her: Oh, I'll cut a bitch. They don't want to try me.

I catch myself smiling for what feels like the first time in days.

> Me: Miss you. Can't wait to get home.
> Her: Hurry back. Love you.

It's times like this I remember why I fell so hopelessly hard for this girl.

CHAPTER 37

HANNAH

"I don't understand what's going on," my mother says, over the canned thunder of the supermarket produce aisle when the sprayers kick on. That used to fascinate me as a kid. "Are you breaking up?"

"No, Mom. Everything's fine." I'm lying on the living room couch with a packet of crackers that I can't seem to eat. Every time I take a bite, I feel nauseous.

"Tommy at the meat counter just said something about an affair."

Tommy at the meat counter should stay in his lane.

"Just some dumb gossip. Don't pay attention to it. I don't."

The rumor mill spins up fast; the moment I opened my eyes this morning, my phone was blowing up with texts and DMs. My group chat with the girls was full of hilarious links from blogs running breathless articles about the naked woman caught in Garrett's bed in California. Churning out all sorts of feverish speculation.

The writers over at Hockey Hotties—and I use the term "writers" loosely—finally retracted their previous speculation that Garrett and Logan are secret lovers. Now they're convinced Garrett is cheating on me with a Palm Springs escort. And Logan is cheating too because apparently he wanted a turn with the call girl. It's the kind of ridiculous, misogynistic garbage I've come to expect from the tabloids, these rags obsessed with the love lives of pro athletes. But the fact that the gossip reached my mother in Indiana is more headache than I bargained for.

"I'm so sorry, sweetie," Mom is saying. "What terrible things to write."

"It comes with the territory." I knew that when Garrett went pro. Though it doesn't make it any easier when you become the main character in the sporting news for the day.

My mom is very good at reading my mind, saying, "Still, these things can take their toll on a relationship."

"It's not my favorite thing," I admit. "You know I prefer to stay out of the limelight these days."

Being a songwriter and producer is something a select few have turned into a highly visible gig, but I prefer being in the background. Don't get me wrong, I have no problem getting up on stage and performing in front of an audience; I did it all the time at Briar. And I don't lack confidence. But ever since my boyfriend became a national hockey sensation, I've come to realize I really don't enjoy the constant attention. I could've tried my hand at a singing career after college, but it holds no appeal for me anymore. The paparazzi, the mean tweets, the public's obsession. Who the hell needs that.

"I hope he knows how lucky he is to have you."

"He does," I assure her.

And while I'd expect my mom to worry about me, the truth is, I put up with all this nonsense because at the end of the day, being with Garrett is worth it.

Once I've allayed Mom's fears, I heave myself off the couch, abandoning my uneaten crackers to go check the mail on the front stoop. The mailbox is stuffed with bills, flyers, more bills, more flyers—and a royalty check from Elise.

I step inside, leaving all but one envelope on the hall credenza. A knot forms in my stomach as I open the flap. Or maybe it's the nausea ramping up again. But Elise did say obscene. She'd said obscene, right?

I close my eyes and take a deep breath before staring down at the numbers on the check.

I see zeroes. And more zeroes. They keep going until my legs get a little unsteady and I reach for a chair.

Three hundred thousand dollars.

I've never seen so much money in my life.

This is a life-changing amount. Enough to carve a big dent in my parents' debt. Maybe even get them out of that house. Oh my God.

The possibilities flood my mind. I'll have to discuss it with Garrett. I heed the silent reminder, trying not to get ahead of myself. But this could be a real opportunity to change my parents' lives.

If they allow it, a little voice reminds me.

Because it's true, the last time I broached the subject of helping with their debts, they'd completely shut me down. Or rather, they'd shut Garrett down. After his rookie year, he'd signed a five-year multimillion-dollar contract with the franchise, so much money we'd both been floored by the amount. And being the amazing person he is, Garrett immediately offered to take care of my parents' debts—to which they'd responded with an unequivocal no way.

And Garrett thinks *I'm* stubborn. I can't even count how many conversations I had with them, but Mom and Dad wouldn't budge. Mom said it wouldn't be right. Dad said he refused to let his future son-in-law incur his debts. I swear, they're too proud for their own good.

But this might be different. Technically this is "my" money, even though Garrett and I share our finances. If I play this carefully, maybe I can convince my folks to finally accept my help.

As excitement eddies in my stomach, I spend much of the afternoon researching home prices in Ransom, Indiana, and the penalties for breaking a mortgage early. I even leave a message for a real estate agent down there so I can ask some questions. Get a sense if this is even a feasible idea. But Lord, how incredible would it be if Mom and Dad could pay off their debts and move to Boston? Or hell, even Philly, if they wanted to be closer to Aunt Nicole. Obviously I'm partial to Boston, but I'd just be happy to have them out of Ransom.

That town holds nothing but bad memories for me and my family. When I was fifteen years old, one of my classmates sexually assaulted me at a party, and life was never the same after that. I was accused of some pretty horrible things, the worst being that I'd made up the entire encounter. My parents were shunned, ostracized, all the while being forced to interact with my attacker's parents, one of whom is the mayor of Ransom.

Fuck that place. If Garrett's on board, I'm spending every dime of that royalty check to rescue my folks, and this time they're not going to stop me.

My spirits are soaring sky-high when Garrett gets home that evening. He'd messaged from the plane earlier complaining that the food sucked, so I make sure to have takeout waiting from his favorite restaurant.

No matter how short the time away, the minute he walks through the door, he greets me like he hasn't seen me in months. Drops his bag in the hallway, grabs my hips, and presses his mouth to mine. The greedy kiss steals the oxygen from my lungs, leaving me breathless.

"Hey," I say, smiling against his lips.

"They've got to stop sending me to these things."

"That bad?"

"I feel like I should give those guys their money back."

"So I guess we can cross pro golfer off your post-hockey retirement plan?"

"Shouldn't seem that different, right?" We head toward the kitchen when he catches a whiff of the food warming in the oven. "A stick and a projectile. But half the time I couldn't even tell where the damn ball went."

I can tell from his posture that his poor performance on the green isn't what's really got him stressed out. In an earlier text, he'd given me the heads-up he'd agreed to do *The Legacy* with his dad, but hadn't elaborated. I hate to broach the subject, but I'm too curious not to.

"So, ah, what made you agree to the ESPN sit-down with you and Phil?" I hedge, handing him a beer.

"I got strong-armed into it," he grumbles before taking a swig. "Basically, the bastard went ahead and accepted on my behalf. Landon said it would raise too many eyebrows if I backed out now."

"Dude. Your dad is *such* a dick."

"Dude. I know." But he's smiling now, watching me over the lip of his bottle. "You look happy. I mean, of course you are, because I'm home—"

I snort. My man is a paragon of modesty.

"But what else is up?"

Unable to mask my glee, I walk over to the side table and grab the royalty check. With a flourish, I hand it to him. "Surprise."

His eyes jump from the paper to mine. "Holy shit! Are you serious? This is for one *song*?"

I nod, bringing my own glass of sparkling water to my lips. "Yup. The one I wrote for Delilah," I confirm before taking a sip.

"This is incredible. Damn, Wellsy. Congratulations."

"Thank you." I'm rather pleased with myself when his bottle taps my glass in a jubilant cheers.

"I mean it. I'm so proud of you." His silvery eyes shine bright. "I know how hard you work. And it's paying off. For real." He pulls me into a hug. "You deserve it, babe."

This is the time, a voice urges. *Tell him now.*

I should. I really should. But this is the first time in ages that I've seen him this relaxed. No tension in his shoulders. Joy in his eyes. The moment I tell him I'm pregnant, this lightness will turn heavy. It'll force us to have days' or weeks' worth of deep discussions that my mind doesn't want to get weighed down by at the moment.

So I bite my tongue, and we sit for a nice dinner. Maybe I'm a coward. I probably am. But I don't want to ruin what is otherwise a brief and perfect moment. We get so few of these lately.

We don't even make it through dessert before Garrett's got his hands on me. Feeling me up while I grab spoons out of the drawer so we can split the huge slice of chocolate mousse cake I picked up from my favorite bakery. But Garrett's not interested in cake, and when he peels my shirt up to squeeze my breasts, I shiver uncontrollably and forget about it too.

Suddenly we're stumbling clumsily toward the living room, because it's closer than the bedroom. Tripping over clothes that are falling to the floor. We follow suit, falling onto the carpet. Naked and sucking each other's faces off.

"God, I love you," he grunts, his teeth sinking into my shoulder.

The tiny sting makes me moan. I squeeze his bare ass and lift my hips to press myself against his straining erection. Being in his arms again, after even just a couple of days, reminds me how addictive this feeling is. The raw chemistry between us. How much I love him.

The shivers return when he starts kissing my breasts. Holy *fuck*, my boobs are hypersensitive and it's making my vision waver.

And after weeks of not noticing my constant bathroom trips and the new development of the smell of eggs making me queasy, Garrett chooses this moment to notice something: my swollen, tender breasts.

"Jeez, your tits feel so full," he mutters, cupping them with both palms. "You getting your period soon?"

I almost burst out laughing.

Do it now, I order myself. *Tell him.*

I mean, this is the perfect opening. "*Well, you see, my period hasn't come in two months. Surprise! I'm pregnant!*"

But then he'll stop doing this—lowering his head to suck on one aching nipple. And it's so sensitive, it sends ripples of pleasure dancing through me. I let out a blissful moan. Oh my God. Maybe pregnancy isn't so bad. Maybe this hormonal hurricane that's wreaking havoc on me finally has some benefits. Like the exquisite agony of Garrett's mouth on my nipple. How impossibly wet I am when he slips his hand between my thighs.

He feels it too, groaning loudly. "Jesus," he grinds out. "Is this all for me?"

"Always," I mumble against his lips.

He kisses me again, his tongue seeking mine, at the same time he plunges inside me, his thick length filling me to the hilt. Then he fucks me on the living room floor carpet that we'd argued about buying for nearly an hour when we'd moved into this brownstone. I'd wanted something more durable, easier to vacuum. He'd argued valiantly for the longer, softer shag. And then after I kept asking why, he got frustrated. In the middle of IKEA, in front of a sales associate whose anxious gaze was ping-ponging between us, Garrett had yanked me closer and growled in my ear, "Because there's gonna be a time when I'm too hot for you to make it to the bedroom, and I'll end up fucking you on the living room floor. Sue me for wanting your ass to be comfortable."

In response, I'd shut up and told the sales guy we wanted the carpet.

Now, I'm rolling Garrett onto his back and straddling his muscular thighs as he thrusts upward, filling me completely. He looks so gorgeous lying there at my mercy. Gray eyes molten, eyelids heavy. His bottom lip is captured between his teeth as he lets out a labored breath, clearly struggling for control.

"Don't fight it," I tell him, my nails scraping his defined pecs as I lay my palms flat to his chest. My lower body grinds him, bringing us both closer to the edge. "I'm almost there."

"Yeah?"

"Yeah."

I squeeze my thighs together, and he groans, his features going taut. "Coming, baby," he groans.

I watch him as he does, loving the noises he makes, the way his eyelids go heavy before closing altogether. The feel of him finding release inside me triggers my climax, and soon I'm the one making noise, eyes squeezed shut as I collapse on top of him.

A while later, we finally make it back to the bedroom, where we take a shower before falling into bed and getting sweaty all over again. As I'm drifting off to sleep in Garrett's strong arms, I promise myself I'm going to tell him tomorrow.

CHAPTER 38

HANNAH

I'M GOING TO TELL HIM TODAY.

I can't *not* tell him today.

I'm reaching the point where I don't think I can delay it any longer. It's been a week since our living room sex-fest, and I still haven't put on my big girl pants and told my boyfriend we're with child. But Allie's right—Garrett is going to start recognizing the changes in me. Last time, he'd noticed my swollen breasts. Who knows what he'll notice next time. And next time, maybe he'll connect the dots.

So today's the day. All I have to do is wait for Garrett to finally drag his ass out of bed so I can tell him. Though in his defense, it's only eight in the morning. I'm the one who woke up at an ungodly hour.

I thought the upside to pregnancy was not having period cramps, but joke's on me. Now I have pregnancy cramps. I woke up at the crack of dawn feeling like I was getting kicked in the stomach by a horse. Even a long, hot shower and some Tylenol hasn't done anything to abate this sensation that makes me long for last week's constant nausea.

No excuses, an inner voice pipes up, that wise part of me that knows I'd been about to convince myself to use cramps as an excuse to stall again.

But nope. No stalling.

Today is the day.

"Motherfucker!" Garrett shouts from the bedroom.

Okay, maybe today's not the day.

Lying in the living room with my laptop and headphones while I work on a new song, I jump at the outburst. Sliding the earphones off, I hear what sounds like Garrett cursing and getting into a scuffle with our closet.

I hurry toward our room. "You okay in there?"

"Do I have to wear a tie to this thing?" He comes out half-dressed with a wad of ties in his hand.

"What thing?"

He spares me a dark look. "*The Legacy* interview. The first taping is in a couple hours."

Yikes. Today is *definitely* not the day.

I'd totally forgotten Garrett was doing that this morning. Stupid pregnancy brain has been kicking in lately, jumbling my thoughts. Yesterday I couldn't remember where I'd left my car keys, searching for twenty minutes before realizing I was holding them in my hand.

"Right." I eye the tie selection. "Normally I would say no, but your agent would probably disagree."

Garrett mutters something rude under his breath and goes back to the closet for a rematch. "The premise of this whole thing is ridiculous to being with. I don't see why they think anyone is interested in watching Phil bullshit his way through a bunch of fond family memories."

"Because they don't know it's bullshit," I point out.

But he's now spinning himself into a small tirade. Not that I blame him. If I had a father like Phil Graham, I'd be spitting mad all the time too.

"Swear to God, if he brings up my mom, I'm going to lose it." Garrett reappears, looping a navy silk tie around his neck. He pulls on it so tight, I'm worried he'll choke himself.

"Did you give the producers a list of no-no questions?" I know a lot of celebrities do that. Every time Nice gives an interview at the studio, his manager steps in to remind the journalist of the questions they aren't allowed to ask.

"Landon told them I don't want to talk about my mother. Gave them the grief excuse, it's too painful, that sort of thing." Garrett's jaw tightens. "But I wouldn't put it past my father to bring her up himself."

I bite my lip. "You know, you don't have to do this. You can just call Landon and tell him you don't want to. He gets paid to say no for you."

"Then what? Answer a bunch of questions about why I backed out at the last minute? Phil knows I can't."

"So you say nothing, ignore it, and in a week or two it goes away. Some football player gets arrested or says he won't play until they buy him a pony and you're off the hook."

But he doesn't want to hear it. It's too late to ease Garrett out of this rage spiral, and the best I can hope for is that he keeps his temper under control while the cameras are rolling. Maybe Landon will have better luck with him.

AFTER GARRETT LEAVES, I WELCOME THE ALONE TIME. I SLIP INTO a pair of cotton boxers and a tank top and climb back into bed, spending the next couple of hours nursing my cramps and trying to get some work done. Eventually I figure out that part of my stomach pains is hunger and get up to make myself a sandwich—only to come back to bed to see a small red stain on the sheets.

When I hurry into the bathroom to check, I realize my under-wear is stained as well.

While it's not a full-blown panic, my pulse kicks up a notch while I change, strip the bed, and text Allie. She gets back to me while I'm putting the sheets in the wash, with the assurance that some spotting is normal.

Me: You're sure? I've felt like crap all morning.

Her: I'm looking at the Mayo Clinic website right now. Says it's common.

Me: When does it become not common?

Her: I'll send you some links. But I don't know. You know what? Call Sabrina. She's probably a better person to talk to.

Me: Good idea.

My first instinct had been to text Allie, my closest friend. But she's right. I should be reaching out to someone who's actually gone through this. And hey, I'll even be able to avoid the awkward news-breaking part, because Sabrina already knows about the pregnancy. Allie the traitor let it slip in our girls' chat.

So I call Sabrina, who picks up on the first ring. I have a feeling she saw my name on the phone and thought, what the hell? We rarely call each other outside of the chat thread.

"Hey. Everything okay?" she asks immediately.

"I don't know." I'm suddenly resisting the urge to cry. Stupid hormones. "When you were pregnant with Jamie, did you ever have any bleeding?"

"Bleeding or spotting?" Her tone is sharp.

"Spotting."

"Light or heavy?"

"Light-ish? Stained my sheets and underwear, but it's not a constant flow."

I can almost hear her relaxing on the other end, as she exhales a breath. "Oh, then yes. That's normal. Any other symptoms?"

"Some cramps this morning, but they've subsided."

"Also normal. My advice is to monitor it for the day. If the spotting turns to bleeding, I'd go to the hospital." She hesitates. "Could be a sign of miscarriage. *But* it could also be nothing."

"Mommy!" I hear a plaintive cry in the background. "I can't find my purple bathing suit!"

"Sorry. That's just Jamie." Sabrina's voice goes muffled for a moment. "Why don't you wear the green one instead, then?"

"BUT I WANT THE PURPLE!"

Jesus. I'm pretty sure Sabrina's covering the phone with her hand, yet I can still hear that kid's shriek.

"Okay, I'll find it for you. One sec." Sabrina returns. "Hannah, I have to go. I'm taking Jamie to the pool and—"

"I heard."

"Call me if anything changes, okay? Keep me updated."

"Will do."

After we hang up, I draw a deep breath and tell myself everything's okay. But no matter how many times I repeat the mantra, I can't shake the idea that something's wrong. Before long, I'm tumbling through my own little spiral as I tunnel deeper into pregnancy blogs and medical journals searching for an explanation. The consensus being that Sabrina is probably right.

Unless she isn't.

CHAPTER 39

GARRETT

"Tell us about one of your earliest memories learning to play."

The interviewer, a former college player turned broadcaster, sits with his pages of questions in his lap. Across from him, my dad and I are in identical director's chairs. The set is a white-hot spotlight surrounded in darkness but for the red lights of two cameras watching this awkward farce unfold. Not unlike an interrogation. Or a snuff film. To be honest, I wouldn't be against someone getting murdered right now. Preferably the Armani-suit-wearing jackass beside me.

"Garrett?" the interviewer, Bryan Farber, prods when I don't reply. "When did you first pick up a hockey stick?"

"Yeah, I was too young to remember."

That's not a lie. I've seen photos of myself at the age of two and three and four, gripping a child's Bauer stick, but I don't have any clear recollection of it. What I do remember, I'm not about to share with Farber.

This guy doesn't want to hear about my father ripping the covers off me when I was six years old and dragging me out in the freezing sleet to make me pick up a stick too big for my little body and slap at street pucks.

"I think you have a picture," Phil says, smoothly jumping in. "One Christmas when he was little, maybe two years old? Wearing a jersey the guys all signed for him. He's in front of our tree with a toy stick in his hands. He took to it right away."

"Do you remember standing up on a pair of skates for the first time?" Farber asks with a schmaltzy TV smile.

"I remember the bruises," I say absently but maybe on purpose.

My dad, clearing his throat, is quick to interject. "He did fall a lot at first. First time we went skating was winter on the lake behind our Cape Cod house. But he never wanted to go inside." He dons a fake faraway look, as if lost on memory lane. "Garrett would wake me up and beg me to take him out there."

Weird. I remember crying, begging for him to let me go home. So cold I couldn't feel my fingers.

I wonder if I should tell Farber how my punishment for complaining was getting on a treadmill with weights on my ankles at seven years old. While Phil shouted at my mother to shut up when she objected. He said he was making me a champion and she'd just make me soft.

"Were you motivated by living up to your father's success?" Farber asks. "Or was it a fear of failure in his shadow?"

"I've never compared myself to anyone else."

The only fear I ever knew was of his violence. I was twelve the first time he actually laid a hand on me. Before that, it was verbal jabs, punishment when I screwed up or didn't try hard enough or just because Phil was in a bad mood that day. And when he got bored of me, taking it out on my mother.

Farber glances over his shoulder, where his producer, my agent, and my father's agent stand near the closer cameraman. I follow his gaze, noting that Phil's rep and the producer seem annoyed, while Landon just looks resigned.

"Can we cut for a second?" Landon calls. "Give me a word with my client?"

"Yes," my dad's agent agrees. His tone is cool. "Perhaps you can remind your client that an interview requires actual answering of the questions?"

Landon pulls me to a darkened corner of the studio, his expression pained. "You've got to throw them a bone here, Garrett."

I set my jaw. "I told you, man, I don't have any good memories growing up. And you know me, I'm a shit liar."

Nodding slowly, he runs a hand over his perfectly coifed hair. "All right. How about we try something like this? How old were you when you realized you were playing hockey for yourself and not for him?"

"I dunno. Nine? Ten?"

"So pick a moment from that age range. A hockey memory, not a dad memory. Can you do that?"

"I'll try."

Once we're seated again, Farber makes another attempt at coaxing anything real from me. "You were saying you've never compared yourself to your father?"

"That's right." I nod. "Honestly, for me, hockey was never about trying to become successful, landing big contracts, or winning awards. I fell in love with the game. I became addicted to the thrill, the fast-paced environment where one mistake can cost you the whole game. When I was ten, I dropped a pass at a crucial moment in the third. My stick wasn't where it was supposed to be, my eyes were on the wrong teammate. I blew it and we lost." I shrug. "So the next day at practice, I begged my coach to let us run the same passing drill over and over again. Until I mastered it."

"And did you? Master it?"

I grin. "Yup. And the next time we hit the ice, I didn't miss a single pass. Hockey's a wild ride, man. It's a challenge. I love a challenge, and I love challenging myself to be better."

Bryan Farber is nodding with encouragement, clearly pleased that I'm opening up.

"I remember that game," my dad says, and I don't doubt it. He never missed any of my games. Never missed an opportunity to tell me where I went wrong.

Farber addresses me again. "I bet having your dad rooting for you on the sidelines, challenging you as well, was a great motivator, yes?"

I clam up again. Damn it, I'm never going to survive this interview. And this is only the first taping. We're supposed to be doing this twice.

An hour into filming, the producer suggests we take a break, and I get off that set as quick as I can. How was that only an hour? It felt like two fucking days.

I avoid the green room and instead grab a drink from a vending machine down some random corridor. When I return to the soundstage and check my phone, I realize I have about a dozen texts and a voicemail from Hannah.

Since she's not one who's prone to drama or panic, I signal to Landon that I need a second, then step away to check the voicemail.

She's talking fast and a bad signal or noise in the background garbles some of the message, but the parts I do grasp nearly stop my heart.

"Garrett. Hey. I'm sorry to do this, but I need you to come home. I…um…"

I frown when she goes silent for several beats. Worry begins tugging at my insides.

"I really don't want to tell you over the phone, but you're filming and I'm not sure when you'll be home and I'm sort of freaking out here, so I'm just going to say it—I'm pregnant."

She's what?

I nearly drop the phone as shock slams into me.

"I meant for us to sit down properly and talk about this, not to blurt it out in a voicemail. But I'm pregnant and I'm, um, bleeding and I think something's wrong. I need you to take me to the hospital." Her voice is small, frightened. It makes my blood run cold with fear. "I don't want to go alone."

"We about ready to get started again?" the producer calls impatiently.

I look over to see Farber and my dad have already taken their seats.

After a brief stuttering glitch, my brain snaps back to the present and the only thing that matters: getting to Hannah right fucking now.

"No," I call back. I rip off my mic pack and toss it at Landon, who's approaching me in concern. "I'm sorry, I have to go. There's been an emergency."

CHAPTER 40

HANNAH

"For fuck's sake. The light's green, asshole!"

Garrett lays on the horn.

We're on our way to the hospital, and I've been braced in my seat since we pulled out of the driveway and almost backed into a passing car. Traffic won't cut us a break as Garrett white-knuckles the steering wheel and alternates between impatient outbursts, worried questions, and angry demands.

"How long has this been going on?" he snaps, scowling at the windshield.

"I woke up not feeling well. I had cramps, felt a bit nauseous. Then it got worse."

"Why didn't you say something then?"

"Because you were all worked up about the interview, and I didn't want to add extra stress on you. I couldn't tell you I was pregnant five minutes before you had to leave the house to see your father."

"I wouldn't have gone!" he shouts. Then he takes a deep breath. "Sorry. I didn't mean to yell. I just don't get it, Wellsy. How could you not tell me?"

"I didn't want to worry you. When I noticed the blood and texted Allie—"

"Allie knows?" Garrett swerves between vehicles.

"—she said I should ask Sabrina if it was normal and—"

"Sabrina knows?" he roars. "Jesus Christ. Am I the last one to find out?"

My hand grips the armrest for dear life. "I meant to tell you," I say through a lump of guilt. "I kept trying to, but it never felt like the right time. I wasn't trying to hide it from you, Garrett. I wanted to tell you."

"But you didn't. The first time I hear anything about it, I've spent all day getting grilled beside Phil, and I check my voicemail to hear you basically in tears telling me to come home because you're pregnant. I mean, what the hell, Hannah?"

"This is why I haven't said anything!" Tears sting my eyes as desperation, frustration, and fear form a lethal cocktail in my throat. I feel like I'm going to throw up. "The last thing I wanted was to dump it on you like this. You had this interview. And before that, it was the awards. And before that, it was post-season."

"You've known about this since post-season?" He nearly sideswipes a utility van that's trying to merge. Horns blare at us from all directions as he speeds up and slips into the left lane. "Christ."

"Don't yell at me."

"I'm not yelling at you," he growls through gritted teeth. "I'm yelling at the fact that you've kept this from me for months."

"At this point I'm sorry I called at all," I growl back. "I should have just gone by myself." Because the louder he gets, and the more the indignation strains his voice while I'm sitting on a pad soaking up blood, the more my own anger rises.

"That's a low blow." He curses loudly. "I can't believe you just said that!"

"You're shouting at me again," I snap in accusation. I could be losing our baby, and this jackass is making it all about himself like I'm not terrified.

"This is exactly the kind of shit my father pulls," Garrett snaps back. "Manipulating me with information. Keeping things to himself."

"Are you serious right now?" I'm so furious, my hands are actually burning with the urge to smack him. "You're comparing me to your father?"

"Tell me I'm wrong."

"Talk about low blows." I can't remember the last time I was this mad at anyone. "You know what, Garrett, if you really wanted to get him out of your life, you could just be honest. I've said this before and I'll say it again: just tell the world what a monster he is and be done with it. You act like you have to keep silent about the abuse and protect the man's legacy. But you've chosen to keep quiet. You do this to yourself."

He glances over, eyes blazing. "What, so I should go on TV and announce to the world that my dad used to hit me? Give newspapers interviews describing the various incidents so they can glorify it and pant over the juicy scoop? Screw that."

"I get that you're embarrassed, okay? And yeah, it's not a pleasant subject. Nobody wants to relive their trauma. But maybe it's time you did."

He doesn't say another word or even spare a sideways look in my direction until we get to the hospital and he checks me in. By that point, I'm relegated to the third person while the nurse asks questions and Garrett takes command. I'd protest more, but I don't have the energy.

Eventually, we're brought into an exam room where I undress and put on a scratchy hospital gown. Neither of us say a single word. We don't even look at each other. But when the doctor enters with the ultrasound machine, Garrett brings a chair over to sit beside my bed and grabs my hand to squeeze it tight.

"It'll be okay," he says roughly. It's the first anger-less thing he's said to me since we got in his car back at home.

"So, Hannah," the doctor says, prepping the machine. She's an older woman in her fifties, with kind eyes and silver streaks in her short hair. "The nurse tells me you've had some spotting and cramps. How's the bleeding now?"

"Like a medium-flow period," I answer awkwardly. "It was lighter earlier, but it started getting worse around lunchtime."

"Any other symptoms?"

"I was nauseated for a couple weeks. Then this morning the cramps were pretty bad."

I was expecting the belly ultrasound like I've seen on TV, but then the doctor turns to me with a phallic-looking wand, and I realize this is a whole different kind of exam. Garrett stares at the floor uncomfortably. Not a milestone in our relationship either of us was prepared for, but I guess we should have thought about that before I got pregnant.

"Some bleeding and discomfort is normal," the doctor says. "But let's get a better look."

A dozen horrible thoughts crash through my brain as I hold my breath. I hadn't decided what my next step would be, mostly because I hadn't worked up the nerve to tell Garrett. Having that choice ripped from my hands before I'd fully gotten my head around all of it feels unfair. Like I've been cheated. My heartbeat accelerates the longer the doctor scrutinizes whatever she's seeing on the screen.

"So, when the body is preparing to carry a baby, it undergoes a number of changes," she tells me, her gaze glued to the imaging scan. "The new rush of hormones can have a number of effects, one of which is changes in your cervix that make it softer. This can lead to bleeding in some cases. Sexual intercourse, for example, or a number of other athletic activities, can exacerbate this. Have you engaged in any strenuous activities in the past few days?"

I bite my lip sheepishly.

Garrett clears his throat. "Uh, yeah. We had some, ah, vigorous intercourse the other night. Like, multiple times."

"Vigorous intercourse?" I echo, turning to sigh at him. "Really? Couldn't find any better words?"

He lifts a brow. "I was going to say I gave you a good pounding, but I figured the doc wouldn't want to hear that."

I feel my cheeks heat up. "I'm sorry," I tell the doctor. "Ignore him."

She looks like she's trying not to laugh. "Vigorous intercourse could do it," she says, her gaze returning to the screen. "And like I said, some bleeding is not unusual. On its own, it's nothing to worry about."

"So that's it?" I ask, confused. "There's nothing wrong?"

"It all looks good from where I'm sitting. You seem to be about ten weeks along. Would you like to hear the heartbeat?"

And then suddenly we hear this wet, whooshing, underwater sound. Like the soundtrack of an alien space horror movie. I listen, dumbfounded, staring at the blob on the screen. How is that noise coming out of me?

Beside me, Garrett looks as stunned as I feel.

"I'd still suggest taking it easy for the next few days," she advises. "Let your body rest and recover. Otherwise, I see nothing to suggest trauma. You're not running a fever, and I have no reason to suspect an infection."

I bite back a relieved laugh. "I feel kind of embarrassed now for coming to the ER. I guess I overreacted."

"You did the right thing," she assures me. "You know your body better than anyone. If something seems off, better to get checked out and make sure."

The doctor takes a few minutes to answer some of my questions and prints out a picture that she hands to Garrett. Though it's so early in the pregnancy, there isn't much to see. He takes the scan without a word. Still silently fuming, I imagine.

Once she leaves us, I quickly clean myself up. Then, as I get dressed, I finally work up the nerve to ask Garrett the question hanging in the tension-thick air between us.

"What do you want to do about it?"

CHAPTER 41

GARRETT

Hannah pulls on her leggings with her back to me while I stare at this monochrome image in my hands. My kid. Inside there. Growing. No idea who he is or what's waiting for him out here. Just this little gooey thing that's about to change our lives forever.

"What do you want to do?" she repeats, slowly turning to face me. Her green eyes are lined with fatigue.

My head starts spinning. How the hell am I going to keep this kid alive? Who in their right mind would trust me with a living thing entirely dependent on me for its survival? Not to mention not royally screwing him up emotionally.

"Fine, I guess I'll go first."

As my mind races in a thousand directions, Hannah's voice cuts in and out. I vaguely hear her saying something about me being gone during the season.

"I'm not thrilled about the idea of being home all alone, raising a baby by myself."

Everything suddenly feels urgent. A loud clock ticking down to the enormity of this new reality. A baby. Our child. How do they just let people have these things? I failed the written portion of my first driver's test, for fuck's sake.

"It's intimidating," she's saying. "I'm not sure if I'm ready to handle that, you know? Like it's a lot. Especially without any family support…"

I start doing math in my head. Thinking about pre-season and doctor visits. Traveling to away games. The baby coming in the middle of the run-up to the playoffs. As panic starts churning in my gut, I wish I had a functional family to tell me how I'm supposed to do all this stuff. Someone to teach me.

"Okay then, apparently I'm talking to myself. Let's go."

My head snaps up, jolting me back to the present. Hannah's standing at the door with her purse. I'm still clutching this picture in my hand, daunted.

Hannah is upset with me, and now I feel like a total dick for getting into a fight with her on the way over. My system just didn't know how to process all that information at once, and I'm a little burnt out, if I'm honest.

"I'm sorry. I'm just…" I trail off.

"Let's go," she says again, turning away from me.

ALTHOUGH IT'S EARLY EVENING WHEN WE GET HOME, HANNAH says we can talk in the morning and goes right to bed. Rather than follow her, I sit at the kitchen table with a beer, staring at my kid. Wondering what he'd think of me. Or she. Could be a girl. But knowing my luck, it's a boy. A son who'll unearth all my daddy issues and make me doubt every parenting move I make, for fear of screwing him up. I sit there for hours, imagining all those ways I could mess up, and wake up an exhausted mess the next morning, having barely slept.

Hannah's still withdrawn as we brush our teeth beside each other at the sink. I want to fix it, but when I shut the water and open my mouth to speak, she leaves the bathroom abruptly. While I'm making coffee in the kitchen, she just sits at the counter eating a piece of toast, watching me. The silence is making the back of my neck itch. Again, I'm about to speak, when her phone rings and she wanders into the den to answer it. I don't catch much of the conversation over the bubbling of the coffeemaker. I peek around the corner to see her write a number down on a pad of paper.

"What was that?" I ask when she returns to the kitchen to finish her breakfast.

Hannah shrugs, not meeting my eyes. "Nothing." She shoves the last piece of toast in her mouth, chewing quickly as she grabs her purse and keys from the side table across the room.

I feel a pang of alarm. "Where are you going?"

"I need to get some stuff from the studio if I'm going to work from home for the next few days."

"You want me to drive you?" I offer.

"No." She ducks into the hallway toward the door, answering over her shoulder. "I'm fine."

Yeah, right. She's far from fine. It's like she can't wait to get away from me. Granted, I was sort of an ass yesterday, but we've got a pretty serious conversation to have. I'd be happy to apologize if she'd stand still long enough to hear it.

After I eat some breakfast and put away the dishes, I give Logan a call. My best friend is hit-or-miss when it comes to giving advice, but God help me, I'm desperate.

"Hey, G," he says. "Good timing. I just got back from the craziest lunch with Grace and her mom. Josie took us to a café near the Eiffel Tower where all the waitstaff were—not shitting you here—goddamn mimes. Can you imagine a worse nightmare scenario?"

"Hannah's pregnant."

That stuns him into silence.

"Wait, I just realized how that sounds," I interject before he can reply. "I'm not using that as an example of a nightmare scenario. I just needed to say it and didn't want to hear your stupid mime story anymore."

"First of all, wow."

"I know, right?" I rake my free hand through my hair. "She totally threw me a curveball yesterday."

"I meant wow, my story wasn't stupid."

I can't help but snort.

"Second of all," he continues. "Wow."

A full-blown laugh slips out. I know it's not the time to be laughing, but I love my friends. They never fail to lift my spirits when I need their support.

"Is this wow about my news?"

"Yeah. I mean, holy shit, G. Congratulations. How far along is she?"

"Ten weeks. She had the first ultrasound yesterday. Actually, that's sort of how I found out. She wasn't feeling well and thought she was losing the baby. Had to rush her to the hospital."

"Oh, damn. I'm sorry. She okay?"

"Yeah, better now. False alarm. But I had no idea." Shame coats my throat. "I was in the middle of this god-awful joint interview with my father when Wellsy called, so I was already in a crap mood. Then she dropped all this on me at once, and I, uh…" The remorse is choking me now. I clear my throat. "I didn't react well."

His voice turns grave. "What'd you do?"

"Nothing. Well, I mean, we got into a shouting match in the car, and I may or may not have compared her to my father."

Logan's expletive thuds in my ear. "Not cool, dude. You can't be yelling at pregnant ladies."

"Yes, thank you. But I was caught off guard."

I pace around the house, trying to walk off the nervous energy building in my muscles.

"You better do some serious groveling," he advises me. "Bust out that credit card and get to work."

"She's pretty mad still. We were supposed to talk, but she basically blew me off this morning."

"Well, yeah, dickhead. She's been all alone in this, and then she's freaking out, tells you, and you flip out on her and tell her she's like your dad? Your dad, who was spawned from Satan's rib? Jesus, bro. She's feeling like shit right about now, and you made it so much worse."

He's right. I know. As he rails into me for my behavior, I wander into the den and notice the notepad Wellsy had written on. I don't even mean to read it. I just happen to glance at it and the name catches my attention.

Reed Realty.

I freeze in place. What the hell does Hannah need a Realtor for? And when did she even have a chance to contact one? She went straight to bed when we got home yesterday—

—at six o'clock in the evening, I realize. And I sat in the kitchen alone for hours, lost in my own damned head while my pregnant girlfriend was in the bedroom. Maybe she hadn't gone to sleep, but stayed up for a while. Also stewing, thinking. And maybe she'd stewed and thought until she'd reached a decision.

To move out.

My blood runs cold with terror. She did just receive that big royalty check. She sure as hell doesn't need me to support her and the baby. And after the way I lost it on her yesterday, maybe she doesn't *want* my support.

Fuck.

My body growing weak, I cut Logan off midsentence. "Dude, I gotta go."

CHAPTER 42

HANNAH

Our engineer, Max, is in the studio with Nice, finessing a track with him, when I get there to pick up my hard drive. The entourage are camped out on the leather sofa, watching some sci-fi show on a laptop. I mean to just grab the drive and go, but when I hear Nice riffing in the booth, I can't help but get sucked in.

At the mic, Nice recites some lines he reads from his phone while Max cues up a new mix of the bridge.

"What do you think?" he asks, calling me into the booth with him. "Came to me last night while we were watching *Farscape*. You ever see that show? It's a trip."

"I like that slant rhyme," I say. "But what if we moved it to the second verse and moved that first bit to the new bridge?"

Max ducks out for a minute while we dig into these lyrics. As always, Nice and I become absorbed in the process, until I notice a figure waving at us through the glass. At first I think it's Max, but then I blink and realize it's Garrett.

My boyfriend stands at the board, silently mouthing words I can't discern.

"Garrett?" I blurt out. "What in the hell?"

He meets my eyes when he hears my voice come through the monitors on his side.

"You have to cue up the talk-back," I tell him, before realizing he has no idea what I'm talking about. "The red button next to the microphone. On the board."

He glances door, frantically bewildered at the dozens of buttons and faders, until Gumby sidles up and points to it for him.

"Thank you," I tell Gumby.

The big man leans down to the mic. "I got you, girl. You know this guy?"

"He's my boyfriend." I scowl at the window. "And he's supposed to be at home."

A sheepish Garrett takes over the mic. He's wearing faded jeans, a black Under Armour T-shirt, and a Bruins cap, looking every inch the athlete and standing out among the hip-hop entourage behind him. "I came to say I'm sorry."

Nice questions me with a look. My face gets warm as a result. This is beyond unprofessional, given that it's his dime paying for the studio time. Well, his record label. But whatever.

I swallow my embarrassment and glance back at Garrett. "Can we do this at home? I was just on my way out, anyway—"

"Don't leave."

I blink again. "The studio?"

Rather than clarify, he keeps barreling forward. "I'm sorry I didn't react better to the news. I know I was asshole. But we can work this out." His husky voice cracks a little. "Give me another chance, Wellsy."

"Ain't you got flowers or nothing?" Gumby chides him in the background, shaking his head. "You gotta at least bring flowers. I got a flower guy if you need the hookup."

Nice straightens to his full height, keeping a firm grip on my elbow. "This guy doing you wrong, Hannah?"

My cheeks are scorching now. "It's fine. Don't worry." I address Garrett in an insistent tone. "We'll talk about it later, Garrett. Please." I'm growing uncomfortable with airing all of this at work.

Nice directs his suspicious eyes at Garrett. "What'd you do, man?" he demands, affecting a tough-guy voice that sounds much older than the kid standing next to me.

"I made probably the biggest mistake of my life," Garrett says, now with the full attention of Nice's entourage. "Hannah, please. Let me try. Don't move out."

"Move out?" The conversation takes a hard left turn and leaves me behind. "What are you talking about?"

The misery on his face is unmistakable. "I saw the number you wrote down from the call earlier. It was for a Realtor."

I release a sigh when the riddle starts to make sense. Then I narrow my eyes as indignation sparks. "Wait a minute, you thought I was *moving out*? You seriously have that little faith in me? I was calling the Realtor for my parents, you dumbass!"

Nice snickers.

"I wanted to see about paying off their mortgage, so they could sell their house and get out of that town," I finish in a huff. "I thought maybe we could use my royalty check to make it happen."

Relief floods his expression. "You're not leaving me?"

"Of course not," I growl. Despite myself, I start to laugh. "Is that why you came all the way over here?"

"What the hell else was I gonna do? Let you walk away without saying a word?"

I bite back a smile. It's sort of sweet, Garrett rushing over here to stop me from leaving. Seeing the panic in his eyes when he thought he was losing me. My heart clenches tight when I realize he was still prepared to fight for us, even with the bombshell I dropped in his lap.

"This guy cheat on you?" Nice asks.

"No." The smile surfaces. "I'm having his baby."

"Oh shit!" Gumby shouts from the control room. He throws an arm over Garrett's shoulder and hugs him. "Congrats, bro."

"Are we?" Garrett asks, entirely focused on me. "Having this baby?"

I shrug, playing it off cool. "I mean, if you're into it."

"Yes," he says, without hesitation. "Babe, I spent all night staring at that sonogram and sometime around three in the morning, it dawned on me—I can't imagine not raising this kid with you. I know the season and traveling will make things more difficult, but we'll get you whatever help you need. Hell, we'll move your parents out here and buy them the house across the street if that's what you want. Anything."

"Yo, that's decent right there," Nice says, nodding his approval at Garrett. "Mad respect."

My smile is so wide, it's liable to crack my face in half. He *is* decent. The best, actually. And I realize that if I'd found a way to tell him sooner, it wouldn't have come as such a shock to the system. Suddenly, seeing that he understands my concerns, makes the whole thing feel less daunting, like whatever challenges confront us, we can figure them out together.

Heart overflowing with emotion, I walk out of the booth and into the control room, where Garrett greets me with a tight hug.

"I am so fucking sorry," he mumbles, burying his face in my hair. "I said some pretty awful shit last night."

"You did," I agree.

He pulls back, gazing down at me with pure remorse. "I need you to know—you're nothing like my father. I think the only reason I said that was because I'd just come from the interview and he was still on my mind. I snapped at you because I was angry with him and you were right there. But I should have never, ever said that. I'm sorry."

I nod slowly. "I know you are. And it's okay. I also know you didn't mean it."

"Are we good?" he asks gruffly.

"Always." I kiss him. With an unprofessional amount of tongue, ignoring the loud reaction of Nice's friends.

Garrett's fingers tangle in my hair. He pulls away for a moment to meet my eyes, staring at me with an expression I've never seen before.

My breath catches. "What?"

"I love you. Maybe more than I ever have."

"We're having a baby," I say, grinning with both excitement and still a bit of trepidation.

"Bet your ass we are."

CHAPTER 43

GARRETT

"Get back in bed. I'll bring it to you."

"It's just coffee," Hannah tells me the next morning, standing at the machine in the kitchen. "I'm not going outside to clean the gutters."

"Doctor said to take it easy."

"I don't think making some decaf and pouring it into a mug is over the line."

Turns out keeping Hannah off her feet is damn near impossible. If this woman makes it more than two days working from home before sneaking back into the studio, I'll be shocked. Already I can tell she's going to be a pain in the ass during this pregnancy.

Hopefully our friends can rally around me and help keep her in check. Last night we put out the word to everyone we care about, sharing the good news and watching the texts roll in congratulating us. Reading the hilarious messages reminded Hannah we're not as alone in this as she'd feared.

Grace is already talking about helping Hannah pick out nursery furniture when she gets back from Paris. Sabrina promised to help out too, though it might be harder for her because in that same text thread we learned that she and Tuck had both accepted jobs in

Manhattan and will be leaving Boston at the end of the summer. I'm happy for them, but I can't help but feel bummed that Tucker, the only dad I know, won't be in close proximity to me anymore.

"I was thinking," Hannah says as she raises her mug to her lips. "We should get married."

I'm in the middle of pouring some orange juice, and my hand freezes mid-pour. "Oh yeah?" I keep my tone casual.

She takes a demure sip, then flashes a little smile. "If you're into it."

It's pretty hard not to throw my OJ glass on the floor, dropkick Hannah's mug out of her hand, and maul her. "Yeah, I could be into it."

"Cool."

"You want me to get you a ring?"

"Obviously. Just don't make it as big as Allie's. I'm not a psycho."

I bite my cheek to stop from laughing. "That's it? That's our proposal?"

"I mean, we love each other and we're having a baby. Isn't that all that matters? Who needs speeches?"

She's right. "Who needs speeches," I echo, grinning. "Now. Please." I take her coffee mug and guide her toward the staircase. "Go back to bed. And don't you dare get up on the roof while I'm gone."

"Can I at least do some vacuuming?"

"Swear to God, I'll send Tucker and Sabrina over here to strap you down."

"I'd like to see them try."

Chuckling, I smack her butt to get her walking up the stairs. But I trail after her, because I still need to finish getting dressed. While she crawls back under the covers like a good girl, I search for a clean button-up and slip it over my shoulders. The nerves slowly work their way up from my stomach and into my throat. There's no part of me that is looking forward to what comes next.

"You never said where you're off to," Hannah says. She's sitting up in bed, flipping through channels on the TV.

"I'm going to talk to the ESPN producer," I admit. "I ran off the set the other day during taping and haven't spoken to anyone since. Landon set up a meeting between me and the producer. Just the two of us."

She looks over sharply. "What are you going to do?"

"What I have to."

WHEN I GET TO THE STUDIO, STEPHEN COLLINS INVITES ME INTO his office. I decline a beverage from his assistant, trying to charge past all the doting and on to the reason I'm here before I find a way to talk myself out of it.

"I hope it was nothing too serious," the producer says, sitting on the edge of his desk. Behind his head, there's a wall of awards and signed sports memorabilia. "Bryan and I were sorry we weren't able to finish the segment. Got some really great stuff out of the interview. We'd like to get you and your father back on set sometime this week, if that works for you."

"I'm sorry. I can't do that," I state plainly.

His polite smile falters. "If we have to push it a week or so, I suppose—"

"I have to pull out of the show, Stephen. I don't want you to air it at all. Any of it."

"Impossible. We have a contract. And we've already put a significant investment in shooting this. People, equipment."

"I understand that, and I'm sorry."

He searches my expression. "Where's this coming from, Garrett? Tell me what the problem is, and I'll work it out."

Over the years I've imagined how this conversation would go. Or a hundred like it. When I finally ripped the veil of this charade. In college it wasn't so difficult, because I didn't have a lot riding on it. But I'm not some unknown college hockey player anymore. I'm in the national spotlight. Now, my career and my image are at stake. The support and respect of my peers.

So for lack of the right way to say it, I just say it.

"My father abused me as a child."

Alarm flashes in Collins's eyes. "Oh," is all he says, and he waits for me to continue.

Despite my itching discomfort, I do.

I'm not sure I even hear myself when I explain how my dad beat, manipulated, and scared me, barely scratching the surface of his cruelty. It's bitter and painful coming out. But like a splinter that's been under the skin so long, you forgot it didn't belong there, the relief is immediate and overwhelming.

For several seconds, the producer is silent. Then he slips off his desk and takes a seat in the chair beside mine.

"Hell, Garrett. I don't know what to say. This is…"

I don't answer. I don't need his sympathy or pity, just his understanding.

But of course, I wouldn't be sitting next to someone in the entertainment industry without them trying to spin it for their own benefit.

"Would you be willing to address this in an interview? Forget what we've already shot. That's scrapped. Consider it in the dumpster." Collins tips his head. "But if it's something you're interested in…"

I laugh hoarsely. "Am I interested in telling the world the salacious details of my childhood physical abuse?" I feel sick just thinking about it.

But I underestimate Collins. Yes, he's definitely trying to use this to his professional advantage, but the suggestion might not be entirely selfish, as he softens his voice and says, "I had a similar experience growing up. Not my dad." His gaze flicks to mine. "My mother. She wasn't a good lady, let me tell you. But you want to know the craziest part? Every time one of my teachers called social services and they sent someone to our house to investigate, I lied. I covered for my mother because I was too embarrassed to admit she was hurting me."

I let out a breath. "Damn."

"Yeah." Collins rubs a hand over his chin. "Anyway. Nowadays, if I had the chance, I think I'd say something. But I don't have a platform and nobody gives a shit who I am. You, on the other hand…" He shrugs. "You've got a name and a platform. You could take this crappy piece of your past and try to squeeze some good out of it."

The words give me pause. I've protected Phil Graham's legacy for so long, but why the hell should I keep doing it? Why am I so afraid of what the world will think?

And what would it say about me as a father if I continued to bury something like this? If I didn't set a better example for my son and then someday someone hurt him, and he was too embarrassed and ashamed to tell me?

There are kids out there, adults, who are still living with these same scars. If I can help some of them overcome their fears, then yeah, I can make the sacrifice and suffer a couple of hours on camera pulling open the wounds.

"Yeah." I lick my suddenly dry lips. "Let's do it."

"You sure?" Collins says, a glimmer of admiration in his eyes.

I nod. "Call Landon to set up a day and time."

God help me, but it's time to officially sever the cord between me and the past.

At home later, after I break the news to Hannah, she's maybe more surprised at my decision than I am.

"I can't believe you agreed to do it," she marvels, her head in my lap while we watch TV on the couch.

"Trust me, I'm not exactly looking forward to it, but I think I have to do this. You were right. It's time."

"Are you going to tell your dad?"

"Nope."

"Good."

Picturing him throwing a glass of scotch across the room at the television when he finds out what's coming for him does get me a little more enthused about the idea.

Hannah sits up to snuggle into my shoulder. "This is a big thing."

"Yeah, kind of."

"I'm really proud of you."

I kiss the top of her head, holding her tighter.

"So proud," she repeats.

Those words mean more to me than she'll ever understand. Truth is, I wouldn't have gotten this far without her. She was the first person who helped me find some kind of peace with my past, and it's with her support I've found my way to the courage to confront it.

She makes me a better man.

And, hopefully, a good father.

EPILOGUE

AUGUST
HANNAH

Sabrina and Tucker stop by about a half hour before Garrett and I are supposed to leave for the doctor's office. I'm having an ultrasound this morning and not looking forward to it. I'm not sure I'll ever get used to being treated like a sunken ship with lost pirate treasure aboard.

"What are you guys doing here?" Garrett asks in surprise, but he looks happy to see them. Especially when he notices Jamie at Sabrina's side. "Gumdrop! Ahh! I missed you!"

He scoops up the redheaded toddler, and she flings her arms around his neck. "Hiiiii!" she exclaims happily. "Hiiiii!"

I stifle a laugh. This kid is so damned adorable.

"We're heading out pretty soon." I glance at Sabrina, who looks stunning as always in a yellow sundress that sets off her summer tan. She's got a pair of dark sunglasses atop her head, and an oversized beach bag over her shoulder.

"Don't worry, we only have a minute. We're on our way to the pool," Tucker explains. Which explains his striped swim trunks and flip-flops. I notice that his gray T-shirt is stained with something that looks pink and sticky.

Sabrina catches my gaze and snorts. "The princess demanded a strawberry creamsicle on the way here and then decided she didn't like it and threw it at Daddy. I told him it wasn't a good idea."

I also notice Tucker's holding a very large gift bag. "What's that?" I ask curiously.

"Jamie picked out a gift for you guys," he says.

"For your baby!!!" the toddler tells us, beaming.

Garrett narrows his eyes. "Jamie picked it out, huh?"

Sabrina and Tucker nod. Either they're telling the truth, or they're the most phenomenal actors on the planet.

"Can we come inside, or should we melt away on your front porch?" Tucker's Texas drawl kicks in as he flashes his good ol' boy smile.

"Come in," I say grudgingly.

We walk inside and go to the kitchen, where Garrett sets Jamie on her feet. Then he and I stare at the gift bag that Tuck sets on the marble island. The only saving grace is there's no way it can be that horrible doll. First of all, it's far too large for Alexander. And secondly, Sabrina swore she and Tuck gave him a burial at sea.

"Open it!" Jamie shouts. And keeps shouting. "Open it! Open it! OPEN IT!"

"Sweet Jesus," Garrett murmurs, "is this what we're in for?"

"Indoor voices, princess," chides Tuck.

Sabrina grins. "You should probably open it before she has an aneurysm."

"All right. Yeah." I grab a pair of scissors and snip the piece of tape holding the gift bag together. "You guys didn't have to do this, but thank you."

"Really nice of you," Garrett agrees.

"Thank Jamie," Tuck says easily.

I reach inside, my hand emerging with a box that looks about large enough to house a basketball. An identical one remains in the bag, but Sabrina says I should do one at a time.

Suspicion gnaws at me as I cut through more tape to open the box. I don't trust them. I'm not sure why, but I just don't. Something about this entire thing feels very, very off—

"A dolly!!" Jamie shrieks when the contents of the box are revealed. "A dolly for your baby, Auntie 'Annah!"

I withdraw my hand as if I'd just burned it on a hot stove.

My betrayed gaze flies to Tucker and Sabrina, who smile innocently before nodding toward their daughter.

"Jamie saw this adorable little guy in Tuck's suitcase when we got back from St. Barth's," Sabrina chirps.

"Can you believe he floated right back to shore like he couldn't bear to part with us?" Tuck pipes up.

"It's like he knew exactly where he belonged." Sabrina nods. "At first we were going to let Jamie keep him—"

I glare. Because, bullshit. They'd never let their precious child have prolonged contact with a doll housing the spirit of Willie the Gold Rush corpse. Never.

"—but when we told her Auntie Hannah and Uncle Garrett were going to have a baby, she decided she couldn't possibly be selfish and deprive the new baby of this joyous gift. Right, little one?"

"Right!" Jamie smiles. "Do you like him?"

I stare at Alexander's smirking red mouth, dread filling my gut.

Then, pasting on a big fake smile, I address the little girl. "I love it," I tell Jamie. While beside me, Garrett mouths *You're dead* to Jamie's parents. He slashes his finger across his neck.

"Oh wait, but there's more!" Tucker is loving every second of this nightmare.

He lifts the second box out of the bag, and my stomach does a queasy somersault that has nothing to do with my pregnancy and everything to do with whatever new horror we're about to experience.

Sabrina offers an evil smile. "Last year Tuck and I did some research on Alexander's history and discovered that he was part of a lot."

"Oh my God," I moan.

"No," Garrett says, holding up his hand as if that'll achieve anything.

Tucker takes up the narrative. "This particular doll maker designed ten dolls, each one custom-made but part of the series. We had an alert set if any other dolls in the lot came up for sale. And last week, one became available! I think they call that serendipity. Maybe. I'm not sure. But it's wild, huh?"

Sabrina nods enthusiastically. "Wild."

"So we said to Jamie, *hey, what's better than one doll for Auntie Hannah's baby?* And what did you say back, princess?"

"I said two!" Jamie dances around her father's legs. This poor innocent child whose parents recruited her to do their malevolent bidding. They had to know that if Jamie wasn't here right now, I'd be trying to shove Alexander in the garbage disposal.

"Two dolls are always better than one," Tucker agrees, and then he pulls out a second porcelain nightmare and holds it up.

This one is a girl doll, with white-blond curls that, oh God, look like they could be actual human hair. Her cheeks are like two red apples, her pink lips stretched in a macabre frozen smile. In a blue dress with a white sash and shiny red shoes like Alexander, she is creepy and awful and I want to punch Tucker in the face with her.

"Her name is Cassandra," Sabrina says, grinning at my expression. "And don't you worry, she comes with a verified biography. It's in the box. Some fun reading for later."

Tucker winks. "We don't want to spoil it for you, but let's just say while Alexander and Willie were traversing the California Trail, Cassandra here served as a wonderful companion for a child in a German insane asylum."

"Yayyyyy!" Jamie starts clapping, clearly ignorant to what most of those words mean.

"Yay," Garrett says weakly.

I glower at our supposed friends. "I'll never forget this."

"Wonderful!" Sabrina says, clapping too. "Hear that, little one? Auntie Hannah says she's never going to forget this gift."

I glance at Garrett and sigh. We need new friends.

FORTY-FIVE MINUTES LATER, WE'RE IN THE EXAM ROOM, BICKERING about the fate of the two haunted dolls we left back at home. I vote we should burn them, but Garrett is too superstitious.

"I think we need to bring someone in to do some sort of exorcism before we burn anything," he argues. "What if the dead kids' spirits exit the dolls during the fire and then haunt the house itself?"

"Ahem."

Our attention shifts to the door, where my doctor stands, eyeing us warily.

"Ignore everything you just heard," I advise her.

"Snitches get stitches," Garrett adds solemnly, and I promptly punch him in the arm.

"Ignore that too," I say.

Chuckling, the doctor moves the ultrasound machine closer and squirts a bunch of cold gel on my belly. I'm still barely showing, but apparently that's normal. Sabrina had warned me that with her pregnancy, she'd barely had a bump the first two trimesters, until at six months she'd suddenly ballooned. Not that I trust anything Sabrina James-Tucker says anymore.

"You ready?" the doc asks as Garrett squeezes my hand.

"Let her rip," I answer, and she laughs at that.

Garrett kisses my knuckles, my engagement ring catching the light. Though I didn't need it, he'd surprised me with a formal proposal a few weeks ago. Got down on one knee and everything. I never thought I'd be one of those pregnant brides waddling down the aisle, but here we are. Funny how life works out sometimes.

"What's in the bag?" I ask, noticing a small plastic bag beside Garrett's chair.

He grins. "Check this out. I saw it in a store window the other day." With a flourish, he pulls out a tiny Bruins hockey jersey with GRAHAM on the back.

"It could still be too early to know the sex," I remind him. "We don't know it's a boy." Though he's been convinced it is.

"It's a unisex jersey," he says smugly.

"I thought so," the doctor says under her breath.

I look over, slightly alarmed. "What's up?"

"I couldn't be sure during your last visit because of the position of the fetus. However, it's quite clear now."

My pulse spikes.

"Something wrong?" Garrett asks, sitting forward as we both stare at the screen.

"Congratulations," she announces with a grin. "You're having twins."

"Twins?" I echo stupidly.

"You serious, Doc?"

"Twins?" I say again. "Like two?"

"Two," she confirms.

Garrett's face collapses. "I only bought one jersey."

"Can you tell the sexes?" I ask, squinting at the screen as if I can discern it myself.

"It's still a bit early. From what I can see, though, yes, I believe we can tell. Would you like to know?"

My pulse spikes as I turn toward Garrett. Our gazes lock, and he nods.

"Yes," I tell the doctor. "We want to know."

"You're having a baby boy…and a baby girl."

The End

Keep reading to discover (or re-discover!) Elle Kennedy's bestselling book *The Deal*, the addictive love story of Hannah Wells and Garrett Graham.

CHAPTER 1

HANNAH

He doesn't know I'm alive.

For the millionth time in forty-five minutes, I sneak a peek in Justin Kohl's direction, and he's so beautiful it makes my throat close up. Though I should probably come up with another adjective—my male friends insist that men don't like being called *beautiful*.

But holy hell, there's no other way to describe his rugged features and soulful brown eyes. He's wearing a baseball cap today, but I know what's beneath it: thick dark hair, the kind that looks silky to the touch and makes you want to run your fingers through it.

In the five years since the rape, my heart has pounded for only two guys.

The first one dumped me.

This one is just oblivious.

At the podium in the lecture hall, Professor Tolbert delivers what I've come to refer to as the Disappointment Speech. It's the third one in six weeks.

Surprise, surprise, seventy percent of the class got a C-plus or lower on the midterm.

Me? I aced it. And I'd be lying if I said the big red *A!* circled on top of my midterm hadn't come as a complete shock. All I did was scribble down a never-ending stream of bullshit to try to fill up the booklet.

Philosophical Ethics was supposed to be a breeze. The prof who used to teach it handed out brainless multiple choice tests and a final "exam" consisting of a personal essay that posed a moral dilemma and asked how you'd react to it.

But two weeks before the semester started, Professor Lane dropped dead from a heart attack. I heard his cleaning lady found him on the bathroom floor—naked. Poor guy.

Luckily (and yep, that's total sarcasm) Pamela Tolbert stepped in to take over Lane's class. She's new to Briar University, and she's the kind of prof who wants you to make connections and "engage" with the material. If this were a movie, she'd be the young, ambitious teacher who shows up at the inner city school and inspires the fuckups, and suddenly everyone's picking up their pencils, and the end credits scroll up to announce how all the kids got into Harvard or some shit. Instant Oscar for Jennifer Lawrence.

Except this isn't a movie, which means that the only thing Tolbert has inspired in her students is hatred. And she honestly can't seem to grasp why nobody is excelling in her class.

Here's a hint—it's because she asks the types of questions you could write a frickin' grad school thesis on.

"I'm willing to offer a makeup exam to anyone who failed or received a C-minus or lower." Tolbert's nose wrinkles as if she can't fathom why it's even necessary.

The word she just used—*willing?* Yeah, right. I heard that a ton of students complained to their advisers about her, and I suspect the administration is forcing her to give everyone a redo. It doesn't reflect well on Briar when more than half the students in a course are flunking, especially when it's not just the slackers. Straight-A students like Nell, who's sulking beside me, also bombed the midterm.

"For those of you who choose to take it again, your two grades will be averaged. If you do worse the second time, the first grade will stand," Tolbert finishes.

"I can't believe you got an A," Nell whispers to me.

She looks so upset that I feel a pang of sympathy. Nell and I aren't best pals or anything, but we've been sitting next to each other since September so it's only reasonable that we've gotten to know each other. She's on the pre-med path, and I know she comes from an overachieving family who would lay into her if they found out about her midterm grade.

"I can't believe it either," I whisper back. "Seriously. Read my answers. They're ramblings of nonsense."

"Actually, can I?" She sounds eager now. "I'm curious to see what the Tyrant considers A material."

"I'll scan and email you a copy tonight," I promise.

The second Tolbert dismisses us, the lecture hall echoes with let's-get-the-hell-outta-here noises. Laptops snap shut, notebooks slide into backpacks, students shuffle out of their seats.

Justin Kohl lingers near the door to talk to someone, and my gaze locks in on him like a missile. He's beautiful.

Have I mentioned how beautiful he is?

My palms go clammy as I stare at his handsome profile. He's new to Briar this year, but I'm not sure which college he transferred from, and although he wasted no time becoming the star wide receiver on the football team, he's not like the other athletes at this school. He doesn't strut through the quad with one of those I'm-God's-gift-to-the-world smirks or show up with a new girl on his arm every day. I've seen him laugh and joke with his teammates, but he gives off an intelligent, intense vibe that makes me think there are hidden depths to him. Which just makes me all the more desperate to get to know him.

I'm not usually into jocks, but something about this one has turned me into a mindless pile of mush.

"You're staring again."

Nell's teasing voice brings a blush to my cheeks. She's caught me drooling over Justin on more than one occasion, and she's one of the few people I've admitted the crush to.

My roommate Allie also knows, but my other friends? Hell no. Most of them are music or drama majors, so I guess that makes us the artsy crowd. Or maybe emo. Aside from Allie, who's had an on-again/off-again relationship with a frat boy since freshman year, my friends get a kick out of trashing Briar's elite. I don't usually join in (I like to think gossiping is beneath me) but...let's face it. Most of the popular kids are total douchebags.

Case in point—Garrett Graham, the other star athlete in this class. Dude walks around like he owns the place. I guess he kind of does. All he has to do is snap his fingers and an eager girl appears at his side. Or jumps into his lap. Or sticks her tongue down his throat.

He doesn't look like the BMOC today, though. Almost everyone else has gone, including Tolbert, but Garrett remains in his seat, his fists curled tightly around the edges of his booklet.

He must have failed too, but I don't feel much sympathy for the guy. Briar is known for two things—hockey and football, which isn't much of a shocker considering Massachusetts is home to both the Patriots and the Bruins. The athletes who play for Briar almost always end up in the pros, and during their years here they get everything handed to them on a silver platter—including grades.

So yeah, maybe it makes me a teeny bit vindictive, but I get a sense of triumph from knowing that Tolbert is failing the captain of our championship-winning hockey team right along with everyone else.

"Wanna grab something from the Coffee Hut?" Nell asks as she gathers her books.

"Can't. I've got rehearsal in twenty minutes." I get up, but I don't follow her to the door. "Go on ahead. I need to check the schedule before I go. Can't remember when my next tutorial is."

Another "perk" of being in Tolbert's class—along with our weekly lecture, we're forced to attend two thirty-minute tutorials a week. On the bright side, Dana the TA runs those, and she has all the qualities Tolbert lacks. Like a sense of humor.

"'Kay," Nell says. "I'll see you later."

"Later," I call after her.

At the sound of my voice, Justin pauses in the doorway and turns his head.

Oh. My. God.

It's impossible to stop the flush that rises in my cheeks. This is the first time we've ever made eye contact, and I don't know how to respond. Say hi? Wave? Smile?

In the end, I settle for a small nod of greeting. *There.* Cool and casual, befitting of a sophisticated college junior.

My heart skips a beat when the corner of his mouth lifts in a faint grin. He nods back, and then he's gone.

I stare at the empty doorway. My pulse explodes in a gallop because *holy shit.* After six weeks of breathing the same air in this stuffy lecture hall, he's finally noticed me.

I wish I were brave enough to go after him. Maybe ask him to grab a coffee. Or dinner. Or brunch—wait, do people our age even have brunch?

But my feet stay rooted to the shiny laminate floor.

Because I'm a coward. Yep, a total chicken-shit coward. I'm terrified that he'll say no, but I'm even more terrified he'll say *yes.*

I was in a good place when I started college. My issues solidly behind me, my guard lowered. I was ready to date again, and I did. I dated several guys, but other than my ex, Devon, none of them made my body tingle the way Justin Kohl does, and that freaks me out.

Baby steps.

Right. Baby steps. That was my therapist's favorite piece of advice, and I can't deny that the strategy helped me a lot. Focus on the small victories, Carole always advised.

So…today's victory…I nodded at Justin and he smiled at me. Next class, maybe I'll smile back. And the one after that, maybe I'll bring up the coffee, dinner, or brunch idea.

I take a breath as I head down the aisle, clinging to that feeling of victory, however teeny it may be.

Baby steps.

GARRETT

I FAILED.

I fucking failed.

For fifteen years, Timothy Lane handed out A's like mints. The year *I* take the class? Lane's ticker quits ticking, and I get stuck with Pamela Tolbert.

It's official. The woman is my archenemy. Just the sight of her flowery handwriting—which fills up every inch of available space in the margins of my midterm—makes me want to go Incredible Hulk on the booklet and rip it to shreds.

I'm rocking A's in most of my other courses, but as of right now, I'm getting an F in Philosophical Ethics. Combined with the C-plus in Spanish history, my average has dropped to a C-minus.

I need a C-plus average to play hockey.

Normally I have no problem keeping my GPA up. Despite what a lot of folks believe, I'm not a dumb jock. But hey, I don't mind letting people think I am. Women, in particular. I guess they're turned on by the idea of screwing the big brawny caveman who's only good for one thing, but since I'm not looking for anything serious, casual hookups with chicks that only want my dick suit me just fine. Gives me more time to focus on hockey.

But there won't *be* any more hockey if I don't bring up this grade. The worst thing about Briar? Our dean demands excellence—academically *and* athletically. While other schools might be more lenient toward athletes, Briar has a zero-tolerance policy.

Fuckin' Tolbert. When I spoke to her before class asking for extra credit, she told me in that nasally voice of hers to attend the tutorials and meet with the study group. I already do both. So yeah, unless I hire some whiz kid to wear a mask of my face and take the makeup midterm for me…I'm screwed.

My frustration manifests itself in the form of an audible groan, and from the corner of my eye I see someone jerk in surprise.

I jerk too, because here I thought I was wallowing in my misery alone. But the girl who sits in the back row has stuck around, and she's making her way down the aisle toward Tolbert's desk.

Mandy?

Marty?

I can't remember her name. Probably because I've never bothered to ask for it. She's cute, though. A helluva lot cuter than I realized. Pretty face, dark hair, smokin' body—shit, how have I never noticed that body before?

But I'm noticing now. Skinny jeans cling to a round, perky ass that just screams "squeeze me," and her V-neck sweater hugs a seriously impressive rack. I don't have time to admire either of those appealing visuals because she catches me staring and a frown touches her mouth.

"Everything okay?" she asks with a pointed look.

I grumble something under my breath. I'm not in the mood to talk to anyone at the moment.

One dark eyebrow rises in my direction. "Sorry, was that English?"

I ball up my midterm and scrape my chair back. "I said everything's fine."

"Okay, then." She shrugs and continues down the steps.

As she picks up the clipboard that contains our tutorial schedule, I fling my Briar Hockey jacket on, then shove my pathetic midterm into my backpack and zip it up.

The dark-haired girl heads back to the aisle. Mona? Molly? The M sounds right, but the rest is a mystery. She has her midterm in hand, but I don't sneak a peek because I assume she failed just like everyone else.

I let her pass before I step into the aisle. I suppose I can say it's the gentleman in me, but that would be a lie. I want to check out her ass again, because it's a damn sexy ass, and now that I've seen it I wouldn't mind another look. I follow her up to the exit, suddenly realizing how frickin' tiny she is—I'm one step below her yet I can see the top of her head.

Just as we reach the door, she stumbles on absolutely nothing and the books in her hand clatter to the floor.

"Shit. I'm such a klutz."

She drops to her knees and so do I, because contrary to my previous statement, I *can* be a gentleman when I want to be, and the gentlemanly thing to do is help her gather her books.

"Oh, you don't have to do that. I'm fine," she insists.

But my hand has already connected with her midterm, and my jaw drops when I see her grade.

"Fucking hell. You aced it?" I demand.

She gives a self-deprecating smile. "I know, right? I thought I failed for sure."

"Holy shit." I feel like I've just bumped into Stephen fuckin' Hawking and he's dangling the secrets to the universe under my nose. "Can I read your answers?"

Her brows quirk up again. "That's rather forward of you, don't you think? We don't even know each other."

I roll my eyes. "I'm not asking you to take your clothes off, baby. I just want to peek at your midterm."

"*Baby*? Goodbye forward, hello presumptuous."

"Would you prefer *miss*? *Ma'am* maybe? I'd use your name but I don't know it."

"Of course you don't." She sighs. "It's Hannah." Then she pauses meaningfully. "*Garrett.*"

Okay, I was waaaay off on the M thing.

And I don't miss the way she emphasizes my name as if to say, *Ha! I know yours, asshole!*

She collects the rest of her books and stands up, but I don't hand over her midterm. Instead, I hop to my feet and start flipping through it. As I skim her answers, my spirits plummet even lower, because if this is the kind of analysis Tolbert is looking for, I'm screwed. There's a reason I'm a history major, for chrissake—I deal in facts. Black and white. This happened at this time to this person and here's the result.

Hannah's answers focus on theoretical shit and how the philosophers would respond to the various moral dilemmas.

"Thanks." I give her the booklet, then hook my thumbs in the belt loops of my jeans. "Hey, listen. Do you…would you consider…" I shrug. "You know…"

Her lips twitch as if she's trying not to laugh. "Actually, I *don't* know."

I let out a breath. "Will you tutor me?"

Her green eyes—the darkest shade of green I've ever seen and surrounded by thick black eyelashes—go from surprised to skeptical in a matter of seconds.

"I'll pay you," I add hastily.

"Oh. Um. Well, yeah, of course I'd expect you to pay me. But…" She shakes her head. "I'm sorry. I can't."

I bite back my disappointment. "C'mon, do me a solid. If I fail this makeup, my GPA will implode. Please?" I flash a smile, the one that makes my dimples pop out and never fails to make girls melt.

"Does that usually work?" she asks curiously.

"What?"

"The aw-shucks little boy grin… Does it help you get your way?"

"Always," I answer without hesitation.

"*Almost* always," she corrects. "Look, I'm sorry, but I really don't have time. I'm already juggling school and work, and with the winter showcase coming up, I'll have even less time."

"Winter showcase?" I say blankly.

"Right, I forgot. If it's not about hockey, then it's not on your radar."

"Now who's being presumptuous? You don't even know me."

There's a beat, and then she sighs. "I'm a music major, okay? And the arts faculty puts on two major performances every year, the winter showcase and the spring one. The winner gets a five-thousand-dollar scholarship. It's kind of a huge deal, actually. Important industry people fly in from all over the country to see it. Agents, record producers, talent scouts…. So, as much as I'd love to help you—"

"You would not," I grumble. "You look like you don't even want to *talk* to me right now."

Her little you-got-me shrug is grating as hell. "I have to get to rehearsal. I'm sorry you're failing this course, but if it makes you feel better, so is everyone else."

I narrow my eyes. "Not *you*."

"I can't help it. Tolbert seems to respond to my brand of bullshit. It's a gift."

"Well, I want your gift. Please, master, teach me how to bullshit."

I'm two seconds from dropping to my knees and begging her, but she edges to the door. "You know there's a study group, right? I can give you the number for—"

"I'm already in it," I mutter.

"Oh. Well, then there's not much else I can do for you. Good luck on the makeup test. *Baby*."

She darts out the door, leaving me staring after her in frustration. Unbelievable. Every girl at this college would cut her frickin' arm off to help me out. But this one? Runs away like I just asked her to murder a cat so we could sacrifice it to Satan.

And now I'm right back to where I was before Hannah-not-with-an-M gave me that faintest flicker of hope.

Royally screwed.

CHAPTER 2

GARRETT

My roommates are piss drunk when I walk into the living room after study group. The coffee table is overflowing with empty beer cans, along with a nearly depleted bottle of Jack that I know belongs to Logan because he subscribes to the *beer is for pussies* philosophy. His words, not mine.

At the moment, Logan and Tucker are battling each other in a heated game of *Ice Pro*, their gazes glued to the flat screen as they furiously click their controllers. Logan's gaze shifts slightly when he notices me in the doorway, and his split second of distraction costs him.

"Hell to the yeah!" Tuck crows as his defenseman flicks a wrist shot past Logan's goalie and the scoreboard lights up.

"Aw, for fuck's sake!" Logan pauses the game and levels a dark glare at me. "What the hell, G? I just got deked out because of you."

I don't answer, because now *I'm* distracted—by the half-naked make-out session happening in the corner of the room. Dean's at it again. Bare-chested and barefoot, he's sprawled in the armchair while a blond in nothing but a lacy black bra and booty shorts sits astride him and grinds against his crotch.

Dark-green eyes peer over the chick's shoulder, and Dean smirks in my direction. "Graham! Where've you been, man?" he slurs.

He goes back to kissing the blond before I can answer the drunken question.

For some reason, Dean likes to hook up everywhere *but* his bedroom. Seriously. Every time I turn around, he's in the midst of some form of debauchery. On the kitchen counter, the living room couch, the dining room table—dude's gotten it on in every inch of the off-campus house the four of us share. He's a total slut and completely unapologetic about it.

Granted, I'm not one to talk. I'm no monk, and neither are Logan and Tuck. What can I say? Hockey players are horny mother-fuckers. When we're not on the ice, we can usually be found hooking up with a puck bunny or two. Or three, if your name is Tucker and it's New Year's Eve of last year.

"I've been texting you for the past hour, man," Logan informs me.

His massive shoulders hunch forward as he swipes the whiskey bottle from the coffee table. Logan's a bruiser of a defenseman, one of the best I've ever played with, and also the best friend I've ever had. His first name is John, but we call him Logan because it makes it easier to differentiate him from Tucker, whose first name is also John. Luckily, Dean is just Dean, so we don't have to call him by his mouthful of a last name: Heyward-Di Laurentis.

"Seriously, where the hell have you been?" Logan grumbles.

"Study group." I grab a Bud Light from the table and pop the tab. "What's this surprise you kept blabbing about?"

I can always tell how plastered Logan is based on the grammar of his texts. And tonight he must be shit-faced, because I had to go full-on Sherlock to decrypt his messages. *Suprz* meant surprise. *Gyabh* had taken longer to decode, but I *think* it meant *get your ass back here?* But who knows with Logan.

From his perch on the couch, he grins so broadly it's a wonder his jaw doesn't snap off. He jerks his thumb at the ceiling and says, "Go upstairs and see for yourself."

I narrow my eyes. "Why? Who's up there?"

Logan snickers. "If I told you, then it wouldn't be a surprise."

"Why do I get the feeling you're up to something?"

"Jeez," Tucker pipes up. "You've got some major trust issues, G."

"Says the asshole who left a live raccoon in my bedroom on the first day of the semester."

Tucker grins. "Aw, come on, Bandit was fucking adorable. He was your welcome back to school gift."

I flip up my middle finger. "Yeah, well, your *gift* was a bitch to get rid of." Now I scowl at him because I still remember how it took three pest control guys to de-raccoon my room.

"For fuck's sake," Logan groans. "Just go upstairs. Trust me, you'll thank us for it later."

The knowing look they exchange eases my suspicion. Kind of. I mean, I'm not about to let down my guard completely, not around *these* assholes.

I steal two more cans of beer on my way out. I don't drink much during the season, but Coach gave us the week off to study for midterms and we still have two days of freedom left. My teammates, lucky bastards, seem to have no problem downing twelve beers and playing like champs the next day. Me? Even a buzz gives me a rip-roaring headache the morning after and then I skate like a toddler with his first pair of Bauers.

Once we're back to a six-days-a-week practice schedule, my alcohol consumption will drop to the usual one/five limit. One drink on practice nights, five after a game. No exceptions.

I plan on taking full advantage of the time I have left.

Armed with my beers, I head upstairs to my room. The *master* bedroom. Yup, I was not above playing the I'm-your-captain card to snag it, and trust me, it was worth the argument my teammates put up. Private bath, baby.

My door is ajar, a sight that snaps me right back into suspicion mode. I warily peer up at the frame to make sure there isn't a bucket of blood up there, then give the door a tiny shove. It gives way and I inch through it, fully prepared for an ambush.

I get one.

Except it's more of a visual ambush, because *damn*, the girl on my bed looks like she stepped out of a Victoria's Secret catalog.

Now, I'm a guy. I don't know the names of half the shit she's wearing. I see white lace and pink bows and lots of skin. And I'm happy.

"Took you long enough." Kendall shoots me a sexy smile that says *you're about to get lucky, big boy*, and my cock reacts accordingly, thickening beneath my zipper. "I was giving you five more minutes before I took off."

"I made it just in time then." My gaze sweeps over her drool-worthy outfit, and then I drawl, "Aw, babe, is that all for me?"

Her blue eyes darken seductively. "You know it, stud."

I'm well aware that we sound like characters from a cheesy porno. But come on, when a man walks into his bedroom and finds a woman who looks like *this*? He's willing to reenact any trashy scene she wants, even one that involves him pretending to be a pizza guy delivering pies to a MILF.

Kendall and I first hooked up over the summer, out of convenience more than anything else because we both happened to be in the area during the break. We hit the bar a couple times, one thing led to another, and the next thing I know I'm fooling around with a hot sorority girl. But it fizzled out before midterms started, and aside from a few dirty texts here and there, I haven't seen Kendall until now.

"I figured you might want to have some fun before practice starts up again," she says, her manicured fingers toying with the tiny pink bow in the center of her bra.

"You figured right."

A smile curves her lips as she rises to her knees. Damn, her tits are practically pouring out of that lacy thing she's wearing. She crooks a finger at me. "C'mere."

I waste no time striding toward her. Because…again…I'm a *guy*.

"I think you're a tad overdressed," she remarks, then grasps the waistband of my jeans and teases the button open. She tugs on the zipper and a second later my dick springs into her waiting hand. I haven't done laundry in weeks so I've been going commando until I get my shit together, and from the way her eyes flare with heat, I can tell she approves of the whole no-boxers thing.

When she wraps her fingers around me, a groan slips out of my throat. Oh yeah. There's nothing better than the feel of a woman's hand on your cock.

Nope, I'm wrong. Kendall's tongue comes into play, and holy shit, it's *so* much better than her hand.

An hour later, Kendall snuggles up beside me and rests her head on my chest. Her lingerie and my clothes are strewn on the bedroom floor, along with two empty condom packages and the bottle of lube we hadn't needed to crack open.

The cuddling makes me apprehensive, but I can't exactly shove her away and demand she hit the road, not when she clearly put a lot of effort into this seduction.

But that worries me too.

Women don't get all decked out in expensive lingerie for a hookup, do they? I'm thinking *no*, and Kendall's next words validate my uneasy thoughts.

"I missed you, baby."

My first though is *shit*.

My second thought is *why*?

Because in all the time we've been hooking up, Kendall hasn't made a single effort to get to know me. If we're not having sex, she just talks nonstop about herself. Seriously, I don't think she's asked me a personal question about myself since we met.

"Uh…" I struggle for words, any sequence of them that doesn't consist of *I*, *miss*, *you*, and *too*. "I've been busy. You know, midterms."

"Obviously. We go to the same college. I was studying, too." There's an edge to her tone now. "Did you miss me?"

Fuck me sideways. What am I supposed to say to that? I'm not going to lie, because that'll only lead her on. But I can't be a dick about it and admit she hasn't even crossed my mind since the last time we hooked up.

Kendall sits up and narrows her eyes. "It's a yes or no question, Garrett. Did. You. Miss. Me."

My gaze darts to the window. Yup, I'm on the second floor and actually contemplating jumping out the frickin' window. That's how badly I want to avoid this convo.

But my silence speaks volumes, and suddenly Kendall flies off the bed, her blond hair whipping in all directions as she scrambles for her clothes. "Oh my God. You are *such* an ass! You don't care about me at all, do you, Garrett?"

I get up and make a beeline for my discarded jeans. "I do care about you," I protest. "But…"

She angrily shoves her panties on. "But what?"

"But I thought we were clear about what this was. I don't want anything serious." I shoot her a pointed look. "I told you that from the start."

Her expression softens as she bites her lip. "I know, but…I just thought…"

I know exactly what she thought—that I'd fall madly in love with her, and our casual hookup would transform into the fucking *Notebook*.

Honestly, I don't know why I bother laying down ground rules anymore. In my experience, no woman enters into a fling believing it's going to *stay* a fling. She might say otherwise, maybe even convince herself she's cool with a no-strings sex-fest, but deep down, she hopes and prays it'll lead to something deeper.

And then I, the villain in her personal rom-com, swoop in and burst that bubble of hope, despite the fact that I never lied about my intentions or misled her, not even for a second.

"Hockey is my entire life," I say gruffly. "I practice six days a week, play twenty games a year—more if we make it to the post-season. I don't have time for a girlfriend, Kendall. And you deserve a helluva lot more than I can give you."

Unhappiness clouds her eyes. "I don't want a casual fling anymore. I want to be your girlfriend."

Another *why* almost flies out of my mouth, but I bite my tongue. If she'd shown any interest in me outside the carnal sense, I might believe her, but the fact that she hasn't makes me wonder if the only reason she wants a relationship with me is because I'm some kind of status symbol to her.

I swallow my frustration and offer another awkward apology. "I'm sorry. But that's where I'm at right now."

As I zip up my jeans, she refocuses her attention on getting her clothes on. Though *clothes* is a bit of a stretch—all she's sporting is lingerie and a trench coat. Which explains why Logan and Tucker were grinning like idiots when I got home. Because when a girl shows up at your door in a trench coat, you know damn well there's not much else underneath it.

"I can't see you anymore," she finally says, her gaze finding mine. "If we keep doing…this…I'll only get more attached."

I can't argue with that, so I don't. "We had fun, though, right?"

After a beat, she smiles. "Yeah, we had fun."

She bridges the distance between us and leans up on her tiptoes to kiss me. I kiss her back, but not with the same degree of passion as before. I keep it light. Polite. The fling has run its course, and I'm not about to lead her on again.

"With that said…" Her eyes twinkle mischievously. "Let me know if you change your mind about the girlfriend thing."

"You'll be the first person I call," I promise.

"Good."

She smacks a kiss on my cheek and walks out the door, leaving me to marvel over how easy that went. I'd been steeling myself for a fight, but aside from that initial burst of anger, Kendall had accepted the situation like a pro.

If only all women were as agreeable as her.

Yup, totally a jab at Hannah there.

Sex always stirs up my appetite, so I head downstairs in search of nourishment, and I'm happy to find there's still leftover rice and fried chicken courtesy of Tuck, who is our resident chef because the rest of us can't boil water without burning it. Tuck, on the other hand, grew up in Texas with a single mom who taught him to cook when he was still in diapers.

I settle at the eat-in counter, shoving a piece of chicken in my mouth just as Logan strolls in wearing nothing but plaid boxers.

He raises a brow when he spots me. "Hey. I didn't think I'd see you again tonight. Figured you'd be VBF."

"VBF?" I ask between mouthfuls. Logan likes to make up acronyms in the hopes that we'll start to use them as slang, but half the time I have no idea what he's babbling about.

He grins. "Very busy fucking."

I roll my eyes and eat a forkful of wild rice.

"Seriously, Blondie's gone already?"

"Yup." I chew before continuing. "She knows the score." The score being, no girlfriends and definitely no sleepovers.

Logan rests his forearms on the counter, his blue eyes gleaming as he changes the subject. "I can't fucking wait for the St. Anthony's game this weekend. Did you hear? Braxton's suspension is over."

That gets my attention. "No shit. He's playing on Saturday?"

"Sure is." Logan's expression turns downright gleeful. "I'm gonna enjoy smashing that asshole's face into the boards."

Greg Braxton is St. Anthony's star left wing and a complete piece of shit human being. The guy's got a sadistic streak that he's not afraid to unleash on the ice, and when our teams faced off in the pre-season, he sent one of our sophomore D-men to the emergency room with a broken arm. Hence his three game suspension, though if it were up to me, the psycho would've been slapped with a lifetime ban from college hockey.

"You need to throw down, I'll be right there with you," I promise.

"I'm holding you to that. Oh, and next week we've got Eastwood heading our way."

I really should pay more attention to our schedule. Eastwood College is number two in our conference (second to us, of course) and our matchups are always nail-biters.

And shit, it suddenly dawns on me that if I don't ace the Ethics redo, I won't be on the ice for the Eastwood game.

"Fuck," I mumble.

Logan swipes a piece of chicken off my plate and pops it in his mouth. "What?"

I haven't told my teammates about my grade situation yet because I'd been hoping my midterm grade wouldn't hurt me too bad, but now it looks like fessing up is unavoidable.

So with a sigh, I tell Logan about my F in Ethics and what it could mean for the team.

"Drop the course," he says instantly.

"Can't. I missed the deadline."

"Crap."

"Yup."

We exchange a glum look, and then Logan flops down on the stool beside mine and rakes a hand through his hair. "Then you gotta shape up, man. Study your balls off and ace this motherfucker. We need you, G."

"I know." I grip my fork in frustration, then put it down, my appetite vanishing. This is my first year as captain, which is a major honor considering I'm only a junior. I'm supposed to follow in my predecessor's footsteps and lead my team to another national championship, but how the hell can I do that if I'm not on the ice with them?

"I've got a tutor lined up," I assure my teammate. "She's a frickin' genius."

"Good. Pay her whatever she wants. I'll chip in if you want."

I can't help but grin. "Wow. You're offering to part with all your sweet, sweet cash? You must *really* want me to play."

"Damn straight. It's all about the dream, man. You and me in Bruins jerseys, remember?"

I have to admit, it's a damn nice dream. It's what Logan and I have been talking about since we were assigned as roommates in freshman year. I didn't enter the draft because I wanted to focus on college, but there's no doubt in my mind that I'll go pro after I graduate. No doubt about Logan getting drafted either. The guy's faster than lightning and a goddamn beast on the ice.

"Get that fucking grade up, G," he orders. "Otherwise I'll kick your ass."

"Coach will kick it harder." I muster up a smile. "Don't worry, I'm on it."

"Good." Logan steals another piece of chicken before wandering out of the kitchen.

I scarf down the rest of my food, then head back upstairs to find my phone. It's time to ramp up the pressure on Hannah-not-with-an-M.

ABOUT THE AUTHOR

A *New York Times*, *USA Today*, and *Wall Street Journal* bestselling author, Elle Kennedy grew up in the suburbs of Toronto, Ontario, and holds a BA in English from York University. From an early age, she knew she wanted to be a writer and actively began pursuing that dream when she was a teenager. She loves strong heroines and sexy alpha heroes, and just enough heat and danger to keep things interesting!

Elle loves to hear from her readers. Visit her website www. ellekennedy.com or sign up for her newsletter to receive updates about upcoming books and exclusive excerpts. You can also find her at:

Website: ellekennedy.com
Facebook: ElleKennedyAuthor
Twitter: @ElleKennedy
Instagram: @ElleKennedy33
TikTok: @ElleKennedyAuthor

THE DEAL

She's about to make a deal with the college bad boy...

Hannah Wells has finally found someone who turns her on. But while she might be confident in every other area of her life, she's carting around a full set of baggage when it comes to sex and seduction. If she wants to get her crush's attention, she'll have to step out of her comfort zone and make him take notice...even if it means tutoring the annoying, childish, cocky captain of the hockey team in exchange for a pretend date.

...and it's going to be oh so good

All Garrett Graham has ever wanted is to play professional hockey after graduation, but his plummeting GPA is threatening everything he's worked so hard for. If helping a sarcastic brunette make another guy jealous will help him secure his position on the team, he's all for it. But when one unexpected kiss leads to the wildest sex of both their lives, it doesn't take long for Garrett to realize that pretend isn't going to cut it. Now he just has to convince Hannah that the man she wants looks a lot like him.

THE MISTAKE

He's a player in more ways than one...

College junior John Logan can get any girl he wants. For this hockey star, life is a parade of parties and hook-ups, but behind his killer grins and easygoing charm, he hides growing despair about the dead-end road he'll be forced to walk after graduation. A sexy encounter with freshman Grace Ivers is just the distraction he needs, but when a thoughtless mistake pushes her away, Logan plans to spend his final year proving to her that he's worth a second chance.

Now he's going to need to up his game...

After a less-than-stellar freshman year, Grace is back at Briar University, older, wiser, and so over the arrogant hockey player she nearly handed her V card to. She's not a charity case, and she's not the quiet butterfly she was when they first hooked up. If Logan expects her to roll over and beg like all his other puck bunnies, he can think again. He wants her back? He'll have to work for it. This time around, she'll be the one in the driver's seat...and she plans on driving him wild.

THE SCORE

He knows how to score, on and off the ice

Allie Hayes is in crisis mode. With graduation looming, she still doesn't have the first clue about what she's going to do after college. To make matters worse, she's nursing a broken heart thanks to the end of her longtime relationship. Wild rebound sex is definitely not the solution to her problems, but gorgeous hockey star Dean Di Laurentis is impossible to resist. Just once, though, because even if her future is uncertain, it sure as heck won't include the king of one-night stands.

It'll take more than flashy moves to win her over

Dean always gets what he wants. Girls, grades, girls, recognition, girls...he's a ladies man, all right, and he's yet to meet a woman who's immune to his charms. Until Allie. For one night, the feisty blond rocked his entire world—and now she wants to be friends? Nope. It's not over until he says it's over. Dean is in full-on pursuit, but when life-rocking changes strike, he starts to wonder if maybe it's time to stop focusing on scoring...and shoot for love.

THE GOAL

She's good at achieving her goals...

College senior Sabrina James has her whole future planned out: graduate from college, kick butt in law school, and land a high-paying job at a cutthroat firm. Her path to escaping her shameful past certainly doesn't include a gorgeous hockey player who believes in love at first sight. One night of sizzling heat and surprising tenderness is all she's willing to give John Tucker, but sometimes, one night is all it takes for your entire life to change.

But the game just got a whole lot more complicated

Tucker believes being a team player is as important as being the star. On the ice, he's fine staying out of the spotlight, but when it comes to becoming a daddy at the age of twenty-two, he refuses to be a benchwarmer. It doesn't hurt that the soon-to-be mother of his child is beautiful, whip-smart, and keeps him on his toes. The problem is, Sabrina's heart is locked up tight, and the fiery brunette is too stubborn to accept his help. If he wants a life with the woman of his dreams, he'll have to convince her that some goals can only be made with an assist.